MILLROY
The Magician

MILLROY
The Magician

PAUL THEROUX

RANDOM HOUSE NEW YORK

FOR SHEILA

All rights reserved under International and Pan-American
Copyright Conventions. Published in the United States by
Random House, Inc., New York, and simultaneously in Canada by
Random House of Canada Limited, Toronto.

Library of Congress Cataloging-in-Publication Data
Theroux, Paul.
Millroy the Magician / Paul Theroux.
p.   cm.
ISBN 0–679–40247–0
I. Title.
PS3570.H4M55 1994
813′.54—dc20   93-25046

Manufactured in the United States of America
24689753
First Edition

Book design by Oksana Kushnir

So I opened my mouth, and he
caused me to eat that roll.

—*Ezekiel, 3:2*

What he liked best was taking things apart, even books, even the Bible. He said the Bible was like an owner's guide, a repair manual to an unfinished invention. He also said that the Bible was a wilderness. It was one of Father's theories that there were parts of the Bible that no one had ever read, just as there were parts of the world where no one had ever set foot.

—*Charlie Fox*

CONTENTS

1

County Fair

1 I was supposed to meet my father at the Barnstable County Fair, and in a way I did, though he was not Dada. And I hated riding that awful bus from Mashpee to the fairground, though I did not have to take it back. How was I to know that it was my own Day One, and that it would end in magic, after that morning had been so wicked?

I had walked from Gaga's in Marstons Mills to Mashpee, where Dada was living with Vera, his Wampanoag woman, and when I got there he was black-out drunk and she was gone. I looked at Dada lying on the floor and made sure he was not dead. He was usually drunk on his day off, but he had promised to be at the fair today. It was nine o'clock on a hot Saturday morning in July. The bus shook and farted on the broken road. I sat on the backseat so nervous I sucked my thumb the whole way.

Millroy was the magician at the fair, famous for making an elephant disappear in a box onstage. I had seen him once with Dada and not forgotten. He had invited a small girl from the audience and turned her into a glass of milk and drank her.

"Jeekers."

Dada had snorted and said, "It's just a trick, Jilly."

But I was still thinking, *Jeekers.*

I walked past the Fun-O-Rama, past the Thunderbolt, past THE WONDERS OF THE WORLD posters and the LIVE FREAKS banners (PIG WITH HUMAN HANDS AND HUMAN FEET, WOLF BOY), past CIRCUS, FOSKETT with Yoyo the Clown and Popcorn the Wonder Dog, past MISTER SOFTEE, SNO-KONES, HOT PEANUTS, SWINE SHOW, and ELEPHANT RIDES, and CHUBBY CHECKER!—LIVE TONIGHT! to the tent with the colored banner of the bald-headed mustached man, BELTESHAZZAR—MASTER OF THE MAGICIANS—Millroy.

When I went in, Millroy looked up in the middle of his magic and his eyes rested directly on me, among all those people, and seemed to lighten from brown to green. Afterward I got to know that look well:

his eyes got a grip on you and, as he said, the rest was simple. I sat down and stuck my thumb back into my mouth.

"I do magic in daylight," Millroy was saying.

It was as though he recognized me from the last time with Dada and had heard me, back then, say *Jeekers*. It made him drop something. He was not fazed.

"This is my first day with my new hand."

He plucked the hand out of his sleeve, squinted at it, then jammed it back on and began juggling with it—three different objects. He juggled a bowling ball, a lighted propane torch, and a *rat-tatting* chain saw, all at once. He filled his mouth with five Ping-Pong balls and threw his head back and blew them around, and then swallowed them, still juggling, still staring.

"I'm doing all this without a net!"

No one had ever stared at me like that before. He was leaning, too.

"Are you Annette?" he said to me.

The people laughed. I was fourteen but even so, small for my age, just under five feet tall, size 2 dress—not that I ever wore a dress, most of my clothes being off the kids' rack usually, junior jeans and little T-shirts and size 4½ sneakers. No bust, and hips like a boy, and short hair. Why would anyone stare at her?

I was so transfixed by him at first I did not hear anything that he was saying. Then I saw him pulling a paper bag from his trouser cuff.

"Would you say I have bags in my pants?"

His eyes were still on me. He was tall and slender, balder than the picture of him out front but with a bushier mustache, gentle in his movements, and he gave the impression of strength without bulk, lots of willpower, mind over matter, a real magician. Watching him, I wondered what had happened to that girl he had turned into milk and drunk.

He wore a tight black suit and riding boots. When he held something like a playing card or even a bowling ball, he did so with the tips of his long fingers. He had a hooked nose, too, and the way he stared and showed his teeth he looked like he wanted to take a bite out of me. I had seen that his eyes had changed color, but they changed again, went paler, and became like a bird's blinkless eyes and pierced me.

Millroy was stuffing a big flapping chicken into the paper bag, but I was so intent on him I did not hear what he was saying. The bird was fat with feathers but did not look twitchy and stupid the way chickens do;

this one seemed slow and agreeable, like an old friend. Millroy twisted the top and punched the bag on its bulge, flattening the thing, and leaving him holding shreds of paper.

"That was Boobie, and that gives a whole new meaning to the expression 'chicken out,' " he said, looking in my direction. "Now let's brighten this place up."

A bunch of flowers popped from his sleeve, and he tweaked another nosegay from his breast pocket. One more bunch exploded from underneath the lapels of his coat. He arranged this bouquet, and while we clapped he wiggled a ribbon of silk from between his fingers, then yanked it—one silk scarf knotted to another on an endless chain—and while he went on yanking he rolled up his sleeves. Where was this thing coming from? By the time the question popped into my mind the scarves lay in a tall pile on the table.

"What was that?" he said. "That sound?"

These questions were all directed at me, and I almost spoke up because just then I heard a clucking sound.

"Get out of there, Boobie, you Chinese chicken!"

He moved his hands over the head of a small girl in the front row and pulled an egg out of her ear and another from her mouth.

"Got that bird worried," Millroy said.

We all laughed, but he was looking straight into me. I kept my thumb in my mouth and locked my finger onto my nose. Millroy was so close I could see that his face and the skin on his bald head were pebbly with sweat, and he was trembling and a bit breathless, as though this performance were taking most of his strength.

The clucking came again like monotonous words in a foreign language.

Millroy said, "That's funny. Come up here, sugar."

Gently pinching her small hand with two long magician's fingers, he lifted the small girl to her feet and guided her to the stage. She was about nine, with skinny white legs and falling-down socks and braids.

"What's your name, honey?"

"Who, me?"

"Yep. You standing there with your teeth in your mouth."

"Lynette Trumpka."

"That's a real pretty name, Lynette. But say, you got a chicken anywhere on you?"

"I don't think so."

"Smile—or if you can't smile, make a funny face," Millroy said, still seeming to be talking to me.

"I'm psyched," the girl said, and everyone laughed.

Millroy walked Lynette Trumpka around the stage so that we could all see she was wearing stiff little pedal pushers and a ketchup-stained T-shirt that had come untucked.

"Hey, what's this?" Millroy said, and pulled two more eggs out of her ears. "You sure you haven't got a chicken somewhere?"

The little girl shook her head; nope, she didn't.

"Okay, Lynette, you've been a good sport, so take a bow."

As she bent over, Millroy pulled a struggling chicken out from one leg of her pedal pushers. Lynette went rigid. It was the chicken he had called Boobie and it flapped and squawked until Millroy gripped its yellow legs; then it relaxed and looked as plump as a feather duster.

"Fatso," Millroy said.

With his fingers sinking into its feathers he weighed Boobie the chicken in his hand.

"But that reminds me," he went on, and leaned toward me. "This is the greatest country in the world—hey, I've got a personal tribute to the USA coming up at the end of Act One—but listen, hasn't there got to be something seriously wrong in a country where the poor people are fat and the rich people are skinny?"

Still plumping Boobie in his hand as though he were thinking hard made him more serious rather than more ridiculous, and it seemed a true question to which there was no obvious answer. But what did it have to do with magic?

"What does this have to do with magic, you're thinking," he said. "The answer is"—the chicken interrupted him, clucking a three-syllable word—"right, Boobie, ev-ree-thing."

He fed the chicken with some corn kernels, and swallowed as the chicken pecked at them in his palm. "That sure makes me hungry," he said, approaching a man in the front row. "I could use a chicken potpie around now, and here's the chicken." Smiling at the man, he said, "You are Kenneth Lesh from Hatchville and I need your carrots and your turnips and your hat."

The man was so surprised at hearing his full name uttered by Millroy that he stood up, flustered, and touched his hat, which was an old farmer cap saying WIRTHMORE FEEDS, as Millroy drew a carrot out of one of the man's ears and a turnip from the other, then lifted off his cap. Before the man could protest, in went the chicken and the vegetables and two of the eggs Millroy had gotten from the little girl Lynette Trumpka, cracking the eggs and chucking the shells along with the goo. Milk squirted from his fist, and by snapping his fingers he produced a sprinkling of flour.

"Bleached flour and refined sugar," he said. "And let's not forget a pinch of salt and a stick of butter. It's an American recipe."

Meanwhile, the hat was struggling and squawking.

"Now let it cook." A match flared from his fingers and he tossed it in.

We were laughing while the farmer down front, Kenneth Lesh—if that really was his name—looked grumpy about his ruined hat and his humiliation.

Millroy passed his fingers across the hat, then turned it over on his table, and when he lifted it up there was a deep, crusty chicken potpie steaming on the tabletop. He broke into the crust with a spoon and brought it out filled with pieces of chicken meat and blobs of fat in the dripping gravy and yellow chicken skin.

"That's death in a spoon," he said, and closed his hand over it, and when he flexed and opened his fingers it was gone.

We laughed hard but did not know why because we did not connect this to anything he had said earlier. As for the hat, it was empty and clean—no damage done, he showed us the inside, and he handed it back to the puzzled farmer. But where had that clucking chicken gone?

"I'm still hungry," Millroy said, and pulled a sword out of the top of his trousers. "Get the point?"

It was a real sword of glittering sharpness about a yard long, silver and gold, with a tassel swinging from its handle. Millroy flourished it and whacked it against the table leg, chunking off a cookie of splintered wood. Then he looked down at me, and I stared back with my thumb in my mouth, my fist in my face.

"This is one way of getting iron into your system."

He gargled, threw his head back and shoved the whole blade into his mouth, straight down, until the handle was jammed against his front teeth. His head was still tipped back, his stomach out, and he unbuttoned his black jacket and his shirt and waggled his finger at the point of his sword pressing against his belly just below his breastbone. I half expected the sword point to pop through his skin.

When he slid the sword out of his mouth the cheer from the audience was louder than ever. He put his hand up for silence, and we all went quiet again out of respect.

"Still awful hungry," Millroy said, and flung a lighted match into a saucer on the table. The spark gasped and flared into torchlike flames.

Using a pair of tongs, he fed himself fiery sponges and chomped on them, then made a torch and chewed on those flames. Smoke and fire flew out of his mouth and seemed to singe his mustache. He was sweating, his head gleamed, his eyes were red in the firelight. I had seen that long sword go down. I could see that these were real flames he was eating, and I was near enough to feel the heat.

Soon there was no more fire—Millroy had eaten it all. He smacked his lips as though he had just had a meal and said, "Delicious, and better for you than some stuff I could name. But fire eating makes you thirsty."

He opened his hand and revealed a pitcher brimming with water.

"Remember the wedding feast at Cana—the very first miracle, according to John? Watch closely."

Still glancing at me, now a bit suspiciously, as though I might be wearing something of his, he poured a stream of water from the pitcher into a glass, and as it splashed, it turned a winy red.

"But just to show you I'm not a one-trick pony, here's a variation that John didn't mention," Millroy said. "Maybe Jesus didn't know it, or was still working on his technique."

Now he had a pitcher of red wine, and some of this he poured into an empty glass and it turned clear and colorless.

"Wine into water—a much better idea in these days of alcohol abuse," he said, setting these pitchers and glasses aside.

He smiled at our applause, lifted a square pane of glass onto the little table, tapped his knuckles on it, and then placed a circular crystal fishbowl on that, giving it a little spin. To the water in the fishbowl he added the red wine from the second pitcher and then carefully wrapped the top of the fishbowl with clinging plastic. He sloshed the red liquid to show us it was sealed, and as it moved in the fishbowl the mingled water and wine had a swimming stripyness, like a drowned flag.

Millroy rolled up his sleeve again. Just the sight of his muscular arm seemed to be a warning that something big was coming, and it was. He shoved his bare arm through the plastic, pulled out a length of silk streamers, and kept pulling until it was hundreds of feet long and a yard wide. We clapped like mad.

But he was not finished. Music played—"Stars and Stripes Forever"—as he dug into the fishbowl again and hauled out a succession of banners that turned out to be a huge American flag, which he hung up on the back of the stage, all this patriotic bunting covering the back wall, where there had only been empty space before. Then he reached into the folds of the enormous flag and using both arms lifted out a live bald eagle, which he held up for us to see.

Our cheering drowned the music, but Millroy did not seem to hear it. He looked dignified holding the flapping eagle, and he turned to me and stared as he had before, and leaned over to where I sat in the second row.

Popping my thumb out of my mouth made the sound of a cork being yanked from a bottle.

Even through the cheering crowds his voice was distinct as he said, "I want to eat you."

So I stayed for his second show.

2 Waiting for Millroy's second act to begin, I walked around the fairground, looked at quilts, watched draft horses pulling slabs of cement, peeked at the baby pigs that had been born at the Swine Show tent earlier that morning. Yet after what I had seen, nothing else looked the least bit interesting to me—not Robinson's Racing Pigs, not Popcorn the Wonder Dog climbing a ten-foot ladder and jumping off, not the giant stuffed panda prizes at the Skee-Ball stand. I spent the last of my money on a root beer float, a chili dog, and a twist of fried dough, then went back for Act Two.

There were boxes and cabinets onstage, their flat surfaces shiny with sequins and painted red and decorated with signs of the zodiac. What caught my eye was a wickerwork coffin with belts in the middle and handles at each end, a lovely object so finely woven that when Millroy heaved it up slowly it stretched and mewed like a live thing that had been disturbed.

"Know what the word 'tangibilized' means?" Millroy asked.

We said no in a sort of moan.

"I'll show you," he said. "But I'm going to need some volunteers. Why more than one? Well, this might not work out. Might lose one. Might need a replacement."

I was laughing against my thumb when Millroy took a stride toward me.

"How about you, miss?"

In the same movement he lifted his hand and pointed to me, near enough for me to take hold of his finger, which I did, as he eased me out of my seat. He led me to the stage with his hot, damp hand on mine. Was this magician nervous, and if so why? It made me think again about his tricks. With a sweaty hand like that he might not do them right.

"And this is your friend?" he said, and beckoned another girl with his outstretched finger. She was younger than me, but about my size, and was black and wore jelly shoes.

I had never seen this girl before, but we were both so nervous we kept our mouths shut and stared at the wooden floor of the stage while the crowd of people laughed at us.

"Something I want you to do for me," Millroy said, leading the girl by the hand. "But first, what's your name?"

"Zula Firkins."

"Lovely little name. You've been eating marshmallows."

"Tons of them."

"Too bad. Now just hop into this basket, Zula, and we'll get started."

"You going to do anything to me?" the girl asked, screwing up one eye.

"Not a thing, Zula," Millroy said. "I just want you to experience the interior of this Indian basket. I won this basket in a psychic duel with a saddhu some years ago in the pink princely province of Rajasthan, in India."

As soon as Zula Firkins was lying inside the coffin-shaped wicker basket and the lid was shut tight and the straps buckled, Millroy opened a box that was filled with swords. He drew out a long, glittering one that looked like the sword he had stuck down his throat that morning. He slashed it in a circle over his head, whipping the air, then plucked a piece of wicker off the basket and whittled it smaller to show how sharp the sword was, and clamped his teeth on this toothpick. Everyone laughed in fear and excitement, and you thought of Zula Firkins flopped on her back inside the basket.

"Watch me," he said.

He raised this sword over the basket, and then drove it into the middle, *ka-shook,* right up to its handle. He picked up another sword and did it again, and this one went in with a tearing of wicker, like someone slashing shredded wheat.

"Go ahead. Take a sword and stick it in. What did you say your name was?"

"Jilly Farina."

"You had a snack, Jilly. Root beer and fried dough." He inhaled. "And a hot dog."

People laughed, but how did he know? I said, "I was wicked hungry."

"Weenie worship," he said. "That's the worst part of county fairs. And what happened to your legs?"

Bruised when I had been thrashed with a strap by Gaga over the broken butter dish, but I hesitated to say so.

"Never mind, don't tell me," Millroy said. "I can't stand violence. Now just pick up a blade, sugar, and start stabbing this basket."

No eyelashes gave him eyes that were so pale and attentive that his gaze did not stop at my face but went so deep into me I felt he knew my whole life and every pure secret and sorrowful joy in my heart. He handed me a sword, which was heavier than I expected, and I pushed it through the long wicker basket into the thick body of Zula Firkins, and it went slow as though making a hole, like a knife into meat.

"Take that," Millroy said. "And that. And—oh, gee—something's leaking out of the basket. Jilly, that gooey stuff—you suppose it's blood?"

"I don't know," I said, not wanting to look down, and the crowd howled at me.

"Zula, you all right in there?" Millroy called out.

No voice or any sound came from the basket, which was now bristling with swords.

"I've been doing this trick for years," Millroy said, "and it's only gone wrong a few times. I hope to holy heck that this isn't another of them. What do you think, Jilly?"

Trying to shrug my narrow shoulders only made me feel smaller. I said, "I don't know."

"I just love that," Millroy said. "Matter of life and death! 'Dunno.' "

His perfect mimicking of my voice and the way I blinked made me feel not weak but secure, protected, as though he had power over me.

"Let's look inside this Indian basket," he said. "That's the only sure way to find out. Undo those buckles, Jilly, like a good sport."

I crouched down and unfastened the straps; then Millroy lifted the lid, propping the basket up. It was empty except for the sword blades, six of them, sticking through the wicker every which way and smeared sticky red.

"Zula's gone," Millroy said. "Zula's disappeared!"

Humming insincere sounds of pity in his sinuses, he yanked the swords out and wiped them clean with a bloody rag. "You're going to have to go look for her, Jilly. Think you can do that?"

"I'm wicked nervous."

He smiled at that and then whispered in a kindly way to me, "Let's roll, sugar—boot it, you'll be fine."

It was my first step into the unknown at Millroy's command and even then, more than climbing into a basket, it seemed like my willing but ignorant descent into a dark tunnel in which I trusted him to make me safe until I emerged from the other side, jarred and shrunk by a blinding light, into a space he controlled like a king yet one I had never known before. I hesitated because the alternative was retreating the way I had come, back to Gaga's on the awful bus, back to my room, my small bed and my posters. Millroy's eyes were on me, but I knew the choice was mine.

The thing creaked as I stepped in, and it went dark as the lid came down on top of me. I lay there holding my belly with one hand and sucking my thumb and thinking, *Let's roll, sugar—boot it, you'll be fine.* Next thing I knew Millroy was talking loudly to the crowd and I was being shaken into a cloth bag, head first, pitch dark, dusty, and no end to it, like crawling through a stitched-up grain sack, a suffocating dream of narrowness, with death at one end and birth at the other.

Meanwhile, Millroy was calling out, "Now you go find Zula, honey. She's down there somewhere. And just to give you some ventilation I'm going to stick some swords into this basket—open it up a little."

Ka-shook! Ka-shook!

I heard the blades going in, slicing through the wicker, but I did not feel a thing, only sniffed the thin, dusty darkness, and still Millroy was talking.

"Strange thing, losing a little girl. Be pretty darned strange if we lost both of them. Ha! But let's have a look—"

The lid creaked open—I heard it not far off, then I heard the crowd laugh in relief and surprise.

"Why, hello there, Zula," he said. "Now you know the meaning of tangibilizcd. But where's our friend Jilly?"

In a sulky voice the small girl said, "She ain't no friend of mine," and I imagined her climbing out of the basket, the wicker creaking against her knees.

"Let's have another look," Millroy said.

The lid crunched, the audience groaned, and in my darkness I heard Millroy saying, "I've had serious lacerations, I've had puncture wounds, I've had splinters. But this is my first disappearance." He sounded worried and helpless. "Maybe she's behind the table—no. Or the curtain, or this box. No, she's gone, folks. She booted it. I am very sorry. I'll try to do better tomorrow."

I'm right in here! I yelled. But it was like the dream in which you panic yet your screech stays in your mouth. I tried again, but I sensed that the sound was trapped inside the bag, if it was a bag.

Things went quiet, and after a while I felt myself being hoisted gently off the floor and carried. When the bag was open I had to squint because of the brightness, the way hamsters do when they are born, blinded and squirming. I was in a small room, a trailer I knew by its tin walls and its narrowness, like the cabin of a sailboat, but with a dog barking outside, the hurdy-gurdy music from the fairground, and in the distance Chubby Checker singing "Come on baby, let's do the Twist," the evening show.

"Time to eat," Millroy said, "and no weenie worship."

The fragrance on his fingers was from a small, cut-open orangy fruit that he was holding to my nose.

"Kind of revives you, doesn't it?"

Filling my nostrils, it entered my head and soothed it with the sweetness of a blown-open blossom.

" 'Comfort me with apples,' " he said. "They knew what they were talking about. Song of Solomon. Two five. By apple they meant apricot, which this is—here, have a bite."

He put it into my mouth and watched me while I chewed it.

There was another, stronger odor clinging in the close-together cupboards of the room, and Millroy knew I was wondering.

"Pottage," he explained.

He passed his fingers over my face.

"Because you don't need meat in your mouth."

I blinked at him to show I was listening and not frightened.

"Or meat in your body," he added. He was smiling, inhaling, enjoying the odors. "Breads. Grains. Bitter herbs. Infusions. Soups. The odd spice."

Chanting this list, he might have worried me the way you are when a strong, bald stranger with a mustache over his mouth blocks your way and utters a garbled sentence and you feel he is insane. Yet I was soothed as though by a promise of well-being and, with the taste of the apricot still on my tongue, sensed a hunger for the food he mentioned rise like yearning in my body, and I wanted to eat.

Setting a steaming bowl of thick reddish paste on the table next to me, Millroy smiled again.

"Parched pulses," he said. "They knew a thing about fiber."

I ate two spoonfuls and felt more secure.

"I don't eat anything with a face," Millroy said.

Thinking hard, I said, "I love fried clams and quahogs and scallops."

He muttered *quow-hawgs*. He muttered *skawlips*. He smiled. And I felt as I had in the show tent, when he imitated the way I spoke—overwhelmed but protected by him, made safe by the way he knew me.

"And I don't eat anything with a mother," he said.

"Sounds good," I said, but what did that mean?

"I suppose we'll have to call your mother and tell her you'll be late."

"I don't have a mother," I said.

He stroked his mustache the way you stroke a cat to calm it.

"Mumma passed on," I said, and touched my face the way I always did when I said the word. He saw me do this and understood. "I have a grandmother."

"What's your granny like?"

"Everyone calls her Gaga."

"I know the type," he said. "And I know she's not very kind to you"—as he traced the welts on my shins with his fingertips, just his touch seemed to soothe them.

"She thrashes me," I said. "Gumpy used to stop her but he passed on, too."

"I'll come up with something," Millroy said, and he sighed.

"She thinks I'm with Dada tonight."

"And where's Dada?"

"Drunk," I said.

"What does he do when he's sober?"

"A whole bunch of stuff," I said.

"Mumma, Dada, Gumpy, Gaga. The front-porch folks from Hell City, USA—everyone's family. I know these people well," Millroy said, and he drew another long breath. "Maybe you would be happier here with me?"

His eyes were huge and damp and gleamingly mirrored my own face.

"Go on, angel, eat some more."

"I can't," I said, choking a little, and still with unchewed food in my mouth, I said, "I don't think I'll be able to swallow until you tell me where I'm supposed to sleep."

Gagging gave me tears in my eyes, which Millroy could have misunderstood.

"In your own sweet safe room," he said. "Will you stay?"

"If you promise not to hurt me, and if you teach me some magic."

Millroy took my hand—did not grip it but let it rest on his soft fingers the way he had held the fragrant apricot.

"I'll never hurt you. We'll be strong, and we'll always be friends," he said. "I know what you're thinking. But don't worry, I'm not a nut-bag."

3 Swallowed up by this stranger, Millroy, was how I felt that night in my own locked room in the darkness of the trailer, and because I had been swallowed I felt different, as though I existed but was blind and blundering and had to be led around in this stomach. It was not as simple as his saying *We'll be friends* and going to sleep. He said the choice was mine; I could call Gaga and tell her where I was, I could phone the police, I could get up and go home the next morning. But I was so sleepy.

"I don't want to let you go," he had said. "I've been waiting half my life for you."

Saying that, Millroy the Magician looked human and weak and sounded whiny in a way that I understood better than magic. Even without touching me he was tugging at me.

"And I don't want to leave this town without you."

A person seeing me inside this strange man's trailer would have told me I was stupid, but I felt safer here than I ever had at Gaga's. There was something about the clean, bright room and the good food he had served; I had never seen or tasted anything like it before, and it had calmed me and made me trust him. There were no bad smells in the trailer, and it was quiet and clean, no clocks, no mirrors, no television set.

"Why not sleep on it?"

His eyes settled on me again, held me in their motion, and as they cooled from gray to blue, I began to dissolve in their yawning pupils and wished only to lie down and let myself fall through the deepness of slumber.

Sleepily I watched him step past me and, sliding a low drawer from the wall, he flapped out its hinged sides and tipped over its front until he had a shelf, which he propped up and called a bed. In a false bottom he revealed a mattress and bedding. He folded out a partition like a pair of shutters, and in a matter of seconds had created a cubicle. It was like one of those collapsing boxes or cabinets, like the Indian basket he used on-stage to make solid objects disappear.

"You will be safe here," he said.

Fool, most people would have said to me, but I knew better, I only felt grateful, and I knew that if there was a risk I had to take it. He was opening a door and nodding for me to step through. I took the step, I shut the door, I locked it, I lay down, and that was when I realized that I had been swallowed and that things would never be the same again.

He was outside, on another shelf, in another cubicle, also in darkness. At first I thought he was dreaming, and maybe he was, but he was speaking to me, his voice muffled in a lovely rumble.

"Something has happened to us," he said. "Yesterday I was just a solitary man who did tricks at a county fair, and I needed someone to trust me. I found you, and now I am a man with responsibilities. And yesterday you were just a child."

He released a long, yearning breath that narrowed to a sigh, drawing itself fine like a wire that found its way through the cracks in my cabinet.

"We were two lost souls, though we didn't know that until we met. Now we are one complex organism."

He was silent for a moment, and my eyes were wide-open in the darkness.

"I believe we are a lot healthier for it," he went on. "This is a totally natural state of affairs, if you see what I mean."

I did not know what to say.

"You took charge of me. Our life will be different from this day onward. Great things are going to follow from this, Jilly Farina."

And I was thinking, *If it gets real bad or strange I can always leave and go back to Gaga,* and I felt that he knew I was thinking that and saying to myself *Wait and see,* and being patient.

Motionless, on my back, hardly breathing, in a dreamless and druggy slumber—that was how I slept, and so when I woke I felt reborn.

But Millroy was gone—I could not find him, and for the first time in the trailer I began to be worried for my safety.

I sat and fretted, and after an hour he appeared in his sudden, out-of-nowhere way.

"Have you just tangibilized yourself?" I asked, trying to make a joke of my worry.

He shook his head. "Just been in the rest room."

He smiled a knowledgeable smile, but I thought, *For over an hour?*

"I spend some of my most productive time in the booth."

I had heard it called a lot of names but never that.

"And so will you."

I was patient because I was excited and felt safe and this was more life than I had ever known, but it was growing odder and odder.

"I was also giving thanks," he said, and seeing me frown because I did not understand, he said, as though explaining, "It's Sunday."

The Sunday Chubby Checker performance in the fairground arena took the place of Millroy's magic hour and because of there being no afternoon show Millroy made more food—even odder: yellow bean salad, wood chips and barley paste, green melons, flat bread with bark-mulch flakes, and grape juice with a kick.

"I never ate stuff like this before."

It did not even seem like food.

"I don't eat anything else," Millroy said, and turned his head and shortened his neck like a nuthatch.

I thought he was being funny.

"Sounds good," I said, feeling desperate.

"It gave me control over nine bodily functions."

He had this way of saying things in English, but even so you had no idea what he meant.

"I didn't know we had that many functions."

"If only you realized how I need you to say that," he said.

"This is great for you," he said, slashing off a hunk of the bread, which was bristling with bark mulch, and stuffing it into his mouth. "They sure knew about fiber."

"You were going to tell me about those magic tricks."

"A lot of that is bodily functions, which is why it's related to food."

"I was thinking about sword swallowing," I said.

"That's a perfect example."

Already he was snatching up the long bread knife that he had used to slash the flat bread. He threw his head back and waggled the blade until it was aiming straight down. Then he made a face, belched, and pushed the knife into his shadowy throat where the belch had come from. Was he smiling with the knife down his throat? He yanked the thing out and wiped the blade on his arm.

"See what I mean?"

And he was swallowing and gulping as though he had eaten the front part of the blade.

"Open that drawer. There's chopsticks inside. Pass a couple over, sugar."

They were black chopsticks with mother-of-pearl inlay in the form of blossoms, probably Chinese flowers. Millroy took them from me delicately, making the chopsticks seem very long as he plucked them up with his fingertips, and then he rotated his head until he was staring at the ceiling and tapped one chopstick into his right nostril and the other into his left, until about eight inches disappeared straight into his head.

He faced me, looking horrible, like a wild animal, the chopsticks looking fangy against his hairy mustache.

"I can stick anything in there. It's not an illusion, and it's not magic. You're looking at it. I've got complete control over these bodily functions."

Saying that, he raised his fingers and slid the chopsticks out of his nostrils, both together, and it was amazing to see them lengthen.

"And I can get anything down my pharynx—just a matter of control. See, the esophagus is a funny little tunnel, and it can be helpful if you know how to use it. It exerts a sort of suction on all bodies that are introduced into it. I can swallow up to twenty-three inches. Long? Course it's long—I can get eight inches into my stomach. Sometimes I stick a tube down, longer than that, because it flexes."

"What kind of tube?"

"For cleaning out my stomach," Millroy said. "For doing inventory. Ever have one of those days when you're feeling logy and you can't remember all the food you ate? Well, my nasal tube would be real useful to you those days."

If I did not know what he was saying, how could I even begin to tell whether he was joking about that flexible nose tube "for doing inventory"?

"Fire eating freaks me."

"Control," he said. "I hold the fire close to my mouth and exhale a lot, making a flamethrower. I blow out the fire as it gets near my lips, and I always use unleaded gasoline."

He demonstrated using a flaming match, biting off the flame and swallowing the burned stick.

"Roughage. I always say forget the cocktail sausage—eat the toothpick and you'll be healthier," he said. "Strictly speaking, there is no fire eating."

"Is there a chicken potpie?"

"There is, but I sure didn't bake it. I used a nesting container with a flange, cleverly separating the pie from the showmanship. In this case, fast talking, doctored eggs and a chloroformed chicken. A trick."

"Did you really change water into wine?"

"Only Jesus ever did that. It's in The Book. John, Chapter Two. 'And when they wanted wine, the mother of Jesus saith unto him, They have no wine.' "

He was jiggling a glass of his own grape wine.

"What you should notice is the technique here. Jesus turned water into wine without ever touching it. He just stood there. He told the servants to fill the pots with water. Then he told them to take it away and serve it. It is perfect magicianship—not even a wave of the hand, just words."

He took a sip of his wine and then gave me some. It was syrupy, grapey, with a little fizz of sweetness.

"What I did was pour a glass of water and alcohol into a glass containing an invisible smidgen of aniline red, which reacts with the alcohol and dyes the water red. Water into wine."

He swallowed the grape wine and smacked his lips.

"As for the other, wine into water, the so-called wine is just a chemical concoction—one gram of potassium permanganate and two grams of sulfuric acid in a potion of water. This fake Burgundy is poured into a glass that contains a few drops of water saturated with sodium hyposulfite. That's why it changes color. Wine into water."

He laughed out loud when I told him that this chemistry and all those names sounded more complicated and mysterious to me than magic.

"That's because you haven't had much of an education," Millroy said. "But stick with me and you'll get A's in chemistry. You'll be mixing up these solutions all by yourself." He put his elbows on the table and leaned over, widening his eyes. "You're going to be my assistant."

Trying to imagine this, I did not say anything.

"You'll get to wear a costume."

I liked that. He picked up his glass of grape wine again and took another swallow.

"A sequined cape. High heels. A sort of slinky bathing suit," he said. "Red lipstick."

"Sounds good," I said, and began to worry about the audience staring at me, and slipped my thumb into my mouth.

"You won't be able to suck your thumb onstage."

I popped it out and remembered what I had meant to ask him.

"What about the Indian basket and the stabbing? And the way I disappeared. How did you do that trick?"

Millroy was smiling and I realized that my thumb was back in my mouth.

"That wasn't a trick," he said, raising his glass. "That was magic."

And he poured the remainder of his wine into my empty glass, and as it burbled it changed color, losing its redness and its fizz, becoming colorless before my eyes.

"Like that. Go on, have a sip."

Water!

Another miracle, and my first full day was still not over.

"Cut it out. Who are you really?"

"No one knows me," he said. "That's another reason I need you."

A black-and-white movie I once saw on TV at Gaga's opened in a small town like Marstons Mills, where a girl working at the appliance department of a store catches a man's eye. When she smiles back at him you know she is very lonely. He buys a washing machine and all at once says, "Will you marry me?" and just as suddenly she says, "Yes, I sure will." That same afternoon they get married and they ride out to his farm, miles from anywhere. They spend a happy night together, and the whole day is like a dream of love at first sight.

But wait. Next morning she wakes up alone and hears a commotion. It is her new husband down below in the yard screaming his head off. He is whacking a sledgehammer against the brand-new washing machine. "I told you I didn't want this one!" he is yelling, and the bride watches him smashing it to pieces. She just stands there looking down, wondering what she's done, and scared to death because of his terrible temper.

Was I going to be that girl? Later in the evening I heard music and said I wanted to go outside and look at the Fun-O-Rama. Millroy said no and that county fairs were not places for innocent youngsters—look at all the riffraff, the chain-smokers, the overweight motorcyclists wearing

Nazi helmets, the women with tattoos, dropouts trying to hide, underaged runaways heading away from home.

Like me, I thought.

"Not like you at all," he said, reading my mind. "You are home." His eyes penetrated me and I saw he was right. "Anyway, it's closing for the night."

"The hot dog stand is still open."

"Crazos eat them. You wouldn't eat those things if you knew what was in them," Millroy said. "Lips, tails, nails, hoof and horn. Gut tubes, hair, bits of skin, fecal matter, udders, all the fat, all the blood and nastiness, the whole strangled animal."

"I guess I'm not hungry anymore."

"Of course not. You had a great meal. That was real food I served you."

"I don't even know what it was."

I knew I should not have said that.

Wearing a wonderful smile, Millroy said, "Then let's have another look at it and I'll tell you."

He quickly poked the rubber tube up his nose, unspooled two or three feet of it into the front of his head, and fitted it with a plunger. He was soon pumping sludge that looked like old fruit salad into a dish.

"It's still breaking down," he said, pumping away. "What have we got here. Bread, bean salad, mashed pulses. Vegetable matter—hardly smells! It's real food."

"It's wicked interesting," I said, and squinted so that I would not see the brimming dish.

"I can show you how to use this thing," he said, toying with his stomach pump, so fascinated he did not notice me looking sick.

A miracle was magic but it was also a shock, and nothing normal here meant I had to ask myself every so often, *What have I gone and done?*

4 Millroy's life was like his magic—I learned that fast—everything was upside down, or amazing, or plain odd. The longer you lived, the less you knew, he said. "Most older people are totally ignorant. I am the exception."

He disliked calendars and clocks: "They give you an erroneous view of time." The healthiest rest-posture was balancing on your head. The best way to eat was standing up straight so that your belly was not creased and the food could go down more easily: "You need a good flow of air in your gullet to digest your food." Sitting in a chair was unhealthy and was a prime cause of many diseases. He claimed he could hold his breath underwater for almost an hour. He said, "I wish I lived underwater." He ate black seaweed, and the parts of plants that other people threw away—the tops, the greens, the seeds, the skin. When he was excited he did not shout, he whispered; his whisper could be heard fifty feet away. The lion roaring loudly from its cage in the Foskett's Zoo enclosure, Millroy said, was not angry but frightened. His skin had an odor of almonds and sometimes of tomato vines. He hated dogs and cats: "I hate their helplessness. I hate the junk they eat." He stared at plants, putting his face against them. "I am watching them grow." He said his bald head and big mustache were indications of his strength. He was always saying, "Punch me in the stomach—go on, hard as you can," and when he was hit very hard he said, "That was better than a handshake."

"But you are much stronger than I am, Jilly Farina," he said.

Most of what Millroy said was the opposite of the little I knew. I was small, I was fourteen, I had no friends outside school. Until I met Millroy I had been alone, living in a kind of cozy boredom: school, television, chores at Gaga's in Marstons Mills, her muddy yard and kitchen garden, her duckpond, the chicken run, all the stinks. I knew the world was somewhere else.

"You have power," Millroy said. "You just don't know how to use it."

"But you have total control over nine bodily functions." Wasn't that what he had said?

"That's just my way of compensating. It's sad, really."

Then why was he smiling?

Listening to what he said, I had to keep reminding myself that he was Millroy the Magician at the Barnstable County Fair.

This was Monday morning, at lunch—crunchable beans, loaves of sawdust, two honeycombs—before his first show. Eating made him think hard about food.

"Virtually everything that people eat is bad for them," he said. "In a way, you can't blame them. Most food in supermarkets is carcinogenic. Cancer in a wrapper."

He had a theory, he said, that some food stayed inside you—never left, just rotted in your guts and destroyed you. There were people, old before their time, and fat, and just looking at them you saw that they contained the residue of most of the meals they had ever eaten.

It made me think of Gaga, and like many of Millroy's theories it helped me see people differently—not as good or evil, or weak or strong, or even happy or sad, but with all those possibilities—because I imagined their insides not their surfaces, and most people were roomy and deep; they held everything. Their dark stomachs and sacs and lungs, and the pipes and sponges of their guts, were filled with the syrupy mixtures they had fed to themselves through their mouth holes. Humans did not explode—they just kept on expanding. They were like bags with legs, and whatever they had inside, they themselves had stuffed there. I saw people as containers, and that was why they looked simple but weren't.

"They show people on TV that are a hundred years old," I said.

"Two hundred should be the goal," Millroy said. "And more is possible. Never mind the Hunzas. Look at Peleg and Isaac. What did they know that we don't? No one ever asks."

"Why don't you?"

"Because I already know the answer," Millroy said. "It's eating right. It's bitter herbage like this." He was holding a clump of green leaves that looked like bunches of chicory and dandelions, or a handful of Gaga's hedge.

"I get it. It's like my friend Missy McClung from school. She's this wicked pious Seventh-Day Adventist, and she's a major food freak, too. She always brown-bagged it for lunch and it looked like meat, but when you asked her what it was she'd say 'Leenies,' or 'Veggie-links' or 'Linkets' or 'Nuteena' or a 'Chik-chop.' The kids used to laugh at her."

"They should have laughed at themselves for gobbling weenies and bacon and sugar and all the rest of it. But as far as I'm concerned they're all burgers, every last one of them, even your friend Missy and her Chik-chops. I'm way ahead of them."

He waved them all aside with his handful of herbage.

"But you're still young enough to be wise," he said. "I knew it the moment I saw you—still pure. Not a kid, that's an awful word, but a young adult." He munched a bite of herbage and went on, talking and chewing. "I love looking down at the faces and seeing young people. Adults have no business going to a magic show like mine. They hardly know what's happening. If I ran this fair I wouldn't let them in. They're just burgers."

"The police would make you."

"I'd use my head. I'd price them out. Twenty-one bucks a ticket, something like that. They'd stay away. Give the youngsters cheap seats. They'd mob the place. They love the show. They laugh, they scream, they cry. No silly questions. Heck, I've had burgers come onstage during a performance and interfere. 'It's a trick'—"

I thought of Dada last year, his exact words.

"—or 'It's all done with mirrors,' or 'Hey, let's see what's up your sleeve.' Rude? You wouldn't believe some of the things. One particularly annoying burger, very persistent, very insolent and interruptive, I made him disappear. I'm not sorry."

"What did the people say?"

"They loved it. Thought it was part of my show."

"Did the burger ever come back?"

Millroy took another bite of his bush of herbage.

With his mouth full, and mushing his words, he said, "I'd rather not say," and sounded as though he meant it.

He made a face, pressed his lips together, blew out his cheeks and chewed some more. His chewing gave him the alert face and squirrel cheeks of someone who was seriously wondering, really grinding away at a mental problem, as though the problem were in his mouth and he was dealing with it, *chomp-chomp-chomp,* thinking hard.

"But listen"—he was looking at me, still wondering, still chewing a little—"if I were going to start a religion I wouldn't let anyone in over the age of twenty or so. Twenty-five, tops. Ideally, they'd all be teenagers. I wouldn't want people who are unteachable. I'd just bring them along slowly.''

"I agree.''

If I were going to start a religion was not crazy. It sounded to me like Dada saying, as he often did when he was jingled, *If I were president,* just as impossible. So I did not think much about it except one night afterward, when Millroy was onstage, as I sat on a stool in the wings those first days. He would not let me out of his sight; he often glanced up to make sure I was there, I was not yet his assistant. And that was when I realized that the way he stood in front of the audience, in his black outfit, working miracles with his long pale fingers, and speaking with such an intense whisper that everyone paid attention—seeing him in that way I knew why his mentioning The Book and his talk about a new religion made sense: he looked like a priest in front of a congregation.

He saw me staring at him. When his show was over, he said to me, "You are happy.''

"You know it.''

"Tell me why.'' He looked at me closely, waiting for my answer.

Because I trusted him, because he made all the decisions, because he believed in me, because he did not scold me, because I slept so well, because I felt healthier, because I was safe with him, because it was so restful hearing him talk, because he listened to me, because I was alive.

"Because, even if it isn't true, I feel like somebody who might matter.''

"But it is true, angel,'' he said. "You matter like crazy. That's why I chose you.''

Thinking about the truth of it made me happier.

That day and the next, there were knocks on the door of his Airstream trailer.

"Doc—you there?''

Someone needing help.

Everyone called him Doc or Doctor Millroy. It seemed he was often called upon to cure the fairground people of their ills. Everyone at Foskett's had some sort of medical problem. The acrobats had the most serious ones; they were prone to sprained ankles, sore backs, muscle aches and blistered hands. Banged fingers were common among the roustabouts, Portugees from the woodlots, who were hired locally. The food people tended to have burns from having been splashed by their Frialators, and the people who looked after the animal pens had bites.

Floyd Fewox was one of those emergencies, a blistered shin from the hot muffler of his Harley, which he rode on The Wall of Death. He limped into the trailer carrying a fat black cat under his arm the way an old woman carries a handbag.

"I don't heal people's pets," Millroy said.

Out through the door went the cat, yowling as it hit the ground. But when Floyd Fewox showed Millroy his injury, he kept glancing over at me. It was as though he had a dead animal hanging in his pants leg, for when he rolled up the cloth, all I saw was raw skin and dead flesh and burned hair, a trampled lump like roadkill where his leg should have been.

"I wrote a book once," Floyd Fewox said, and it sounded like a geteven threat. "I could show you a copy. You'd probably be scared. It's really frank. You don't believe me."

His spiky graying hair was stuck in little bunches like doll's hair to his scalp, and it was growing in neat scabby rows, as though it had been planted. Even his hair's sticky wildness did not cover these plugs and punctures, and you could not look at his hair without thinking of all the real baldness underneath. He had yellowish Italian skin, and his nose was twisted sideways, as though he had tried to straighten it but failed, leaving it looking pinched. He wore high boots, greasy jeans with a silver studded belt, and had a tattoo on his arm that said BORN TO RAISE HELL. His sweaty skin steamed of beer. He was stubbly, he smelled, he wore a filthy T-shirt lettered HARVARD.

"I used to teach at Harvard," he said. "They said I was trouble. You don't believe me."

At first I did not see that he had teeth missing, and so I suspected Floyd Fewox was deliberately trying to frighten me when he suddenly widened his mouth in a gappy smile. He worked his lips at me as Millroy scissored open his pants leg and bandaged his shin.

"If you're looking for trouble, you came to the right place," he said. He was munch-mouthed and his floppy lips got in the way when he talked.

The black holes where his teeth should have been made him look violent, but also weak and nasty, like an old man with a grudge.

"Folks call me Harley," he said. "They don't realize I'm an educator. You got a name, babe?"

"Get out," Millroy said, and jerked the man over to the Airstream door and flung it open. He moved the man easily, using his fingers like pliers and pinching his elbow.

Afterward Millroy said he was sorry he had let the man into the trailer, but he had learned something important.

"I did not truly know that man until I saw the way he looked at you," he said. "You see how I need you?"

The way Millroy disposed of Floyd Fewox in the darkness outside—I heard this rider on The Wall of Death begging Millroy not to hurt him and then calling his cat—made me confident that no harm would come to me. I had never known anyone as strong as Millroy.

"Are you a real doctor?" I asked.

"Of course not. Real doctors are unhealthy. They die from the same diseases as their patients. They're like priests who commit the same sins as the people they preach to. Commit sins with them, for that matter. Funny how they're all in the same boat. People who use the word 'sin' are sinners. Ill health is the issue—it begins there, and where science and religion should overlap they diverge, and that leaves people helpless. Christian Science—were you going to mention that, Jilly? I'm very sorry, but you'd be wrong if you did. How can you take any religion seriously if it leaves out nutrition? A fat priest is a sinner, a sick doctor is a quack. I'm a healer."

"Gaga used to make me go to church every Sunday," I said. "Mashpee Baptist, across from the town hall."

"I never found a church I agreed with. They all seem to lead straight to damnation. Start believing them and you're lost."

He was energetic and seemed happy talking this way, as though he had been turning these thoughts over in his head for ages but that this was the first time he had actually spoken them out loud. He seemed relieved, eager to have me listen to him, and I was proud that he had chosen me to hear him.

"People are obsessed by the way they look," he was saying. "But that's the exterior. What about the inside, which is much more important? You have to know the condition of your stomach and your gut. Do you realize how dramatically people's lives would be changed if they looked in a mirror and saw their kidneys and their liver and their lungs? Your innards are knowable, but no one wants to look.''

For a moment I thought he was going to take out the flexible rubber tube and force it up his nose and spill some soupy chunks out of his stomach for us to admire. But he was so intent on what he was saying, and so eager for me to understand, that he had stopped coiling the gauze bandage that he had cut for Floyd Fewox's shin. He was leaning on the table flap and I was thinking how hard it was to know someone's true expression when they had a big mustache covering their face—even a smile was guesswork on the part of the watcher.

''How can you have a religion that forgives sins and purges you of evil, and yet leaves out the stomach pump and never mentions regularity?''

''You're wicked interested in that, huh?''

''Overwhelmingly. It's impossible to have a sincere interest in food without an accompanying and just as powerful interest in your bowels singing like a harp. America won't be strong until America understands the magic of health.''

''Like your water into wine?''

''You could call that a chemical reaction,'' he said. ''This is magic.''

He put his hands on his face and wrenched with his fingers until he had dislodged something from his mouth that I first took to be a rosy mottled fruit. It was his tongue, pink and twitching in his open hand, like a whole muscle, a hard sausage of flesh. He held it out to me, panting from the effort and then he whimpered, his mouth a great gaping hole, his eyes blazing with ecstasy, and the thing vanished from his hand, leaving a slight ripeness of breath in the air.

At last—that one flourish had exhausted him—he said, ''See what I mean?'' and went straight to bed, sealing himself in his cubicle.

In the morning, as though remembering an unfinished thought, he said, ''And I didn't understand myself until I saw you. Now I know who I am and what I can do.''

Millroy disliked elevators, he said, and other people's locks. He said things like *I picked that up in Mexico,* or Egypt or India. He could play hymns on the harmonica with his nose, jamming the instrument against his nostrils and snuffling. He believed that music had healing powers; certain notes and chords, especially the sound of crickets, not only healed you but induced visions and opened up hidden parts of your mind.

He said, "Once you have healed a person they are related to you. Once you have fed a person, they are a part of you."

He had a powerful sense of smell. "I like your flavor," he said to me. He knew from a whiff of my head that Gaga smoked. He said he could judge a person by his or her odor—their whole life was in that aroma. He could forecast weather by inhaling. He did exercises—push-ups, sit-ups, chin-ups, jumping jacks.

"I could never perform magic if I weren't as healthy as I am. Houdini? Mainly an illusionist and escape artist. No spirituality. His secret? He was a great physical specimen. I would like to be more akin to Saint Joseph of Copertino, who defied gravity and could levitate himself by physical strength and the power of prayer. The philosopher Leibniz saw him in 1677 floating in midair, the height of the treetops."

Millroy made it a point to drink two gallons of distilled water every day. He was very clean. He preferred showers over baths. He had an aversion to public swimming pools, public bathrooms and restaurants. "For starters, I could never use anyone else's cutlery." He said he could not exist without his own trailer. "I need to be near all my own facilities." He was neat, he was handy, he could sew, he made all his own trick boxes and caskets. He repeated: *I eat nothing with a face. Nothing with legs. I eat nothing with a mother. I take no meat into my body. No meat into my mouth.*

He regarded the county fair as dangerous and the other performers as cheap, vulgar or plainly criminal. After that one encounter with Floyd Fewox, he kept me away from all the other employees. He was suspicious of adults. He trusted children. He liked me.

5 In less than a week Millroy's trailer seemed like home, but happier and more familiar than anything I had known except the long-ago comfort of Gumpy's lap or Mumma's arms: Millroy's food, his talk, his big, belly-shaped Airstream, all smooth and buttoned-down silver, like a cradle, like a coffin, very quiet, very clean. "You could eat your dinner off that floor." My first thought after his crunchy vanishing trap of the Indian basket had been: *What if he won't let me go?* Now my great worry was that he would send me back where I came from. It frightened me to think of him saying *Go away, get out of here.*

His Airstream was parked beyond Robinson's Racing Pigs and the Pulling Arena, behind the draft horses and the dumb, clanking blue-ribbon cows, the steaming animal pens and the dripping dung of the chicken cages and the tables and shelves of prize vegetables in the distant and dustier corner of the fairground, nowhere near the Fun-O-Rama or the other trailers that he called "the gypsy camp."

The more familiar Millroy and his trailer became, the wilder the fairground seemed. I felt dangled there, just floating, as though I were snorkeling across all that strangeness. It excited me to see it, and soothed me when I surfaced in the silent winking windows, safe in the belly of the trailer.

Hugging a big wrinkled doctor's bag of creaky leather to his chest, Millroy said, "We've got a little repair work to do, angel."

From the clinks inside the bag I imagined scissors and bottles and knives. He tied a bib around my neck, slipped a plastic shower cap over my hair and sat me down on a stool.

"We've got a show to put on tonight."

He knelt in front of me, unfastened the flap on the doctor's bag and took out his bottles and tools and all the rest, arranging them on a little table—damp sponges and six different brushes and a dozen compacts of powder, tins of color, sprays and tubes of lipstick. He worked on my face first, using the brushes and sponges, and then his fingertips, like a blind man examining my face, moving his fingers like spider legs, working the powder around my cheeks. When he finished, he dealt with my eyes, dabbing them with mascara and drawing the color across my lids and all around. He did not speak, though his face was nearer to mine than it had ever been. He breathed, and the pressure of his breath, the scrape of this air through his nostrils, told me he was enjoying this. But he was so gentle, he touched me so lightly, I knew there was a layer of powder between his fingertips and my skin. I sensed strongly that he was giving me a mask, making a picture on my blank face, but I also felt that his tender gestures were more like a blessing than just another of his tricks.

You listen for one thing and hear another. I expected Millroy to speak, so my ears were open. I heard the chirpy whine of crickets under the trailer, the whistle of cicadas, and the fairground music, which at this distance was no more than a thumping, like someone rolling a barrel. All the talking and shouting had combined to make a shrill crazy-house crackle, and it was hard to hear any of those sounds without imagining blinking lights. Then there was a cowbell, the scratching of more insects, a nagging dog, the *rat-tat* of the shooting gallery. I was listening for Millroy, but he was listening too.

He remained silent and seemed to grow sadder as he worked on me; when he finally unsnapped one of the little compacts of powder, swinging the mirror disk from its hinge, and held it to my face, he shrugged, looking helpless.

"Anything wrong?" I knew he disliked mirrors, but this seemed more serious.

He looked away and said, "I have to be very careful."

But hadn't he been careful? He had given me a new face. I was another person—older, smarter, brighter, with large lovely eyes and shapely lips, and a pale pretty face—no freckles, no marks. It was a happy face, and not a girl's but a woman's.

"I don't recognize myself."

"Gilding the lily," he said. "But that's the point."

"Who am I supposed to be?"

He smiled with more assurance and pleasure than I had seen so far.

"Take a guess."

But I knew. It was as though in putting this makeup on me that he had given me more than a face. He had remade me, and so, with this face and in this mood, I was his.

As he had promised, I became his assistant. He wrapped me in an old coat and put a floppy hat on my head and we set off for the evening performance. He said, "You can't imagine what these people are like. But if anyone asks, call me Doc."

He kept his eyes down, sort of tugging me and not looking either left or right. I tried to do the same, but it was hard.

Dodging the animal pens, the staring cows and shuffling goats, and the Elephant Rides—closed for the night: Millroy used "Packy" in his show—we moved forward into the Fun-O-Rama crowd and I saw immediately what he meant. These people were older than the ones I knew from the daytime. Instead of children, there were lots of young rowdy couples and greasy bikers and prowling boys with their hats on backward.

Millroy seemed to hesitate and look up as we entered the midway, a wide strip with food concessions on either side: pizza stalls, burger wagons, the stands with signs in big flashing lights spelling out HOT PEANUTS, CHILI DOGS, TEXAS BURGER (PORK KNOBS! BEEF NUGGETS!), SNO-KONES and OLD-FASHIONED ROOT BEER FLOAT. At FRIED DOUGH a man ladled brown twists out of a brimming pot of dark bubbling oil, and at FOSKETT'S FLUFF a man spun cotton candy onto paper spikes. It was all steam, gas burners, sizzling fat, the splat of popcorn and the gleaming racks of burned and burst-open hot dogs.

"They are compromising their immune systems," Millroy said. "And it's not just weenie worship. Look at that wedge of pie. Look at those Twinkies. Junk food is for people who believe in UFOs."

Yet he had slowed down and was watching these eaters with such bright eyes and such a big disgusted smile that he had hiked up his mustache and I could see his teeth.

People were looking at us; I could sense their inquiring eyes, people at Custom Air Brush and Handwriting—Personality—Love—Horoscope. They even turned from the shooting galleries, from the knockdown dollies and wooden milk bottles, Water Fun Gun, Frog Hop, the fishing games, the darts into limp balloons and playing cards, Chuck the Hoopla and rifles with popping corks. People looked up as they waited in line at Super Loops, Mirror Maze, Cobra, and Thunderbolt, and even the dizzier ones spilling out of Gravitron glanced up when Millroy went by with me in his shadow, feeling in my hat like a dwarf under a mushroom.

"Don't look up." Millroy spoke in a muffled mumbling voice like a ventriloquist. He knew when someone was staring at him, even when his back was turned, from the pressure of the person's eyes. From under the low brim of my hat I saw, near a sign saying THE WALL OF DEATH, Floyd Fewox, the yellow-faced man with spiky planted hair and tattoos, who clicked his teeth as we passed.

"Doc and his young friend. Hey, I'm talking to you. Get over here and jam with Fearless Floyd," he said. He was wearing his dirty Harvard T-shirt.

Something about the way these fairground men stared made me feel even smaller than I was, and Floyd Fewox had Millroy's own habit of looking as though he wanted to take a bite out of me, but his missing teeth made it a frightening thought.

Floyd Fewox—I could see his greasy boots—was walking alongside the enclosure lettered LIVE FREAKS and the painted banners COW WITH SIX LEGS, SHEEP WITH FIVE LEGS, DUCK WITH FOUR WINGS, GOAT BORN WITHOUT EARS, MIDGET HORSE, ZONKEY, WOLF BOY and PIG WITH HUMAN HANDS AND HUMAN FEET.

"How do they know it's not a human being with a pig's head and body?" Millroy said in his ventriloquist's voice.

"Over here," Floyd Fewox said.

"Just keep walking," Millroy said, and I was glad for the way he loomed above me, hiding me.

Nearer the tent entrance Millroy took longer strides, and then he threw open the flap and hauled me in, seeming very agitated.

"Until today I hadn't realized how much I disliked this fairground," he said. "I've been working magic here for Foskett's for almost three years, but it wasn't until I saw it with your eyes that it dawned on me how dangerous and disturbing a place it is."

In his dressing room he unstrapped his valise and took out his cape, baton and some oatmeal fingers, which he had made that morning from his own recipe.

"And how I have no business here."

He walked entirely around the Indian basket without touching it.

"Which is another reason I am grateful to you."

And kept walking through the door, backstage, ignoring the smiling stagehands, to peek through the curtain at the audience.

"You inspired in me the feeling that I am a messenger," he said. "That I was cut out for better things."

Looming over me, he turned again, casting his shadow.

"And if I didn't think that you were, I would have left you in your twenty-five-cent seat that day, wouldn't I?"

The stagehand with the baseball hat and mouthful of gum disentangled a hanging rope and took a step toward us. He looked like shapeless Floyd Fewox at The Wall of Death—the same hair, the skinned knuckles, the black fingernails, the missing teeth, the loose lips, the tattoos.

"No, Doc."

Millroy smiled, he was grateful, he looked relieved, but I was glad to have that name for him. He had a gift for names. At various times I heard him call himself Felix, Archie, Chester, Galen, Prospero and Max. He was so powerful that the one name Millroy was perfect, yet I was happiest calling him Doc or nothing at all.

Sitting me down, he gave me instructions about how to walk and use my hands, showing me the gestures, and then he was on, saying *I do magic in daylight.*

Round and round, juggling above his head, went the chain saw, the bowling ball, the propane torch, the saw *rat-tatting* and a blue flame shooting from the torch.

"I'm doing all this without a net!"

Millroy was still juggling in a way that made the people in the front rows wince.

"So come out here, Annette, and give me a hand!"

They laughed at the joke but that was my new name. He had shown me how to walk onstage as though I knew where I was going, and I did, feeling like a different person in my high heels and new face. I was always to stand at the side, perfectly still and pointing to Millroy except when I was handing him something.

"Annette will now bring me a bottle of the best French wine, an excellent Beaujolais, which I shall turn into the purest spring water. Annette, my flagon, if you please."

I handed Millroy the bottle he needed—"Always use your fingertips, make it a gesture." Then I cleared the tables, but mainly I watched, standing in his shadow and applauding—"Stand straight, head back, on your pretty toes"—applauding while holding my hands up, as he had instructed, so that the audience would imitate me.

And when you get them applauding, point to me with both hands—a kind of presentation, he had said.

This meant extending my skinny arms and twinkling my fingers at him to emphasize that he was the star of the show. I did the rest of it, shut off the chain saw, turned off the torch, and boxed the bowling ball. I disposed of the paper bags, took charge of the youngsters from the audience Millroy had sent crawling into the basket, and the hoarse, heavy-breathing boy he had locked in the cabinet he called ''The Thorn Variation.''

He turned wine into water, water into wine, rammed chopsticks up his nose, then set them on fire and ate them.

''What's your name?'' he asked a young girl.

''Polly,'' she said shyly.

''And I am polyphagous!'' Millroy cried out.

He swallowed broken glass, more fire, live slugs, and something I had never seen before. Shoving a long sword down his throat, he pulled only half out, leaving about a foot of it—the pointy end—in his guts. He ate part of an omelet and vomited whole unbroken eggs, which he turned into three large chickens. The chickens were pushed into a pot, the pot became a pie, the pie became a cake with fourteen candles and the monogram *AF*—and he presented this to a girl in the front row.

''Tell us your initials and your age,'' Millroy said.

''A.F.—for Amy Feerick, and I'm fourteen.'' Then she screeched, ''Awesome!'' and looked scared.

I was not frightened, but I was amazed because Millroy's magic was more powerful and shocking close up than from the audience; I could see things transformed, could smell the burning and hear the sizzle and squawks, could taste the water and wine.

After Millroy took his bow—I was still pointing and presenting—and the curtain flopped down, he stood in the dust flecks sifting past the bright lights and looked sad.

''I hate the way they stare at you, angel.''

He crammed the big-brimmed hat on my head, covered me with a cape and wrapped himself up as well, and we walked the long way back to his trailer, past the little zoo where the animals looked badly fed and deeply unhappy, sick, vicious and miserable, Packy chained to his post, the bony lion boxed into its big loose cage, where it coughed and roared itself hoarse. We hurried past the Fun-O-Rama and Live Freaks, and the terrifying food and all the people eating it. *Don't look up,* he said, but he was slowing down and staring hard and wearing an exhausted smile.

Back at his Airstream trailer he said, "Tell me the truth. What did you think of the show from up close?"

"It was awesome, like that girl said."

"But what did you think?"

"They were all, like, going nuts," I said. "About a million eyeballs all looking at you."

"And you," he said. "Tell me more."

"Magic," I said.

Until then the county fair had just been a summer event that appeared out of nowhere and vanished after two weeks, leaving only injured Portugees, worn patches on the ground, trampled grass, garbage and splotches of spilled engine oil in the dirt that had dripped from the gears of the rides. It was a strange little temporary town of canvas, RVs, trucks and trailers, odd-shaped laundry on lines and big yapping watchdogs wherever you went.

During the day it was bright and blowsy, but at night the fairground could be wicked: the shadows were sharper, the shows different, louder, and weirder, and so were the spectators. Instead of the daytime families and children, at night there were crowds of loud boys with their baseball hats on backward, big sunburned lobstermen, farm boys, Wampanoags in torn shirts, clammy-skinned couples hugging, and babies screaming because they were up too late. It was all glary and louder, the sort of marbly light and dark of a stormy sky that seemed to have gaps and cracks wide enough for you to fall through—where you might vanish. The days were hot and disorderly, the nights were black and violent.

Most nights, from under the wide brim of my floppy hat, on those long walks from the trailer to the show tent and back, I saw much more of the county fair than Millroy wanted me to.

Through the flap of a heavy canvas tent behind the Fun-O-Rama, a pale fattish woman walked back and forth in front of silent, staring men while loud music played. She was naked and had a cruel, shaking way of walking, and her body wore a teasing expression, as though it were a huge bearded face with popping eyes. She laughed as she passed the men and snatched off their hats and eyeglasses, and she looked like a witch in a roomful of wheezy children.

The yellowish man, Floyd Fewox, with the wild planted hair and the Harvard T-shirt and greasy jeans, sat on his motorcycle and gunned the engine as we passed by Live Freaks. He made finger signs to Millroy and me.

"I wrote you some poems," he called out. I noticed he kept his cat in his lap. "You don't believe me!"

Some nights I saw him riding sideways up The Wall of Death, and his crazy laugh was louder than his motorcycle.

The lion with the rotten teeth became hysterical at night, growling and hiccuping while people stood watching or gargling back at it, tossing peanuts at it and smacking the bars.

You often got a fight when it was very late at the Fun-O-Rama, two drunks pushing or wrestling each other and kicking, and their girlfriends screaming and other men egging them on.

Neither my big hat nor any amount of hurrying from Millroy could prevent me from seeing those faces or smelling those smells. Then I knew that it was one thing to visit the county fair for a day, but a whole other thing to live there. When I saw someone I knew, I hid because it was like seeing them in a dream in which they were real and I was not, or as though they were dreaming me.

"That's true," Millroy said when I told him. He gripped my shoulders in his excitement. "And what's dangerous about unreality is that it tends to shorten your life. Who wants that?"

We were passing Sno-Kones, Texas Burger, Chili Dogs, Fried Dough, Pizza.

"This is one of the saddest places in the world," Millroy said.

Prince Vladimir, the acrobat, attached lighted sparklers to his buttocks so that he was bristling, and stood on his head. He wagged his butt to the music, which was his trick.

"I taught him that," Millroy said. "How to gain complete control of one set of muscles."

One night Vladimir attached too many sparklers and generated so much heat with his shaking buttocks that he set off the sprinkling system in the show tent and drenched the crowd.

Millroy's show was canceled while they set up pumps and dried the seats.

"What do you see when you walk through this hideous place?" Millroy asked me.

"A whole bunch of stuff," I said.

He thought about this for a moment, and then said, "I'm sorry you have to see it."

But I liked hearing *I'm working without a net!* and *Why, here she is—Annette!*

One night after Millroy's show, a woman in the audience came up to me quickly as I was leaving the stage and I thought she was going to hit me. She was potbellied, her face was hairy, and she wore a baseball cap and muddy sneakers.

"I know you. You're Jilly Farina from Marstons Mills. Listen, kiddo, does your granny know you're here dressed up like that?"

"Madam," Millroy said, "you are mistaken. This young woman, my assistant Annette, is a recent immigrant from the Baltic republic of Latvia and does not speak a word of English."

He fixed the woman by enlarging one of his eyes and leaning forward and back.

She said, "Sorry!"

"That was close," Millroy said.

That same night I lay in bed alone in my wooden cabinet listening to Floyd Fewox's motorcycle sputtering up and down The Wall of Death, and to his crazy laugh drowning out the *rat-tatting* of his engine, and after the applause and the music at the end, I still heard the motorcycle as though it were zigzagging through the fairground. I was not imagining it. The next thing I knew, the motorcycle was revving outside the trailer. Millroy turned on the light and went to the door. I opened the flap to my cubicle and looked out.

Floyd Fewox stood on the trailer steps holding a can of beer.

"Get your shoes on, babe, and let's wail," he said. "You're going for a ride you'll never forget."

Millroy turned his back on the man and said, "It's true—this man taught at Harvard. He wrote a book which got respectful reviews. But he was fired for writing threatening letters to his colleagues and for persecuting students. His irrational views were incompatible with those of a great institution. He spent a great deal of time sobbing his heart out in the university infirmary. He was heavily sedated, and finally was discharged."

"Hey, I'm not denying it," Floyd Fewox said. "I'm wild. You don't believe me."

"He once went into the kitchen for a glass of water for his late wife and disappeared. He showed up three months later wearing nothing but a pair of army surplus combat boots, with the laces undone."

Floyd Fewox laughed, showing the black gaps in his teeth, and took a slug of beer, spilling foam over his stubbly chin, wiped his mouth with the blue tattoo on his arm, and laughed again, like a dog trying to talk.

"You know his problem?" Millroy said. "He's not wild. He's not an outlaw. He's just selfish. He's an intellectual."

"This babe's coming with me," Floyd Fewox said.

He made a move toward me and I thought he was going to touch me, when Millroy took a step and blocked his way.

"I'm challenging you to a duel," Millroy said. He was very calm. His mustache was smooth. His head was dry. He was taller than Floyd Fewox, and more muscular, and pink with health.

"Anytime, buddy."

"A psychic duel," Millroy said.

"I'll rip your ear off and spit in the hole," Floyd Fewox said.

6 Floyd Fewox had been crouching, hunkering down, but the way he stood up with his elbows out told you to make room for him. Then they stood face to face, Floyd Fewox, cackling the way he often did when riding The Wall of Death, and Millroy the Magician.

"Get lost," Floyd Fewox said.

He showed the gaps in his teeth and his terrible wood-colored fangs, and when he opened it wide to laugh at Millroy, his mouth was a dark hole with brown teeth and a black tongue. He slouched in front of Millroy, his thumbs sticking out sideways, squeezing his can of beer in one hand and pinching a cigarette in the other. His greasy jeans were tugged down and I could see the deep shadowy navel in his hairy belly.

"I'm taking this little lady for some Chinese food."

He swigged his beer, let it dribble from his chin, and then wiped his hands on his Harvard T-shirt.

"Pay no attention to him, angel. He's a case of serious mind-fry."

"I'm okay," I said. Millroy was still calm, staring with electric eyes, as though he could see straight through Floyd Fewox and maybe even straight through the walls of the trailer.

"He's had too much to drink," Millroy said. "But that is not the point."

I wanted to say, *Drunks—tell me about them,* as if I had not seen Dada's wet eyes brimming stupidly with Old Grand-Dad enough times. That seemed to be the way it always was with people like that, big messy men who drank and drank, and then just leaked all over, sweating, steaming, nose running, drooling, whatever.

"You're a liar, Millroy."

Even his saying that was familiar, and typical of Dada saying *There's nothing in my hand* when he was holding a bottle, or *I haven't had a drop* when he was falling-down drunk and talked with a wobbly hinge on his jaw.

"The point is that this man is constipated."

"Dada gets wicked constipation, too," I said, and when both Millroy and Floyd Fewox suddenly looked at me, I realized that I had mentioned this because I had been following my train of thought about Dada.

"You think you're strong, huh?" Floyd Fewox said. "Okay, smart guy, pick up this oyster." And he spat a clot of phlegm on the trailer floor.

Millroy smiled a pitying smile.

"She's coming with me. To the China Moon!"

"Not just yet."

Floyd Fewox staggered and then propped himself up by snatching the towel rail beside the sink counter.

"Don't you see that I am challenging you to a duel?"

Floyd Fewox opened his dark hole again, and an angry Wall of Death laugh came out like a bark, and then he bumped the sink.

"But I'd rather you didn't sit down," Millroy said.

Lifting his arms, Fewox looked eagerly for a place to throw his staggering body. He saw a low stool beside the sink, plopped on it and grunted. Millroy's face was blank, his mouth was shut, but there was great confidence in his eyes.

He said, "Go on, Floyd, frazzle me with your power. Make me afraid."

Floyd Fewox leaned forward, showed his dark teeth at Millroy and said, "I'll kill you."

Millroy did not flinch. He said, "Though he became a thug at Harvard, Floyd is an intellectual from Canada. He's ninety-nine percent buffoon. *Neendy-neen.*"

Hearing Millroy mock him with these Canadian words, Floyd Fewox put on his *I'll kill you* face again.

"Say 'Good morning,' " Millroy said, and then, "*gid merning!*"

"I'll break your neck," Floyd said.

"Want one of these?"

Millroy opened his hand and produced a glass of whiskey, and as Floyd dropped his can of beer and reached out, the glass burst open, making a watery explosion that became a bunch of flames. Millroy licked the fire from his fingers and a hissing sound came from his head, like spit on a griddle, and this sound was weirder than the sudden fire.

Floyd Fewox stood up crookedly in surprise, or maybe fear, his arms down and his thumbs rigid.

"Now that I have your attention, perhaps we can continue," Millroy said.

"You think you're better than the rest of us—you and your Airstream trailer. But you're the same. That's what I want your little friend to know." His lips were wet with drink spittle and his face was twisted. "You're the same as us."

"No, I'm not," Millroy said, and seemed to smile. "Are you righteous? Do you have one of these?"

Saying that, he reached into his own ear, pulled a fluttering bird from his earhole and released it. It was a whitish canary, which flew to the windowsill over Floyd's head and began to sing a cheeping song, starting the same three-note tune over and over.

The small, frail bird seemed to taunt Floyd, like someone laughing at his gloom and making him aggressive. When he snatched at it, the bird flew to the sink faucet, tootled again, and took off, Floyd still after him. That was when Millroy put his hand on Floyd's ear, took hold and twisted out a shiny black rat.

Crouched on the back of Millroy's hand, the rat sniffed Millroy's knuckles and whipped its raw tail around his wrist. Its wet browny-black hair—more horrible than its teeth—was pasted flat against its plumpness, and it stank like a sewer.

"This is your own rat," Millroy said, "still slimy from being inside your body."

"Get that thing away from me," Floyd Fewox said.

Millroy glanced at me. "No one likes his own rat. See how disgusted the man is? Whereas the rat is kind of cheery."

Lowering its head, the rat twitched the whiskers on its pink nose.

"This rat came from deep in the bowels of Floyd Fewox," Millroy said, and faced him again. "You've spent your whole life feeding this rat."

"I told you to get it away." Backing up, Floyd hit the wall and lost his balance, sitting down with a grunt on the floor.

"Feed the rat," Millroy said.

And spilled the rat onto Floyd's lap. The man cried out, but the rat did not move. It hung on to the filthy cloth and its wet body softened like tar, then sank and grew small, liquefying to several patches of gleaming oil on the thighs of Floyd's jeans.

"That rat is fluidified," Millroy said.

Floyd Fewox stood up again, slapping his legs and whinnying like a dog too spooked to bark. But when Millroy stared at him he seemed to grow dizzy and sat down again with his back to the wall.

"You couldn't hurt me with your hands—not these hands," Millroy said, and pinched off one of Floyd Fewox's fingers.

He held it up and showed the man the soft white flesh as he snapped it into two pieces. It was impossible to tell whether it was a human finger or an uncooked sausage link until I saw the dirty fingernail on the end.

"You have made yourself into bad meat," Millroy said, and smiled for the first time. The smile had an immediate effect on Floyd Fewox, or was it the cold fire blazing in Millroy's eyes?

Something in Floyd Fewox worked loose, became unstrung, as though allowing an important organ to come unstitched and begin to slip. He stumbled to his feet and went lopsided, then got clumsy. He was moaning *no, no, no, no,* and was trying to keep Millroy away, holding up his hand with the finger stump.

"This Harvard man is crawling with vermin," Millroy said, pushing Floyd's damaged hand aside and removing a smaller rat from his ear, which he held in the palm of his hand and then compressed into a black pellet.

"And what's this?"

He found a tiny egg the size of a finch's egg in Floyd's mouth, making the man gag as he retrieved it.

"No ordinary chicken's egg, that's for sure," Millroy said. He cracked it open in Floyd's face, releasing from the broken shell a wiggly snake, like a green worm. It was active and fat, with a white film of slime over its eyes.

"I hate snakes," Floyd Fewox said in a pleading way. "I hate rats."

"You would," Millroy said, "on account of you're crawling with them. And you're probably not too fond of spiders either."

The thing was hairy and purple, with black legs, and it came straight out of Floyd's mouth, clawing and snagging his lips as it passed through.

The man howled, "What are you doing to me?"

"I wanted to have a psychic duel," Millroy said, "head to head, to give you an eternal brainstorm. But you don't have the mind for it, you don't have the body, and you've got infestation. Look."

There was a cockroach in Millroy's hand, which he had plucked from Floyd's nostril, and when he let it go it flew into Floyd's face and clung to his eye until he clawed it off.

"I'm showing you what you're made of," Millroy said. "Are you aware that you are filled with crawling, sniffing critters?"

The trailer had gotten hot and smelly—not the usual sticky summer-stink of swamp water and skunk cabbage, but something wetter and more rotten. Millroy saw me making a face and knew what I was thinking.

"This man is unmercifully constipated," Millroy said.

Floyd Fewox cowered at the side of the trailer looking sick and wearing a strained, grunting look of fear.

"Here, angel, give him your hand. That's what he wants."

Before I could draw away, Floyd Fewox involuntarily reached out. He did not touch me, and yet when he closed his hand he was holding a flower with a big blossom, like a large blown-open rose. He smiled and brought it to his face, and it went limp, flopped over his fingers, and turned to a smear of thin yellow liquid.

"Everything he touches turns foul," Millroy said calmly, almost sweetly.

Floyd whinnied again and tried to shake the slime from his fingers.

"I can scorch you," Millroy said. "I can make you itch. I can blister you and drive you mad. You'd be in such pain you'd be better off dead.''

This time Floyd Fewox stood and roared—not at Millroy but all around him, as though demons had attacked him with stings and set his skin on fire.

A cup of water materialized in Millroy's hand and he showed it to the whinnying man.

"Drink this."

The man guzzled it, choked and yelled, spitting out flames. He pushed past Millroy, holding his mouth, opened the trailer door and clawed his hair, uprooting some of the scabby plugs that had been planted.

Millroy had hardly touched him. He held a nest of flames in the palm of his hand.

"If you ever look at this little woman again, I'll blind you," he said.

And closed his hand on the flames.

We were left in the scorched silence of the trailer. Millroy said nothing for quite a while. He was slow and exhausted, as though the magic had taken all his strength.

"Jeekers," I said.

Millroy was still breathing.

"That was awesome," I said.

At last he said, "You made it possible," and took another breath into his noisy lungs. "Don't tell anyone what you've seen—not a word of it, not yet."

Who was there to tell? Anyway, it had all frightened me, especially when I remembered that I was sharing the small trailer space with this huge magician.

Millroy went to bed and slept for nine straight hours, as though he were dead, while I lay awake among all the smells and the memory of those sights.

In the morning, before the noon show, Millroy hitched his Ford to the trailer.

"I have nothing to do," he said.

But when I looked at him he was smiling.

"So I think I'll do it tomorrow."

He was still smiling his magician's smile.

"Nothing," he said, and we drove out of the fairground.

7 Heading into the Mashpee rotary behind a huge jingling Coke truck, all the bottles wobbling, Millroy said, "I can hardly believe what I've just done. *I quit my job!* Why are you making that face?"

"I'm, like, why is he so pumped about it?"

He shook his head and smiled the way frustrated people smile.

"Muffin," he said in an unusual voice, forcing himself to be calm, "I am a magician."

Which was exactly why I was making the face. For him, hopping into his Ford and driving his Airstream down the road was a more amazing thing than pulling a full-grown rat out of a man's ear, or eating fire, or making an elephant vanish in a collapsible box.

Millroy thumped the steering wheel and said, "It's you. Tomorrow the fair is going to Cherry Hill, New Jersey. I would be going with them except for you. You did it!"

This made me feel terrible—responsible for all this, the cause of the whole disruption, the reason for the psychic duel and Floyd Fewox's ordeal. But I said nothing. Several times on the road I felt sorry for Millroy and wondered what I should say, but then I remembered that he was a magician, and not just of tricks but of real, baffling magic, creating something out of nothing.

"So where are we going?"

"The thing of it is"—he was smiling a real smile now—"I don't know."

That was one of the times I thought, *Millroy the Magician!*

"Dada lives down that road," I said as he was rounding the rotary. "That's where Gaga thinks I am. At Dada's."

"And Dada thinks you're at Gaga's?"

"Kind of."

"That can't last, but it's good for now." He was slowing down. "I'd like to see this Dada of yours."

He spun the steering wheel and took the Mashpee shortcut, Waquoit Road, racing past the Senior Center and the low, shaded houses and chicken runs. Some barefoot boys and a woman in a torn dress were sitting on a front porch; a pig was loose under some trees in a yard on Crocker Road.

"Most people see a fat pig and think of mustard," Millroy said. "It's so sad."

Mashpee Baptist Church came up on the left, River Bend Motel on the right, then the fire station and Mashpee Town Hall, and Lucius Hooley's wooden roadside stand with an arrow sign, FRESH SQUASH.

"High fiber, high residue, high in beta carotene," Millroy said. "Mentioned in Jonah. That man is rendering a valuable service."

"He's a Wampanoag," I said.

Millroy looked at me.

"An Indian," I said.

Millroy turned left at the town hall.

"I mean, a Native American," I said. "And Dada's down there."

Saying his name made me curious about him because the last time I had seen him he was flat on his back, blacked out and gurgling on the floor of his trailer.

Millroy did not hesitate. He headed along Snake Pond Road, past the Indian Museum and the waterworks, and kept going past Ma Glockner's chicken restaurant and the stove shop and the Cheapo Depot.

"Dada's gas station is on the left, next to Mister Donut."

Millroy said, "You took the bus from here to the fairground?" .

"It's safer than bumming," I said. "Plus I didn't have to take it back, right?"

"You will never bum a ride ever again," Millroy said, and it sounded like the noblest promise I had ever heard.

All the trees hereabouts were bluey-green and brilliant in the morning sun, the pitch pines and the dense maples crowding the narrow road.

"So your father owns a filling station?"

"Dada pumps gas," I said, and because it made him sound like an underachiever, which he was, I added, "And he's a motor mechanic."

"I have great respect for anyone who can repair an automobile," Millroy said, again nobly, and I could see that quitting and driving away from the county fair had put him in a good mood.

He pulled off the road against a stony sandbank, beside a stand of pitch pines.

"Better hop in the trailer, angel."

I did so, crouching under a side window so that Dada would not see me at the Gas and Go.

What was it that Millroy had said about Fewox? *This man is unmercifully constipated.* I remembered this when I saw Dada appear from the office, a greasy rag flopping at his pants pocket. He seemed plump and pale next to Millroy, and he looked a wreck. He must have had a heavy night, but that was not what I noticed most. He seemed almost lifeless, half-dead and cranky, self-pitying and trembly. Millroy stood straight, he smiled, he was pleasant to this grumpy man, even got out of the car and flipped open the gas flap. Dada's name patch said RAY. All this was odd because I had been expecting the two men, Millroy and Dada, to be more alike.

"Fill it up?" Dada asked, already sounding disgusted. He looked ill, but I knew Millroy was diagnosing bad diet.

"All the way."

"Cash or charge?" Dada said, jamming the iron nozzle into the gas tank.

"Cash," Millroy said, inhaling and glancing around, taking in the gas station and the trees and Mister Donut. "What a lovely morning."

Dada blew air through his nose with a sound like sandpaper.

"Makes you feel glad to be alive," Millroy said.

Dada faced him and frowned. "I wouldn't go that far."

Meanwhile, the gas pump was *ping-pinging* and Dada had kept one hand behind his back. Now he showed it; he was holding a cigarette. He put it to his lips and sucked hard on it.

Millroy said, "Smoking is not mentioned anywhere in the Scriptures."

Dada stayed silent, believing he was being criticized. He hated God, he once told me.

"Which is not very surprising, seeing as how they didn't grow tobacco in the Holy Land."

Dada gave Millroy an uncomprehending grin.

"But I was just thinking of the fire hazard," Millroy said.

"That you, still talking? Funny, for a minute there I thought I left the radio on," Dada said. He sighed loudly, spat on the ground, and then clicked the trigger of the gas nozzle rapid-fire, watching the gasoline splash down the side of the Ford. I disliked him and felt sorry for him at the same time.

I did not concentrate on how Dada and Millroy were different—different sizes, different heights, different in complexion. Dada was grubby, Millroy was clean. Dada was fattish, the sort of man who looks strong, but I knew that Millroy was stronger.

No, the longer I looked at them, the more I was amazed by their similarities. Dada was shrewd and could be funny, like Millroy. They were both unpredictable. They were about the same age. They were alike in many ways. Dada was sometimes a con man, and his magic was making money disappear. He had schemes and always talked about having great ambitions, and changing the world was one of them. In the end I decided that Dada was a failed version of Millroy.

"Eight dollars," Dada said.

"I used to smoke three packs a day," Millroy said, holding up a credit card.

"You said cash." Dada's jaw twitched. He seemed weak—that was it, the main difference—and his weakness made you feel unsafe.

Twisting the credit card into his fingers, Millroy manipulated it until it softened and turned green, then unrolled it—a twenty-dollar bill. It was a wonderful trick.

Dada shrugged, refusing to be impressed. "You don't have anything smaller?"

Millroy folded it into his fingers and turned it into a ten, which Dada took without blinking.

When he came back with Millroy's change and counted the two bills into Millroy's hand, Millroy said, "Mind looking at the plugs? She's misfiring."

"I don't work on American cars," Dada said. "For philosophical reasons."

Later, when we were on the road again and I was in the front seat, Millroy said, "He was kind of funny. You have to respect that. And he's not stupid."

I kept my eyes on the road.

"But he has no leadership qualities. He's not goal-oriented. And his health is a little worrying."

"He drinks," I said.

"He's got Smoker's Face. He's got Smoker's Voice. His skin's a mess, lost a lot of porosity. He's not regular at all. I'm not a fanatic, muffin, but your Dada could use a conversion."

He was steering us through Forestdale, a place I loved for its small houses and big trees.

"I used to go to camp here."

Millroy did not hear me. He was still thinking about Dada. "He could be precancerous," he said, "but then most Americans are."

Soon we were on the Mid-Cape Highway, heading west.

"Want to go back?"

I shook my head and Millroy laughed joyfully.

"You saved me. This is another life—it's wonderful."

It was a beautiful day, the sun whitening the road, the trees thrashing in the sea breeze blowing up from Falmouth, the other cars whistling past us, our old rounded Airstream trailer jogging along behind.

Millroy said, "That's why I am so grateful to you. I was hungry and you fed me. With inspiration."

I wanted to say, *Wait a minute, you're the one who does the magic, not me.*

"And that's why I need you, pudding."

It worried me greatly, his saying that.

"What's wrong?" he asked, because I had cringed and looked miserable.

"I don't know what you want me to do."

"Don't do a blessed thing," he said, and smiled and smacked my leg, and I cheered up.

He pulled into the outlet mall near the Sagamore Bridge, explaining that with an Airstream trailer you did your shopping according to which place had the best parking lot. In Wallace's Family Clothes Factory, he fumbled through the clothes and made a pile—blue jeans, shirts, a pair of sneakers. He asked me whether there was anything I wanted.

"Maybe something like a tank top."

"Too revealing," he said.

He bought me a loose long-sleeved shirt and a baseball hat, a short leather jacket and a sweat suit. Then, the trailer still parked, he took me inside, sat me down and pulled the window shades.

"What now?"

He towered over me, holding a pair of scissors, going *snick-snick* with them.

"I'm going to make you nice and cool," he said. *Snick-snick.*

But I trusted him. He put his hot face near my head and cut my hair very short. When he was through, he said he would leave me alone so I could change into my new clothes. I put on the blue jeans, polo shirt, and sneakers. Wearing them, I felt shapeless and younger. I yearned for the sequined dress and the cape and the lipstick I had worn when I had been his assistant, Annette—"It's dangerous working without a net!" But he had bought these clothes for me with his money and it seemed ungrateful to refuse to wear the hosepipe pants and the kid's shirt.

We crossed the bridge and followed the signs to Buzzards Bay, where he pulled over at a roadside telephone. He talked for a while and listened intently, squinting into the mouthpiece of the phone.

"That was a trailer park."

I did not know what to say. The Cape was full of trailer parks. Dada lived in a trailer in Mashpee.

"It's run by a preacher, the Reverend Baby Huber. Ever meet him?"

"Never even heard of him."

"That's good. He has a Fat Voice."

Now I understood that Millroy knew what a person was like from the way he or she looked: Fat Voice, Smoker's Face, all that.

Pilgrim Pines Trailer Park was located on the canal side of Buzzards Bay, near the railway bridge. A sign said HOOK-UPS AVAILABLE—ALL FACILITIES. Millroy swung his Airstream into the lot, where a fat little man in a baseball hat was waiting with a clipboard.

"How long you planning to stay?"

"Days or weeks, I'm not sure," Millroy said. "We're on vacation, aren't we, son?"

Son?

Was he talking to me?

8 After we got hooked up and were inside the trailer, I wanted to say to Millroy, "I didn't appreciate that."

When a truthful person tells you a lie, he turns into someone else, and if you don't say anything about it, so do you. Then you have to think hard about everything else he has ever said to you. I had trusted

Millroy for his being true—it had encouraged me to go with him. I believed I would be safe. Now with this *Aren't we, son?* business, I was not so sure.

But that was what he had said to the Reverend Baby Huber, manager of the Pilgrim Pines Trailer Park in Buzzards Bay, and I became seriously worried, more worried than when he had whispered to me, *I need you, pudding.*

"Where are you going, sugar?"

"Rest room." It was his usual word.

Millroy said, "Just take your time."

It was not what he thought. It was my period, not my first one but the strangest one, because this was my first day as a boy and I was not feeling boyish. I was crampy and weak and leaky. I attended to my bleeding, then looked at my reflection in the mirror.

My face was small, I had freckles, my nose was sunburned and peeling, my eyelashes and eyebrows were sunbleached like my hair, though most of it had been chopped off in the crewcut Millroy had given me. Because of the short hair, my ears stuck out. I wore a baggy shirt and loose jeans, the rolled-up kind that Little Leaguers liked. Now I knew why Reverend Huber had not blinked.

Never mind how I felt; I had passed for Millroy's son. I could see that I was more convincing-looking as Millroy's son than as Millroy's anything else. And in the way that I had seen a resemblance between Millroy and Dada, I also saw one between Millroy and me—the same resemblance.

Yet I began to think that Millroy was sorry about the lie, because it was one of those lies that you had to keep telling the next day and the next, because I had to go on being his son and wearing these clothes as long as we stayed at Pilgrim Pines.

"You're regular," he said when I came out of the rest room. "See, they knew something about high-residue diet, too."

I said nothing. He knew nothing about my period. He thought that I was brooding about his lie. I could tell he wanted to be forgiven.

"What would you be doing right now if you were at your Gaga's house?" he said.

It was about seven-thirty at night, mosquito time, cricket harmonizing, skunk hour, just getting dark.

"Probably watching TV."

Without another word Millroy hurried into Buzzards Bay and bought a twelve-inch Panasonic TV set. He jammed in the rabbit ears, put it on the prop-up dining table and turned it to face my bunk.

"All the comforts of home," he said.

Millroy's trailer, a Wally Byam Airstream, was set up like one of his magic boxes, full of secret compartments, panels and sliding doors. He said that everything he owned, all his tricks, all his books, his whole wardrobe, was in that little trailer. The biggest, whitest, warmest room was the rest room, set up like a vanishing cabinet, with pull-down facilities, fold-away plumbing and pop-out drawers.

Millroy had a magician's ability to conceal large objects in a small space and to make other things disappear. He kept his trained birds in a special rack that hung on the rounded rear end of the trailer. "I'm always fighting contamination." They clucked and cooed in a series of boxes like pull-out drawers with holes drilled in them. Inside the trailer were pull-down tables and fold-out chairs. The sink was a pop-out, and so was the stove. My sleeping cubicle had walls that swung aside like shutters, a foldaway bed-shelf and a door with a triple lock. It was just like the ones in his magic act in which he took an unsuspecting little girl from the audience, locked her in the box and made her disappear. I was not worried by that. I was glad my cubicle was designed like a vanishing cabinet: it meant there was plenty of room inside where I could hide.

I was in it right now, looking at *Julia Child's Art of French Cooking* but not paying much attention to the old woman with the big wooden spoon.

"I wish you wouldn't watch that, angel."

He was very gentle, still trying to please me, still wanting to be forgiven.

"I'm not watching it," I said. "I'm thinking."

"What about?"

"Tons of things," I said. "Like seeing Dada at the Gas and Go, the way you were talking to him, and those clothes you bought me at the outlet mall." Then in a panic, my eyes hurting, I put it to him: "Plus I was wondering why you called me your son."

"Because you're underage," Millroy said, "and people always jump to the wrong conclusions. Particularly someone like the Reverend Baby Huber."

That was the main thing, but there were other things. I could see

Millroy being extra-careful, trying to avoid scaring me. Our going-to-bed ritual had became elaborate and fussy.

"Now I'll just step outside while you put on your jams."

They were boy's pajamas with flapping sleeves and a drawstring on the big legs. I put them on fast. In those first days, I never felt nakeder than when I was naked in Millroy's trailer, but I soon ignored the fact that in his act he bugged his eyes out and said, *I can see through walls!*, because he was so kind to me.

He gave me time to change and then, returning to the trailer, always announced what he was doing so as not to spook me. "I'm locking this door tight," he said when he was inside. "I'm drawing the curtains, and fastening the walls on my bedshelf"—the vanishing cabinet across the room that he slept in. Then, two clunks on the floor: "They were my shoes, angel." I heard him breathing softly; he had a strong man's way of breathing, a sort of steady purr of powerful lungs. "Now I'm climbing in and locking up. See you in the morning, pudding."

I imagined him on his bedshelf, wrapped in his blanket like a parcel, purring through the wool.

In the darkness that first night at Pilgrim Pines, after a summer silence—crickets, the wind in the pines, the mooing of the foghorn at the canal entrance—he cleared his throat, sounding like a drain emptying.

Then he piped up, "And because of something else . . ."

He was resuming the talk we'd had earlier in the day. It startled me. I had thought he was asleep, but his wide-awake voice filled the room.

"Because I believe I was you in a former life," he said.

A former life? This just confused me. I had been listening to boats passing through the canal, trying to make out from their sound or the wash of their wake against the banks whether they were big or small, freighters or sailboats.

Often, figuring what Millroy said was like doing arithmetic.

"If you were me in a former life, huh, who was I?"

"Good question," he said. There was a dark, buzzing little pause, interrupted by the foghorn. "The answer is, you were me. We were each other."

"Sounds okay," I said because I did not understand it.

What did it matter, either way? It did not change anything. It was perhaps more magic, trying to make something so by saying it was so. What he did with his hands, his magic manipulation, he often did with words. So what he said—the words, the meanings—was often like something out of nothing, colorful, shocking, unexpected, funny and bright, even reassuring. He could talk magic. He had talked me into being a boy.

"That's why I could never hurt you."

"Sounds good."

I was happy enough being a boy. When I was supposed to be Annette in my sequined costume and cape, Millroy had seemed not dangerous but a little steamed, giving off simmering vibrations and a hesitant surge of heat, like a toaster just before it pops up. I had felt it as we walked down the Fun-O-Rama midway with Floyd Fewox and the others looking. I could even feel it onstage from people in the audience. It made me feel small and white. But as a boy I did not feel this surge. No one looked at me, not Reverend Huber or his son Todd, or any of the other trailer people at Pilgrim Pines—the Silverinos, F. X. McEachern, Franny Grasso, Bea Rezabeck, the Glenn Branums, the Lucas Huffmans, the Blevinses, Thressa and Ross Lingell, Tike Overmore, Lee and Chuck Reddish and their daughter Misty, who Millroy said I could not play with. Millroy relaxed. When we walked along, we did so like father and son, and that suited me. Now I had an inkling of how my being a boy affected him—no surge, no steam, and no one was suspicious of him.

As a girl I had sensed that he was strongly a male—a man. But as a boy, his so-called son, I began to regard him as my father, not Dada but a safe one, generous and protective, big and friendly. He would take care of me. With Dada I had always felt I was in danger.

He was happier too, and less guilty about having made me vanish in the Indian basket and then driving off with me.

And it was fun being someone else. The past was rubbed out. I was starting all over again new, and I was not alone, even though sometimes I felt like it.

It was Millroy's TV watching. He had bought the set for me, but then he became interested in it—at first in an offhand way, sort of turning his head to look, and then in an unstoppable way, with his face flat against the screen. He began watching *The Hour of Power, Festival of Faith, Faith for Life, Reasons to Believe,* and *Healing Hands, with Pastor Walter Murray Clemens.*

He smiled, stroking his big mustache as though it were his pet. He was fascinated, not happy but disgusted.

"They're awful, they're subversive, they're all about money."

It was true. All the programs asked for donations to keep the program on the air, they said, to spread the word.

"I had no idea they were so rapacious."

Millroy said that since joining Foskett's Circus Promotions he had not paid any attention to television, but this was better than any midway show. It reached more people, it was technically better, it was simpler, more direct, more entertaining and conveyed more information.

"But you said they were awful."

"I'm describing their potential, sugar."

The Bible programs were only half of it. The other half was children's shows. Mostly he watched early in the morning—cartoons, puppet shows, *Scooby-Doo, The Flintstones, Balloony and Muttrix, Quackerbox, The Chippies, Voyage to Candy Mountain.* Sometimes I heard him watching even before I woke up, when it was still dark.

Where are you going with that hamster, Muttrix?

Hamsterdam, of course, you bean brain!

Now and then I heard Millroy's unmistakable chuckle, pumping little bursts of air through his nose. He watched *Sesame Street* and *Captain Kangaroo,* many of them reruns of programs I had seen when I was five.

"That man used to be Clarabelle the Clown," he said. "Bob Keeshan. Kind of low-key and lovable."

Millroy was looking at the man, Captain Kangaroo, a big man in a blue uniform with a mustache similar to his own.

"But a dietary disaster."

Millroy was smiling in pity, and then he turned to me.

"Howdy Doody? Mister Bluster? Buffalo Bob?"

I shook my head.

"You're so young, angel."

"I used to watch *Captain Kangaroo,*" I said. "I liked *The Flintstones* better, though."

"I can go with the immediacy, but I'm uncomfortable with the unreality of cartoons. This fellow's very talented."

He meant Captain Kangaroo, who was talking to the simple skinny man, Mister Green Jeans.

I'm just going to put my bales of hay in my wagon, Mister Green Jeans said. *And then we can eat some of that cherry pie.*

"All over America, children are yelling, 'Ma, I want a piece of cherry paahhhhhh!' "

I laughed at the way he imitated a small stuttering child, but then he became very serious.

"The power these people have," he said. "A county fair magic act is nothing to this. I needed to be reminded of that."

He went on watching Bible programs and the children's shows, and soon it was all children's shows, the early-morning ones, the late-afternoon ones, some of them new to me, many of them reruns: *Teenage Mutant Ninja Turtles, The Mickey Mouse Club, Big Brother Bert, Robby the Parrot, Whiskery Pete in the Yukon, The Jingle Family and Their Dog Fred, Yogi Bear.* He never missed *Paradise Park with Mister Phyllis,* a Boston show that was on every morning between eight and nine.

"Why do you like that show?" I asked him one morning when he was sitting in front of *Paradise Park.*

"Who said I liked it?" he said, keeping his eyes on the screen.

I felt lonely and excluded when Millroy watched these shows. He often watched them while doing yoga exercises, sitting in total silence, wrapped tightly, or with one leg flung around his neck, or stretched out with his arms twisted backward like a human pretzel. He could hold his breath for an hour or more—for an entire episode of *Paradise Park,* he said. "I have total lung control. I've been buried alive in a sealed box. I hold an underwater record." His elbows and knees were double-jointed. He could put himself in a trance, sitting or standing. He could shut off his nerve endings, he said, so that he felt no pain at all. He could eat glass. He could stick pins into his body and still watch TV.

This made me feel lonely, too, but I never felt lonelier than the night he yelled in a dream into the darkness of the trailer, *I ain't ready!*

He did not explain it. The next morning he was tying himself in knots and saying to me, "Punch me in the stomach! Go ahead! Hard as you can!"

This Reggie Bear is precious, Mister Phyllis said. *Look at his lifelike eyes, just warmly glowing. Isn't he super?*

"How do I do it?" Millroy said. "How do I resist pain, perform magic, sleep like a log, multiply six-digit sums in my head, swallow and hurl razor blades?''

Chickens, do you have a bear that you take to bed? Mister Phyllis asked, peering out of the TV screen at Millroy.

''Because I know health,'' Millroy said. ''Simple as that. It has allowed me to gain control of nine of my bodily functions.''

I had seen him stand on his head in front of the television set and watch an entire program that way. He could hoist himself twenty-two times doing one-arm push-ups. He stuck lighted matches under his fingers. You could punch him in the stomach as hard as you wanted and he just laughed.

I know a song about warm furry bears, Mister Phyllis said.

''I can make any of these organs obey me.''

I was thinking, *Organs? Which organs?*

''Not everyone can say that.''

This sort of talk made me wonder what I was doing in a trailer park in Buzzards Bay on a Saturday morning dressed as a boy with a big middle-aged magician standing upside down on his bald head and watching a children's show on TV.

I would have asked Millroy that very question if I could have thought of a way of putting the words together. With each passing day it became harder for me to ask, and, though I could not explain why, less urgent. I accepted this man as he had accepted me.

Meanwhile, Millroy spent most mornings in front of the TV set, in a yoga posture, arms and legs looped together, clenching and throbbing.

''I am not afraid of anything mortal,'' he said. I did not mention his dream, when he had yelled. ''It is wonderful that we are together, that we have each other, that we have everything ahead of us.''

Some bears are frightful snobs when it comes to elevenses, and they want fresh jam and clotted cream with their hot scones, don't they, Titch?

''Two hundred years,'' Millroy said.

''*—sits there on his little bottikins . . .*''

''Because I have an exemplary set of bowels,'' Millroy said. Then he laughed very hard, and I did not know whether he was joking or serious. I had no idea what he was talking about. I had never heard anyone talk so much about the inside of their body. Millroy often described his kidneys—how he flushed them out. His lungs—the way he hyperventilated them. His heart—how he got it pumping, sluicing its gates and chambers. He could activate his intestines while you watched, his stomach roiling like snakes squirming inside a bag. "Peristalsis," he said. "That's control."

"So they come in sets," I said. "I don't think many people know that."

That made him happy, and he looked at me closely. He said nothing, but it was his *I want to eat you* face.

The Reverend Baby Huber's son Todd often came over to the trailer in the morning and asked me to go out and play. "How about a game of horseshoes?" "Want to shoot layups?" "I know a neat place to swim."

Millroy said we were occupied with his project. *Paradise Park* was playing in the background.

"I hate that guy," Todd said, looking through the trailer door. "Plus he thinks he's English."

"We're busy," Millroy said.

"Wicked busy," I said.

"My dad's been on TV. *Festival of Faith.* He led the offerings. We got the video."

Millroy showed his teeth, rolled up his sleeve, showed Todd an enormous blue and red tattoo of a dagger on his forearm and then made it vanish.

Todd was not impressed.

"So what about it? I've got the horseshoes."

"Let go, sonny," Millroy said, and shut the door. Then he said, "Kids that age have an animal intuition. Or did you tell him something?"

"I don't talk to him, being as I don't even have a name," I said.

Millroy said nothing, but that night at the pajama hour he said, "Time for bed, Alex."

We were so near the Cape Cod Canal we could not only hear the ships passing through, but also their chains clanking, the men on them, their voices sounding small and sometimes cross. Just behind our trailer, men on the embankment cast long lines for bluefish and ate sandwiches.

Those late-August days were hot and humid, hottest when the skies were gray, but there was often a breeze after lunch springing up from Falmouth and the islands, blowing through Woods Hole.

The trailer park was surrounded by a grove of tall, restless oaks and pitch pines, and all around us a deep layer of old leaves and reddish pine needles covered the ground. At night in the dark there was a strong piney smell, but if the tide was out there was a syrupy stink of mud flats, of clams and kelp and old rope and sea salt from Buzzards Bay, and there were always more birds at low tide. After ten days or so, being with Millroy was my way of life, and I never asked or dared to wonder what was coming next.

One night around this time, the air thick with low tide and the *rat-tat-tat* of boats motoring up to Sandwich through the canal, I was lying in my bunk on my shelf in the cabinet, all my shutters locked tight. Millroy's voice started in the darkness. It was his wide-awake voice. He had been sleeping.

"But what about this Gaga of yours?" he said, and paused to hum. "Won't she be wondering about you?"

"Not really."

"You're sucking your thumb, angel."

I slipped my thumb out of my mouth.

"She thinks I'm with Dada."

Millroy hummed a little more, the sound of him thinking.

"Does she ever worry about you?"

"There's nothing for her to worry about."

After a shorter hum, just a phrase of it, Millroy said, "Not even when you're out and about all alone?"

"I never go out and about all alone."

"You were alone at the fairground, sugar."

"Because Dada was dead black-out drunk and couldn't take me."

"You were still alone, though."

"And Vera was probably fishing."

Millroy considered this; I could hear him, and now I was wide-awake, too, in the darkness, with all these questions. I was dreading more. I did not have to wait long.

"Doesn't your Gaga worry about you and boys?"

"Which boys?"

"Any," Millroy said, and cleared his throat.

"Boys are just trouble."

"That's what I mean, pudding."

"I don't pay any attention."

"But your Gaga might worry about them bothering you."

"She knows I don't stand for any fooling."

"And yet," he said smoothly, "she thrashed you."

"That was for other stuff," I said.

Millroy was silent.

"Sulking," I said.

"Why were you sulking?"

"I wasn't. I was just sad, missing Mumma and feeling bad about Dada."

"Someday death and illness will be rare occurrences, but even so."

I could tell he was trying to think of another question.

"What did your Gaga say when you came home late?"

"Who says I came home late?" I sat up straight in the darkness. My thumb had gotten cold from being wet. "I never came home late."

"Bunny, do you want me to believe 'never'?"

"Please don't call me bunny," I said. "Hey, I never went out with boys in the first place."

"What about dating?"

"I hate that word, plus I'm, like, 'What does it really mean?'"

Millroy hummed again, thinking hard.

"Wasn't there someone special in your life?"

Slowly I lay down on my bunk again. I did not answer. I thought, *Why didn't I pretend I was asleep when he started these questions?* The last one was the toughest one because it made me think again of Mumma, and I felt small and lonely, back to my old life. I looked behind me and saw myself at Gaga's in Marstons Mills as a silent solitary person with no friends, someone people picked on because she was small and the rest of the world did not know or care about her. Most days I did not believe that I really existed, and I felt like a harmless ghost haunting the world from behind a big window because no one spoke to me or saw me or paid any attention. Was this why I had gone with Millroy so easily?

"Wasn't there someone you opened your heart to?" Millroy asked. "Someone you trusted?"

I was still silent, thinking, *I trusted you, Doc.*

"Someone you would offer anything to, and wouldn't draw the line anywhere?"

Now the air surged with heat and pine scent, and I saw in a stifling way what he meant by his questions.

"No," I said in a croaky voice.

Millroy went very quiet. I could hear the purring of his breath through his blanket, and I knew he was rigid in his own cabinet, thinking of what I had just said. My boys' pajamas were stuck to my skin, my hair was plastered to my head and my hands were damp. The thumb I sucked when I was alone felt small, like a whittled-down stick.

In that same croaky voice, half-sorrowful and half-defiant, I said, "Nobody ever touched me."

There was something like a gasp from Millroy's corner of the trailer, as though he had been holding his breath.

"Good girl," he said.

"And if anyone ever tried anything funny like that with me I'd get wicked angry and try to kill them."

Thinking about it, I started to cry, then stuck my thumb back into my mouth and felt better.

Millroy said nothing else. After a while I fell asleep, and in the morning, as usual, he was watching *Prayer Line* and *Paradise Park with Mister Phyllis,* doing yoga upside down. Even so, I could tell that he was glad to see me, and I felt safe again.

"Morning, sugar. There's a breakfast plate in the pantry, melon balls, wheaten loaves and honey."

I was looking at Mister Phyllis.

"What is it about that guy?"

"He's twisted," Millroy said, "but this show could be licked into shape."

He watched nothing except *Paradise Park* for a week after that, ignoring even the Bible shows.

That was the week after Labor Day, and the summer was over. No matter how hot it was during the day it was cold at night, cold enough that I needed a sweater and had to start wearing socks; and the more clothes I wore, the more I felt like a boy—Alex, as far as anyone else was concerned. For the first time, for as long as I could remember, I would not be heading back to school. It made me happy to think I would not have to deal with all that, but the thought of explaining it to Gaga and Dada worried me. Most of all I was afraid that the school would get to them before I did.

"I'll take care of them," Millroy said, reading my thoughts. I was grateful to him for caring about me and liking me and surprising me with his magic.

A few days later I smelled cold leafmeal from beneath the trees, and my nose was pinched by drier air, and it was quieter at night—fewer cars on the roads, fewer boats on the canal, ducks in the sky looking distant and frantic. I knew the summer was over and that we had to face them after all this time. But at least I was not alone anymore.

9 The trees of the Upper Cape were bright with September streaks—yellow patches here and there, a few bunches of orangy leaves, splashes in the maples, fluttery rust-red leaves in the stuck-out boughs of the pepperidge trees, and every back road crowded and overhung with buttery branches that the school bus always banged into. We saw one do it just off Cotuit Road.

"Miss school, muffin?"

"I stunk at it."

"Smart kid like you?"

"They said I had a learning disorder. A.D.D. Attention Deficit Disorder. I used to stare at stuff for a wicked long time. I never heard them when they talked to me at school."

And the longer I had stayed away from Gaga's the less I wanted to go back.

"I like it when you stare."

Millroy called Gaga from the public phone at Pilgrim Pines ("This is Dicktronics Telemarketing," was all I heard him say). He could tell by the sound of her voice that she abused her body "violently."

"She has a Fat Voice, a congested heart, and labored breathing from the tar on her lungs," Millroy said. "I don't even want to think about her muscle tonus."

Never mind her health; that was no excuse. My supposed reason for being away from her was a lie, and growing bigger and stranger, and now that I had been away so long—almost six weeks—the lie was such a monster that I was afraid to uncover it.

Maybe Gaga and Dada knew I had run away, and maybe they were mad. Maybe they had already called the police. I did not want to face that crazy old woman and that drunken man. But Millroy said we had to, or else.

"I want the best for you, even if it means losing you. Your future is what matters most."

"They'll go coo-coo."

"No."

"Gaga will scream wicked loud and Dada will hit me."

"Let me handle them."

That word made me remember that I had once seen him juggle a bowling ball (big), a chain saw (going) and a blowtorch (lit). He had made an elephant disappear. I also remembered his saying that he was good with kids but did not have much luck with adults.

"I have to be careful. They'll get the police after me," Millroy said. "Ever notice? The police are very poor listeners."

He had unhooked the Ford from the Airstream, and I got into the front seat with two sandwiches of alfalfa sprouts, a jug of grape juice, a pomegranate and a cantaloupe to eat with a spoon. We drove on back roads toward Marstons Mills, the Ford slanting and curving under the trees that had just begun to turn.

It was a Sunday in that slow, uncertain time of year, the last hesitating days of late summer. On the Cape in these weeks, it was as though the weather had feelings—mostly regrets, but also plenty of pride. Except for the first hot days of May, I liked it better than any other time. It was a month of clear skies, cold lawns, browny cornstalks, too many tomatoes, squashes and pumpkins, and empty roads. People started to wear socks again. The bushes and the trees were thick with green leaves and those occasional blobs of color. Soon all the leaves would be brown, dead and torn off and plastered against the house. After that, fall and winter were a time for holding your breath.

The weather and the trees at home were familiar to me, but home was so strange—nothing like Buzzards Bay, which was not even far. I had last been on the road the week of the Barnstable County Fair. Then I had run away with Millroy the Magician. Now he was heading back, and I wondered whether the road had always been so narrow, the houses so small, squatting against the grass, the wood shingles so weatherbeaten, the spaces between the trees so dark. I felt younger and more helpless here, and yet I knew something important—the way out.

"I feel different," I said. "It all looks different."

"It's the way you're seeing it. And you *are* different," Millroy said. "Stands to reason."

We were passing the grassy runway of Marstons Mills airport, just a wooden shed and an airstrip, which lay like a flat meadow beside the straight road.

"You're regular," Millroy said. "You think it doesn't affect your eyesight?"

"This is the airport."

"All I see is grass." Millroy was driving and glancing. "Regularity is very important."

"It's a meadow. A field, anyway. But planes still land on it."

"Ah, yes. There's a windsock."

"Dada used to work out of here."

"Flying planes?"

I nodded.

"Licensed pilot? Lots of hours on his log?"

I nodded again.

"Charter flights?"

"No. Dada used to be a tuna spotter. You fly out over the ocean and look for tuna fish."

"The tuna is specifically forbidden as food in Leviticus Eleven," Millroy said. "Moses probably wrote that book, by the way. 'Hath not scales,' 'an abomination,' et cetera—all the standbys of the school cafeteria. Never mind, it's one of the more misleading prophetic books. Most of those proscribed animals were worshiped by so-called pagans— Egyptians, desert crazies, what-have-you. Take the pig—worshiped. Take the snake and the eagle—worshiped. Lizards—they were on their knees to them. 'Pay no attention' was what Moses was trying to get across."

We were in the woods again, but when the road straightened out Millroy turned to me.

"Your Seventh-Day Adventist is a sort of tuna spotter, too."

"After Dada got his license revoked on account of his drinking he couldn't go tuna spotting, so he ended up on the pump at the Gas and Go."

"Some people would call that despair," Millroy said. He was twisting his head to look up at the sky. "But not me."

Some black ducks were flying in formation among wisps of cloud. That was another thing about this time of year, always ducks overhead, flying toward Rhode Island.

"Your Dada just lowered his sights. Got a job that allowed him to go on drinking."

"You want to know anything about Gaga?"

"I already know she's not vertical, and I've monitored her emissions on the telephone. That's enough for now. Just point me in her direction."

Gaga's house was a gray frame saltbox with a chicken run behind it, set just off the road in the cold shade of two towering oaks. It needed paint so bad it looked like driftwood, the same splintery dry-bone color. Never mind the flat, weedy yard and stone walls. Never mind the sandy soil your feet sank into, the pitch pines, the bent-over scrub cherries, the sick and scabby maples, the poison staghorn sumacs with leaves turning into yellow knives. Never mind the desperate vines of sour grapes snatching at everything. They were the same as ever. What bothered me was Gaga's house. It was smaller and uglier than I remembered. It startled me like a sudden horrible face. Was it Gaga's old hairy face with the bones showing? Anyway, I did not want to go inside.

The house looked somewhat different, but I did not mind that; Millroy had accustomed me to differences. The way it was dark inside: it had always looked that way. I imagined myself walking in and disappearing, in the way any house swallows you up and never lets you go peacefully but sometimes spits you out.

"You're afraid," Millroy said.

He could tell.

I said, "Not much."

He was silent. He knew I was lying.

"It's just that I'm not ready for this."

"You're regular," he said. "You're ready."

He was steering the Ford into the driveway, which was two wheel-tracks in the weedy yard.

"I believe in you—do you believe in me?"

"Yes."

"Then you believe in yourself, muffin. Let me do the talking. In the meantime, stay in the car."

The fat cat, Yowie, stared and did not hiss at Millroy as he went to the door and knocked. Pretty soon I heard the old *yakkety-yak* of Gaga's complaining voice, then the whisper of Millroy's, then silence.

In a very short time he was back at the car. He knew from my eyes that I wanted to know how she was.

"She's big and angry and crammed with pork, and she looks like Babe Ruth, and where are her teeth?"

He glanced back at the house.

"You think she's sober, but no. She's a dry drunk."

Millroy was still peering at the house and I thought I could make out Gaga's shape, standing perfectly still, her big body in the kitchen.

"Yet she's open to suggestions."

Whatever that meant.

"Come on, angel."

I followed, but I was still afraid that she would yell at me and maybe hit me and call me a tramp. But when she saw me entering the house, she just smiled and wiped her hands on her dress the way she did when they were wet or she had sticky jam on her fingers. She seemed unsteady, as though she was on the verge of tipping over.

"Hi, Jilly," she said.

That made me want to duck. I looked for Millroy but did not see him.

"I like your friend a whole lot," Gaga said.

"Anyway, where is he?" I began to panic.

Gaga was smiling. "Carrying out his inspection. He's servicing the house, and that."

Was she drunk? She wore a silly grin, and her head was cocked to one side; her eyes were half-closed and looked cruel and slitty. The woman terrified me. I thought her grin was a trick. At any moment she was going to attack me—grab my head and begin bashing me. She could be violent and, in spite of her large size, energetic—huffing and puffing and harmful. But today she looked big and soft, with crazy, crinkled hair and those squinting, nutso eyes. Was this what Millroy meant by her Babe Ruth face, plump cheeks with fur on them, like a baby monster?

"The man said he can repair all my appliances." Gaga was trembling quietly, as though her motor were idling. "He says he has to carry out a property inspection first."

I kept out of her reach. I said, "He can fix anything."

Gaga tottered at me again.

"He's wicked strong, too," I said to make her hesitate.

Just then Millroy appeared, so confident you would have thought he was in his own doorway.

"It would be a very great privilege to see your rest room."

Only I knew what this really meant, and why. Millroy sort of held his nose as he waded in.

He was not gone long. His expression was pained and disgusted, his mouth turned down. There was an obvious tingling in his fingers.

"Quite a lot of work to be done in there," he said. "Full of distractions. Drips and stains. Hopper's the wrong height. The seat is a beast. Frankly, I'd gut the whole business. And the other one?"

Gaga stared at him, her goony face wavering.

"You mean you have only the one rest room, ma'am?"

Millroy's eyes were fixed on hers.

"A rest room ought to be clean and comfortable enough to read the Scriptures in," he said. "Something I often do."

Now I realized that Gaga seemed a little sad as it sank in—you could see it in her eyes—that Millroy was flunking her.

"I'd love to see what you've done with your kitchen," he said.

I could not imagine what Gaga would say to this. Would she hit him? No, she smiled instead, shuffled her dirty slippers and showed him the way.

To me she said, "As you know, I have great respect for the medical profession."

A lie, but she seemed to believe it. It was then that I noticed she was breathing normally, not wheezing. She was relaxed, tired perhaps. It was her after-dinner mood when she was full of food, having finished a huge meal of take-out fried clams and onion rings from Winky's Clam Shack or a Centerville pizza, when she heaved herself into a chair to watch the news, when she might even burp and say, "That's funny,

Jilly. I'm not hungry anymore.'' I could see she was not going to hit me. She turned her moo-cow eyes from me to Millroy.

He was opening the refrigerator door, and when the sticky rubber seal sucked apart, a small whimper of pain escaped his lips as the smeared shelves lit up: whole-fat milk in a half-gallon jug, ''Tropical Cocktail'' in a rusty can, pork sausages, hard, cracked cheese, dead Yoo-Hoos, leftover meatloaf getting gray, last week's Jell-O, a gnawed ham bone, two opened cans of cat food for Yowie, a yellow fried-chicken thigh, half a loaf of white bread, a carrot that looked like a screwdriver, black seaweedy lettuce, a jar of Miracle Whip, a bitten-off piece of Mars Bar with teethmarks in the chocolate, bottles of pink wine, plastic bottles of diet cola.

Millroy was thinking: *death and damnation.*

''You eat these puppies?'' he said, and pinched a mouse out of a plate of burned pork sausages.

The pink and black mouse squealed under Gaga's nose, and she looked at it sadly as Millroy tucked it back onto the plate, where it curled up, imitating a sausage link.

''Chicken thigh's fresh.'' Gaga's tongue was gray as she spoke.

''Just the word 'thigh,' angel.'' Millroy was shaking his head at me. ''You wouldn't eat this on a bet, and even if you did you'd lose.''

''I eat everything,'' Gaga said, swaying, ''that's put in front of me.''

''Murder,'' Millroy said.

Gaga seemed sad and was growing sadder, as though Millroy had found her valve and was letting air out of her.

A slope had been hacked into the chopping board, which was dull gray with meat grease. Millroy ran a fork across it, making tracks.

''Botulism,'' he said. ''Think of all those carcasses. Don't scrub it, burn it.''

Smiling sadly in her drugged and dreamy way, Gaga seemed to agree with him.

But she could be so tricky. *I won't touch your loose tooth, I just want to look at it. Open up.* She would breathe these words into my face just before she stuck her sour fingers into my mouth and clawed my tooth out. Even now, she might still explode and snatch my hair and kick me in the legs and tell me I was creepy and cost too much money.

''This is all very discouraging,'' Millroy said. He lifted a plastic bowl with a quivering mass inside it. ''Does this have a name?''

"Salad," Gaga said. It was red and white and brown.

"Ingredients?"

"Jell-O, can of crushed pineapple chunks, peanuts, and Cool Whip. It's nice on a hot summer day, ain't it, Jilly?"

Millroy made wild eyes at me and plucked a pink, struggling mouse from the bowl, making Gaga wince.

This house was a dusty trap, containing all my lonely past. I felt sick, I felt small, I wanted to go. I was afraid I might enter my bedroom and be trapped again. All this time I longed to be back in the Airstream in my little cupboard, away from this witch's cottage.

But I was grateful that Gaga did not attack me. She seemed peaceful the way she went humping back and forth behind Millroy. He reached under tables and chairs, moved lamps, lifted rugs. Was he searching for one thing or many? He fished from one room to the other, and then he saw me looking at him and read the question on my face.

"I'm looking for signs of life."

After a while he stood still and seemed to size up the rooms he had checked—the bathroom, the kitchen, the hallway, the parlor with its catstink, TV set and bowl full of goldfish ("Probably the only edible thing in the entire house").

"We've got a problem," he said.

Gaga's sloping smile tightened with anxiety.

"I hope you're not mad," she said.

"Not mad," he said. "Disappointed."

"Is this going to cost me anything?"

That was the old Gaga.

"Not a cent," Millroy said. "But there are other consequences."

Gaga lost all expression, and her big, blank face with pale eyes and big jaw was like the front of her own old car.

"We've got a serious health risk on the premises," Millroy said.

Gaga accepted this, nodding.

"You want this little girl to be healthy," Millroy said, "eating nutritious whole grains, soups, breads, porridges, honeys, and tree-ripened fruits."

I could see these words enter Gaga's brainpan and rattle around, making her head wobble a little.

"You are going to leave her with me. You are grateful that this opportunity has arisen," Millroy said. "Take care of yourself as best you can, and let me handle Jilly."

At first I thought that Gaga was twitching and hesitating, but in fact she was nodding her head, not the wobble of a moment earlier, but a positive movement meaning okay.

"I understand that Jilly used to work odd weekends, sweeping and cleaning at Shockley's Cash-and-Carry, and some baby-sitting," Millroy said. "And that she contributed to your household expenses."

She called me lazy, she used a strap on my legs, she demanded half my money in the summer, she said I would never amount to anything, that no one would ever want me. I was stupid, I was obstinate, I was deaf, I sucked my thumb, I had made her suffer by wetting the bed for months after the funeral, A.D.D. was just another word for stupid. I had told Millroy all this, but even so, you looked at Gaga and knew it on sight.

"Here is a little something to ease the passage of time," Millroy said.

A thickness of bills, General Grant's face on the fold: fifties.

"This will come in awful handy," Gaga said, and I sensed she was glad to sell me.

"You want me to look after Jilly," Millroy said, issuing her an order.

Gaga was not listening. She squeezed the money, trapping it in her fist so tight it looked like a stain in her hand. But even now I thought that she might spring forward, casting a great, stinking shadow on me, pushing me over and crushing me against her fatness, smothering me on the floor under her knees. Yet she stayed mild, with the same silly eyes and goofy grin, her hairy face turned toward Millroy. It was a doggy obedience I had never seen in her before, but I wanted with all my heart to get out of this house.

Millroy said, as though to an employee, "I will be telephoning you with further instructions. You will know what to do when you hear my voice."

Gaga nodded again at this, looking unsteady on her fat ankles and broken slippers. Her mind was made up. Her face was turned away from mine and fixed on Millroy the Magician.

Then Millroy and I were out the door, in the car, across the yard, on the road, racing away. My heart was whole.

"Bet you hardly recognized her," Millroy said.

He was looking pleased with himself. I had seen that face just after the elephant vanished, as the razor blades spilled onto the glass table, when he opened the Indian basket for the last time.

''She was open to suggestions,'' he said.

''What did you do to her?''

''Straightened her out, helped her listen.''

He drove down to Route 28 and hung a right nearer Falmouth. We passed Mashpee Intermediate.

''They're probably doing geography with Miss Buckwack.''

''Let them.''

Millroy was very happy.

''So as things stand,'' he said, ''I have total control over nine of my bodily functions, and one or two of your grandmother's.''

Whatever that meant, though I felt I had nothing to fear from her.

''And I memorized your room,'' he said, still being mysterious. ''Now where's our tuna spotter?''

10 He was not at the Gas and Go, and he should have been. He was not at Ma Glockner's, nor at the Cheapo Depot. He was not at Mister Donut, not at the Trading Post, not at the Rod and Gun Club, where he often drank. Dada had to be black-out drunk, though it was not even noon, and I was sorry because I knew what he was like sober, but I could never predict what he would be like drunk.

''There are so many black children here,'' Millroy said, looking out the window as we crisscrossed Mashpee.

''I guess so. I never really noticed.''

I just wanted to go away without seeing Dada or even saying good-bye.

Millroy said, ''He must be home.''

Home seemed the wrong word for the place where Dada lived.

He too had a trailer, but his was an old rattrap the shape of a shoe box, on a sandy back road the color of stale cornmeal in some pitch pines near Moody Pond, Mashpee. The trailer bottom had burst with rot like an old barrel, slipped off its cinder blocks and fixed itself to the ground. Some weeds reached to the windows. It was made of scratched metal sheets riveted together with aluminum strips that were whitened by decay. The whole thing looked rotten and immovable. All around it were scattered bottles, rubber tires, twisted metal, burned boxes, the back end of a car and a Jeep with no wheels.

"There's a dog. You never see him. He just growls behind a hung-up blanket."

"What's his name?"

"Muttrix."

"The power of television," Millroy said, and smiled twitchily. "I'm great with dogs."

At the window, the thing that looked like the most torn part of the torn curtain was the face of Dada's Wampanoag woman wondering what to do. Her eyes were wide open and her mouth was pressed shut.

"Vera Turtle," I said.

Millroy raised his hand to her in a friendly greeting. His big mustache bristled around his teeth and made them bright. He said nothing. His hand was still upright. He folded his fingers over, then opened his hand and produced a blue parakeet. It perched on his forefinger, swiveling its head and squeaking.

Looking out the window at the fidgeting bird on his finger and not at Millroy's face, Vera became calmer and started to smile.

"He's sleepun," she said in a whisper, pushing on the door. She seldom said Dada's name. "Don't wake um."

The warped door stuck and then sprang outward with a twang like the cut-open lid on a can of fish. That was the smell, too—fish, coming out of the doorway. And the hum of flies frisking in sour dust. The smell of frying pan, cigarettes and the sweaty dog, Muttrix.

"Hi, Jilly. Got a haircut, eh?"

"I like yours better."

The way Vera's hair was stiff and wild and burned blond at the ends, and her small, smooth face, which was browny-gold, made her pretty. Her eyes were greeny-gray and such a pale color they always looked slightly wet and lovely. Her lips were full and pink, and she was so shy that she smiled with her lips pressed together, not showing her teeth.

She hung on to the door with her slender fingers, keeping us out, and was in such a timid shrugging posture that her body was lost in her loose cotton dress.

"This is for you, dear," Millroy said, lifting the blue parakeet. The bird nibbled and squeaked at her.

"Hi, Vera," I said. "We thought we'd stop over and see you guys."

But Vera was looking at the bird. She put her fingers to her mouth and chewed where the pink polish on her nails was chipped.

"So what am I gunna do?"

"Just relax, Vera," the bird said in a small, squawky voice.

"He was drinkun last night with Al Shockley," Vera told the bird. "He was down for workun at the G. and G. this mornun, but then he starts throwun up and everythin gets stinkun. I goes, 'Ya late because I wanna do some cleanun.' He goes, 'Except I'm sick' and starts drinkun again, and I'm, like, 'What's go-un on?' "

The bird began tweeting back at her.

"No point botherun with um, so I bombs over the canal for fishun and caught some blues, about a ton of um."

That was the smell coming through the door—fish guts and scales, and flies, crazed by the hot stink of gutted bluefish, buzzing in the enclosed heat of the sunny trailer room.

"He goes, 'So what's up?' "

She seemed more talkative than usual and I guessed that she was frightened and lonely.

"Then he starts snorun."

She glanced around into the rusty trailer, and now her damp-looking eyes made her seem sad.

"He's still sleepun."

"Why not say hello to my little friend," Millroy suggested, moving the bird on his finger closer to Vera's face.

Vera said, "So where have you been hidun, Jilly?"

But her soft nose was near the bird's glittery blue feathers.

Millroy said, "Tell Vera Turtle how glad you are to see her."

The bird said in its squawky way, "I was, like, 'Are we really going to see Vera?' "

Vera's mouth had dropped open, her eyes seemed wetter, she had let go of the warped metal door of the trailer, and her hands were open, as though to clutch the bird.

The bird said, "I'm here to help you relax. I have come all this way to show you how I can sing. I will sing you to sleep. I am too small to do you any harm.''

The lids of Vera's eyes were drooping, and now I could see her tongue swelling behind her teeth as her lips parted. She seemed dazed and happy, and all at once very soft.

''Can we come in?'' the bird asked in a low, gargly tone.

''But don't make any noise,'' Vera said. She led the way. ''I don't want him go-un and wakun up.''

She moved beneath her dress and then her dress moved as she went swaying barefoot through the old trailer. It was not big but the smell of warm fish guts made it seem smaller.

Millroy said, ''Please sit down, Vera.''

She did so, putting her wrists on her knees and swinging her legs together.

Then I knew what he had done to Gaga: hypnotized her, made her smile and obey. In his Millroy way he had turned terrible Gaga into someone who was peaceful and agreeable.

It was happening to Vera now. It was like a dentist giving her gas. She breathed deeply and listened and became calm. Her voice was steady. She smiled at Millroy and his talking bird. She sat up straight, listening as the small bird fluttered to the top of a chair back.

''And you do all your cooking here?'' Millroy asked, pausing near the sink and the stove.

''Don't do much cookun.''

''Food preparation.''

''Whatever,'' Vera said. ''Guttun blues and then fryun um up.''

Millroy turned to me and said, ''When you consider the time we spend eating our ancestors!''

''Ray ain't much of an eater.''

Speaking his name made her seem as though she were divulging a secret, something out of her heart, and by saying his name she made Dada exist.

There he was, lying stiffly on a bedshelf at the far end of the trailer in the hot shadows. His face was pale, with blue bristles of beard, and he wore a T-shirt and jeans, his white, twisted toes sticking up. He slept motionlessly with his mouth open, stinking and sighing and gulping like a frog.

Vera was smiling at me without showing her teeth.

"Guess ya still suckun ya thumb, Jilly."

In my nervousness, I had slipped it into my mouth. I pulled it out quickly and did not tell her how it calmed me, nor how, when I locked one finger over the end of my nose, it helped me to think clearly.

Millroy was nodding at Dada and jingling the loose change in his pocket.

"His heart's bad. He sweats." Millroy sniffed and made a face. "There's corruption in his lungs. I am not condemning him. I am merely remarking on his physical condition."

A hiss like a slow leak came from Vera, who had picked up a small aerosol can and was spraying out air.

"Sometimes he's usun this for breathun."

"And he has some difficulty walking."

"Walkun, talkun, runnun, you name it."

Millroy had turned to look up at the shelves, but he took everything in at a glance: the boxes of breakfast cereal, their names, the cans—all their labels—and the bags of chips.

"If you'da told me you were gunna come over I woulda made brownies or somethun," Vera said. "And cleaned this place up."

Now she was seeing everything with Millroy's eyes—the trailer and Dada and the big TV with the pilgrim doll from Plymouth on top. The ashtray full of butts. The sticky telephone.

Millroy touched her shoulders with his fingertips and kept them there until Vera smiled.

"Mind if I use your rest room?"

I had been dreading this.

"Have to step outside," Vera said.

It was a privy in a shed. I had not known how to warn him. Never mind, he ducked out, went inside, and was back in the trailer in seconds.

"I see."

It meant everything the way he said it.

"Jilly, you gunna have a drink of anythun?"

I shook my head.

"Matter of factly, I got some tonic in the cooler. I got some of them slices of baloney. I could make you a peanut-butter sandwich. Or what about some marshmullahs?"

She had begun squeezing and crinkling the bag of marshmallows. The bag swelled and spoke in her fingers.

Just her mention of these forbidden things made me fearful and breathless, and I could sense Millroy stiffen as she named them. I was sad, too, that she did not know what was in them and that she ate them with such innocence.

Millroy turned to Dada. "That man is not well."

"He always goes, 'I can look after myself.' "

"He ever talk about his daughter?"

"Not too much." She had dropped the marshmallows and was twisting her dress in her fingers. She was sorry, but it was the truth.

What did I care? I felt strong. I had Millroy. *Don't talk to strangers,* Gaga had said. But this stranger protected me. I had never felt safer. And when the need arose, he had magic.

Millroy said, "Take care of that body of yours, Vera. Don't punish it. Be good to it."

"I don't do much drinkun."

"Try to eat right, I mean."

"Do my best."

All this time, the blue parakeet had been silent. Now it twittered again from the chair back where it had perched. Millroy extended his finger and the bird hopped on; then he wrapped it in his hand and the bird went silent as he squeezed. When he opened his fingers again there was money in his palm and a glint of gold.

"My," Vera said. Millroy dumped it all into the pocket of her dress, and it jerked her dress down with its weight.

"That's for fresh fruit."

"I love an apple."

Millroy was leaving, motioning me out.

"I will call you. You will remember my voice and do as I say. But you won't remember me. You won't remember Jilly was here. And you will never smoke again. Smoke rhymes with choke, Vera. The taste of a cigarette will make you gag."

She just stared at his head. Behind the clothes rack, on the bedshelf, Dada gulped and shifted his arms, hugging his dirty shirt.

Then Dada sat up straight.

"Heard every word," he said in his crumbly Smoker's Voice, smacking his lips. "You can watch a thief but you can never watch a liar."

At the sound of Dada's voice, the dog, Muttrix, began yapping.

Millroy simply pointed; both Dada and the dog rolled over and sighed.

Driving down Route 28, Millroy slowed the Ford at the first pay phone he saw. I gave him Gaga's number, then Dada's, and watched him enter the phone booth, where he made the calls, two of them, very brief ones, but during each one, as he spoke, he motioned with his arm, moving his fingers in a steady command.

"Think of the responsibility," he said when we were on the road again. "The power of having someone totally in your control. You need great restraint." He was driving, but he took his eyes off the road and set his gaze on me. "You can get them to do anything."

Back at the trailer he told me to wait a minute, and then said, "It's okay to go in now."

My room was changed. It was now my room from Gaga's, with all the old paraphernalia that I loved and she hated: my music box, my two stuffed bears, my bedside lamp with the frilly shades, my Michael Jackson poster, my Tall Ships poster, the stuffed squirrel I won last year at Squirt Gun Fun, my Mashpee Intermediate pennant, the framed dollar bill from my first paycheck at Shockley's, my Cape Cod Melody Tent program for the Olivia Newton-John concert, a quahog shell with a face of pebbles glued on it, a gold tassel I found at the Annual Mashpee Powwow two Julys ago, my own pink pillow, and a small box with a locket inside containing—how did Millroy know this?—a picture of Mumma in her wedding dress.

Even so, that night I woke up worried.

"Promise you won't ever do that to me," I said into the darkness.

Millroy knew what I had just remembered, and I did not even hesitate to wonder why he was still awake.

"I promise, angel."

After a while, from the other end of the trailer, he spoke again through the darkness that separated us.

"And I know how you must feel."

I wanted him to tell me because I hardly knew.

"I left home myself. I had spent years telling them things they needed to know. Then I realized that no one was listening to me, so I went."

That was not it.

"You're sad," he said.

"Not only," I said. "But I also wish they were like other people's folks."

Millroy's voice was like sparks in the shadows of that dark trailer.

"They are exactly like other people's folks," he said. "They're burgers."

"Rachel Wolfson's father's a dentist, she was at Camp Farley with me, and they live in a big house in Osterville, and he's not like that."

"Dentists are the worst burgers of all," Millroy said. "They are *all* like that. Only their shapes are different, and their shapes can be truly monstrous."

He sounded so sure of this that his voice was rumbling like someone on the radio, and I could tell he was sitting upright now. His voice lit up the trailer.

"Every last one of them is the same. Walter and Lorraine Millroy, of El Jobean, Florida, for example. And is your Gaga different from old Grammy Gert Millroy? No, she is not. If you stayed with them you'd end up living like them and dying like them."

There was a sound like small birds that told me his hands were flapping, and his voice went on rising and falling.

"You think your own folks are uniquely horrible, but I tell you, no, they are average. Give or take a few pounds of pork, they are the brother and sister of most burgers in America. That's why you're afraid of them."

It was true. Fear was that suffocation I had felt, a sensation of thirst and nausea.

"Afraid they'll drag you down."

Or just keep me indoors.

"Which is why you should pray for them."

I tried to pray. I shaped the words *Please God* with my mouth, and let God read the rest of what was scrambled in my mind.

"Because people like that, people in general, will eat you alive if you give them half a chance."

Millroy was angrier than I had ever heard him, and although I had been afraid of Gaga and Dada I had never felt that angry with them. He was still talking and by now I was too upset to pray anymore.

"They can't get their teeth into you now, angel. You're free."

But all I saw was their teeth glinting in the darkness.

''Get some sleep, princess. Big week ahead.''

At some point in the measureless darkness I went to sleep, and woke to the sound of *Paradise Park with Mister Phyllis* playing on the TV in the room beyond my own folding walls.

''He's a twisted old fruit,'' Millroy said, ''but this program has potential.''

Then I remembered where I was and how I had gotten there; I knew I was free. I had no doubts now, but I trembled at the memory of having been trapped. Millroy had rescued me, but it had been a close call.

II

Paradise Park

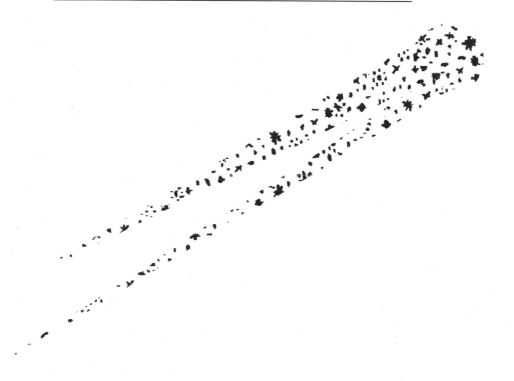

11 Millroy had a powerful sense of smell, not only for food, his favorite subject, but also for what he called "the unphysical world."

"It was not always this way with me," he said, squinting as though into his past, but not mentioning anything that he saw.

He could smell bad luck, he could smell disorder and corruption, he could smell the future. ("Much of our future has the tang of fresh bread.") A person's lie created a strong odor that reached him. Premonition was another odor. He could smell trouble, he could smell truth, he could smell colors in the dark. The physical world was simpler. "That's why I could happily walk around with a blindfold," he said. "My nostrils are like a keen pair of eyes."

Children a certain age also had an unusual sense of smell, was his theory, especially where adults or the opposite sex was involved. "And most intuition is in your nose, angel." He said this was why Todd Huber was still lurking, though there was something dumb in his patience; he did not know why he wanted me to roughhouse with him, though Millroy and I were well aware of it. Todd would lose this gift soon, Millroy said, "because if you're not conscious of it, your capacity atrophies."

"You have all these gifts when you're young, and one by one you lose them unless you work on them and fine-tune them," he said. "And I can smell error, I can smell complex fractions, I can smell the past."

Millroy's nose was larger than normal, he could wrap his whole hand around it—he often did so when he was thinking—but even though it was big it was soft, it was not fearsome, it made him seem friendly. He had started out the same as everyone else, his nerves had been no different, it was just that he had gained mastery over his body.

"As I say, it was not always this way."

He did not elaborate until one night just before bedtime he said suddenly, "I was a lost soul once. I'll tell you all about it sometime. How I ate the flesh of innocent animals. I was full of dead meat—meat rotting inside me. That was all I could smell—my own self. Can you imagine how that cuts a person off from the spiritual world?''

He was at the door of the trailer looking out at the rest of Pilgrim Pines: music playing, other people's TV sets, a grumbling dog, the sound of frying, the Silverinos, F. X. McEachern, Franny Grasso, Bea Rezabeck, the Glenn Branums, all the others.

''Excuse me, muffin, but I was farting pure methane,'' he said. ''I was like most people, a walking fire hazard. I had flamethrower breath. I was combustible.''

Our little settlement of pets and laundry lines and people murmuring in tin trailers and recreational vehicles reminded me of the gypsy camp employees' quarters at the Barnstable County Fair. I was too tired to tell him this, and I was even a bit sorry that he had raised such an interesting topic so late at night. That was a habit with him, even speaking up in the darkness to say something frightening, as though he had just woken from a bad dream.

''I was once like those people,'' he said, looking at the other trailers. ''I don't deny it because it is important to consider how I transformed myself.''

Now he was staring past the Blevinses and the Lingells, at the Reverend Baby Huber's mobile home. The smell of cooking, the sound of sizzling fat, came from that trailer. It was Huber preparing his specialty, which he wanted to put on the market under the name ''Huber's Real Good Fries,'' as a nonprofit company, and use all the money for what he called ''prayer fairs.''

''Magic isn't an accident,'' Millroy said. ''It's good health. It's aligning your body and mind. I made myself into what I am with God's help, by eating right. Hey, I got creative.''

''Some people say there is no God.''

''God is just another way to spell 'good.' ''

''I believe in God,'' I said.

''That's kind of premature—a mistake, angel, and anyway so does Reverend Huber, but never mind.''

''What's wrong with believing in God?''

''If you eat right, your head clears, you get power, you get an odor of sanctity,'' he said. ''You don't need faith. Listen, if you live the truth—

and I'm talking about food here—you don't have to take anyone's word
for the Almighty.''

He swallowed hard, he hesitated, and then he turned to me.

''Eat right and get regular and you will see the face of God.''

I was smiling at the thought of someone with a full stomach of pottage, honey and wheaten loaves looking up and seeing God in a white
robe like a full spinnaker, with a huge beard and blazing hair.

''No,'' he said because he knew what I was smiling at. ''It's not as
though God is someone else. You will be looking at your own face.''

I was thinking how Millroy did not even go to church.

''Church isn't the answer,'' Millroy said, again reading my thoughts.
''A church is just an empty building. The trouble with most religions is
that they make you feel so miserable on earth that you know you're
going to feel equally miserable after you're dead. Think about it. The
Catholics? The Jews? The Mormons? The Baptists? The Reverend Baby
Huber's Pentacostalists? Who wants to spend eternity in their particular
kind of heaven?''

He was looking out of the door of the trailer, but not at Pilgrim Pines
or at any particular mobile home or RV. His eyes were raised above
those roofs, as though he were looking at the world.

''Did you go to church?'' he asked, without turning his head to me.

''Most Sundays,'' I said. ''With Gaga.''

''Which church?''

''The one with the gold rooster on the weathervane in West Barnstable. And when I was staying at Dada's, Vera took me to Mashpee Baptist.''

''It should be real easy to choose a religion,'' Millroy said. ''You walk
in the church building and you ask yourself, 'Do I want to look like these
people—I mean, physically resemble them? Do I want to live for all
eternity in a heaven populated by burgers like these?' ''

''I never really thought about it that way.''

''It's even simpler than that. You don't need church if you've got
The Book,'' Millroy said. ''A man like Huber thinks the church comes
before The Book.''

I reminded myself that he meant the Bible.

He said, ''A true religion would tell you how to read it, to harmonize
your body and mind. Most of them think they're bigger than The Book.

They preach about themselves instead, and that's another reason I can't join.''

All this talk about God, religion and the Bible should have made Millroy seem a severe and scolding preacher himself, but he was the opposite, chuckling as he talked, inhaling the cool night air of Buzzards Bay, and occasionally chewing a fig. He wore black boots and a shirt with roses embroidered on the back—buds and blossoms, green leaves and thorny stems, a beautiful piece of needlework. He looked priestlike without seeming religious. No matter where he was, even here in Pilgrim Pines, he looked like a magician, with his great mustache and shining head and small gold earring in one earlobe. Handsome.

''You're probably thinking, 'But I could learn all about that in school!' ''

I was not thinking this at all.

''What about food technology and science? You're cogitating hard on that.''

Whatever cogitating was, I was not doing it because I was not doing anything except looking at Millroy.

''Listen, muffin. Technology eventually catches up with scriptural principles and vindicates them.''

My dim smile was a one-word question: *meaning?*

He knew it, and said, ''See this fig?''

The wrinkled fruit was in his hand. He popped it into his mouth and chewed.

''That's what I mean,'' he said. ''The Book is full of figs. Make you healthy. Keep you right. It seems simple but this could be the secret of life, muffin.''

He was still munching the fig.

''I'm talking longevity here. The Book's specific about years.''

''Like how long?''

''Four hundred isn't unusual. Shem lived six hundred.'' Chewing the fig was his way of thinking. ''I want to be looking at two hundred–plus, and why shouldn't you?''

That night Millroy woke up and interrupted the darkness, saying, ''I am so grateful to you, princess. If it weren't for you I'd be talking to myself and thinking I was crazy.''

• • •

"Letter for Doctor Millroy," the Reverend Baby Huber said one morning soon after this. He delivered the mail. "A doctor's always handy in the trailer park. Now I know where to come."

"You will receive all the attention you deserve," Millroy said.

The letter was from Big Brother Bert of the TV show. He wore a buttoned-up sweater and never smiled. The lights blazed off his glasses so that you could not see his eyes.

Millroy said it was not the one he had been expecting. This reply suggested that Millroy might be five years old: *I too am very concerned about good eating habits, and I hope you tell your mom and dad that you want to eat right.*

More letters arrived. One was from the president of the United States, with a big gold eagle on the flap. Reverend Huber handed it over without a remark.

"I was going to write to the Surgeon General," Millroy told me afterward. "I wanted him to consider banning all food advertising on television. Most of that stuff's as bad as cigarettes or alcohol. Then I figured I'd go directly to the president."

Your letter to the president is one of many thousands received by the White House on an average day, it began, and it was not so much a reply as a thank-you for writing.

Millroy did not mind. "I'm on file," he said. "That's the important thing."

He had also begun to write letters to the TV programs, giving his reactions and explaining his thoughts about the food habits of Americans today.

Thank you for your communication. We wish it were possible to provide a personalized reply to each and every letter we receive, the answers usually started. They were from the characters who appeared on the programs and from the people in charge.

"They think I'm a nutbag," Millroy said. "You don't think I'm a nutbag, do you, angel?"

"No," I said, and he knew I meant it. "You're amazing, and I also think you're kind."

"I'm regular," Millroy said. "It's all to do with time. For most people time is an avenger, the enemy. But I eat right, so time is my friend."

He had time for everything, he said, which was why he not only watched all the TV shows but also wrote letters to them. Besides the president of the United States, he wrote to the governor of Massachusetts, the local Board of Health, and the mayor of Buzzards Bay on urgent matters of health and personal hygiene.

"This could be the big one," Millroy said one morning when a letter came from *Paradise Park*. It was different from the others. *We would be most interested in hearing more about the presentation you mention. Please get in touch with our program secretary. . . .*

The letters nearly always thanked him and signed off for good. This was the first letter I saw in which Millroy was encouraged to write back.

Because of this sympathetic reply, he watched *Paradise Park* every morning.

"I smell breakfast, I smell Reverend Huber's bacon, I can hear the snap of his Rice Krispies and the thud of his Real Good Fries. Does he know the Seventh-Day Adventists invented American breakfast cereal?"

He was watching the show with the windows open. Mister Phyllis had shrunk on the screen to the size of the tiny puppets called the Mumbling Humptulips, who lived in Paradise Park with the Frawlies and all the rest of the little people.

"Gaga used to fry up eggs and bacon all the time. I liked the smell."

"It's a misleading aroma. It is blood and the meat of strangled animals. You would have been so much better off with this."

He meant the breakfast he had just finished: homemade wheaten loaves, fruit and nuts, and his drink of juiced grapes.

"They're all getting the wrong message," he said. Mister Phyllis was now normal size, talking with his face against the TV screen. "Children who listen to adults like that will grow up to look just like them. They'll be just as weak and tricky. Muffin, the wrong people are in charge."

He changed channels—*Sesame Street*, noisy cartoons, *Big Brother Bert, The Jingle Family and Their Dog Fred, Balloony and Muttrix, Reasons to Believe, Doctor Walter Malone, The Chippies, The Hour of Power,* brightly colored animals, fat-faced people, loud music, shouting.

"People don't know how to live. They're taking the wrong road. It's pathetic."

"What should they do?"

I knew that he wanted me to ask that.

"They should be asking themselves questions like yours, sugar."

He was smiling. He looked at me with gratitude, that *You saved me* expression.

"They should listen to me," he said. "Start all over. Get back to basics. Declare Day One."

I was not surprised when the letter came from WBNT, the station that broadcast *Paradise Park*.

"I was right," he said. "It's the big one."

Thank you for your brief but effective synopsis of your presentation, the letter said. *We would be very interested in meeting with you and discussing the matter further. Please call . . .*

The envelope was addressed to *Dr. H. Millroy.*

It was much too late for me to ask him what the *H.* stood for. It was not for any name I knew—Max or Felix or any of the others.

We had no telephone, and so that no one in the trailer park would overhear him, we drove to a public phone in Buzzards Bay.

Afterward, Millroy said that he had spoken to three people—a Thin Voice, a Fat Voice and a Smoker's Voice. Fat Voice had the grumbellies. He was not being frivolous, he said. Physical facts revealed inner states, and even the spirit of people.

"People are instruments of Divine Will," he piped up suddenly on the way back to Pilgrim Pines. "Even when they are unimpressive they might be essential. A bum may be necessary to your enlightenment. Or a nagging woman. Or an epicene oldster in makeup, wearing glasses and baggy pants on a TV show. Or a small girl who is no more than a face in the crowd."

"With her thumb in her mouth." I knew what he was saying.

"An angel," he said, correcting me and looking thankful. He cleared his throat and went on. "The main thing is to obey the call without questioning it, and then do your stuff."

12 We were in our suite at the Hathaway Hotel in Boston, Millroy prowling the rooms while I pretended not to be nervous. It was not Millroy, it was not the desk clerk's smirk as he said, "I'll need Dad's signature." It was all the rest. Hotel was only a word to me. I had never stayed in one in my life. Some things I had never done seemed so unbelievable that I did not even mention them to Millroy, who had done everything. Next to him I was nobody. I had felt this strongly on the trip up to Boston, and told him so that he would not be disappointed.

"I'm nothing," I had said.

He had not denied it, which made me feel awful.

"I'm a blank."

"Yes." And gave me his thankful face again. "I wouldn't have you any other way."

We were headed up Route 3, Millroy at the wheel of the Ford.

"See that?"

It was a large American flag flapping in front of a restaurant just off the road. Now, with the leaves turned and many of them blown to the ground, you could see what was behind the trees.

"That flag's not patriotism," he said. "That's just an attention getter, so that they can sell grease dogs and fat burgers and rubber chicken."

All morning Millroy had been talking, as though psyching himself up for his interview. He had always been talkative before his shows, and afterward he went silent, fading in the trailer. He admitted that magic exhausted him, and his talking was often magic, too, making you see something you had never seen before.

"That house," he said—it, too, been revealed through the trees by the fallen leaves—"all spiffed up."

It was a brick-fronted mansion with Greek pillars, white window shutters, a black wrought-iron fence, and a fountain in front surrounded by beds of orange and yellow and purply-blue flowers that might or might not have been chrysanthemums.

"That's not a young person's house, princess. An older couple lives there. They spend all their time and money beautifying and renovating it, buying expensive shingles and the best landscaping and window treatments available. Because the older people get, the more they spend on their houses.''

He was now half-turned in his seat, glancing back at the house.

''Why? They'll be dead soon, so it's a kind of tomb. A house of that sort is just an expensive sarcophagus.''

He shook his head, still smiling in disapproval.

''How much better it would be if they renovated their bodies and made themselves healthy from within instead of hiding in those pretentious houses. They'd learn to love life then instead of being busy dying.''

He seemed confident, talking the whole time, a kind of soundtrack for the trip up to Boston. He dug some dried fruit out of his pocket, picked the lint off and offered me some little leathery apricots.

''This is one serious interview, no question about it,'' he said, ''but who's interviewing whom?''

His blinkless eyes searched my face for a reaction.

''Hah!''

He could smell success, I knew. I was getting used to his facial expressions, and the reasons for them. He did not boast—he beamed instead, and a warm light showed in his whole face, which looked like a Christmas ornament most of the time because he was so healthy and happy. He raised his hands and clutched the air with eager energy.

''Meanwhile, the Reverend Baby Huber is leading the hymns at Pilgrim Pines—all that suffering, all that mercy and money. Pass the hat and don't forget the barf bag. That's the way to heaven with the Sinister Minister.''

He went on talking about life after death—how it was different for everyone, according to what you believed, and if you thought it was eternal darkness you would get eternal darkness, or if a paradise then it would be a paradise. ''Let's face it, belief in the afterlife is just a test of your imagination.''

After this, Boston the city was sudden and ugly; it had a sour, soapy smell of food, gas, dust and low tide. Our car went slower on the side street to the hotel than the people walking on the sidewalk.

We passed clubs and bars and movie houses.

''Don't look,'' Millroy said after we parked the car, and he said nothing more, just frowned and sheltered me with his shadow and height as we walked through the noisy streets, Millroy carrying the bag, to the hotel.

Then it was *I'll need Dad's signature.*

"We're short of double rooms," the desk clerk said after Millroy had signed the card, "so we're upgrading you and your son to a suite."

Soon Millroy was prowling the room and I was pretending not to be nervous, thinking how I had never been in a hotel before, and how I was a blank.

The suite overlooking the Public Gardens was full of armchairs and tables and footstools, all of them with skirts. There were two bathrooms, a desk, two TVs, flowers in vases, bowls of fruit, pictures in gold frames.

"I hate ashtrays," Millroy said. "And other people's rest rooms can be traumatic."

Away from his trailer, from his food and his facilities, he was edgy. He did not eat strange food, did not trust strange plumbing, did not sleep well in any bed but his own, and it was hard, he said, to work magic in unfamiliar places.

"Never mind, we'll be home tomorrow," he said.

"But are these flowers real?"

Millroy snatched one and let me sniff it, then stuffed it into his mouth with a bunch of the flower's green leaves. He chewed and swallowed.

"Nasturtiums are a tasty flower."

Circling the room, he reached into the fruit bowl, broke off a cluster of grapes from a bunch and began eating them.

"The Book's full of grapes."

He was striding and flinging his arms out as he talked, taking possession of the space. He went for the sofa, dug at the cushions, yanked them apart, heaved them up, made a bed, smacked his hand on it and lay down.

Now I noticed there was a live tree in the far corner of the room, taller than me.

"Is this luxury? Maybe yes, maybe no. The thing is, I know what to do with it. I could be right at home here, whereas the average person would be totally lost, sitting in his underwear with all the lights off, bewildered by all the amenities and appliances. But I simply extend my hand."

He opened the little refrigerator of the mini-bar and made a face as he took out a bottle of wine that was lying on its side.

"Wine maketh glad the heart of man," he said.

He popped the cork and swigged some. He switched on the TV—a game show. He stowed his clothes in the dresser. He finished the cluster of grapes. He said "Yours" and "Mine" at the doors to the different bathrooms, and he kept opening drawers, examining bags, matches, sewing kits, shoe mitts, stationery, pens and postcards, until he found what he was looking for, a book.

"Room service," he said.

It was a thick brown book with tissuey pages. What was odd was that from where I sat I could see on the desk top a binder lettered IN-ROOM DINING MENU, nothing like the thing that Millroy was holding. He flipped the pages of his book with a moistened finger.

"Is that the Bible?" I asked. "The Book?"

"Yes and no," he said.

Yes and no?

"It's also the room-service menu," he said.

At times like this I wished someone else could hear and see this man, he could be so unexpected.

He was still licking his finger and scraping at the pages. Finally he found the page he wanted and read, " 'We remember the fish, which we did eat in Egypt freely, the cucumbers, and the melons, and the leeks, and the onions and the garlic.' " He smiled at the open book. "Numbers, eleven five." He picked up the telephone.

"Room service? This is suite forty-two twenty-five. I'd like to order dinner for two."

Melon appetizer, fish of the day—it was fresh scrod—with leeks, and a mixed salad of cukes, garlic and onions.

When it was delivered by a silent, paunchy man in a dark uniform pushing a steel trolley, Millroy was still holding the Bible and smiling. The man unsprung the trolley, turning it into a table, set up our meal, and then glanced at me because I was staring at him. I was thinking that Millroy had taught me how to look at people, how the ones in the food business could be unhealthy, what a strange thing that was, and how he would say this man was a living contradiction, dishing up health but unhealthy himself. Even "paunchy" was a Millroy word.

"This is Alex," Millroy said, as though challenging the man to deny it. He still clutched the Bible.

Looking furtive—perhaps because of the way Millroy was swinging the Bible at him like a brick—the man excused himself in a foreign accent, and backed out of the room.

"I was saved by a Gideon Bible," Millroy said to me.

He ate, cutting his food carefully, like someone carrying out a delicate operation, poking, slicing, forking, lifting and scrutinizing. He hated sauces. He never put food into his mouth until he had squinted at every forkful.

"I was trapped inside my huge body," he said. He spoke in his magician's voice, sounding wise and powerful. "I was blinded by the darkness of my body, in a limitless wilderness of insensible fat. I was miserable."

He was eating, but slowly and in very small amounts, and speaking of fatness he seemed to be talking about someone else, someone far off and monstrous, because he was slender and strong and bright.

"I was fat. Picture me fat."

I could not manage it.

"Cheeks like this"—he plumped them out for me—"face full of pork. I taped out at just under three hundred. I was a burger. Lost? You have no idea."

Yet he was slender, his skin was clear, the dome of his head glowed with health, his legs and arms were muscular ("A lot of magic is muscle power," he often said), and when he walked the body of the room shook, not his body. With a fat person it was the other way around.

"Know what a great meal was to me then? It was finger foods, dead eels or fish eggs on toast or weenies with toothpicks, and two so-called cocktails, nine-to-one martinis, followed by thick, milky soup, say cream of rabbit, and you could just about taste its long ears. It was wine with the fish course, and the fish was fried in animal fat. It was more wine and an animal entree, something beefy, a chunk of it, with the blood still running out of its severed circulatory system. It was surrounded by pale boiled vegetables. This was all followed by dessert, a lardy cake, toxic black coffee, and hundred-proof brandy. Can you conceive how lethal that combination was?"

He was still eating slowly, which was surprising, because the next thing he said was, "I'd almost be willing to eat a meal like that again just so I could pump out my stomach and actually demonstrate to you what a mess it is. Practically indigestible. Probably no sooner get it onto the table and it would explode—spontaneous combustion, *ba-boom!*"

He had not pumped out his stomach to show me its contents for several weeks, nor had I thought of it, but from time to time I tried to picture what a stranger would say if he witnessed Millroy the Magician pumping chewed food out through a nose tube and poking at it seriously on a plate. This was one of those times; I still could not imagine the stranger's reaction.

"I ate because I was bored. I smoked and drank because I was bored. I buried myself in fat. I hadn't read Psalm Forty-five. Ever looked at it? I did not know that the 'oil of gladness' is low in cholesterol."

He sniffed a morsel of fish and his eyes registered the smell, their color wavering like two little meters. Then he clamped his teeth on the morsel and tugged it off the fork.

"Loneliness is the worst illness in the world. And everyone is lonely who does not have the ability to see . . . I hate the word 'God,' let's say 'Good.' A person thinks, *'I am alone, I am no one, I don't matter'* . . ."

It was exactly how I felt most of the time, and had even said those very words in my upstairs room at Gaga's. He was talking about me.

". . . and because they imagine that they don't matter, anything they do is okay. They think to themselves, *Who cares?*"

I had said that, too.

"And every night before they go to sleep they think about themselves and the world, and they cry."

So had I, and I wanted to tell him so, but he was still peering at pieces of food on his fork and talking.

"I suppose it does them a lot of good, in a way. After dark, most people in America murmur to themselves, *Am I alone?* and they weep because they know the answer. So they eat themselves silly and get fat and drunk. The shapes of people! The way they swell and stick out—all the bags and bulges! Did you see that poor man who brought this food up to us, how paunchy he was?"

I nodded. I was learning.

"You're too young to be able to imagine how they hate the way they look. And when they get sick they're glad because they enjoy feeling sick, the way guilty people do."

He sniffed his food and ate slowly, chewing the way people chewed gum.

"Do fat people ever think about being fat?" He swallowed and answered his own question. "Yes, they sorrow every waking second of the day. And at night they have nightmares about it. They resort to quackery, they take big multicolored capsules—Fat Blockers, Fat Melters, Fat Magnets, 'Dream Away' diet pills that are supposed to draw fat off while you're asleep. They wear 'diet sunglasses' that project appetite suppressants on the retina. They sweat inside rubber sauna suits and become dehydrated. But nothing works—they stay fat, they keep eating, they're afraid of starving."

Millroy kept eating too, but his way made him look patient and sensible and strong. The fat people he was talking about sounded sad and addicted. What they were doing was out of control and demented and beyond eating.

"They're abused for being fat. Because they're seen as self-indulgent sinners, it's okay to mock them. People go out of their way to watch them eat, they grunt at them, they make mooing noises, they go 'oink-oink,' they throw food at them."

"The kids used to throw food at Shannon Slupski in the school lunchroom. She was huge."

"They threw food at me, angel. And it made me sick, body and soul. Like most other chubbies, I didn't think I deserved to feel well. And that's why when I meet someone like Floyd Fewox or the Reverend Baby Huber, who looks like a turnip, I understand them, I can deal with them. I know their pain."

The only thing I could think of to say was, "Couldn't you help them get healthy?"

He was chewing as he said, "It would take too long. They're too old. They'd try and drag me down. No, there are other ways, sugar."

He put his fork down. All the food he had rejected he had pushed to the edge of his plate.

"Health, strength, willpower, wit and nutrition. The Book saved me. I'll tell you all about it sometime."

He had finished eating. Now I knew he would be very quiet, digesting his food, settling his stomach. The last thing he said before he squatted on the floor was, "But consider this. Was Jesus ever under the weather? Does The Book ever speak of Jesus coughing or being afflicted by gas or having pneumonia? Was the Savior ever sick? Think about it."

Soon he was snoring softly in his own separate room. He needed sleep, he said. Magic came from strength.

When I was alone with the flowers and the tree in my big bed, I thought of how Millroy had said Americans cried at night. Though I had been frightened at times, I was glad to be with this man, no matter how strange this setup might seem to someone else. But I did not want to hear him say he was alone, because that would have meant that I was, too.

Now I was used to his speaking up in the darkness. That night, after the lights were out, he said in a clear voice, "Don't you think America should know what I know?"

13 In each different place and sometimes at different times of day I could see that Millroy was a different man and an odd man—odder than anyone I had ever known in my life. The next morning it was another place and another Millroy. We were in a yellow taxi going from the hotel to the studio for the audition—my first taxi, my first hotel, and what was an audition?—when Millroy turned to me and asked, "Who are you?"

Just like that, in a stranger's voice, with his big face near mine, and with his eyes on me, waiting for my answer.

I blinked back at him. His eyes were dark, depthless and gentle, but they did not help me. He looked straight into me. The very way he asked a question and set his eyes on you could make you feel secure, or else the opposite—make you squirm. I was worried, verging on desperate, and he knew it.

"I can wait," he said. "I've got all day."

I was glad there was a pane of glass between us and the driver. Tears came to the edges of my eyes because I was thinking again, *I am no one,* and then I said it.

"That's not true this morning," Millroy said, so sure of himself that I blew my nose and brightened up.

But I thought again, as I did every time I got worried, *What am I doing here?* Whenever I felt stupid I realized I was in danger, and never mind who *I* was, who was *Millroy?*

That was his next question.

"You are Millroy the Magician," I said. "You made me disappear, you live in Pilgrim Pines Trailer Park in Buzzards Bay."

"What else, son?"

That stopped me. I blinked at my tears, pushed my hands against my blue jeans to wipe the dampness off my palms, and said, "You're my father."

"And who are you?"

"Alex?"

"You're learning," Millroy said.

He leaned back in the seat and glanced out of the taxi window at a cop directing traffic.

"Do you realize that every minute I am with you I am breaking the law?"

My hair was cut short and felt like a shoe brush. I was wearing a boy's clothes and sneakers. Millroy was a wizard, but there was so much to remember because of the way we lived. Now I was worried again. He could calm me one minute and make me fret the next.

"But the law is ignorant and the world doesn't know that I will never hurt you." He was frowning at the taxi driver, and added in a whisper, "That man has been eating a Danish pastry ever since we left the hotel."

At the TV station, Millroy paid the driver and said, "I am not trying to scare you or exaggerate for effect, but that Danish pastry will do you more harm than smoking dope. Next time you feel a craving for pastry, say to yourself, 'I think I'll have an apple!' "

"Let me worry about that," the driver said.

"I would, except that you're not worried at all," Millroy said, "and you should be, with that dangerous thing in your hand."

The man drove away angry, and Millroy smiled a fatherly smile of pity and protection.

It was lucky that we'd had that talk in the taxi, because almost the first thing the woman at the TV station said to me was, "I bet you're real proud of your dad."

"I sure am," I said, and I was. I also realized that it was easy calling him Dad because I had no other name for him.

At that moment Millroy was saying, "You have the most interesting name, Mister Mazzola. I want to hear all about it."

"My ancestors were Italian, as you might have guessed," the man said, and began describing how poor and miserable they had been when they came to America.

"Europe's still a very unhealthy place," Millroy said.

I was looking at Mister Mazzola's hair, the way it was lopped, strand by strand, across the top of his head from back to front, arranged there and stuck down like an ornamental plant. I knew Millroy was studying it, too, and that afterward he would say, as he had of Floyd Fewox, *Hair! It's the great giveaway. Never mind that hair loss is directly traceable to poor diet, bad circulation and iron deficiency. Imagine the amount of time such a person spends in front of the mirror! The top of that man's head is an alarm bell, signaling deep insecurity.*

Millroy also claimed that he had many reasons for shaving his own head, which he did every few days with a buzzing razor, and one was that it gave other men a sense of superiority.

Meanwhile, he was encouraging Mister Mazzola, who was head of the whole TV station, calling him Eddie. Walking down the corridor toward the studio, they were laughing like old friends, though the man was doing all the talking.

Then Sondra Spitler, the producer, was introduced to Millroy, who said, "I've got an uncanny feeling that your birthday is October twenty-second."

"Right! That's amazing," Miss Spitler said. "How did you guess?"

"It's not a guess. I knew. I'm psychic. You probably hate that word! But it's my birthday, too."

The woman was so pleased she patted the chair beside her and said, "Tell me more."

"You're so kind," Millroy said. "The number three"—he was waggling his fingers in the air and squinting, as though he were getting signals from the sky—"I am receiving that number from your pulsations. Three has a strong meaning for you."

"I have three children," Miss Spitler said.

"The third one," Millroy said. "You are very concerned about your third child. I am receiving a T."

"His name is Thomas."

"Yes, that would be it," Millroy said. "I am sensing a sharp pain in the stomach—here," and he touched the front of his shirt.

The woman said, "My son Tom has been diagnosed as having diverticulitis. I haven't slept since I heard. I almost didn't make it here today, and I'm supposed to be running your audition."

"It is very important that you came today and that we met," Millroy said, and took the woman's hand. He had once held my hand that way, and it was as though he had tugged my soul out of my fingertips. "I want you to stop worrying about your son."

"I keep picturing him in pain, and all those antibiotics," Miss Spitler said, "and drinking barium."

"I can feel that," Millroy said, closing his hand on her fingers. "But you need a second opinion. Your own opinion."

"All I know is what the doctor told me. I don't know anything about diverticulitis."

"Your doctor is overweight," Millroy said. "Why would he care about bulgy pouches in his colon?"

The woman said nothing, but she was looking slitty-eyed and probably thinking, *Yes, our doctor is kind of fat.*

"Massive gas buildup? Rectal tenderness? Constipation? Crampy gut? Nausea? Bloating?"

"Tom's had just about all of those symptoms."

"Diverticulitis is a McIllness, and Tom is full-figured, too," Millroy said. "He likes fat burgers with big soft buns, hot dogs, Froot Loops, fizzy drinks, sugary snacks. He's like most youngsters, and like most youngsters this low-residue diet is not reaming his colon."

"The doctor has him on antibiotics."

"Bitter herbs. Sound familiar? Numbers, nine eleven. The inner bark of pau d'arco is a natural antibiotic. Boil it and get him to drink buckets of it. After the inflammation has eased and his colon's open, get some whole food into him. He needs fiber. He needs garlic. No sugar, no fat." Millroy had lowered his head and was looking into the woman's eyes. "Diverticulosis is precipitated into full-blown destructive diverticulitis by diet—too much junk food, not enough roughage. If Tom is ill—"

Now another woman approached him and said, "We need you in makeup, Mister Millroy."

"Doctor Millroy," he said. "But you can call me Uncle Dick."

Before he was led away to the makeup room, Millroy turned to Miss Spitler and said, "Don't worry, dear. No doctors." He released her hand, touched her head like a priest touching someone at the altar rail, and said, "We'll want to get his weight down, first of all. And I can tell you the treatment in two words." He smiled and said, "Dietary control. Feed him."

Miss Spitler, Mister Mazzola and two other men waited at the studio entrance for Millroy. When I peeked inside I saw what an audition was: a room full of kids and the four adults on their way in. He would get the job if he managed to please all these people.

There were seventy-five or a hundred children in chairs surrounding the studio stage, and they were restless and fidgety, all colors, all ages up to fifteen or so.

"You'll have to sit in the peanut gallery for now, angel," Millroy said to me when he came out of the makeup room with his face rouged, his mustache combed straight, and a dustiness on his bald head. "But you know what to do."

At the doorway, Mister Mazzola introduced Millroy to the two other men, Otis Godberry and Mister Phyllis, whom I did not recognize at first because he was still wearing his smock from the makeup room. Then I saw his pink socks.

Otis Godberry said, "We've got some kids here from the projects in Dorchester"—he said "projects" in a certain way, meaning ghetto—"and I'd appreciate it if you could make them feel especially welcome. They find it awfully hard to fit in with other kids."

"Because they're horrid little beasts. You might have to employ persuasion," Mister Phyllis said, and puckered his wrinkly mouth. "Like a massive clout on the earhole."

"They're part of our target audience," Mister Mazzola said in a stern voice.

"I'll keep them in mind," Millroy said.

"You'll be lucky if you can just shut them up," Mister Phyllis said. "*Paradise Park* has never had a live audience before, and I don't see any reason to start now."

"This is just a pilot program," Miss Spitler said. "See how it goes."

"And who do we have here?" Mister Phyllis asked, turning his wrinkly face on me. "You're quite the little charmer."

"This is Alex, he's going off his bird," Millroy said. "You know how impatient youngsters can get."

Then we all walked into the studio and Millroy went to the center of the stage, opened his box of tricks, and took charge, silencing the studio by dropping his chain saw and making an enormous crash.

"Excuse me, this is my first day with my new hand."

He plucked off his hand, then screwed it on again and flexed his fingers. Now he had everyone's attention. He started the chain saw and juggled it with a bowling ball and a flaming torch, all the while telling the children how hungry he was.

"But I brought my lunch."

He stopped juggling and licked all the flames from the torch, guzzling the fire. He swallowed a sword—shoved a two-foot sword into his mouth and pulled out the handle and a few inches of the blade ("I needed some iron in my system"), and then found his chicken, Boobie, in a small girl's purse. He did his chicken-potpie trick and ate some of that. He turned a studio technician's cellular phone into a banana, peeled it and ate it, and produced the sound of a ringing phone in his stomach. He made a little boy named Darren disappear in the Indian basket. Darren turned up in a bureau drawer at the other side of the stage, wearing a Harvard sweatshirt and a crimson beanie, and looking confused.

Next Millroy produced a puppet, and the puppet conjured Boobie the chicken, feathers and all, out of the pie. The puppet clapped a silver dome over Boobie, shrieked "Lonny"—the name of a boy in the front row—and when he removed the dome there were ten pieces of fried chicken where Boobie had been. The children loved it and cheered, but Millroy said that greasy chicken was no good for you, and after more business with the puppet and the lid, made a pile of plums appear where the greasy chicken had been.

"If you eat what I eat, you'll be able to work magic like me," Millroy said, and did twenty one-arm push-ups while pinching a spoon behind his back and bending it.

He had placed the puppet on a table, where it lay limp and lopsided like a broken doll. Millroy said the puppet had been so helpful that he wanted to make it into a real kid. The puppet wore a red shirt and a baseball hat and blue jeans.

"He deserves to be a real boy," Millroy said.

I knew my signal, and where to go and how to vanish by bunching myself up in the box offstage. I did not see Millroy make the puppet disappear, but I could hear him asking the kids whether he should make the puppet into a real boy.

The children screeched, "Yes!" over and over and went on squawking like parrots as Millroy persisted with his questions, winding the kids up, and the next thing I knew he was whacking the top off my box with a hammer. I stood up dressed like the puppet, whom I resembled, in the red shirt, baseball hat and blue jeans I had put on in the box.

Millroy calmed the cheering and whistling while I dropped out of sight, and said that Uncle Dick had some questions for them—Uncle Dick's history lesson.

"How many of you know what grandparents are?"

A boy in the front row answered that they were your dad's and mom's parents.

"And what are *their* parents called, your grandparents' folks?"

"Great-grandparents!" Several children competed to shout this.

"And if you've got four grandparents and each of them has parents, how many great-grandparents does that make?"

Eventually they got it right: eight great-grandparents.

"Now Uncle Dick has a real interesting question for you youngsters," Millroy said.

Even the adults were listening closely to this, Mister Mazzola, Miss Spitler, Otis Godberry and the frowning Mister Phyllis.

"How many of you can say that all eight of your great-grandparents were born in the USA? If one of them was born in Ireland or Puerto Rico or Italy or somewhere else, just sit there. But if you know that all eight of your great-grandparents were born in the USA I want you to stand up."

There was a little shuffling and then—how did Millroy know this?—twelve black children stood up, smiling proudly. And then a big person was standing, the last man on the judging panel, and he was black too, Otis Godberry.

"You were here first, guys," Millroy said. "You were waiting for us. Let's have a cheer for these early Americans."

Everyone began to clap, with Millroy leading the applause.

That was the show, most of it—and then Millroy went upstairs with the big people for the interview.

. . .

"You were the hit of the show," Millroy said back at the hotel as we were getting ready to leave for the Cape. He was a new man here, gathering our things, putting his box of tricks together, clearing out.

"I didn't do anything," I said.

He looked up from packing his suitcase.

"As usual," I said.

"You were there," he said, leaning toward me. "You are here with me."

"And what am I doing?"

"Seeing it all."

He was in a great hurry to check out of the hotel and leave, and already talking about how in one hour we would be back at Pilgrim Pines and have our own food, our own space, our own rest room.

On the road, relaxed, a different man again, he told me about the interview.

"I let them talk. I listened. Everyone is so lonely. You think important people are going to be strong, but they're much weaker than the average person." Millroy was shaking his head. "Much easier to manipulate. Their egos are bigger. They need help managing their egos. What's so funny?"

"I thought you said 'eagles.' "

He laughed out loud, then said, "When someone says, 'I really want to talk to you,' what they mean is, 'I really want you to listen to me.' "

But I was thinking of the history lesson he had sprung on them, and the black children and the man Otis Godberry, when they had stood up, how proud they were, and how their faces shone when they were applauded. I felt lucky to be there, and had never admired Millroy more.

"I got the job." He said it casually, as though there were nothing more to say, that there had never been any doubt of it. "It's not a trashy show. It teaches reading and numbers. It's got intelligent cartoons and good graphics. It's funny and educational, and it's still a Boston show, but as it gets stronger it will be picked up by lots of other stations. I got them to accept a live audience—all youngsters."

"Mister Phyllis said he doesn't want them."

"His name is Sidney Perkus," Millroy said, "and I am sure I can handle him."

"What else are you doing?"

"I've got a slot." He turned to me and wiggled his mustache. "They liked my ideas about eating. 'Mealtime Magic.' What do you think?"

"Sounds good."

Millroy was in a wonderful mood, and I knew that it was because he was back in the world again. He had not liked being unemployed. Leaving the Barnstable County Fair so suddenly had confused him, and he had told me how he disliked looking for work, as though he were going around asking people for permission to work magic. Now he had found a job on his own terms, and it was a job he wanted, even though it seemed strange to me, to want to be a magician on a children's television show. He was his old self, Millroy the Magician, the one I had first seen at the county fair, who worked magic in a tent, lived in a trailer and did not own a TV.

That evening he must have been thinking the same things. Breaking the silence, he said, "If it hadn't been for you I wouldn't have watched that show—wouldn't even have bought the TV set. I dislike TV evangelists, I hate the unhealthy food advertised on TV, and most children's TV shows are utter trash."

I was looking at him, thinking, *Then why are you going on this show?*

"Exactly," he said, reading my mind. "Because I'm the logical answer, I'm Uncle Dick of 'Mealtime Magic.' "

He did not say anything more until after the food, after the rest-room sessions, after the baths, after the lights were out. He called through the darkness from his own dark box of a room.

"I need you, muffin," he said.

I twitched suddenly, a spasm down one side of my body, as I wondered whether I had bolted and latched the swing-out shutters to my little bedroom.

"As a martyr," he said.

For an instant I felt important, because the word was so strange.

"Know what martyr means in Greek?"

I was going to say that I did not even know what it meant in English.

"They didn't teach you that at Mashpee Intermediate?"

He did not wait for me to say no.

"Martyr," Millroy said in the dark. "It means witness."

14 *Paradise Park,* the children's TV show, was famous for being educational and having cartoons and safety tips, as well as the Mumbling Humptulips, a bunch of oversize bees, and the Frawlies, a family of mice who lived in a log, Princess Vanya in her castle in ''Crystal Palace,'' Pignut and Dogfish, a pair of peddlers, Alpha Betty and Her Dancing Letters, and many other puppets and stuffed toys. But until Millroy joined and became Uncle Dick, the only live person on the program had been Mister Phyllis.

''There's something about that guy,'' Millroy said.

Mister Phyllis had short, flattened-down hair that was purply-blue and scraped forward, and a tiny, wrinkled mouth in a narrow face. He looked like an elderly child, Millroy said, or an anxious monkey. It was his twitching.

I knew Millroy had hated it last Thursday, the day of the audition, when Mister Phyllis had said to me, *You're a charmer.* I almost expected Millroy to challenge him to a psychic duel, as he had with Floyd Fewox. But he said nothing, only watched and listened closely.

It had been Millroy's idea to have live children in the studio. He got his way, and on the day of the first real show the studio was full of children.

That day Mister Phyllis said to me, ''Sit up front where I can see you, chicken.''

Millroy winced. I knew it was the word ''chicken,'' and he hated strangers talking to me, but he said nothing. He stood behind the cameras with Otis Godberry. It was seven minutes to showtime.

''Where is my chair?'' Mister Phyllis said. ''Some career criminal has pinched my chair.''

He went through the studio fussing and waggling his fingers.

''Didn't I tell you these kids were a mistake? I want someone to find the vandal who annihilated my hat—find her and scratch her cheeks. And if I catch the person who oversweetened my tea I'll chop her little fingers off.''

Earlier someone had sat on his newspaper. ''I can see the imprint of his horrid botty on my *Globe.* He has made it physically impossible for me to touch it, much less read it.''

When he complained about being hungry and Otis Godberry brought him a brown-bag lunch, Mister Phyllis said, "That's the ugliest sandwich in the whole world."

With only minutes to go before the show started, he began to search for his cat, Tinkum. Where was Tinky's portable cat box?

"Find your places, people," the studio manager said, clutching his earphones.

"Get stuffed, sunshine," Mister Phyllis said. He was groping behind a chair.

"Quiet on the set. The clock is on—"

"Shove it up your jumper."

He wore a white and red sweater, striped like a candy cane, pink pants, pink socks and bright new sneakers that creaked as he walked. When he lifted his arms his bracelets jangled. This morning he wore makeup, but its color—the gloss on his lips, his rouged cheeks, his powdered nose—made him look like a wicked doll.

"We're hearing your jewelry, Phil," said a bottled-up voice on the studio loudspeaker.

"Why do you think they're called bangles, peckerhead?"

"Lose them," said the same voice.

"Don't get your knickers in a twist!"

Otis Godberry sighed each time Mister Phyllis spoke, and hearing this last shriek, said, "He's kind of—I don't know—is it high-strung? I can't think of the word."

"I hate the color of the new set," Mister Phyllis was saying. "I've seen more attractive vomit. The curtains look like a dog's breakfast. I might as well stick pins in my eyes."

"Maladroit," Millroy said.

He could always think of the right word.

Otis Godberry smiled.

"Epicene," Millroy said, and noticing that Otis looked vague, added, "Fruity."

Otis covered his mouth and chuckled, his eyes shining over his fingers.

"Hyperbolic," Millroy said. "But I guess he puts his best foot forward when the cameras are rolling."

It was true, because when the man with the earphones raised his hands and said, "Quiet, please. Five, four, three"—silence dropped like darkness and the camera moved up to the little kitchen—Mister Phyllis began to whisper slowly and winked the way he had with me and crinkled his monkey face into the camera.

". . . whole new show and masses of new friends here at Paradise Park," he was saying.

He leaned over his tin sink and turned the faucet handle. Long blobs of water plopped out and made rapping sounds on the metal bowl.

"Listen. What is the water saying?"

He crouched to put his small round head nearer the faucet.

"It's saying splish-splash, splish-splash."

Smiling into the camera, Mister Phyllis picked up a bar of purple soap, showed it, smelled it, drew a harsh breath, and held the soap near his mouth, as though he were going to eat it.

"This is my soap. It smells scrumptious. Now what am I going to do with this bar of soap?"

Blink-blink-blink, and all the wrinkles in his face were smiling. There was a pause before he spoke again.

"Yes, that's right. I'm going to wash my hands." He was still blinking. His fingernails were pale, his fingers pinky-white and smaller than mine. "I'm going to scrub them until they're immaculate. That's a big word, isn't it? It means very clean. That's how I like to be."

He slapped at the water and twisted the soap in his hands, lathering suds onto his fingers.

"I know a song about washing hands."

He smiled, chewed, swallowed, and made monkey cheeks.

> *Scrub a dub, rub a dub*
> *Cakes of soap, to make us hope*
> *For clean and happy hands that . . .*

"And if he says anything else to you, I want to hear about it," Millroy said, then realizing that Otis Godberry was listening, he added, "Okay, Alex?"

When Mister Phyllis was finished singing, he scooped up his cat, Tinkum, and began brushing its fur. Turning his back to the children in the studio seats, he put his face into the camera and said, "I bet your cat would like her fur brushed like this." In the same slow voice, he told Tinkum how to cross the road and look both ways.

Then two strange things happened. While I watched Mister Phyllis on the TV set in the studio, he started to shrink, and shrink until he was so tiny on the screen I could hardly see him.

He was as small as a mouse; I knew this because the Frawlies were mice, little sniffing balls of cloth with button eyes and stiff whiskers. They lived in a tree stump in Paradise Park and Mister Phyllis and Tinkum sat by the stump watching them.

It was a trick of the camera. Millroy said that the lens shrank Mister Phyllis and his cat, and moved them. They were still big as life in the studio and nowhere near the Frawlies, who were fooling with their lunch and making useful words with their alphabet soup.

That was the first strange thing: tiny Mister Phyllis and tiny Tinkum.

The second was when the man wearing earphones picked up some stuffed toys and Tinkum's deep dish on the set and said, "They're in the shot."

"Take your fat fingers away from my props or I'll chop them off," Mister Phyllis said.

The man hesitated, then began to speak.

"Go pick boogies out of your big nose!" Mister Phyllis said. He crossed the studio, threw himself into a swivel chair and spun around so that his back was turned to the audience and the technicians.

I was so surprised that I stood up and gaped at him, and some of the children giggled, hearing Mister Phyllis's loud voice abusing the man.

"Shut up, or this will be the last time you ever set foot in here!"

Instantly the children went silent, but no one else heard Mister Phyllis—none of the Frawlies, none of the people watching the show on their TV sets.

"His mike's off," Millroy said in a duck-like voice, "and that's not all."

He was talking to Otis Godberry, who was frowning nervously at his own big shoes, probably wondering where the voice was coming from. Millroy could talk in five or six different voices without moving his mouth.

Under the hot lights, Mister Phyllis was saying, "Either get those beastly Frawlies off the monitor or else pass me a two-gallon barf bag."

"Thirty seconds," came the cramped, bottled-up voice from the speaker on the wall.

"Take a flying jump at yourself," Mister Phyllis said.

"Fifteen," the voice said after a few seconds.

"Your lights are frying Tinky," Mister Phyllis said. "Find the deep dish and fill it with clean, fresh water. There's something on my shoe—chewing gum. Oh, bull!"

"Ten, and counting, nine, eight—"

"Not on your nelly, bean brain!" Mister Phyllis had opened his tiny mouth wide to screech this, but as he spun around in his swivel chair to speak into the camera, he made his cute monkey cheeks again and said slowly, "That was fun, wasn't it, kids? The Frawlies will be back tomorrow, but in the meantime here are some more adventures from Pignut and Dogfish. Let's watch."

He did not watch the cartoons, for just then a woman in bib overalls put a dish of water on the floor behind the camera.

The lights dimmed, Mister Phyllis hoisted himself out of the chair and kicked the dish of water, wetting his foot and the leg of his pink pants.

"That's not Tinky's deep dish, you space case!"

In the cartoon, Pignut and Dogfish, wearing mushroom caps, were learning how to make the letter M. It was large and blue and loomed over them. Although they struggled to prop it up, it kept falling over and turning into the letter W.

"—then get stuffed!" Mister Phyllis was saying.

Without moving his mouth, Millroy said, "This is all seriously distracting."

He could not work magic unless he was able to concentrate.

"I would guess that man takes in vast infusions of processed sugar," he said. "It's addictive. He's manic and emotional. He's constipated." He was still not moving his mouth. "Apples have all the fructose you need, and you can cook with honey or fruit juice, substituting it for white sugar."

"Is that so?" Otis Godberry said, looking confused and probably wondering what the connection was between Mister Phyllis's loud outbursts and the food he ate. But he was game. He said, "Just give me a piece of fresh fruit and I'm happy."

"Though you'd want to harmonize it," Millroy said. "Pottage is a good harmonizer."

"A mess of pottage," Otis said, and smiled. "Like Jacob and Esau made."

"Jacob was the cook, Esau the hunter who sold his birthright," Millroy said. "And the fact is that lentil pottage is more important than a birthright. In harmony, it keeps you regular, with big buoyant stools."

Otis Godberry smiled a painful, confused smile at the turn this conversation had taken.

"Pull your finger out and find it," Mister Phyllis was saying to a studio technician. "It must be near that barf-colored wall."

"You just want that man to rethink everything he shoves into his mouth," Millroy said, with his lips pressed together like a ventriloquist.

The chewing, crunching sound was Pignut and Dogfish walking down a gravel path, satisfied with the monumental letter M they had raised. As the images flickered out, the studio lights brightened and Mister Phyllis leaned forward in his chair.

"Can you make the letter M? I want you to try. Draw me some nice M's and then think of words that start with the letter M."

His eyes were half-closed, his mouth slightly parted.

"Like mouth. And mother. And muffin."

He nodded suddenly as though he had just remembered something.

"Magician begins with an M."

"So does monkey," Millroy said, because Mister Phyllis was pursing his firm little monkey mouth.

"I know a magician. He is our new neighbor. Yes, he is. A magician has just moved to Paradise Park. He lives here all the time now. He does magic for us. His name is Uncle Dick. Shall we go over and visit him?"

Only the camera moved. Mister Phyllis remained in his swivel chair, his legs crossed. He had taken off one of his white sneakers and was scratching his pink sock.

"I wonder if Uncle Dick has a last name," he said.

Millroy smiled, but it was a defiant one, and I knew he was happy being on this show, with a large audience in the studio and all those people watching him on television. He seemed to swell and become physically larger when he was pleased, and I had not seen him this size since that day at the Barnstable County Fair when he had made Packy, the elephant, vanish for the last time.

"I was wondering if you had a first name, Mister Phyllis," Millroy said in a teasing voice, "and what it might be."

"That doesn't sound like magic to me," Mister Phyllis said in a similar taunting way. "Does it to you, kids?"

Millroy said, "Lots of things don't sound like magic. 'Chicken' doesn't sound like magic, but if you say it a certain way and really mean it . . . Chicken,'' he said in an intense whisper of pleasure and celebration.

In that same instant Boobie was sitting on the back of his hand, clucking in the direction of Mister Phyllis.

''I don't know about you youngsters, but I'm real hungry,'' Millroy said, and began conjuring vegetables out of his sleeve and his ear—carrots, potatoes, celery stalks, onions, and ripe tomatoes out of the tips of his fingers. ''It's natural magic.''

I was watching intently, trying to decide whether Millroy was working magic or performing tricks. It seemed to me that on this first television appearance he was working real magic. His magic made the world seem amazing, unfamiliar and a little frightening because there was always a hint of danger in it, as though he had reached down deeply and stuck his hand into another, darker world in order to produce these wonders. It was the sort of magic that exhausted him. Afterward he would sleep, lying flat like a dead person.

There was no other explanation but magic for the way he scribbled a note, shoved it into his pocket and then asked everyone to look into his or her pockets. ''I've got it,'' a small boy shouted and held up the message with Millroy's writing on it. Millroy had done it without touching the boy, and though anyone watching could have said it was a setup, I knew it was nothing of the kind.

Soon he was juggling torches and eating fire, and while I watched, a person next to me breathed hard in a kind of catlike hiss and said, ''Want to hold Tinky?''

It was Mister Phyllis, who had crept over to sit next to me, but I had not been aware of it until he spoke. He had a powerful perfumy aroma of powder and flowers that stung my eyes.

''Sounds good,'' I said because I did not know what else to say.

Mister Phyllis saw that my watery eyes were on Millroy.

''He's got his own chicken. You can be my chicken.'' Mister Phyllis's breath was sweet and dangerous-smelling, with a cover-up aroma of candy.

I was suddenly fearful of the foody smell of his breath and the nearness of his body, that surge of heat.

''He's not really your dad, is he?''

I wanted to cry as Mister Phyllis leaned over, pushing his vicious lips at me.

"No," I said, and heard him sigh with pleasure.

Just then there was a clang and I looked up. Millroy had dropped a silver ball he had been juggling.

Mister Phyllis was smiling at me, as though he wanted me to repeat what I already regretted saying. I hated him for asking me that, I hated myself for telling the truth. I was glad that Otis Godberry had not heard what I said. He was watching Millroy's magic, "the sacrifice of the vegetables," making meals out of them and talking about health and strength.

"Now you're not going to tell me that you've got a girlfriend," Mister Phyllis said.

I shook my head and said no, glad that I could tell the truth.

"That's a clever chap," he said. "They spill things. They smell. They always pretend they're so helpless."

I hated him again and wanted to say to him, *I am a girl.*

"Like that one."

Millroy was helping a little girl named Kimberly into his Indian basket. She was giggling nervously, sucking on one hand and tugging her sock with the other.

"I saw her before the show. She was with her silly friends. She has filthy knickers. She doesn't brush her teeth."

Mister Phyllis leaned toward me again, and I could feel the rising temperature of his breath.

"Do I hate a dirty mouth?" he said. "Not half!"

Millroy was tapping the basket, fixing the hasp and reassuring Kimberly that everything was going to be fine.

"You've got precious little lips," Mister Phyllis said. He spoke to the cat on his lap. "Doesn't he, Tinkum? Yes, he most assuredly does."

Kimberly vanished from the basket and reappeared blinking and saying "Gosh!" in a mirror that turned into a window: magic!

"So who is he then?" Mister Phyllis said. "Some kind of special friend?"

At that moment Millroy was talking about butter and honey and making more food, peeling fruit, slicing it and serving it to the children in the audience. He was active, manipulating a silver platter, passing the fruit segments around, and yet he never took his eyes off me.

In any case, by then I had recovered.

"He's my dad," I said.

After the show everyone congratulated Millroy on his performance. He seemed appreciative but deaf, simply nodding but keeping his eyes on Mister Phyllis. When the little man approached him and made monkey cheeks and began to speak, Millroy said, "Be very careful."

"I can look after myself."

With an electric jolt, Millroy magnetized the man, and half-pushed, half-steered Mister Phyllis to the side of the studio where no one could hear.

"Your name is Sidney Perkus and you come from abroad."

"England, in point of fact."

"All those places are the same," Millroy said. "And what's this?"

Millroy reached beneath the candy-striped sweater that Mister Phyllis was wearing and lifted out a black, greasy rat that squirmed in his hand as he held it. Mister Phyllis gasped, and Tinky screeched and leaped to the ground.

"I hear everything," Millroy said, and passed the rat back. The creature twitched, became a splash, solid to liquid, and dissolved on the little man's arm, leaving a damp stain on his sweater.

Mister Phyllis looked disgusted and frightened.

"This is my show," he said, clawing at the stain on his sweater. "Remember that."

15 I was thinking, *Why did he——?*
This was in the trailer at Pilgrim Pines, four shows later, toward the end of that first week, just after we hurried back for our food and facilities.

Millroy had decided that eating elsewhere, sleeping in another bed or

using any rest room except his own was unacceptable, even "an abomination." I had been wondering about something else.

"Anything wrong?" he asked, sizing me up and seeing me with my
thumb in my mouth, thinking hard. He was confident and jaunty, always
trying to think up new angles for his "Mealtime Magic" appearance on
the show, at which he had become a success. Already he was getting
phone calls, and the first letters from watchers had begun to arrive.

I pulled out my thumb.

"No, Dad," to get myself into the habit.

But several things were wrong, as I had been thinking when he interrupted me. One, why did he claim he could hear what people were saying fifty yards away, and that he had actually heard what Mister Phyllis
had said in the studio? And two, I knew that what had happened was that
he had read Mister Phyllis's lips.

He was great at this. He could watch TV with the sound turned off,
reading lips. He said it was more convincing if you could not hear their
voices. Lip-reading had been one of his tricks at the Barnstable County
Fair, but he did not admit it.

"It's these ears of mine," he said.

Why claim to have superhuman hearing when what you really have is
good eyesight and a superhuman ability to read lips?

I wanted to tell him the sort of thing he was always telling me: the
truth is always more interesting than you think. Be proud of what you
are good at. If so, why call yourself Uncle Dick and shave your head if
your name is Max Millroy and you have an excellent head of hair?

I felt that he did not want people to know him, and I understood.
"It's so restful to be anonymous." But didn't he realize that *I* knew,
much more than he guessed, various secrets—never mind that they
were small—that he was hiding? It was hard not being able to say how
wonderful he was, maddening that he was brilliant at something he
could not admit to. Or maybe it was all different, maybe I was supposed
to know everything, even these secrets, because he had told me enough
times that he wanted me to know everything, that I was doing exactly
what he wanted me to do.

Mister Phyllis believed that Millroy had magic powers of hearing, but
he went on whispering, and perhaps the lie did not matter at all because
Millroy knew exactly what the man was saying. He read his lips.

Anyway, with all this stress I was back sucking my thumb in the front seat of the Ford early this dark September morning as we drove to Boston.

Dressed as a boy I looked different, but so did Millroy dressed as Uncle Dick. And sometimes when he bought gas and was heading back from the office having paid for it, I would look up at this man hurrying to the car and wonder, *Who's that?*

It was him, mustache, skinhead, muscles and all, though these days he had taken to wearing sunglasses, no matter what the weather. Even in his dark glasses I knew he was happy. It was the audience, he said; he liked working with young people.

"They're—what?—eight, nine, ten years old. Young preteens. You can shape their lives. You can show them the right way to eat and drink and play. You can determine what the whole next generation of Americans will be like. You can shape the world."

He was silent a minute, staring at the road ahead.

"When I say 'you' I mean me."

Even the people who produced the program were young, not young enough but still all right.

The problem was Mister Phyllis. What he had said was true. *Paradise Park was* his show, and Millroy's slot on the program was no larger than the Frawlies' or the Mumbling Humptulips'. The two men had disliked each other on sight. Mister Phyllis had not liked the changes—the children in the audience—and Millroy said he knew that Mister Phyllis was trying to find ways of getting rid of him.

"People always put on perfume to cover up a bad smell. Whenever I come across someone wearing perfume I know it's a disguise. That's why perfume always smells horrible to me. Perfume stinks."

That was Millroy's thinking about Mister Phyllis, and I agreed because the man reminded me of the kind of peppermint disinfectant that always made me think of toilet germs.

"Physically I can't bear to be near him."

In this first week, Millroy was anxious on the way to the studio, knowing that he was going to have to see Mister Phyllis, and talk to him, and perform with him.

"He's afraid of me, but so what? Most older people are afraid of me. Most of them hate me because I'm happy. It's only the kids who are on my side. Mister Phyllis is afraid of what I'll do. He thinks he knows that I am capable of a certain amount of magic. If he really knew he would be scared.''

I had the feeling that Millroy was mentally doing battle with him as we drove up to the show.

''There's so much wrong with him,'' he said.

He squinted at the road ahead, calling up an image of Mister Phyllis's face.

''He's got Smoker's Face. It's gray. It's stale and dry. Like uncooked pastry that's been handled too much. Like crunched-up paper, dead at the edges. I'm talking about troubled circulation. Smoker's Face is a horrible, revealing mask.''

There was Smoker's Hand and Smoker's Fingers. Mister Phyllis had these too, Millroy said, and further proof of his bad circulation was his bald spot, covered by his brittle, scraped-down hair.

''Don't be fooled by his teeth. He's had them capped, but underneath they're bad—yellow and bony. The gums are spongy. They're not pink, they're purple. My guess is that they're inflamed.'' He tapped his own front teeth. ''It's not necessarily diet. You can destroy your teeth by saying certain stupid things over and over.''

He swallowed and made a face.

''And I don't want to think about his diet.''

Then Millroy winced, as though recalling something that disgusted him.

''Muffin, I have an instinctive distrust of people with bad breath.'' He shook his head and sniffed. ''Mister Phyllis's breath reeks. There is something rotten inside him.'' He turned to me frowning, and said, ''He's foreign, he has night sweats, he's got blockage.''

The traffic had been building as we drove north on Route 3, and by the time we got to the Expressway the traffic was so heavy that Millroy said nothing more, just steered and braked and accelerated in the mass of cars packed together and moving fast in three lanes.

''And not only that,'' Millroy said when we were nearer our exit— he had a knack for picking up an interrupted conversation. ''It is incontestable that they're unclean and unhealthy, but I also think that people with bad breath are lazy, cheap, sneaky, tell lies. That's why their breath smells.''

Mister Phyllis's breath was thick and foul; it stung your eyes, made you turn away, came from deep inside him, Millroy said.

"Listen, a smell is invisible but it tells all. It is everything the person has ever eaten, everything he has ever thought or done. It is a powerful glimpse of your insides, and yet no one knows what he or she smells like."

He was scowling now, looking like a wizard with dark glasses.

"I would like to make his smell visible."

Millroy's face was lit golden by the sunrise, a flash, and in that light the cluster of tall Boston buildings slid onto the lenses of his glasses.

"Or audible."

Now we were on the Chinatown ramp, and now turning, and now there were hospitals on the left and Chinese restaurants on the right.

"As you know . . ."

He often said this, and I never knew.

". . . I don't believe in evil. I believe in right and wrong, and very often they are the same thing."

I looked at him. How could right and wrong be the same thing?

"What I did with you—taking you away," Millroy said. "That was both."

That Friday morning, to celebrate the first full week of the new *Paradise Park,* the producers gave a little party in the Green Room before the program: sandwiches, a chocolate cake and ice cream. Mister Phyllis, looking stinky, started off boasting.

"I was ordained a Buddhist monk," he was saying to Otis Godberry as we entered the room.

"They cut off the crusts," Millroy said, ignoring Mister Phyllis and looking at the plates of sandwiches. "Too bad they didn't keep them. That's the only part we eat."

"Have you just driven up from the Cape?" Otis asked.

"Buzzards Bay," Millroy said.

"What in the world do you manage to do down there?" Mister Phyllis asked.

"Eat and sleep. The two most important human activities. I cook food. I make soups and breads. Bean soups. Unleavened breads."

"We're at Pilgrim Pines Trailer Park," I said, though as soon as I said

it I felt I had made a mistake and that Millroy disapproved of giving out
this information.

We sat at opposite ends of the room, Millroy in his magician's cloak
and boots, uninterested in the food, Mister Phyllis in his pink pants,
white sneakers and peppermint jersey, telling Otis Godberry and the
others how he had been a Buddhist monk.

He is unbearable, Millroy said in his low ventriloquist's voice. *He is a
nightmare.*

"This was years ago," Mister Phyllis said. He was nibbling a little
white triangle of bread and wagging his head with satisfaction, the sandwich in one hand, a cigarette in the other.

He'd be better off eating the cigarette, Millroy said. *Or smoking the sandwich.*

Mister Phyllis said, "In Bangkok."

"Thighland," Otis said.

"Exactly," Mister Phyllis said. "This was long before it became a
tourist trap. The Thais are so sweet—oh, bother, there isn't a thing on
this plate for Tinky. He'll be absolutely furious." He cocked his head.
"Listen. The monkeys are here. What a racket."

The audience, he meant. *The monkeys with no tails,* he had started calling the children in the audience. He cringed when he heard the sound of
their voices and feet, and a look of hatred tightened his wrinkled face.

If only they could smell him, Millroy said, staring across the room and
not moving his lips. He took a slug from his glass of water and gulped it,
talking all the while. *If only they could hear him and see what he eats. I
shouldn't even call it eating. See what he sticks into his mouth.*

"Danny Kaye," Mister Phyllis said, licking his fingertips, "one of my
oldest and dearest friends, introduced me to a Thai prince in Los Angeles. I was on the Coast doing a benefit for Marge and Gower Cham-
pion, and Art Linkletter was begging me to be on his show . . ."

Millroy watched Mister Phyllis making horrible faces, fishing among
his molars for a snagged scrap of food.

"The prince embraced me. He said, 'I believe we are brothers. I
command you to come to my country and I will treat you as a prince.'
One does not turn down an offer of that kind."

He fed himself another sandwich, tapped the ash from his cigarette and smiled at Otis Godberry as though challenging him to ask another question. But Otis was flummoxed. He was thinking, *Buddhist monk?*

"He was wearing a fabulous saffron robe," Mister Phyllis said, stroking his peppermint sweater with his fingertips to show how the robe flowed. "I am entitled to wear a robe like that. Will you listen to that pandemonium in the studio? They should asphyxiate every last one of them. Put a sock in it, kids!"

"You were actually ordained a preacher in that faith?" Otis asked.

Millroy was so impatient, a noise like hot steam shot from his nose and mouth.

"Ordained, yes, but not to preach," Mister Phyllis said.

"Doggone," Otis said.

"There is no preaching in Buddhism."

Buddha himself preached, Padmasambhava preached, Guan Di did it, too— 'The way that can be told is not the constant way'—they all gabbed, how else could they spread the word?

Millroy looked pained as he squeezed these words out of his nose.

"Buddhism is more a way of life," Mister Phyllis said, and glanced around. "I do wish I knew where Tinky was."

Otis said, "So you spent some time out there?"

"Three weeks," Mister Phyllis said. "That was when I took my vows."

Millroy looked up and said flatly in his penetrating voice, "It takes longer than that to become an Eagle Scout."

"I had been studying Buddhist texts for years," Mister Phyllis said, stiffening and straightening, as though angrily trying to levitate himself out of his chair. "Four years anyway."

"It still takes longer to become an Eagle Scout," Millroy said, "and what's the point?"

"It is one of the world's great religions. It teaches wisdom, piety, moderation, compassion, correct behavior."

"I hadn't noticed," Millroy said. "But as you say"—Mister Phyllis squinted: what had he said?—"there's beliefs and there's believers."

"Danny Kaye wanted to be on the show," Otis said. "His agent was calling us day and night."

"He was a lovely man," Mister Phyllis said. "And so talented."

"An audience junkie," Millroy said. "The worst kind of addict."

Mister Phyllis's small wicked face looked tormented and poisonous, but Millroy was talking to Otis Godberry.

"As you know, he used kids as props, to advance his career. Totally insincere."

Mister Phyllis lit another cigarette. He smoked using a carved holder that was brown-stained and chewed.

"Why don't you smoke on the show?" Millroy asked. "Wouldn't it give your hands something to do?"

"I just want Tinky at this point. Hasn't anyone seen him?" Mister Phyllis said. "Oh, Danny often came to dinner parties. I had a lovely home on the north shore—Manchester-by-the-Sea—do you know the Cape Ann area, Otis? So many show-business personalities and celebrities came to dinner. Arthur Godfrey, Ed Sullivan, Pinky Lee, Art Linkletter, the lot. If only they could see that I ended up here entertaining these dreadful kids."

"You won't end up here," Millroy said.

"I gave lavish parties. You would have hated my parties, Mister Millroy."

"How do you know that?" Millroy got out of his chair and walked over to Mister Phyllis.

"The food. It was fabulous."

"Food is my favorite subject," Millroy said. "Guess what I had for breakfast?"

Looking wicked again, his face stiff with glee, Mister Phyllis said, "I cannot imagine. Do tell me."

"I can show you," Millroy said, and picking up an empty bowl from the table of cut sandwiches and cake, with a little bark vomited efficiently into it. Then he held the bowl of steaming yellow chunks before Mister Phyllis's face.

"You are disgusting!"

Whirling his hand into the bowl with a scouring motion, Millroy made its contents disappear, and then the bowl itself. He folded his arms, and when he unfolded them he was holding the cat, Tinkum, which lay across one of Millroy's arms, licking its fur.

"Come here, Tinky, come here, darling," Mister Phyllis said. "Don't let that man torment us."

But the big soft cat had its flat face turned to Millroy, who held it as though in a beam of light from his eyes.

Mister Phyllis squashed out his cigarette and screeched, ''Get over here, you big soppy thing. Tinky!''

But the cat was looking at Millroy, who was making a low, fruity purring in his throat barely loud enough for me to hear.

''I am talking to you!''

''Normally I don't like cats,'' Millroy said. ''I don't like the things they eat. But I could wean this little fellow onto vegetable matter.'' He stroked Tinky's head and scratched behind its ear, and the cat responded by licking Millroy's fingers.

Just then, there was laughing in the studio.

''The children are waiting,'' Millroy said.

''Goddamn those kids, Millroy. They can get bent. Give me my Tinky back.''

But the cat compressed its face and sat compactly without turning or blinking or even twitching a whisker while Mister Phyllis said more filthy words.

16 Millroy's eyes changed color according to his mood—what was he looking at? what was he thinking about?—whitish and blinkless when he saw something he wanted, bluest when he was happy, yellow-green when he was suspicious, reddish when he was lecturing about food and hunger, and so on. Never mind colors, just the single word ''hamburger'' made his eyes go dead; they darkened with concentration, and if they went black you were done for.

Mister Phyllis was smiling into the camera and buttoning his candy-striped sweater with precious gestures. The *Paradise Park* theme song had begun to play

> *Wear a smile, all the while,*
> *In Paradise Park,*

> *We are free, you and me,*
>> *In Paradise Park . . .*

Millroy was intent, almost prayerful, in the way he regarded Mister Phyllis. He positioned his head like a weapon, and his eyes glittered like chips of coal.

"If you think there are two Mister Phyllises, the one that smokes and swears off-camera, and the one that smiles and simpers into the screen—if you think that, you're wrong, but it's a common misconception. There is only one Mister Phyllis."

If you didn't know that he smoked and boasted and swore and said, *Chop her silly fingers off,* wouldn't you think this smiling man, buttoning his colorful sweater, was a nice person?

"See, it's not a smile, for one thing," Millroy said. "It's a snarl. He is very unhappy."

Mister Phyllis was saying, "I know a song about buttons—want to hear it?"

"And it's all written on his face, the details of this deeply imperfect man." Millroy was half whispering, half ventriloquizing. "You just have to know how to read him. Yes, he has Smoker's Face, and you can tell from the slant of his mouth and the color of his teeth that he rarely has a good word for anyone. But listen, even if he were on the radio I'd know from the sound of his voice that he was . . . I'm not going to say diabolical, but how about pernicious?"

Mister Phyllis was singing flat and off-key with his sour-shaped mouth

> *Buttons big and buttons small*
> *Squeezed inside a buttonhole*
> *Keep our clothing . . .*

Millroy's eyes flashed at Mister Phyllis, then he closed them and sighed, pinching his fingers.

"Gah," he said. "That whistle, that lisp of self-love, the way he enjoys listening to himself. His singing reveals everything—his bad circulation, his fibrillating ticker, his black lungs—and that's just the dumb drone of his body. Is this the message we want to send America's children?"

Turning from the man himself to the studio monitor, he shook his head.

I wonder what the Frawlies are doing on this fine sunny day? I bet they're being sweet little Frawlies and keeping nice and clean in their tree stump in Paradise Park.

Mister Phyllis pushed his face into the TV screen of the monitor and made his famous monkey cheeks.

Do you keep nice and clean?

"Pillow-biter," Millroy said. "That man is just selling poison cookies."

The Frawlies' mouse music played, *tumpty-tumpty-tee,* and Mister Phyllis put his hand to his ear.

I think I hear our favorite tinies. Can you?

"A malign influence," Millroy said.

Of course you can! And, look, there's Wally Frawly!

Somewhere in another part of the studio, under the eye of another camera, a puppeteer was whacking Wally Frawly up and down the tree stump, and when the music swelled Mister Phyllis turned from his microphone and, seeing Tinkum, made his voice nasty and said, "Get over here!"

But the cat hesitated and crept away toward the audience of children, where a little girl wearing a badge that said TRISH stroked Tinkum's head.

On the screen the Frawlies were gathering cans and brushes and talking about painting their tree stump.

"Get your filthy hands away from my cat," Mister Phyllis said.

The little girl knotted her fingers, pressed her lips together and looked as though she were about to cry.

"Don't think I don't know how to warm your backside," Mister Phyllis said.

The Frawlies were singing

> *Shall we paint it blue or green,*
> *red or yellow or . . .*

Mister Phyllis was making threatening gestures at Tinky.

"Even if he had a bag over his head and didn't say a word—even if he was not in this room, and overseas, and not on television and I happened to be sitting here, I'd know he was dangerous.''

Millroy was gathering up his magician's pots and pans, slipping objects into his sleeves, vegetables into his pockets, making himself ready for "Mealtime Magic.'' "I say 'dangerous' because he's an authority figure. Innocent children look at him and think he has the answers.''

"But if he was overseas"—I was still trying to figure that one out—"how would you know he was dangerous?''

Just then Mister Phyllis disappeared as the Frawlies chased around their tree stump, dumping cans of paint on each other.

"By his smell?''

"By his cat,'' Millroy said.

Tinkum glanced over to him as Millroy said this.

In another part of the studio Mister Phyllis was saying, "I will talk as loud as I jolly well please. I want a cup of hot tea with three sugars for my parched throat, and I want my cat!''

Millroy was staring at the microphone hanging above Mister Phyllis's head as he complained. By now the children in the audience had become used to Mister Phyllis's outbursts, and were watching the Frawlies roughhousing with the paint cans on the studio monitor.

"His cat is a cushion, a hair bag, a loose piece of meat. It is overweight and needy. Its eyes are cloudy, its fur is dull. This animal's muscle tonus is poor. It has the reflexes of a shoelace. Forget for a moment all the canned meat it has ingested. Consider the cigarette smoke this cat has passively inhaled by being in Mister Phyllis's slipstream. I knew Mister Phyllis was in trouble when I saw Tinky.''

Only then did he turn from staring at Mister Phyllis's microphone and set his dark eyes on Tinky.

"When I say 'in trouble' I mean a loss of elasticity. The pair of them.''

Millroy beckoned to the cat by extending his hand, releasing his fingers.

"Animals trust me. They are never rivalrous. They don't smell meat on me. They don't smell blood.'' As the cat lifted its nose against his fingers, he said, "And children feel the same. But as you know, some adults resist me.''

I could tell that as he said this, he caught Mister Phyllis in his gaze.

The man was making a witch face at him, and what made it worse was the mouthful of unswallowed coffee bulging like a hard ball against his cheek.

The Frawlies had stopped fighting. They were now covered with fresh paint and making music, and all you saw and heard on the monitor were these mice, opening their mouths wide, singing loudly.

"Tinky belongs by my side and not with some irresponsible twit," Mister Phyllis said.

It was his normal Tinky spasm. When the Frawlies were on the screen without him, he tramped up and down beneath his turned-off microphone being bad-tempered. It did not matter. Pretty soon he would be shrunk by the camera, a silent little guy in a striped sweater, with his tiny cat on his lap. No one ever heard him on the puppet or cartoon parts of the show.

And where was his cat today? It was crouched in front of Millroy, who was whispering to the soft, misshapen creature. The cat looked around, then took careful, tottering steps toward the children's chairs, its belly swaying.

"Get over here," Mister Phyllis said, scooping backward with his hand.

Tinky paid no attention and went on padding toward the kids, who had begun to make soft kissing noises to call it.

No one heard Mister Phyllis say, "Leave my Tinky alone!"

Millroy was now concentrating on the Frawlies.

Holly's acting strange, man.

Don't upset your brother!

All I said was—and the little mouse, Holly Frawly, blinked her long eyelashes—*I'd like to eat a cat for a change. I mean, eat it alive.*

This unexpected joke upset Mister Phyllis, who called out, "No!" and Millroy said, "Look, he's unhinged." He was smiling.

Mister Phyllis was hacking the air with his hands, motioning for his cat.

"You'll be sorry," he called out to the children in the audience, who were stroking Tinkum's fur.

The fact that his microphone was off during the Frawly segment always gave him confidence, but today he was hyper, spitting and swearing.

He should have been warned, not only by the darkness of Millroy's eyes but by the brightening of the studio lights above his head, as though at Millroy's command.

"Stop that stupid nonsense, you feeble-minded midgets . . ." He should have been warned when, as though all by itself, a camera turned upon his sad, shriveled face.

He went on working his furious lips and then shrieked, "I'd love to have a carving knife right now!"

He looked like a hairy-faced woman with a black hat in an old story.

The studio seemed bewitched, it hummed with heat and light. The laughing children in the audience were playing with Tinkum, and on the screen Wally Frawly was singing his revenge song, about mice eating live cats. And Mister Phyllis was also on the screen, with a white catlike face, raging.

"What's going on?" Otis Godberry said, appearing from the door to the control room.

Hateful bratty children—it was Mister Phyllis on the monitor, clawing the air and showing his small teeth—*chop their goddamned fingers off!*

In that instant, like another wicked word, a rat's snout poked from his mouth and choked him as it slid out and bounded to the floor.

"The hell was that?" someone said. "Are we still on the air?"

"His mike's live, but what's he doing there?"

"We're going to lose our license," Otis said.

Mister Phyllis was still on the screen, squawking and looking horrible.

"We just lost the picture," a cameraman said.

Hawaiian music began to play mockingly.

Millroy was smiling, but he looked exhausted, as though he had just lifted something very heavy. He was panting and a little damp and pale.

"He lunched it," Millroy said, "and he doesn't even know it."

Because Mister Phyllis had not stopped hissing—and was that his purple tongue or another rat in his mouth?

Someone said, "Shut him up."

The children were teasing Tinky, the Hawaiian music was playing, and Mister Phyllis gagged on the next thing he said. Then he was silent and seemed very small next to the security man's big blue belly.

"Cue Uncle Dick."

Millroy was already in position, framed by his Uncle Dick curtains, and when they jerked apart, he stepped forward smiling and produced a flock of white doves from the cuffs of his flapping sleeves.

"It's time for Mealtime Magic!"

The children looked up at the circling birds and cheered, and when they looked back at Millroy he was spinning two plump yellow melons on the upright index finger of each hand.

At that moment I saw Mister Phyllis glance from the studio exit door, where he was being helped away by the security man. Now he knew what magic meant.

He was in the Green Room, still looking small, when Millroy entered after the show was over and offered his hand in consolation.

Mister Phyllis worked his little purselike mouth around a short wicked word and there was spit on his lips.

Millroy showed Mister Phyllis his empty hand and magically conjured a quarter from his fingertips.

"Your name is Sidney Perkus," he said, "and you've mentioned your mother several times."

This softened Mister Phyllis's expression.

"Here's a quarter, Perkus. Call your mother and tell her you've just gotten yourself fired from a major TV series."

17 That was how Millroy took over *Paradise Park*. He just stepped in smiling and produced those doves, and then the melons, which he spun on his fingers and divided among the children. Though there were only two melons and a hundred children, there were enough segments to feed each child. No one remarked on this little miracle, and all that Millroy said as he served it was, "Magic is natural."

In came Uncle Dick.

"So often in life," Millroy told me, "you hear or see something, and you think, 'I wish I hadn't heard that.' "

He was wincing at the thought of Mister Phyllis.

"I wish I hadn't seen that."

Out the door went Mister Phyllis, looking beaten, the dead lights decomposing in his eyes, the air seeping out of his face. No definite color with his makeup rubbed off, he seemed like a wrinkled beach toy with a slow leak, so soft, so old, so sad, so suddenly frail, like someone stripped naked, that Millroy said he felt sorry he had told him to call his mother and tell him he'd been fired.

Going away slowly, Mister Phyllis looked different, not just punctured. He had been growing smaller, and defeat reduced him further, until he was very small. He walked strangely, sagging slightly, lopsided with failure, as though learning how to limp.

"But I am glad you saw it, angel," Millroy said. "You had to."

Mister Phyllis had seemed strong, as people do when they are in charge, but it had not taken much to destroy him, and so I realized how weak he had always been.

"Some fresh fruit, a bit of that melon, would do him an awful lot of good right now," Millroy said. "His blood-sugar level must be very low. You can tell."

Millroy and I were in the executive conference room waiting for the verdict about Monday's show. With Mister Phyllis gone, an emergency had arisen. There was a live *Paradise Park* every weekday morning from eight to nine. Would Uncle Dick take over the show, or would a whole new format be proposed?

"I'm glad you're here, angel. Can you see how I'm right at home in this room?" Millroy asked.

He had a method of levitating tables with his fingertips, and he did this while he was speaking. Up went the long conference table, and as it shivered in the air for a few moments he made a spider of his fingers on the tabletop and pushed it slowly down with his fingertips.

His magic sometimes made me nervous, and this was one of those times. I never wondered whether the table would crash down, but I felt flustered when I thought that at any moment Otis or Miss Spitler or Mister Mazzola might open the door and see their mahogany conference table three feet off the floor. It was not that I was embarrassed or fearful, but was it right to work magic with someone else's table?

"Don't worry," Millroy said. "Work magic is all you can do with someone else's stuff. You can't do anything better with it."

Lowering the table into place, he said that at this moment everyone was probably worried about the show, but that when he began doing it they would relax and be glad that Mister Phyllis was gone.

"But it wasn't me. He pulled the chain."

Millroy was stroking his mustache with his long, slender fingers as he thought this over.

"There was so much that I could have done. I get scared when I contemplate the power of it." He made a thoughtful kissing sound against his fingertips. "I could have destroyed him, but that would have been a devilish thing to do. Instead, seeing straight through him, I let him destroy himself."

He raised his eyes to me, and they were the happiest blue I had ever seen.

"That's what God does. He doesn't punish us. He watches us, and there is something terrible in the brilliance of his steady gaze, like a light searching our hearts. That's how he lets us punish our own selves."

He was smiling as he took my hand.

"I was merely an instrument of his power, and you were a reliable witness."

My small damp hand rested in his large dry palm, and he seemed to weigh it appreciatively as he lifted it, as though it were a baby vegetable.

"That is why I need you, angel. Not now, but someday you will have to tell what you have seen. I want you to remember everything."

I said, "But you did do something to Mister Phyllis."

"Not much."

"Was it magic?"

Millroy shook his head.

"Animal magnetism," he said, looking around the empty conference room. "Call it Dicktronics."

Bright daylight was framed in the window and dazzled like something beautiful spilled on the long, polished table. The sunlight seemed odd to me, because normally we were on our way back to Buzzards Bay at this time of the morning. We had arrived at the studio just at daybreak, when the sky was pink or gray, the clouds—the whole Boston sky—like cat's fur, and all the streets damp and blacker with the night's dew. Early in the dim light of these fall mornings, Boston seemed vague and unfinished, but by the time the show was over the day had turned hot and bright, the sun was over the harbor, and the city seemed old and overbuilt. Then Millroy was eager to leave, to be back at the trailer for food and facilities.

"I can't find anything to eat in this city," Millroy said.

He brought out two hunks of bread and a honeycomb, and made a sandwich of them, which he broke in half for us to share. As always, he ate slowly, chewing carefully, as though examining each bite, concentrating on the taste. It was not like eating at all, but as if he were testing with his mouth.

He ate looking at the door where the show's producers were holding their emergency meeting.

"They're trying to decide whether I can do the job." He munched. "They're wondering whether I can fill Mister Phyllis's shoes." He swallowed and smiled. "His tinky-winky shoes."

"It was kind of sad seeing him go," I said, and saw again the little old man in the striped sweater limping away, carrying his overweight cat.

"Like death," Millroy said. He said it briskly, without much feeling. "Just like death. How do I know?" He took another bite of the sandwich and chewed it, nodding at me. "Because I've been there—I died."

He became very attentive, waiting to see what this word would do to me. I only blinked and let him go on because I knew he wanted to talk about the day he died.

Day he *what*?

"Remember how I told you that prophets and messengers are tested with all sorts of temptations and sufferings?"

I said no, he had not.

"Remember how I told you I was fat? Cheeks out like this? Hamburger face? Fat Voice? Breathless? People mooing and throwing food at me?"

He said this lightly, nibbling the edges of the honeycomb sandwich.

"I was so fat I should have had numbers on my back. People told me to jog or use a rowing machine. I lasted about five seconds. They let me off the hook—claimed I was exercise intolerant."

He sat at the far end of the conference table and stared down its gleaming length, remembering.

"How was I to know that I was trapped in the darkness of my body?"

"You told me about that," I said.

"But why didn't the doctor find me abnormal and realize that I was doomed?"

What I was wondering was, *Why is Millroy smiling?*

"Because the doctor was fat," he said brightly. "And he smoked. Imagine his fingers—Smoker's Fingers—poking me and trying to find something wrong. He scanned my gallbladder and found nothing wrong. Why? Because it was plugged solid. Single stones didn't appear. It was one solid stone."

He had finished his sandwich and was dabbing at crumbs with a damp fingertip, tidying the shiny surface of the table.

"One morning I died. You think it's going to be a huge earthquake, with music. But it was no great event. I had been dying for years. I just slipped under. My heart stopped. No blood could get through the fat in my arteries. Call it heartburn—that's what it felt like."

He stood up, looking so strong it was impossible to imagine him any other way, and yet I saw this other man he was describing lying in bed like a great heavy heap.

"No one tried seriously to revive me. Why should they bother when they could use me for spare parts? My eyes and liver were still functional. They could transplant my corneas. They'd bury the rest in a toxic-waste dump."

Hearing footsteps behind the door, he became alert and spoke quickly, looking hopeful.

"I just lay there cooling," he said. "And I had a vastation." He heard something far off, and repeated, sounding happy, "I had a vastation of the person I had been—not recently but long ago, and I saw myself as a child of six—healthy, happy, full of hope, able to work magic. Gifted. Innocent. Like the kids on the show. Like you, angel, the day I first saw you."

There were people outside the door, moving fast and talking.

"I rose from the dead, sugar."

Otis was opening the door, Mister Mazzola and Miss Spitler behind him.

"You want me," Millroy said.

They all laughed hearing that, because it was true. They shook his hand, congratulating him, and then sat around the table.

"Your new contract is being drawn up," Miss Spitler said. "We ought to have something for you by the middle of next week."

"Money is not a particular concern of mine," Millroy said. "My decisions are made without reference to remuneration."

"It will be based on Mister Phyllis's contract," Mister Mazzola said.

"People lose the fat off their personality as they get older," Millroy said. "Humorous people get less funny, eccentrics get crazy, and the worst of it is, they don't know it."

"He was our first host," Miss Spitler said. "No question, Mister Phyllis left his mark on the show."

"His contribution was nugatory," Millroy said, placing his fingertips on the table.

"That is a fact," Otis said.

"He lost the fat off his personality," Millroy said. "His sharp edges stuck out."

"You could see them," Otis said.

"He'll find something," Miss Spitler said. But the scripts would stay the same until the end of next week. All Millroy had to do was read Mister Phyllis's lines on the TelePrompTer. The week after, she said, he could develop his own material.

They went on talking but I stopped listening. They all seemed pleased, though the atmosphere was stark and a little shaky, as though a storm had just blown through.

"Now we have to go back home," Millroy said. "Buzzards Bay."

He was absentmindedly levitating his end of the table by tugging the tabletop with his fingers.

"Seems an awful long way," Otis said.

"Got to eat," Millroy said.

Now they were all staring at the table jiggling off the floor.

"Let's go, son."

Thump.

Millroy came on playing the *Paradise Park* theme song ("Wear a smile, all the while . . ."), with a harmonica jammed against his nose, snuffling the notes as he juggled six raw carrots with one hand. He used Mister Phyllis's script but he spoke it differently, and he introduced the children in the audience—talked to them, got them to comment on the puppets and cartoons.

What Millroy enjoyed most was speaking to the children, giving them little jobs to do, and watching them fuss with pots and pans and bottles and little gadgets. He did not touch anything, so that in carrying out his directions the children worked magic. But they did not know what I knew, that Millroy rejoiced in making magic with words, and that in directing and announcing a miracle he had been inspired.

"The Book is full of look-no-hands magic," he had told me. " 'Rise, lift your pallet and go home,' and the cripple walks away. Or, 'Go home, your son's alive,' and the nobleman's son has recovered from his fever. Or to Peter, 'Go catch a fish, open its mouth and you'll find a coin.' And there's the coin, just as the Lord said! No hands!"

Even the first day he was the host he did it, instructing the children in the audience to pack a mass of vegetables in an empty silver container.

"Now put the lid on, and everyone place your hands on the lid. You feel anything?"

"No, Uncle Dick!"

"Now take the lid off and look in and tell me what you see."

The vegetables were gone and in their place was liquid, which Millroy directed them to pour into six glasses of reddish vegetable juice. Looking fearful at first, they tasted it but ended up drinking it all.

"Isn't that the greatest stuff you ever drank?"

Millroy said there was a stern logic and a pure motive in every bit of magic he worked, whether it was look-no-hands or total involvement. He turned big brown spuds into mashed potatoes, flour into bread, and milk into yogurt and then into fat-free ice cream. He passed this food around to the children in the audience, and there was always enough for everyone, and even some left over.

"It's natural magic," he said after the show on the following Wednesday. "Come to think of it, that wouldn't be a bad name for the whole show. *Paradise Park* has a ring of unreality about it. It sends the wrong message."

Otis Godberry agreed with Millroy, but the others—Mister Mazzola and Miss Spitler—said no, that name recognition was important, and this was why the show was staying popular even without Mister Phyllis.

"Or how about *Eat with Ernie?*" Millroy said.

They gave him a certain silent look that meant *Never mind.*

"I'd change my name to Ernie," Millroy said.

This confused them, because how were they to know that Millroy was always changing his name?

"I like you as Uncle Dick," Miss Spitler said, not knowing that it too was made up.

"What do most people do when they watch TV? What do all children do?" Millroy was still on his feet, still pitching. "They chew gum, they chomp popcorn, they snack, they suck candy, they lick their fingers. They seek oral gratification. In a word, they eat."

"We have a very reliable format," Miss Spitler said. "We have Mister Phyllis to thank for that."

"Mister Phyllis was unhealthy. He was sick and weak because he didn't eat right. He smoked. He was irregular—that was visible. This is a breakfasttime show. Seems to me we can take advantage of the timing."

None of them saw what he was driving at.

"Get the kids eating right," Millroy said. "Instead of habituating them to seeing unhealthy people and irrelevant puppets. Let's face it, the Frawlies are vermin, the Mumbling Humptulips are insects."

I knew what he was leading up to because he had been talking about nothing else even before the day Mister Phyllis left.

"Forget *Paradise Park*. Call the whole show *Mealtime Magic*. Fill it with nutritious foodstuffs."

"Kind of a *Fun with Food* thing?" Otis asked.

"No," Millroy said. "A serious thing. Talk about eating in general. About sickness and death, health and magic. Open a whole world to them. The children might want to know why their parents are big and breathless and sweaty. Why they smell awful, why they're unfair and bad-tempered, why they die."

"Why they die?" Miss Spitler asked.

With a patient expression and a soft voice, Millroy said, "Your son Tom, who had diverticulitis, whom I talked to you about two weeks ago in this very office—how is he?"

"Much better. He made a full recovery." Miss Spitler looked confused and grateful and unsure of herself until she stepped away, as though from Millroy's magnetic field, and said, "But you're talking about completely changing Boston's top children's show."

"Left to itself, Tom's colon might have been completely rerouted into a colostomy bag," Millroy said. "I have a message, daughter."

"I don't get what you're proposing," Mister Mazzola said.

Millroy said, "Explain to me why Americans who work in restaurants and supermarkets, of all places, always look unhealthy."

" 'Cause they don't eat right," Otis said.

"This man's eyes are open," Millroy said.

Still standing away from Millroy, Miss Spitler said, "We're keeping the format."

Without an objection or another word, Millroy accepted this. Afterward I followed him down the corridor to the station lobby.

"There is only one fat person in The Book," Millroy said, throwing his arm around Otis Godberry. "His name is Eglon and he is stabbed. Where? In the rest room! There are old people and there are sick people, diseases of all kinds are mentioned, not only leprosy and boils, but infections and dropsy and other afflictions. Yet apart from 'Eglon was a very fat man' in Judges, obesity is never mentioned. I want you to think about the implications."

"What about Jeshurun, who waxed so fat in Deuteronomy that he was covered in fatness and forsook God?" Otis asked.

Millroy had started shaking his head as soon as Otis mentioned Jeshurun.

"Jeshurun wasn't a man," Millroy said. "It's just another name for Israel. You're confused."

Looking more respectful, Otis agreed, and followed us to the Ford, saying that Millroy was an amazing man and it was a shame no one recognized this.

"What's the other thing you remember from The Book?" Millroy said, then answered his own question. "That people lived an average of two hundred and thirty years. It's true. I've done the numbers."

So the name "Paradise Park" stayed the same, but the material was Millroy's: more magic, more food, more humor, fewer puppets, children everywhere. The show was more popular than ever. Each morning there was a long line of children waiting in the six o'clock darkness to get into the studio to be part of the audience. Some came with their parents, some in little packs looking wolfish, others were alone. When I told Millroy that these were the ones I felt sorry for, he chose them first—"Who's here alone?" There were eighty seats, but within a week there were two or three hundred children waiting to get in.

I stopped sitting backstage in the Green Room, the control room or the rear of the studio—a lonely little guy waiting to go home to eat with his dad, nothing else to do. With Mister Phyllis around, Millroy had tried to hide me, but from the day he took over the show, I was in the audience with the other children. They were small, sweaty, loud and happy, and Millroy said they—not he—were the heart and soul of the show. They were much happier than when Mister Phyllis had been in charge because they had known how much he hated them. They were more eager these days because Millroy had a way of whipping people up, children especially. He said he loved seeing children twitching and squirming with excitement.

"What time is it, guys?"

"It's mealtime!"

"Who says mealtime is magic time?"

"Uncle Dick!"

By expanding this eating segment and shrinking "Puppet Time" and "Cartoon Carnival," Millroy got his way—the sort of food show he had asked for—without changing the name. He still kept his magic boxes and cabinets, but he also had kegs of fruit and vegetables, and bowls and jugs with his name on them, and a juicer he called "DJ" because he refused to advertise any commercial products.

"What should I do with this bushel of apples, guys?"

"Juice them!"

"And what about the juice?"

It turned out to be a half gallon of frothing brown liquid.

"Drink it!"

He drank it down—he could pour that much and more down his throat at one go without gulping or spilling—and he finished it before the children stopped yelling.

Children like making noise, Millroy said. They hunger to scream. It is a physical necessity, like blinking and yawning. After those screams they need rest; storms and calms make up a youngster's disposition, which was why they are capable of working magic.

"I need a volunteer," he said one day. "Who wants to help Uncle Dick?"

Every child in the studio jumped up and waved, trying to attract Millroy's attention. But he chose me.

"What's your name, son?"

"Alex," I said.

It pleased me that no one knew my secret, that I was a nobody girl from Marstons Mills named Jilly Farina, and not a boy named Alex, Millroy's teenage son.

"You're going to be my little helper," he said. "It seems young Herma-Rae over here has lost her new wristwatch."

It was not until this moment that the little girl realized her watch was gone, and there was panic on her tight, tearful face.

"Some magicians just tease you," Millroy said. "People who tease you are burgers and sadists, especially grown-ups. Uncle Dick will never do that to you"—he was speaking to all the children on the sloping bank of seats—"so let's find that wristwatch, Alex."

I hesitated and then thought, *Alex—that's me.*

"This little guy is going to be my dowsing rod, and don't worry about that job description. When he's finished, you're going to know what a dowsing rod is."

How it happened I don't know, but without touching me Millroy steered me across the studio and my whole body focused on the boom microphone, hanging over Paradise Park like a fishing rod. The wristwatch (how did it get there without anyone seeing?) was buckled around the top, fifteen feet from the floor.

After handing the watch over to Herma-Rae, Millroy changed a boy's signet ring into a Bing cherry, and I ate it.

"That's full of fructose," Millroy said in his Uncle Dick voice, "and it doesn't cause cancer like the cherries you get in ice-cream stores."

The signet ring turned up in the Frawlies' tree stump.

At the end of the show we did the Indian basket, but this time Millroy himself crawled inside, and after I tapped the basket with a magic wand he vanished. Opening it, I revealed not Uncle Dick but the whole family of buzzing Humptulips. While they jostled in the basket, looking demented, the alphabet cartoons started, Pignut and Dogfish discussing the letter T and all the words you could make with it.

"Did you miss me?" Millroy said, reappearing in the Indian basket after the cartoons.

The kids screamed, "Yes!" and were happy making noise for a while, as though they had drawn a deep breath.

"Are you sure you missed me?" Millroy asked, and encouraged them by adding, "Let it out, guys!"

You could hear their loud voices ringing against the pipes and tubes of the metal chairs and vibrating in the steel hoods of the bright lights. Their yells set the whole studio twanging.

"Now where's my little helper?"

"Here I am."

"Little Al," he said.

I liked being Little Al. I put the Indian basket away, turned the crank of the wind-up record player, passed more Bing cherries around, pulled the curtains, scooped up Boobie. I chose a small girl from the audience to help me clean the blackboard.

I was not nervous. The day before, in the trailer at Buzzards Bay, Millroy had coached me for three hours. I was prepared for it all. His magic filled me with confidence.

I thought to myself, _I'm on TV._

Riding back in the Ford later that morning, I kept thinking how easy Millroy had made it for me, and what fun it was to be under the bright lights of the studio, with the cameras on me, my face in the monitor, part of the show.

I said, "I liked doing that."

It made me uncomfortable when Millroy did not reply.

I said, "I mean, you never see ugly little guys like me on TV."

It was as though he had disappeared inside his own body. He was not just unusually quiet but simply not there, and so silent, so absent, that I stuck my thumb into my mouth.

I was looking at the wooden totem pole at Exit 5 when he suddenly said, "You gave me an idea."

18 _I'm going to be on the show again,_ I thought. _Might even be in charge!_

Millroy had the power to fill anyone, even someone like me, with confidence. I thought then in the car how he should have had children of his own, lots of them, and how they would never fear him, never lock their bedroom door, never hide when he raised his voice, never leave home when he began to drink, but only love him. He could make the weepiest person feel happy; after a pep talk from him you believed in yourself. I was Little Al, full of beans. Maybe I had a hidden talent for magic myself!

You're going to live for two hundred years, was the sort of thing he said, *and you're going to be happy the whole time.*

After his coaching me and when I looked back on my performance on the show, it did not seem strange that he might say, *You did so well today that you can do it all by yourself from now on.*

Wasn't that what he was going to tell me? Not that I wanted to be a star. I was just sick of sitting around.

Why shouldn't I be eager for him to give me this job and costume? He had turned me into Little Al, so the next logical step was to give this boy something to do. I imagined how it might be for me as Alex, or Little Al, or even Crazy Al, helping out each time there was a job to be done. I liked the idea of being the sort of favorite sidekick and helper that I had been for him that week at the Barnstable County Fair, when he had dressed me up in a sequined dress and a cape and called me "My lovely assistant, Annette," and I went *click-clicking* in my high heels across the stage.

He had changed my life. I could hardly remember the person I had been. I was stronger—still small, but tougher. I ate big, fibrous, beany meals and piles of fruit, flat bread and honey and broiled fish. He made porridgy soups out of barley, and red-lentil pottage. He allowed sour yogurt and sour cheese, but hardly any meat, only lamb when I had a meat fit, and even then he called it a sacrifice. He made salads of flowers and vine leaves, he offered me handfuls of alfalfa sprouts. He was crazy about figs, and he was very big on garlic ("It's a natural antibiotic—completely mends your immune system"). Now and then he mixed some water with a grapey liquid that tasted like weak, inky wine.

In Millroy's Airstream trailer, I slept soundly, dreamlessly, hardly moving, and woke up feeling bright, my head completely clear. At Gaga's I had always felt weary, fearful, guilty and a little weepy—anxious at the thought that without warning the old woman might hit me or scream at me, or just yell at the walls, freaking out in frustration. I was calmer now, I was healthy. I told Millroy how different I felt.

"Your body's working nicely," he said. "You have spirit. That's the whole point. Your hair's healthy, your skin's elastic, you've got tonus. And you feel like a good person, sort of virtuous. Unapologetic.''

It was true, it was a sense of strength, and he had done it. He had fed me and looked after me.

"I know that feeling," he said.

Though I did not dare say so, I also felt that part of me belonged to him because he had improved me and made me healthy and happy, that he was responsible, and that it would not have happened without him. He had taken over the care and operation of my body the way real parents were supposed to do. But I did not say it because I did not know how to put it into words, to thank him for it, without making him think that my body was his to use. It was small and skinny and he was helping it grow healthier, but did that give him any rights to touch me? He did not try or even seem interested, but even so the answer was a flat no.

"It's neat," I said. "I love feeling like this."

He was sluicing barley and beans in a shallow pan, washing them and picking out the pebbles. *I'm just fooling around here, experimenting with an amazing bread recipe.* The Bible was open on the counter to the Book of Ezekiel.

"Stands to reason," he said.

He went on flopping loops of wet beans in the pan, like a prospector panning for gold.

"Because you're regular," he said.

It was his favorite word, and was a major feature of his daily routine. It took longer than most meals, and just the thought of it made him serious. It was also a form of meditation, he said.

"It's more than purging—it's purification. Get all those poisons out of your body." He always told me to take my time. "And it's usually a good idea to reduce your restrictive clothing and to loosen all your garments."

Even a hat, tight shoes, or a knotted necktie could be serious obstacles to digestion, never mind regularity, he said.

I had my own lock for the rest room in the trailer, my own section in the two-basin sink, and my own hopper. So did Millroy. It was important to him, he said.

"If I ever have to travel without my Airstream—which, God forbid—I would never go anywhere without my Soft Seat."

He took this contraption to Boston every morning in his Uncle Dick briefcase.

"Is that a life preserver?" I had asked when I first saw it. It was the sort of rubber ring you sometimes found floating in kiddie pools.

No, it was an inflatable toilet seat, a doughnut-shaped cushion for when he was away from the trailer. It was his own invention, and soon after we started going to Boston every morning, he made one for me. But he said it was not a good idea to develop a dependency on it because the seat was only part of the problem, it was the room itself, the locks, the atmosphere, the lack of privacy, the sudden noises, the stinks and perfumes, the sight of other people's feet.

"Gaga was always banging on the door and telling me to hurry up."

"See what I mean? Your grandmother's worse than a burger. She's a savage."

Millroy was odd, he was unexpected, but he was gentle and fun, and I felt more comfortable now as a boy than I had as a girl. I was the right size and shape for a young boy: I was a small fourteen-year-old girl but I looked like a normal twelve-year-old boy. I realized Millroy had been right. It was easy for a boy to be living this life with him in the trailer at Pilgrim Pines, and going with him to the TV studio. It would have been very hard for a girl—all those questions like *Who is this guy?* and *Where's your mother?*

Millroy made it even simpler by treating me like a boy, never crowding me or intruding when we were inside the Airstream, and always calling me Alex when we were outside. He almost convinced me that I was a boy. I began to look at boy's clothes with a new curiosity and interest that Millroy himself encouraged. *Neat pair of sneakers there, Allie,* he might say, or, *That is one very cool baseball hat.*

Millroy was always in disguise, too, not just his clothes but the hats he wore, the dark glasses, the way he trimmed his mustache. Floyd Fewox would not have recognized him. Did the Reverend Baby Huber have any idea that the bulgy silver Airstream trailer in Space 28 belonged to Uncle Dick, the star of Boston TV's *Paradise Park*? He was Millroy there, and I was his silent kid, but as soon as we set off we became Uncle Dick and his talented son Alex.

It was a long way to travel from Pilgrim Pines to Boston and back, almost sixty miles each way.

"It strengthens me," Millroy said.

"Coming all the way back here to eat?"

"Yes, but most of all to watch Reverend Huber eat."

By this time he had washed his soaked beans and was kneading them with the barley, wheat flour, lentils and butter, still glancing at the Book of Ezekiel from time to time.

"It's human of course," Millroy said. "We love to hear that someone has a terrible weakness."

I was thinking, *Do we?*

"It really does my heart good to hear Huber saying, 'I love hot dogs' or 'I can't stop munching nachos,' or see mayonnaise smeared on his lips, or a dab of ketchup on the tip of his nose as he eats his so-called Real Good Fries."

I was thinking, *Does it?*

"It gives me such a boost to see him gnawing a bucket of hot wings from Kentucky Fried Chicken. I don't say it makes me feel superior, but it makes me feel powerful within myself. Strengthens my resolve."

"You would have loved Gaga and Dada if you had gotten to know them better."

"I know them well. I see them clearly, and I want you to see them as I do."

He trusted me, he said. He believed in me. He said that I gave him ideas, and that none of this would have happened to him if it had not been for me. He would still have been Millroy the Magician, making an elephant disappear at Foskett's Fun-O-Rama. But I had liberated him. He had followed me, not the other way around, and together we had taken over *Paradise Park*. He owed all his success to me.

"You are my secret," he said, "and you are much bigger than you think."

I did not ask why. I did not want to think about the reason. Yet all this talk made me happy. It meant I had a purpose, a life to live, real work, I was not just someone he pitied, tagging along. And it meant that my disguise was complete. I was a whole made-up person, Little Al.

I looked out of the window at the cold Cape Cod Canal as Millroy slipped his lump of dough into the oven. It was now early November, and school had been in session for almost two months—classes, books, teachers, dullness, work, rain and muddy sports. The yellow school bus with Mister Pocknett at the wheel had stopped flashing its lights in the morning at the corner of Prospect Street and River Road, and they no longer waited for Jilly Farina, but just drove off, the other kids muttering, *Jelly-fish must have moved.* Yes, I was somewhere else, and I did not want to go back because that meant that I would have to turn into a small girl once again, afraid of bigger people and loud noises, heading nowhere in the dark.

In the summer I had always felt free. I could do as I liked, could dream without interruption as long as I was alone. In the hot dusty summer air, in the yellow woods of Marstons Mills, or even during my usual week at Camp Farley in Mashpee with the 4-H Club, I had visions of happiness. When September came I had to wake up and go back. But now it was November and I had no wish to go back—ever. Millroy had shown me that life could be simple and you could be fearless and have fun, eating right and praising God—"or Good, as I prefer to call the Almighty"—by doing so. Living well was a form of prayer. Taking care of your body was a way of giving thanks because your life was a gift to treasure and endow with health, not just for now but for two centuries.

So Millroy said, in just those words, and he claimed I had succeeded.

"I can tell by looking at you that you're faithful, angel."

In a short time after he had shoved his beany dough mixture into the oven, he removed it, hardened and browned, like a failed cake or a huge ugly cookie.

This year would be different from any other, I thought. I was rescued, and even though I did not know where I was going I was sure that I was better off with Millroy than without him. He swore that he felt the same about me.

"I am going to call this Ezekiel Four-Nine bread," he said, breaking it into two hunks and handing one to me.

Then he gave me the bad news, and the worst was that he thought it was good news.

"Muffin, you have given me a dynamite idea for this show," he said.

It was later now. I was trying not to sulk, and we were eating bowls of pottage with fitches and figs and thick slices of Ezekiel bread. I had been waiting for nothing except to be disappointed.

"When you were walking back and forth, calling the kids by name, arranging the props, setting up the tricks, I was marveling at your authority. You saw how those little guys looked at you?"

Yes, just dying for me to do something wrong—drop a pot or trip over a wire so that they could laugh at me. I said so to Millroy.

"Exactly," he said. "They weren't afraid. They weren't nervous. If they performed something it was an exercise of their own free will."

"They would have done the same for anyone, even someone like Mister Phyllis."

"Heaven help them."

"They would have been pumped."

"But he would have intimidated them."

So what? Some of these kids looked dangerous and stupid, and drooled and smelled and laughed too loud and wore their baseball hats on sideways and backward. Why not intimidate them a little? I would not have minded if they had been afraid of me.

"See, this is a children's show," Millroy said. "It's their own show. Because of that, it should be run by children. Real tinky-winky children."

Expecting that he was handing me the job, I waited, smiling a little and trying to look capable and intelligent and bigger than I felt.

"I am going to put children in charge," he said.

I was standing there waiting for the job.

"And I'll take a backseat," he said.

I was still standing there. Was he planning to give me this job? If so, he was going about it in the most roundabout way.

"From now on we're going to see children in front of that camera all the time. Children talking to children."

"Like what I was doing?"

"Right," he said. "Only more of it. Will you help me, sugar?"

This gave me the jolt I wanted and I said, "Yes, sure," two or three times, blinking like mad.

But all he said was, "You're going to find me the right youngsters."

"Find you the right youngsters?"

Find him the right youngsters?

"To run the show," he said.

I almost cried. I said, "I wanted to run the show."

He gave me his Uncle Dick grin and said, "You're going to run the youngsters."

• • •

"Mazzola thinks it's a great idea," Otis Godberry said after the next day's show in the *Paradise Park* studio.

We were waiting for Mister Mazzola and Miss Spitler to show up, as they did every morning to make a comment on that day's program.

"And so do I—kids in charge, kids running the show, kids' faces in the camera, goofing off."

But even as Otis praised the scheme Millroy was frowning.

"I think you have reservations," Millroy said. He could smell doubt as strongly as though it were a bucket of hot chicken wings.

Otis pinched a twist of hair and fussed with it before he answered.

"Not about that, but I was thinking that with all these new ideas and the rehearsal time, shouldn't you be thinking about living up here in Boston?"

"Can't do it."

Holding on to his twist of hair, Otis said, "That traveling back and forth must be real tiring."

"I have to go back to Buzzards Bay." Millroy was not moved. "To eat."

"I see."

I knew that Otis did not see at all and that he was just pretending this made sense.

"I need to get back to my trailer for so many things."

"Lots of business," Otis said, trying to help him out.

"Not business," Millroy said. "But health issues. Nutrition and general hygiene." Then he laughed because it was all so obvious to him. "My kitchen is there, my bed is there." He dropped his voice and became more serious. "And my whole support system is there."

"Home sweet home," Otis said. He was still uncertain, and still held on to the twist of hair, which was now curled on his clumsy finger.

Millroy said, "These aren't luxuries—they're necessities. And you want me to stay in Boston." He laughed again in a defiant way, as though Otis were being totally unreasonable. "Where would I eat?"

Millroy was so sure of himself that Otis agreed that to commute to Boston every day, over an hour up, the same down, longer on Fridays, much longer when there was an accident or a traffic jam, so that he could fire up his cooker, sleep on his bedshelf and use his own hopper and bathtub made perfect sense.

When Miss Spitler and Mister Mazzola showed up, they said the children-in-charge idea was wonderful and how surprised and pleased they had been when they saw me on the show working the Indian basket and talking to the other children.

"I sometimes wonder what you'd do without your Alex," Mister Mazzola said.

"I'd be lost," Millroy said.

He spoke with such force and feeling that he generated a warm, silent cloud of embarrassment that hung over us for a long moment.

"We just have to find the rest of the children," he said, breaking the silence, "and I have Alex working on that, too."

Feeling their eyes on me, I tried to look worthy and competent.

"We don't need more puppets," Millroy said, his voice croaky and emotional—he was still getting over having said *I'd be lost.* "We need more food, more nutrition. We've got to go for health and happiness."

They had blinked when he said *more food,* and now they were watching him closely. He knew he had made them curious.

"Is this *Eat with Ernie* again?" Mister Mazzola asked.

"No, but I see bread being a very significant element in this show."

Otis had not stopped blinking, trying to understand by repeating various words. He said, "Happiness." He said, "Bread."

"The bread of life," Millroy said. "I see fresh fruit—grapes, peaches, lemons, apples. I see mentions of ambrosia and nectar. Honey, of course. Nourishing soups. Nuts, grains, barleys."

The three people watching him moved their mouths—not talking, but sort of tasting the food he mentioned. It was hard to tell whether they liked the taste; they were still staring and their tongues were swelling in their open mouths.

"Pottage," Millroy said. "Figs."

They were still staring.

"Fitches," he said. "Or vetches. Same thing."

"This is that old food show again," Mister Mazzola said in a warning voice.

"No," Millroy said.

This seemed to surprise them, and they blinked again at him.

"Because the show is staying *Paradise Park,*" Miss Spitler said. "Putting kids in charge is a good programing idea, but we're keeping the format."

"As a celebration of life," Millroy said.

He did not smile. He turned slowly from them, moved his head and raised his eyes, leaning his whole body toward the window. They did the same, though more awkwardly, and I looked, too.

"Do you see what I see?"

The signs said POPPY'S PACKAGE STORE, DISCOUNT TIRES, PRESTO COPYING and DUNKIN' DONUTS.

"The future," Millroy said.

"What exactly are fitches?" Mister Mazzola asked. "Kind of bird?"

" 'When he hath made plain the face thereof, doth he not cast abroad the fitches?" Otis quoted. "Isaiah."

"I love this man," Millroy said, and hugged him.

Mister Mazzola still did not know.

"You sprinkle them on bread," Millroy said, "and the bread I suggest is the Ezekiel loaf. I just baked a batch. Tell them about it, Alex."

I smiled because their own smiles were so bewildered, the sort of grin that said they didn't have a clue.

"I feel that including children in the show could be a huge success," Miss Spitler said.

"Or chaos," Mister Mazzola said.

"Maybe both," Millroy said, and now he was smiling at his watch. "Look at the time. I'm getting the grumbellies."

"So you're heading back?" Otis said, walking us to the lobby. Millroy had his arm locked in a friendly way around Otis's shoulder, his usual hug.

"Correct," Millroy said.

"Back to your kitchen."

"Food is very important," Millroy said.

"Sleep in your own bed kind of thing."

"And don't forget my rest room."

"Got to keep clean."

"Clean outside and in," Millroy said.

This seemed to fluster Otis, so he wagged his head and made an anxious sound in his nose. But Millroy was smiling.

"My tub, my shower bath," he said, and tightened his arm around Otis and looked him straight in the eye. "My hopper."

Otis was trying to speak.

"Punch me in the stomach, Otis. Go on—hard as you can."

Otis opened his mouth to speak but no sound came out.

"Guess my age. You'll never get it," Millroy said. "I'm regular, Otis. If I wasn't regular, you wouldn't want me."

After two tries, Otis said, "Anyway, your children-in-charge idea is just great."

"Children are the answer," Millroy said.

He was excited. He had gotten his way. When he was triumphant like this he seemed bewitched and brilliant.

"Children are about seventy-five percent water, you know that, Otis? That's more pure liquid than the average piña colada. You could drink most kids."

Otis had gone mute again and seemed to have trouble breathing.

"Just joking," Millroy said, "but the water content of a child is very important."

"Sure thing." That was what Otis's mouth said, but his eyes said, *Oh boy.*

19

"I am fed up to the roof of my mouth with those puppets," Millroy said on the puppets' last day to Leo LaBlang, the floor manager. Millroy had—magically, right on the show—made the puppets collapse, go limp and die.

Leo was swinging some of the crumpled puppets in his hand, one bundle of Frawlies and one bundle of Mumbling Humptulips, to bury in the prop room.

"I'm going to miss these characters," he said.

"See? They subverted you!" Millroy snatched them and tossed them aside. "I hate fake animals with silly faces and horrible costumes—mice especially. Mice should be naked. And by the way, who ever heard of a fat mouse? No talking animals. I want human spontaneity. Alex has found us some real people."

He wanted cheerful children, boys or girls, it did not matter. If I liked them when I saw them in the audience, he signed them up.

"I want happy youngsters who know how to listen."

On the next show there was Willie Webb, big for fifteen, baseball hat on sideways, smiling at Millroy and chiming in, saying things that Millroy repeated. Another happy echo was a twinkling little girl named Stacy. I had already had them in mind when I saw them in the audience on previous shows. I wanted to impress Millroy with my brisk efficiency.

"Type of youngster I look for is open to suggestion," Millroy said. "Almost inevitably they've been leaned on by a burger—parenthetically, what child hasn't been?—but it would be kind of nifty if you found me a few more natural youngsters like these. And remember that health is more important than looks. No cutie pies, please. I want human beings."

Willie Webb had bright, appreciative eyes and a good, deep laugh, and when he wasn't laughing he was listening and picking at his elbow.

"Come here, son," Millroy had said when I brought Willie to him, and he lifted the boy's head gently by touching his chin, and calmed the fearful upturned face by saying, "Listen. And look at my nose"—Millroy's nose began to throb in a strange, beaky way—"I need you to help me."

Willie stood squarely on short, reliable legs. He wore big sneakers and a sweatshirt that was lettered PROPERTY OF TUBMAN JUNIOR HIGH ATHLETIC DEPT. I liked the way his faded clothes fitted him. He had beautiful teeth, and his posture and the way he moved made him seem strong. I had felt safe when he was seated near me, which was why I picked him. He was much bigger than me, and I had the idea that he was careless and happy.

Millroy held him motionless with his fingertips, touching the roundness of the boy's shoulder. I knew that a surge of soothing energy was passing through those fingers to Willie Webb's body. Millroy had touched me that way with no other motive than kindness.

Certain animals, such as Yowie and Muttrix, growled and grew calm when they were touched like that, and afterward you saw them twitching and eager to please, like Willie just now.

"You're going to walk out there and take over."

Millroy was speaking without moving his mouth, and it was as though his voice were coming from high above his head.

" 'Hello, brothers and sisters, and welcome—it's Day One of *Paradise Park!*' And if you can't remember that you just look into the camera lens and read the words you see in the TelePrompTer.''

Willie's eyes glistened and, though he did not say a word, all his energy was making him tremble.

"You're not going to be nervous, because everyone is your friend. You're going to hold your head up and keep your mouth open when you talk. 'Let's see what's happening! Let's feel good!' ''

Millroy's fingers had drawn away, and he held the boy by making his eyes tiny and intense, encouraging Willie and filling him with strength. I knew how it felt. He had done it to me when we rehearsed my part in the show. And when he talked without moving his lips, it was impossible to tell whether that hovering voice was something in your mind or his.

Willie's face was blank and beautiful and he seemed to be purring through his chest like a cat as he listened. He did not blink at all.

That same look, Willie's holy shining face, became Stacy's expression, and lit up her teeth as she put herself into Millroy's hands to receive his instructions.

"This is the way it should be," Millroy said afterward in his Uncle Dick voice. "I hate puppets, and anyway who needs them?"

The rehearsals these days were often better than the shows—funnier, with lots of bread and beany food that Uncle Dick served.

I am so pleased that they always arrive here hungry, he said.

He put Willie Webb and Stacy in charge and gave a long, slow speech, and made faces, and encouraged them. They followed his suggestions and worked magic.

Everything is falling into place was what he said to praise us. He seemed to be talking about something more important than this children's show, something as big as the world. Many times in the middle of the rehearsals he marveled in a low voice to me, *I didn't realize that it would happen this way. I had no plan, yet I was strong in my desire. I simply trusted that eventually my message would be delivered. I waited for a sign because I didn't know how to bring it about. And then I saw you in the audience. Everything since then has happened because of you.*

He always knew I was thinking, *I didn't do a thing!*

Because of what you are, he said. *Who you are.*

Today we were sitting on the old sofa that the puppeteers used to sit in, holding the Frawlies and the Humptulips and the rest of them in their laps. But all Millroy had in his lap was his hands.

"This old basket has swallowed her up," Willie Webb was saying as he removed the lid. "And in her place is an apple. Or is it two?"

Willie picked up the apple, massaged it, closed his hands around it and produced another one from nowhere.

"They are born with amazing gifts. They can work real magic. But in the course of time they lose the knack, the gift vanishes, and they become dull and pedestrian."

Watching Willie rehearse, Millroy kept his hands upright in his lap like a pair of gremlins and conjured with his fingers.

"If they start early enough, kids can get mastery of three or four bodily functions. Think about it."

"Is that enough?"

"It's a good start."

Willie was crawling into the basket and saying, "I think I'll go look for Stacy. So Kayla, when you open the lid you might not see me, girl."

"Some people call it yoga, but it's because I have always been a child," Millroy said.

He winked and I knew he was half-joking.

"Which is why, when I first saw you alone sucking your thumb at my show at the Barnstable County Fair, I knew you hadn't lost it. And you're what? Fifteen?"

"Fourteen." My birthday was next month.

"Whatever," Millroy said, but looked startled. "You don't know how rare you are."

"Gone," Kayla said as she raised the lid on the basket. "That boy is out of here."

"But like I say, I'm a child myself," Millroy said, croaking and sounding as though he had a dry mouth.

He saw that I was distracted, looking at the Indian basket for signs of Willie Webb and Stacy. He sat forward on the sofa, raised his hands and said, "Take your places, people."

His voice was even, and though it was not loud, it was distinctly Uncle Dick speaking, audible all over the studio.

At the sound, Willie and Stacy materialized, he from the basket, she from behind a screen, both of them on their feet, smiling, listening, ready to take another order.

"This is good," Millroy said.

Willie Webb had fixed his eyes on a boy named Dedrick, who was fifteen or older, black like most of the others, with tight, plumlike skin, tiny ears, big spotty eyes, and a growly and breathless way of talking. He would be a useful one, I thought.

The music started. Willie and Stacy positioned themselves at the gates of Paradise Park, welcoming the other children in to play. The music was *rumpty-tumpty-tiddly-ump,* like staggering rabbits.

Millroy's way of rehearsing was to make it a party—the food first, then letting them fool around on their own, try out the props, and listen to the music, all the while rousing them with the intensity of his gaze, as though they were performing for him alone. When he asked me what I thought, I always said, "Sounds good," or made a suggestion. The minute I recommended Dedrick he was on the team. After this party, when they were relaxed and slightly tired, they would run through the show together, Millroy standing aside and Willie and Stacy doing most of the talking.

"You want me to read that again, Uncle Dick?"

"Nope. That's fine, Willie. If you memorize it you'll sound like a robot. Keep it spontaneous. Don't watch the clock."

"I can't tell time anyway."

By playing music and switching cameras, Millroy could always keep track of time, as one segment glided into another.

"Children talking to children. That's what counts."

Willie was talking to Kayla, and Stacy was showing the new boy, Dedrick, how to string beads in his hair.

"Do you think they're good?" I asked because I did not know.

"It doesn't matter whether they're good or not as long as they're themselves. They're real, and they're always watchable. That's what matters about children—that they are slightly perfect."

Watchable was the word. They stumbled, they stuttered, they giggled, they bobbled the props. Millroy just looked on, smiling his Uncle Dick smile, and when he talked his lips did not move. I knew he was

happy from the wiggles of heat that came from his body and the brightness of his head and whole glowing face.

''It's Day One,'' Willie Webb had said on the first morning when the
children were put in charge of the show.

He said it on the second day, too; he could not get the words out of
his head.

''It's Day One.''

''I like that,'' Millroy said. ''That's true. Every day is a new day.
Every day is Day One.''

It did not matter to him that Willie Webb was excited and careless
and too lazy to think that it was Day Two. For Millroy it was an important discovery, and there were many more of them. On every show
something unexpected happened. Millroy liked that. *Keep it loose, guys.*
That was what he wanted.

There was laughter but no applause. Even the best and most unexplainable moment of magic produced cheers and yells but no clapping.

''It's because with children running the show everything looks natural. Children inhabit a world where magic is normal. They believe in it.
They expect chickens to disappear. They would be surprised if I *couldn't*
swallow a sword, or if it stabbed me instead of sliding down my throat.''

He was watching Willie Webb and Stacy in the Mouse House, where
the Frawly puppets had once lived, and I could tell from his expression
that he was pleased by the way they were taking turns juggling oranges
and talking about juice to the camera.

''That's my only excuse for being on the show—because I can still
work magic. An adult who can't work magic is a burger and has no business here.''

His was food magic these days, tricks with certain fruits, illusions
with unsuspecting vegetables, the tall stack of assorted food that he piled
up, held vertical on the dome of his head, and called ''the balanced
diet.'' He gave strange food lessons in which edible items simply materialized, a whole collection of similar ones, like the morning he did Animals Without Faces—clams, oysters and jellyfish. ''But they all have
mothers,'' he said.

Dedrick turned out to be a tease and a trickster, sometimes hogging
the show, but he ended up eating raw oysters and making everyone
laugh when they saw his face.

"See, we don't need puppets," Millroy said.

There were no cartoons either. To take their place, he introduced an item called "The Bread Truck."

"Here comes Uncle Dick's Bread Truck," Willie said.

Millroy drove up in a blue van and took out a loaf of bread—a different type every day—and described what was in it by making a new loaf with flour, water, grains and magic, just like that, so that we could all try it.

"Have a hunk?"

He broke it apart. You saw his hands on the screen, but not his face. Most of the time all you could see were Millroy's clever fingers working magic.

"Never use a knife on it. Never slice it or stab it. Don't bully it, don't butter it up. If it's good bread you can eat it as it is. Its sinews have more tonus than muscles."

He smelled it, showed how it was so fibrous you could make a coat out of it and wear it. It was thick and elastic. He snapped it and crunched its crust.

"Good bread is like a live creature, full of the bloom of health. You could be forgiven for believing that bread has a soul."

Still breaking it into pieces, he shared it, and we were all shown chewing on camera. He said he hated the taboo against seeing people on TV munching and eating. "Eating is the greatest of life's pleasures." The music started as we chewed, a munching music he hoped would help us eat at the healthiest speed. Now we were all eating the daily loaf, and somehow there was enough to feed us all.

Most days The Bread Truck also contained "a piece of tape," a video or a film clip of older people eating. They were usually fat and stuffing themselves with the wrong food, cakes, pies, TV dinners, and "the half-burned parts of dead animals."

These grown-ups ate without any pleasure, just pushing food into their mouths. Their strange shapes—stranger than any of the puppets or cartoon characters—were often frightening: you thought they were about to collapse or explode, or spring a leak and drizzle onto the ground. They were either squat and sealed and looked like large tight bags, or else loose and jowly, with odd wobbly arms and pumped-up faces, their eyes squeezed shut. Some of them looked as though they were filled with water, so that they shook and shuddered when they walked. They were pale and anxious, and they gasped and sweated when they ate.

Watching fat people eat was like watching drunk people drink. It was not the chewing noises, nor the way their poor faces swelled, nor the droplets on their foreheads. It was the desperation and pain, as though because they could not explode they would only become dangerous. You became afraid.

Millroy was silent—what was there to say?—and the music was gulps, trombone blasts, drumrolls, and a pressure of squeaky violin strings that sounded like indigestion.

It made you mistrust this kind of food, this kind of grown-up and this kind of eating. It looked like sickness and crime, even sadness. It looked like dying.

"This is all you need to know," Millroy said in his Uncle Dick voice.

I remembered when he had told me that he had been fat, and how other people had laughed at him. *They mooed at me, they made oinking noises, they threw food at me. It was tragic. I was lost in the darkness of my body.* I wondered if he had looked like those eaters.

Millroy seemed so healthy when the lights went back on after a film clip of the huge, unhappy-looking people.

"I can make this apple disappear," Willie Webb said, and ate it.

This was an Uncle Dick line if ever there was one.

"You can do it, too," Stacy said, and ate a handful of figs. "We can all be magicians."

That was the meaning of mealtime magic, they said.

"It's the secret of life."

Music was also magic: a child picking up a misshapen object and producing sweet sounds was working magic, too. They had never played before. Millroy taught everyone on the show how to play a particular instrument, and when they all played together it was exciting to hear. Then they put their trumpets and flutes and drums down, and danced and did push-ups and somersaults, and you envied them for being like little rubber people full of bounce, and before the show ended they always pleaded with Uncle Dick to take a bow, which he did, bouncing higher than any of them, and finally so high he simply vanished, and that day's show was over.

• • •

The new *Paradise Park* continued to be a hit. There were more letters and postcards than ever, and they were from children, not parents. And Millroy said he was not surprised.

"If I had taken over and done my version of Mister Phyllis, they would have compared me. But the children are running the show—and who is seriously going to compare those youngsters with Mister Phyllis? It's a whole different ball game. It really is Day One every day."

He wanted to change the name of the show to *Day One,* but the producers refused.

"We've got to stick to the formula," Mister Mazzola said.

What formula? The program was completely different. It was a food show using the old name. It was a music show. It was the only real children's show that had ever been shown on television. No one had ever seen a show that taught children how to eat so that they would live for two hundred years.

It was magic, too, that everyone in Boston knew who Uncle Dick was, and no one knew Millroy. He had known beforehand how to keep his secret, and mine.

We went on commuting, Buzzards Bay to Boston and back, every day—up before dawn for the early trip and the rehearsal, then the show from eight to nine, then returning to the trailer in time for lunch.

Lunch at Pilgrim Pines was always something that Millroy had prepared—Ezekiel bread, fish, vegetables, barley or pottage, raisin cakes, sour cheese, a waxy wedge of honeycomb. Then we went for a walk, lounged around planning the next day's show, read fan letters—Millroy took the comments in children's letters very seriously—had a snack and went to bed early. "All good people ought to be in bed by eight." Then we were up again at four, on the road by five, eating our breakfast in the car or in the rest area at Exit 5, where there was water, and in the studio for the first rehearsal at six-thirty.

One afternoon later in November, Reverend Huber watched us drive into the trailer park and made a point of walking over with a green-handled rake in his hands. He had fat dimpled hands and his body rotated as he walked. He wore a baseball hat and sneakers.

Millroy smiled at him and said, "Guess my age."

"I have compassion for you," Huber said.

"Compassion is the one thing I don't need."

"Don't you believe in the power of prayer?"

Millroy said, "You need prayer and you need action."

"Prayer is my meat and potatoes," Huber said.

Millroy laughed at him. "Then you're lost. You'll get indigestion."

"I cured myself of a tumor, brother," Huber said. He touched his big belly where his shirt was tight. "It was the size of a grapefruit."

"Everyone talks of tumors in terms of food. Quite right."

"Prayer alone removed it."

"I am not saying it did or it didn't, but you might have asked yourself how that tumor got there in the first place."

"It was his will. 'The Lord giveth and the Lord taketh away.' "

"Making the Lord responsible for your bad health and your nibbling fingers isn't right," Millroy said. "Take the blame yourself. Face it, like an American."

"I am spreading the word," Huber said. "Sin is everywhere."

Millroy frowned, then said, "That word is not in my vocabulary. You can't have a word for something that doesn't exist."

"I serve the King," Huber said, and walked away swinging his rake.

Millroy said, "It's no use arguing. He's overage, he's mad, he's unwell. Some people cannot be saved. He's the proof. And you wonder why I concentrate on the young?"

"With your show?"

"It's much more than a show, muffin."

After that conversation with Reverend Huber, Millroy was more careful. He said such people were easily roused, especially when they smelled a skeptic, so he avoided the man, and when he spotted him, said in his ventriloquist's voice, *That's all pork.*

But Huber came over more and more, trying to start a conversation, and though Millroy would not let him into the trailer, one day the plump little clergyman stood at the door and stuck his face against the glass, looking in at Millroy, who was cooking.

"Something on fire?" he asked.

Millroy unhooked the window and swung it open, one of his contraptions, and faced Huber the way he had once faced Floyd Fewox. I was expecting the worst—rats, mice, howls of pain.

"I was searing some vegetables," he said.

Reverend Huber smiled but was silent, as though Millroy had said something obviously wrong.

"It breaks down the cellulose. It seals the juices."

Huber's face looked like an uncooked piece of meat when he shook it from side to side.

"Then I'm going to seethe some fitches," Millroy said.

"You need a stove for that?"

"Course I need a stove."

"Thought you might just say 'Abracadabra.' "

"What good would that do?"

"You tell me," Huber said with an unholy smile. "Uncle Dick."

"Uncle Dick doesn't say 'Abracadabra.' "

But when Huber went away, Millroy got into bed. I had only seen him look that sorrowful when he was telling me how he had once been trapped in the darkness of his fat body. This afternoon he looked as though he had been struck down with an illness, and when had he ever been sick before? He lay still and silent like a wounded animal, not breathing, not blinking, in his buried-alive mode.

At last, after dark, he spoke in a voice that had a dry, clawing sound, like a pencil scratching on a sheet of paper.

"I don't want him to know me. I don't want anyone to know me." He took a breath like a long, slow drink of water. "Except you."

But it was too late. Huber had called him by the name I never used.

A day or two later, suspecting he was strengthened in knowing Millroy's secret, Huber said to Millroy and me, "You're probably wondering where Todd is."

I was not wondering. Todd was always after me to go skateboarding at the up ramp, fishing in the canal, or shooting layups at the Pilgrim Pines backboard. He still did not know that I was a girl. *That would make him so much worse.*

"As a matter of fact"—but who had asked?—"he is in school."

Millroy had not yet turned to show his face to Huber.

"What school do you go to, sonny?" Huber asked me.

"You've never heard of it," Millroy said.

The following morning after the show we hitched the Airstream to the Ford and towed it up Route 3 to Wompatuck, just south of Boston, at Exit 14, past HAROLD HECHT PREVIOUSLY OWNED AUTO LEASING, a farm stand with fresh produce, PIZZA TO GO, MARIO'S MINI MARKET, and Star-of-the-Sea Church.

"This way we can get up half an hour later for the show," Millroy said.

It was deep, cool November, and every night at Wompatuck I could hear the acorns bursting off the oaks and plopping into the dead wrinkly leaves.

20 A red-faced man named Sharkey, with yellowy-white hair and a tight necktie, stopped Millroy on his way into the *Paradise Park* studio one dark morning and said to him, "Got a minute?"

"Sorry," Millroy said, and I thought of how he had once said, *Hair! It's the great giveaway,* because this man's hair was piled up and flopped over to one side like a hairy potholder with no roots underneath. Millroy must have been thinking, *What is he trying to hide?*

Sharkey's face grew redder, and as he exerted himself dimples appeared in his cheeks. He touched his hair and put his face near Millroy's.

"I don't know what kind of a contract you've got here," he said, "but my people could put together a package, and when it's a done deal you could be a very happy man. Your kids' show has tremendous cable potential."

"I don't think of them as kids," Millroy said, loud enough for some of the waiting youngsters to hear. "Who are you?"

"We are breakfast cereals, we are juice drinks, we are health snacks, we are a key player in the thirty-billion-dollar weight-loss industry," Sharkey said, leaning across the station entrance to block Millroy's way, "and we are looking for a vehicle." He put his hand on Millroy's. "I believe we've found it, Uncle Dick."

Then, making a sour mouth, the man snatched his hand back from Millroy's and held it to his face in the glare of the doorway.

Sharkey was gripping a dead rat with grinning teeth and a price tag stapled to the top of its slimy skull. He shook it from his hand and choked when it splatted like a wet, grubby rag onto the hard floor.

"That's all you'll ever find, brother."

In that startling moment Millroy pushed past Sharkey and went into the studio to get ready for the rehearsal. He did not look behind him, but I knew from the way his skin was bunched at the back of his neck that he was smiling.

"Lock the doors," Millroy said every morning after that, breathless and glancing sideways before each rehearsal. "We don't want any burgers in here."

Then he walked around the *Paradise Park* studio with nothing in his hands, and stood aside, or smiled at you, or else took your chin and tilted it up toward him the way a dentist does.

"No one gets through that door."

We loved him for that.

The idea that this was all ours, private, a secret, where no adult—not even parents— could intrude, pleased us all and made Millroy seem like one of us, another conspirator. In the way he laughed and fooled and egged us on he really was one of us, but now and then he would work some magic, like Sharkey's sudden, grinning rat, or a singing bird from his sleeve, or he would swallow a bunch of keys to remind us who he really was, not one of us at all.

One day, just for fun—the rehearsal was going slowly—he showed the children his stomach plunger, stuck it down his throat and emptied out his stomach, his whole breakfast in a plastic bowl, to demonstrate his good food and his powers of digestion.

"It's totally gross," a girl named LaPrincia said.

Her eyes were shining in fascination, and so were the others'.

"They're disgusted, they love it," Millroy said, seeing how the rehearsal had been enlivened. "I've had adults faint dead away on me when I've done that."

Our run-through was usually fast: Millroy jumped out at the children, catching them and whispering, looked intently into their faces and then sent them on their way. He behaved more like another child than a coach, and sometimes he was not there—he would vanish without warning, and then we would be alone, getting ready for the show.

Yet even when he was far away or out of sight you could feel him next to you invisibly, humming softly like a black light, or right behind you, as though you only had to turn around quickly to see him.

Mostly, rehearsals were a free-for-all confusion, and so the show it-self surprised me—surprised everyone else, too—all that energy and fun, with perfect timing. Except for Willie Webb, who was the best performer, no particular child was in charge, just one after another, rushing around and talking to the camera.

"It's all yours," Millroy said before each show.

He always raised his hands when he saw Otis or Miss Spitler or Mister Mazzola—lifted his hands and smiled as though to say, *Nothing to do with me, guys!*

"You show them what to do?" Otis had asked.

"I don't show them anything—this is spontaneity. These aren't pup-pets, they're youngsters. Children are capable of attaining perfection. That's what this program is all about."

The original *Paradise Park* became famous because Mister Phyllis had been fired for cursing the children. People had kept watching, wonder-ing what was going to come next.

Millroy's show was altogether different, and it kept changing. From a clever magician on Mister Phyllis's show, Millroy turned into a sort of spectator, a little silly and slow, who needed things explained to him—how plants grow, what the heart and lungs do, what the digestive tract looks like when it hasn't been emptied for a week and is full of chocolate cake, and facts about salt.

Millroy rolled his eyes when these processes were explained.

"You mean good old peanut butter's deadly?" he would ask.

"Yo."

"How about running that past me again?"

"Yo. See, the Seventh-Day Adventists invented peanut butter so they could have spreadable protein without meat . . ."

Some of the shows became famous the same day they were broadcast. Something on the show in the morning would be repeated as a news item on *Eyewitness News Update* at six o'clock.

One show was still talked about the next day because of the "True Stories" slot. In this segment the children told stories to illustrate the workings of the human body. One of Berry's was about a woman he said he knew, Mother Bunshaft. We had an actual photograph of this fat, lov-able old woman in her starched apron. She looked a little like Gaga—tiny eyes in a big meaty face, her poster on the wall behind Berry as he told his tale.

"Mother Bunshaft was a murderer," Berry said.

"No way!"

"Poisoned her whole family using plain old sugar, the kind you all have at home."

Berry poured a cup of white sugar onto the Mealtime Magic table.

"She fed it to them, tons of it, and they died five different ways. Straight up."

"No way!"

You looked at the old woman on the poster and wondered again at that smile that was not a smile anymore but, rather, the expression of a person who is just about to swallow a mouthful of forbidden food.

"One of her kids swells up and chokes to death. One explodes and leaves a mess on his chair. One goes into shock and turns rigid. One has a heart attack. One gets a manic spasm and jumps out the window."

Then Berry turned to go, but as he did he glanced back at the camera and winked, as though he had just remembered something.

"Hey, Mother Bunshaft wasn't bad. Not evil or wicked. Just not very bright or helpful. But too old to change. She was a burger."

"And she got real mad when her kids talked about toilets," Brenda said, popping into view.

Brenda was a little blonde, her hair in two bobbing ponytails with ribbons, and a way of blinking her eyes that made you think of lights flashing. She had chubby knees and cute feet.

"I knew Mother Bunshaft, too," she said. "She screamed if you said 'poo-poo.' "

"She used to ask, 'Do you want to do a tinkle or a yucky?' "

That was Kelly, seeming to make it up as she went along.

"Which is just plain silly."

Now the big photograph of Mother Bunshaft looked like the portrait of a very dangerous and stupid person who would scold you for using the wrong word and then poison you with a chunk of her homemade fudge.

"She could have called it 'elimination,' which is a value-free word," Stacy said, holding her chin as she pondered this. "But she wanted to make it seem dirty."

Snuffling a little so he would not laugh, Willie said, " 'Got to drop a log,' she used to say."

"Want to relieve yourself?" Dedrick said to Stacy. When we started to laugh, he said, "Mother Bunshaft would have said that, right?"

"Listen, everybody, you know why this is better than an English lesson?" Kayla said. "Because bowels are more important than vowels."

Even before the show was over, the phones were ringing. Millroy headed into the conference room and I stayed outside, listening to the voices go back and forth.

Where did they get this toilet stuff?

Let's see the script. We're going to be asked for written verification.

The phones were going, too many to answer. A ringing phone that no one answered sounded like someone yelling in the dark for help.

The hell's this all about?

Millroy's voice was low and reasonable when he replied.

Children are always talking about toilets. It's instinctive, and like all instincts this one is healthy.

Tell Eddie Mazzola that.

Mazzola was the general manager, and because he was seldom around these days he seemed more powerful and unpredictable as a name than as a real man.

Eddie Mazzola ought to know that already, one would think.

It sounded infantile.

In the good sense, Millroy said quietly.

They were actually talking about crapping.

Who was it said, 'Drop a log'?

Interesting choice of words. Yes, and they were talking about digestion. About bodily functions. About toilet training.

We've got to stop it.

How? The children are in charge, Millroy said. And after more talk he came out smiling, to the sound of ringing telephones.

"They're looking for someone to blame."

There was an air of emergency in the station, as though something exciting and eventful had happened. No one knew what to do, Millroy said, because they didn't know whether this was bad or good.

"It's magic," he said.

The next day before the morning rehearsal, Otis was smiling. He said, "We're famous again."

By this time Millroy had met Norman Fredette, who owned Norm's Diner, one street over from the studio. It was on Church Street, behind the Statler Hotel, next to the Star of Siam restaurant, across Park Square

from Legal Sea Food, the Greyhound terminal and the sooty stone buildings of the University of Massachusetts in Boston. It was a busy area,
people everywhere. It was the only area I knew because it was where we
parked, and waited, and saw the children gathering on those early mornings for the program, and from which we left to go home.

But we left later and later. Having a successful program meant more
interest, more phone calls and requests from photographers. Millroy did
not cooperate with any of these people—no pictures, no interviews,
nothing—but even his refusals caused delays, and he got too hungry to
make it all the way back to Wompatuck.

On one of these mornings he stopped at the diner, partly to hide but
also to get some boiling water for his mint tea.

"Uncle Dick," Norman Fredette said, recognizing him. "Do some
Mealtime Magic."

"That's what this is," Millroy said, stirring the tea.

"I want you to wow me."

Millroy stopped stirring, showed Fredette the spoon, clinked it
against his cup, and swallowed it. Then he gulped and took a deep
breath.

"I'd give anything to learn how to do magic like that," Fredette said.

"That's not magic, so you're in luck," Millroy said. "It's a trick."

"Show me how."

Millroy looked around the diner. "I'm just wondering what you
could do for me in return."

Within a few days, in exchange for giving Norman Fredette lessons in
doing magic tricks, Millroy was cooking his own meals in the kitchen of
Norm's Diner. He made his bean and green salad, his pottage, pistachio
pie, figgy loaves, cinnamon baked apple, barley soup and Ezekiel Four-
Nine bread. He had started doing it because he was hungry and because
he wanted to feed me on time, but it also calmed him to cook, and Fredette's was so near the studio that he could go there afterward, cook his
meal and have a place to eat it. If he did not live on his own food, he said,
he would turn into someone else and look like a zoo animal and not be
able to work any magic.

"And I need to be away from those television people," he said. "The
advertisers, the merchandisers, the money changers."

Even though *Paradise Park* was on a nonprofit, public-broadcasting
channel, the program made money—Millroy himself was given a sal-

ary—but he hated the idea of the show's earning an unfair profit or accepting support from food companies. He knew he was cantankerous, but the thought of it made him laugh.

"They can't handle me, muffin, because I am not interested in money," he told me one day at Norm's Diner. "That's why I will always get my way."

We were sitting in a corner booth, eating Millroy's own food. While he was talking, Norman came over, working a stained sponge around the edge of the table, and then lingered near us.

Norman Fredette was a pale, bony-faced man with greasy, pushed-back hair, nervous eyes and a panicky smile that came and went, sometimes two or three times before he finished a sentence. He had a way of sniffing loudly that gave you the impression he had troubled thoughts.

"Don't hover," Millroy said. "It's bad for your digestion if someone hovers. I'll show you a trick in a minute."

"That's okay," Fredette said, but still he lingered.

Already he could swallow spoons, guess playing cards, manipulate eggs and do a little light juggling.

"I just wanted to tell you it was a great show today."

Millroy put down his forkful of pottage, looked straight at Fredette and said, "Tell me."

"A tremendous show."

Norm was twisting an egg around his fingers—hiding it, revealing it. There was an aspect of magic and trickery that seemed to appeal to nervous people by giving them something to do with their fumbling fingers.

"The TV is on in the corner. The kid goes, 'Toilet,' and the whole counter starts laughing. Then there's that business about forty-four pounds of—what did they call it?"

"Fecal residue," Millroy said.

"Right. Staying inside your body. The customers start screaming. I takes a frying pan and whacks it down on the stove. 'You want a hit in the head?' They're still yelling, so I goes, 'Shut up and listen. You might learn something.' "

He was still rolling the egg on the back of his hand as Millroy had taught him.

Millroy took a bite of bread, an Ezekiel loaf that he had baked in Fredette's kitchen. He looked satisfied with what Norm had said. He ate slowly, as always, biting bread, forking up a gob of pottage, drinking, without spilling, juice from his own jug.

"Home cooking," Fredette said. "My customers are always asking me. They say, 'What's he eating? I don't see nothing like it on the menu.' I'm, like, 'Mind your own business.' "

"Wholesome cooking," Millroy said. "Real food."

He reached over, took the egg from Fredette, wrapped it in his napkin and then shook it, making the egg disappear.

Fredette blinked, wondering where the egg had gone.

"You were making me nervous."

"I wish I could do that," Fredette said, his lips looking greedy.

"You're impressed by a little trick like that. Why aren't you impressed by the power of nutrition, the transformation of your bodily functions, and the force of your bowels?"

Instead of replying, Fredette looked over at the row of people eating at the lunch counter. They were staring at Millroy with that *What did he just say?* expression on their faces.

"First, eat right. Food is the first step."

"I'm interested. Plus I'm in the food business myself."

"If your food was right I would eat it."

"I see what you're saying."

"If you desire to be pure in body and mind you'll be renewed by this food." Millroy was eating again. "And you will perform magic. Alex, juggle those eggs."

He handed me four eggs, which I juggled easily, first whirling all four with both hands, then simultaneously juggling two with each hand.

"Fidem scit," Millroy said.

"Now they got *you* doing it!" Norman Fredette said.

I looked at the faces of the people in the diner. *What did he just say?*

" 'He knows faith,' " Millroy said. "That's Latin. He is pure, he eats well, and so he can manipulate those eggs."

"That's what I'm aiming at."

"You will be regular."

Millroy smiled and showed Fredette how to do the egg-in-napkin trick.

Afterward, when we were alone, Millroy said, "What I'm going to say might sound strange to you."

So I knew it definitely would.

"I made an exception when I cooked in his kitchen, yet I will not bend when it comes to his toilet. You know I have an inflatable seat—patent pending. But I feel strongly that when I use someone's rest room I'm doing that person a favor—bestowing something on that person, leaving a bit of myself behind. Using their facilities is a profound show of trust. It is an act of faith—but no, Norman is not ready for that."

Back in our trailer at Wompatuck we tidied up and were silent, and when we were hungry we worked with barley, parched corn and pulses, baked beany bread and drank Millroy's weak, inky wine. I dreamed like mad. Our life was elsewhere these days, on the show.

The Boston Globe ran a news story about *Paradise Park*—short but on page one—about how people were phoning the station all day, some complaining but most praising, and many of them were children. We were told about the newspaper story ahead of time, and the next day on our way to Boston we saw stacks of the papers in vending machines, and people reading it on the Plymouth and Brockton commuter buses.

"Notice I'm not reading the story? I'm looking at people reading the story. I'm not worried."

"What about Otis?"

"I'm treating him for headaches. Guess how."

Millroy could be very talkative, even in the early morning, even now on the Expressway in the before-dawn darkness, which was gray and grainy like a blow-up of an old photo.

"Relieving his constipation. He has major blockage, and it's building in his passages and pressurizing all his other bodily functions."

We were passing another bus—people reading the *Globe*.

"I have him on a low-residue food program. But he's easy. He knows his Book. I have him on mint tea. He understands. He knows that Matthew heard the Lord himself speak the word 'mint.' "

I pulled my thumb out of my mouth because I could feel a yawn coming on.

That morning *Paradise Park* had another rest-room segment. After "Mealtime Magic," some Uncle Dick Bread Truck videos, and music—the youngsters playing instruments and singing their song "The Function Room."

"Hey, if it's not the most important room in the house," Berry said, "then why does it always have a lock on the door?"

LaPrincia said, "We should talk a little bit about nutrition and fat. 'Eat no manner of fat,' it says in the Bible. That's good advice."

"Yo, and remember that butter sounds like buttock," Kelly said.

We all laughed at that.

"It just popped into my head," she said. "People don't talk about it, because it's the one part of your body you never see."

"Yo. If you could see inside your body you wouldn't wreck it," Willie Webb said at the end of the show, tilting his head at the camera and pushing his face into the lens.

He was staring and breathing hard.

"So watch what you put into it. But there's only one way of knowing what's really going on in your body. Have a real good look at what comes out of it. Bye, guys. See you tomorrow at the Park."

"What kind of little kids' show is this supposed to be?" a man asked Millroy in Norm's Diner one morning when we were eating there after a broadcast. The man must have watched the show on Fredette's TV. He sounded resentful and sulky the way some people are when something bewilders them.

Millroy told the man what he had told Sharkey ("I don't think of them as kids"), and what he told Otis, Mazzola and the rest of the producers. These days, feeling confident, he never raised his voice, but he had a whisper that could silence a whole room.

"These youngsters are going to live a long time and be very influential, so it's important that they know the truth. They will be the first people in America to live more than two hundred years. That's the goal. Imagine how people will look up to them. They'll want to know how and why."

The man thought for a moment, and then said in the same sulky voice, "What's that you're eating?"

"It's not on the menu," Norman Fredette said.

"But if it was," Millroy said to the man, "maybe you'd have some idea of what I was talking about."

He went on eating. He liked saying things that forced people to think, baffling them and then pretending not to notice their bafflement.

No one argued with him today.

"Except for Otis, the producers don't like the show, for their own pathetic reasons," Millroy said. "But it works, so what can they do?"

The new *Paradise Park* was proving to be very popular ("I could have told them it would be"), but no one knew whether it was simply a good combination of children and stories, or all the toilet talk mixed in with "Mealtime Magic." But because they did not know, they were afraid to change the new format that Millroy had been steadily tinkering with.

After three weeks the program's viewing figures exceeded those of *Sesame Street,* the other Boston children's show. Millroy was glad because he hated that show. "Henson's a puppeteer, not an educator," he said.

"All those misshapen puppets and quacky voices. Their literacy is just whimsical and their notions of cultural relativism are actually subversive. It does matter what country you come from. They stick things in their mouth in Africa and China that are no good for you at all. No, *Sesame Street*'s a bad joke. We know what youngsters need."

That Friday, after the producers' meeting, after the release of the viewing figures, after the meal at Fredette's diner, we headed back to Wompatuck in the Ford, and Millroy was glowing with certainty.

"Of course I let them blame me for the show," he said.

His head was alight, and he seemed to know the secret of this gray winter world. Cormorants drooped on the black posts stuck in the water near the big ugly building of the Dorchester Yacht Club.

"Because in the end they'll have to give me credit for the show's success."

Now we were passing the gas tanks, which were candy-striped and conspicuous.

"I think something good is happening, angel—something I've been leading up to my whole life."

Hearing that, I felt sure he was talking about more than a children's program on morning TV. It was his *I am a messenger* voice.

21 Holidays seem to make even a humdrum event dramatic or strange by giving it specific decorations, like a Christmas wreath on the door of a burned-down house, or a *Merry Christmas* sticker on the bumper of a wrecked car. Holidays were different, too, because of the days you had off, or the extra time you worked, and you usually remembered the weather, and always the music, and there were surprises. All this Millroy told me, but I knew that Christmas was a time of disasters, drunkenness and tears. My birthday was the twentieth, so close to Christmas that I did not even mention it to him. I turned fifteen but stayed the same size.

"People are intensely together on holidays, or else intensely alone," Millroy said. "And holidays always mark shifts in people's fortunes. Ours, for example. Think of the Fourth of July at the Barnstable County Fair."

Now Christmas was coming.

"I sense something in the air," he said, tapping his nose, getting a sniff of the future.

Thanksgiving and the alternative turkey show was past; these days it was Christmas carols in the elevator at the TV station, and the producers asking Millroy about his plans for a Christmas show. He said he would deal with it, of course, because Christmas was his favorite time of year.

"And I insist on using the word 'Christmas' on the show," he said, "not the all-purpose secularity of 'Happy Holidays.' "

There were more surprises, even for me, and I had thought that living with Millroy had prepared me for everything.

On one early-December show, Willie Webb was talking about people who used to be fat, and how they felt now that they were the right weight.

"And we're going to hear from one of them," he said.

I sat up, curious about hearing a fat person's story. I liked life histories that were full of facts—what their Dada said, what they watched on TV, what they ate for breakfast and especially what they worried about. I wanted to hear a story about a young girl who no longer lived at home, and how she was happier than she had ever been, and the good things that had happened to her. I wanted to hear that everything had come out right. Millroy was a story man in just that way, his struggle stories were always successes, and they had as much magic in them as his conjuring.

"Yo." Willie was nodding. "We have someone right here with us who used to be very fat."

I looked around, wondering who that person might be, and I saw that everyone else was looking, too. In the middle of the searching and silence I heard my name spoken out loud.

"Alex?"

I glanced up and saw Willie staring straight at my head.

"Want to tell us your story?"

I said, "What story?"

"About the time you were fat."

About the time I was *what*?

I had no story, but as soon as I stood up and opened my mouth to deny it, a story came out.

"Yes, it's true, though it's probably hard for you to imagine me porky," I said. "But they used to see me and say, 'Hey, it's Chub, the basketball smuggler,' and they oinked at me. My belly was out to here and like a lot of fat people I had wicked body odor. I shook when I walked, and sometimes when I was quiet I couldn't stop my body from jiggling. I yawned all the time and I fell asleep on buses. I used to steal food. The only time I didn't eat was at mealtimes, when there were other people around, and—"

"Alex was in denial," Willie said.

"There were other people around at mealtimes, and why would you want anyone to see you eating if you were so fat? The whole rest of the time I was scarfing food. If I saw anything that would fit into my mouth I shoved it in, no matter what it was. I usually ate three cookies at a time, making them into a sandwich."

I was talking so fast I was almost out of breath.

Willie said, "Come on down here, Alex, so that we can get a real good look at you."

I left my seat with the other children and went to join Willie and Stacy. Maybe Stacy had a fat story, too? But if so, she had to wait for me to finish because I was talking all the way down. I wanted Millroy to hear this, but where was he today?

"I told people I had disturbed glands. I dreamed of dying, I was suicidal, I looked about thirty-five. I heard there was this machine that sucked fat out of you, could pump about a gallon of fat out of your thighs. I wanted the treatment so I could go on eating.''

I started to laugh so that this would not seem such an awful story. But as I was telling it I believed it and grew sad, thinking of myself as huge and horrible and foul-smelling.

"You should have seen me''—I was still trying to laugh—"I looked like a burger. I hated seeing myself in a mirror but I learned to check out my reflection without getting upset. I looked very closely at my face in a very small mirror.''

Pretending that I had a small mirror in my hand, I peered in, biting my cheeks and trying to shrivel my face.

"After a while, I realized that being fat was making me a bad person. Ever thought of that? It turned me into a liar. I lied about my weight. I lied about food. I said I was on a diet when I wasn't. 'I only had one of them cookies, Gaga' kind of thing. Being unhealthy can make you bad. I got into a program on fat acceptance. Then I thought about killing myself by sticking my finger in a light socket. I got depressed when my finger wouldn't fit, and depression made me eat more, so I got even fatter.''

Everyone was listening intently.

"Jeekers," I said. "Fatness makes you tricky.''

I could tell that thousands of people were seeing me on their TV sets, fascinated and sad. I could sense all those eyes.

"Then I heard Uncle Dick talking about Mealtime Magic. He goes, 'It's all in The Book. The Book is full of food, plus a lot of menu suggestions. He goes, 'Try it.' It's fruit and fish and vegetables and nuts and beans.''

With mention of Uncle Dick and The Book, there was perfect silence.

"That was Day One for me," I said. "From that day onward, everything got better. I'm happy, plus I'm healthy inside and out.''

I smiled and took a bow while the youngsters whistled and whooped, looking at how skinny I was.

"What a neat story," Willie said. "Hey, thanks, Alex.''

Yes, it was a neat story, but where had it come from?

I was going to mention it at Norm's Diner later that morning, but Millroy was teaching Fredette how to eat razor blades.

"It's not magic. It's a real trick, because they're not razor blades and you don't eat them," he said.

Then I was going to mention it on the ride back to the trailer park at Wompatuck, but Millroy began telling me about holidays ("They are times for confessions and summaries and new beginnings"). Back at the trailer he was silent, so I knew he was thinking about tomorrow's show and did not want to be disturbed.

I waited until bedtime, which was eight or so, the usual. I did not speak until he had put the lights out and had stopped fumbling with his pillow. He was at the other end of the trailer on his own shelf, in his own cubicle, sighing, submerging himself in sleep as he had taught me to do.

"I never was fat, you know."

He heard me but said nothing.

"I was small. I had a slim little figure. I wasn't fat."

"Maybe 'fat' is a figure of speech," Millroy said.

"Like I'm supposed to know what that means?"

Was his silence a way of telling me he was sorry he had said that?

"And you sure didn't make me thin."

"Are you the same as when we met, muffin?"

That had to be a trick question, because the answer was no.

"But don't think about it," he said.

It was always obvious to me when he was smiling in the dark. I could almost see his teeth showing bright white under his mustache.

"That wasn't my story."

"It's yours now, muffin."

I could hear his brain buzzing, the wheels turning, the throb of the hubs, the wind in the spokes.

"Maybe it was glossolalia," Millroy said. "Speaking in tongues."

"Jeekers."

"Like Joel says, 'Your sons and your daughters shall prophesy.' "

"How come?"

"Because these are the days of the latter rain, muffin."

"Jeekers."

"Aren't the floors full of wheat and the vats overflowing with wine and oil?" he asked.

"I guess so."

" 'And ye shall eat in plenty.' "

So there was nothing I could do, but that was not what bothered me most. All night I lay in bed wondering where I had gotten that story, and what if I got any more of them?

My story was popular. Parents and children wrote in to say it was helpful. It made them feel better about themselves, they said. And they asked about Uncle Dick's food—did he have the recipes, and what was the book I mentioned?

On the next "Mealtime Magic" slot, Uncle Dick made figgy loaves, passed them around and said, "It's not so much a diet as a way of life. Yet it's satisfying enough to be a religion," and he repeated some recipes.

"If this show wasn't so popular you'd be in trouble," Eddie Mazzola said.

Millroy just laughed, and because he laughed so seldom, when he did he sounded like a cackling wizard. But there was nothing the producers could say, each week the show's viewing figures increased even more.

Then there were what Millroy called "administrative warnings"— that Christmas was coming, that religious messages were not allowed on *Paradise Park;* neither was talk about toilets or mentioning racial groups.

Dedrick was the one who had described different races.

"Ever wonder about the Japanese?" he asked. "They eat tons of fish. If you take a real good look, you'll see that they've gotten to look like fish."

Because the children were laughing, he did not stop at that. From eating pork, the Koreans looked like pigs. Vegetarian Hindus had come to look like vegetables, skinny and lumpy. Dutch people looked pale and soft, like their own cheese. Americans looked like burgers.

It was too much. Millroy was reprimanded, Otis delivering the administrative warning from Eddie Mazzola.

"These youngsters aren't racists," Millroy said, "and you know there's a grain of truth in what Dedrick said."

"You mean you believe that stuff about people getting to look like the food they eat?"

"How are your headaches?" Millroy asked suddenly.

"Gone," Otis said.

"Can you put your hand on your heart, Otis, and say that the Japanese don't look like fish?"

When he was warned again about not submitting a script for the Christmas show, Millroy shrugged and said he was not worried. He judged the reaction at Norm's Diner to be typical. The early-morning customers all watched the show, and Fredette reported the things they said. They liked the children on *Paradise Park* for being themselves, funny, enthusiastic and unpredictable. No puppets, no bullying Big Person, no fantasies.

"They're winging it," Millroy said. "They're on their own now."

He had no control over the youngsters, he said, and the reason for the immense popularity of *Paradise Park* was that the children devised all their own dialogue and skits.

"They got creative."

Fredette and the rest of the customers at the diner believed what Millroy said, not because he was persuasive but because his food was on the menu at last and they said it was delicious. His food was the proof of his message, and it made him believable.

He said to Fredette, "I know you're interested in learning magic, but this food is much more important than these tricks, and I think you'll agree that it has a magic all its own."

Christmas came, not the day but the seasonal show, with no prior warning, no script in advance, just the word that something special was going to happen.

"Don't ask me," Millroy said to Otis on the way in. "The children are in charge."

It was a Wednesday. We locked ourselves into the studio for the rehearsal, and there was the usual confusion, five or six groups of youngsters working separately, Millroy passing from one group to the next, fixing them with his eyes, the youngsters singing, Millroy whispering.

After the show started, Millroy did the Uncle Dick turkey trick that had been such a hit at Thanksgiving, bringing a roasted turkey back to life in his "Mealtime Magic" oven.

First he showed the big basted bird on a platter and held it up.

"Those drumsticks are the legs—this bird used to strut on those legs," he said. "That neck once supported a lively head. And look at those burned appendages—they were once real feathered wings. This creature was capable of sustained flight. Imagine, this roasted bundle of meat could actually fly in fresh air . . ."

But not even Millroy's vivid description could help you see the turkey fly. He seemed to realize this, because soon he slipped the bird into his oven, not an ordinary oven but a magician's tin box with panels and flaps.

"Perfectly empty," he said in his Uncle Dick voice.

He showed the inside of the oven, poked his whole arm through, wagged it up and down, then slipped the roasted bird in.

"I ask you to energize this carcass through the power of prayer," he said. "Help me. This dead bird had third-degree burns over one hundred percent of its body and needs your prayers."

We concentrated hard. I made myself see a fat black turkey beating its wings over Marstons Mills with the fleshy flannel of its red comb flopping as it flew.

Millroy passed his hands over the tin-box oven and slid the side panels up.

The live turkey gobbled and seemed to swell as it burst out of the box. All feathers and motion, it was loud and live, a very proud bird, like the eagle I had once seen Millroy yank out of the folds of an American flag.

"That turkey is saying thank you," Millroy said, and as usual what you saw most of was Uncle Dick's arms and legs on the TV screen.

Willie Webb gathered up the grateful turkey and Stacy said, "Why should a beautiful bird like that have to die just so you can have a merry Christmas?"

"Yo. Eat an apple," Berry said.

"There are so many other foods you can eat," Dedrick said. "Everyone likes squash and nut stuffing, which is nutritious and fibrous. Why not try making a meal of that? Gourds are pretty cool."

"How about barley soup and figgy loaves, bro?" Kayla said.

"Let's see what's in the Christmas Bread Truck this morning," Dedrick said.

A whole assortment of new food was laid out on the Mealtime Magic table. The back-from-the-dead turkey watched it all and even ate some of the stuffing.

"That's the best way to stuff a turkey," Willie Webb said.

"So much for the eating part of Christmas, which everyone talks about every year," Dedrick said. "But what about the other part that no one ever talks about?"

I was thinking, *What other part?* but the rest of the children seemed to know what he was talking about because they were already wheezing and giggling.

Millroy was nowhere in sight. He had gone as soon as he had brought the roasted turkey back to life. It was a sign of something. He was never more conspicuous than when he was out of sight.

"The main problem at Christmas is going—I am talking rest-room time," Dedrick said. "Where to go and how to go. I am talking high-volume residue here, guys."

Several of the children laughed out loud, and I could hear Dedrick's deep-throated *haw*.

"If you eat this good, clean-burning food we have here and drink plenty of liquid, you'll want to go real quick. But at Christmas there are always lots of people at the table. So first of all, check out the rest room and make sure you can get there when you want to. Examine the lock and verify that it works okay. That way you're not stressing."

Now the children were settling down and laughing a little less so that they could hear what Dedrick had to say.

"The main thing is timing," he said. "Don't hurry. Lock the door so that no one can bother you. And it's a good idea to loosen all your clothes. Maybe you pushed your pants down, but that can be bad. Often it locks your ankles together. You get stressed, plus it may make your deposit real difficult."

"Yo. So what's the best way, Dedrick?" Willie asked, and when someone whooped he added, "Chill, guys. Listen up."

"The best way is to get naked, no matter what anyone says. Always take your shoes off. Yo, even a shirt or a sweater can seriously inhibit your freedom of movement."

"Hear that?" Willie said.

But all I heard was an adult voice squawking out of a cameraman's earphones. *We've got a problem.*

"Whether you are male or female, always sit down on the seat. Don't even think of doing it standing up. Hey, guys, it's not a test of marksmanship! And like I say, don't rush it. It's better to sit and wait than to force it and risk muscle strain, cramps, piles or whatever. If you're relaxed, you're ready. Then you just wait and you'll be real amazed at how much freedom of action you have."

"You'll be real surprised at the results, too," Willie said. "You'll get control over your bodily functions."

I just do not believe this.

"You'll have power."

I thought to myself, *It's too late. This has already happened. This is the future.*

"And why not bring a book to read? Never read when you eat, guys, but always read when you go make a deposit," Dedrick said, holding up a thick book. "Your folks might say no, but listen, the rest room is a great place to read. Everyone remembers what they read in the function room."

"Amen."

It sounded like Millroy's voice, but where was he?

"Don't laugh," Dedrick said, though he was still smiling. "You could read this in there. It would be a real neat seasonal touch."

He held up a book, The Book.

Millroy's mustache appeared on the screen, just this huge hairy mouth, starting to open.

"*Fidem scit*," Millroy's mouth said.

That's it—we're off the air.

III

Day One

22 "We're not fleeing," Millroy said in his *Remember this* voice. "We are waiting."

We had come straight back to the trailer park in Wompatuck after the show without saying a word to anyone—just slipped out of Boston and hurried down the road and into the Airstream. The program was off the air again.

Millroy's eyes said, *I told you so,* but he kept his mouth shut, and when his picture appeared in the paper his face looked harmless and out of place under the big black headlines HIT CHILDREN'S SHOW CANCELED —"TASTE" FUROR CITED—STATION DELUGED WITH CALLS, MANY IN SUPPORT.

"I am well pleased," Millroy said, but when he glanced in my direction his eyes were not focused on me and no light came out of them. They were the pale, penetrating eyes he gazed with when he told his audience, *I can see through walls. I hear everything.*

He was listening. He went very quiet; he knew something that I didn't. His concentration was entirely inside his head, and there was no telling from the outside what he was thinking. Still he listened, his eyes fixed and staring, his nose and ears twitching, the rest of him motionless and alert, like a squirrel on a branch just before it darts up a tree.

That first day he said, "I have to be in contact with food," and started sorting chick-peas, looking for stones before he soaked them.

"I need the consolation of cooking. My fingers, my nose, my taste buds, this tongue, these eyes. I would love to be feeding the multitudes and stirring a huge tureen. If I had a loaf of bread I would be tearing great hunks out of it."

Saying this, he began to mix flour and water in an earthenware crock with beans, millet, barley, and was soon slapping big pale cheeks and jowls of dough with floury fingers to make a batch of Ezekiel bread.

"I am convinced that this is how bread came into being," he said.

"Someone in the remote past needing to lay hands on pliant dough—had a yearning to hold it and work with it. Someone waiting and giving thanks."

Though his eyes were bright and eager, they were fixed on a distant object or idea, and not on me.

"A kind of offering."

He was still breathless, pinching and squeezing the fat little loaves.

"Showbread."

He liked the word, and swallowed when he said it, gulping and saying it again, another mouthful of it.

"They're looking for me."

At last he seemed confident, with the air of inattention, carelessness, and casualness just before he performed a wonderful trick. The whole technique of working magic, he said, was to look the other way, turn your back on the business, gesture sideways, smile at the wall, and then, as though a trap had been sprung, the magic happened and everyone said, "Ah."

"Waiting for the call," he said, and seemed to be finishing a sentence he had started a while ago.

There was no telephone here at Wompatuck, no delivery of mail, no telegrams even. The trailer office had a private phone but refused to take messages. Trailer and RV owners sometimes complained, but Millroy said, "It suits me fine. I've been in the wilderness before, so I know this isn't the wilderness."

There was no way that either Millroy or I could be reached at the Wompatuck Trailer Park.

"I know my attitude must seem overwhelmingly Olympian to you," he said.

He was wearing his Mealtime Magic T-shirt, a floury apron and trampled slippers, and there were flecks of whole wheat flour in his mustache and eyelashes, smears of butter and flour on his fingers, pellets of barley stuck to the backs of his hands. He was walking up and down the Airstream, making it sway with each jouncing step. He was happy.

This happiness of his made him seem brighter and freer than anyone I had ever known. I did not know what Olympian meant, but Millroy seemed weightless and wonderful.

"When you get your name in the paper they're sending you a message,'' he said. "Your picture in the paper? That's special delivery, your name writ large.''

"Like skywriting,'' I said, and imagined dribbles and puffs of cloud spelling MILLROY in a blue sky.

"Exactly,'' he said. "The whole world witnesses your being summoned. Skywriting!''

He liked that. He took me aside and showed me his name picked out in the clouds in the sky. He was always kind to me, but I was especially grateful to have his approval, the sun shining on me. He was my safety.

I also felt that, with all the fame from the disgrace of his canceled program, he was in danger—the whole of Boston and beyond was looking for him.

"Listen, angel,'' he said, "it's all the better when people can't find you. Then they value you more and realize your ultimate importance. They don't take you for granted. Am I in anyone's pocket?''

Even two days later he was still smiling his flat satisfied smile under his jerked-up mustache, as though he knew they were talking about him, as though he could actually hear what they were saying. This made him calmer than ever.

"Are we ever going up to Boston again?''

"I'm there,'' he said, winked and looked the other way.

He said it again, *I'm there,* as he pushed a shopping cart through Purity Supreme Foodland in the Hingham Mall with his *I never look hungry* face, turning his stern attention to the vegetables. The vegetables seemed to stare sternly back at him.

"In spirit.''

He scrutinized the fruit, sized it up without touching it.

"I'm conspicuously absent. Bigger than I would ever be if I were there in the flesh.''

He began choosing melons, rattling them, squeezing them, pressing his thumbs into avocados, shaking bunches of grapes, taking hold of bananas, poking plums, gripping apples, sniffing lemons—testing for ripeness.

"I know they're looking for me.''

Raising a pale honeydew melon as though holding the planet Earth in his hand, he pressed his fleshy nose against it, said, "No one but you has the slightest idea of who I am.''

And slowly bowled the melon into the corner of the shopping cart.

"This is a tremendous moment of anonymity," he said. "Because to be truly anonymous you need to have once been well known. If no one ever knew you, what difference would it make? But if everyone knows you and no one sees you, then you're truly walking through walls."

We were still walking through Purity Supreme Foodland, the aisles jammed with shoppers pushing full carts, stocking up for the Christmas holidays.

"If only they knew."

He was triumphant among the fruits and vegetables, more pleased with himself now than he had been doing magic at the Barnstable County Fair, or as Uncle Dick in *Paradise Park*. He had been like this at rehearsals—happy, hopeful, confident, working magic with no hands.

"You don't just call someone up and expect him to jump."

Still choosing fruit—squeezing, sniffing, weighing, bowling—he seemed jaunty.

"The person you're pestering might be food shopping. Or eating. Or sleeping. Or praying. Listen, he might be in the rest room—on the hopper even. A call at that moment could be traumatic."

The shelves of beans and pulses were nearby. Millroy clutched the little sacks, throttled them with his thumbs, and then brought them to his nose, as though venerating them as he smelled them.

"It's a question of being in a state of readiness, and that's as much a spiritual thing as it is physical. You wait until the summoning occurs and you get the call," he said. "And when I say 'you' I mean me."

All the shopping was done, but why had he bought so many sacks of flour?

"An experience of humility," he said.

He baked thirty loaves or more of Ezekiel bread. We stacked them in the backseat of the Ford and drove from street to street in small towns on the South Shore—places like Egypt, Greenbush and Marshfield—on two rainy December days during Christmas week, selling them. Millroy quoted the recipe in Ezekiel 4:9.

"I am that bread of life," he said. "These loaves have no price. I am simply asking for a donation—anything they wish to share for this show-bread."

He insisted that I go with him to each door to meet the bewildered people, half of whom would not even open their storm door to look at the bread, but just put their blurred, fearful faces against the pane of glass while someone in another room screamed, *Who is it?* Millroy said that because I was with him they would not turn us away, and they would be more careful how they treated an evangelist with his small son braving the winter weather to bring his message of hope. Yet he seemed almost pleased by their indifference, and was delighted that he was not recognized as Uncle Dick.

"Do we need the money?"

"No, angel. But these people need the experience of encountering a messenger."

"How much did you collect?"

"Four dollars and change."

When the bread was gone at the end of that day we stopped this tiring routine.

The next day, over lunch, Millroy hardly ate, but wearing his listening face, mouth pressed shut, head tilted so that the sounds would drain into it like a hole, said, "Angel, I hear something."

Millroy called Norman Fredette from the public phone in the entrance lobby of Purity Supreme.

"They're looking for you," Fredette said.

"I know."

"Guys wearing suits."

They had come to Norm's Diner to find Uncle Dick because they had heard this was where he sometimes went to cook his food after the show. Some of the people were journalists, some were fans or parents with kids, and the ones wearing suits were television executives.

"They were asking a lot of questions," Fredette said.

Millroy smiled because of course Fredette did not have any answers. He seemed particularly pleased that all this interest in finding him had centered around the pale, blinking figure of Norman Fredette.

"I told them I'd keep my eyes open," Fredette said, being important, "so it was a good thing you called."

"I knew it. I heard it."

Fredette made his silence into a nagging question.

"Vibrations," was Millroy's answer.

"So what else did the guys in suits say to me?" Fredette asked, trying to be jokey but really challenging Millroy.

"They stressed the urgency of the matter. They tried to deputize you. They urged you to go looking for me, said they'd make it worth your while if you did. And of course you looked, because business is not so good at the diner.''

''That's putting it mild.''

''You're thinking of selling,'' Millroy said.

''I haven't put it into words.''

''Until now.''

''I guess not.''

Millroy said, ''Can you be at this number tomorrow at noon?''

Fredette said yes, and Millroy hung up. But he did not call back. He paid a visit in person instead. *If I had told him I was coming he might have spread it around.* We drove up in the Ford, Millroy intimidating in a black leather biker's jacket and sunglasses, his mustache shaggy, and I a boy in boots, two inches taller than I really was.

Fredette was startled to see us, but Millroy just kept on marching into the back office, and Fredette followed.

''This is my assistant, Rusty.''

''New assistant?''

''Same assistant, new name,'' Millroy said. ''Mind if I use your facilities?''

Toilet, he meant, and not use but look at because he would never use anyone else's rest room. It was his way of seeing what kind of person Fredette was, and his state of mind, which the condition of the fixtures and especially the hopper often revealed, he said.

''Those guys were after him like you would not believe,'' Fredette was saying to me. ''I wish someone wanted me that bad.''

When a grown-up spoke to me I could never think of an answer. I just hummed and did not reply. After a while Millroy entered the office. He had heard Fredette from two rooms away, he said, not the words but the sounds twanging in the air, which he decoded.

''Maybe if they really knew you,'' Millroy said, ''they would be after you, too.''

''Every day.'' It was a Boston expression meaning never.

''I mean it.''

''I could get used to it,'' Fredette said, still a little gloomy. ''When people want you that bad there's always good money involved.''

Millroy was peering at the room and beyond it, looking through the walls. It was a cramped office with a fine layer of grease on the plaster, an adding machine on the desk, bills stuck on a rusty, upright spike, telephone numbers scribbled on the blotter, and business cards tacked everywhere. It was cluttered with papers, magazines, cooking utensil catalogs, cutout pictures, a few thumb-tacked postcards and a calendar picture showing a woman in a bathing suit leaning against an industrial dishwasher.

I knew that Millroy was holding his nose. He hated rooms like this— the clutter, grease, dirt, unswept floor—and his disgusted face told me that he had also just had an experience in the bathroom.

"You find the john?"

"I found it, but you'd never be able to pray in there, or even use it without extensive renovation. Norman, it needs work."

"It's for employees."

"That's very much in its favor," Millroy said, "but let's talk about you."

Dishes were clinking and cutlery clanking in the diner on the other side of the wall. Someone said, *Dog with everything, and a side of fries,* and Millroy winced.

"I don't get it," Fredette said. "I'm supposed to find you for these guys in suits, and here you are, and you go, 'Let's talk about you.' "

"Did you say you'd deliver me?"

"I said I'd try."

"That shows a little humility, Norman. Now can we talk about you?"

"Business is lousy. There's nothing to talk about."

"Maybe you're in the wrong business."

"Cooking is all I know." Fredette was tugging on one ear. "Food and beverage, catering, short-order stuff. You know—you done a little cooking in here."

"But you're also pretty good at communicating on the lower frequencies."

"What, mind reading and that?"

"Vibrations have to be sent before they can be received," Millroy said. "I got your message, Norman."

This pleased Fredette, who began to touch his own face like a blind person touching an old friend, running his fingertips over all the contours of his cheeks for the sheer joy of it.

"And you know a trick or two," Millroy said.

Fredette's smile gave him a bigger, scarier face, with hunger showing on it.

"I could teach you control over two or three more bodily functions. Ever juggle?"

But Fredette was thinking about his diner. He said, "The rotten thing about food and beverage is the hours. I never get to bed before two. I'm here again at six, heating the deep fat in the Frialator, revving the salamander, defrosting the hamburg, slicing baloney, mixing up the juice, making the batter."

From the look of distress on Millroy's face you would have thought he was being forced to taste these things rather than just hearing the words.

"You could put that all behind you."

Fredette was not convinced, but he was thinking.

"You could sell and relocate."

"I've got a good mind to," Fredette said, and looked as though he wanted to kick the wall and leave, slamming the door behind him.

"Florida's lovely."

"Maybe sit on the beach."

"Or work magic. With your juggling and your control of functions and the right motivation you'd have enough skills to put on a show. And think of the financial resources you'd have as a cushion from the sale of your diner."

"It's more a question of who's going to pick up the rest of my lease."

"Whatever," Millroy said. "With that money you could invest in your future. Buy some equipment. I've got props I could sell you—caskets, pedestals, boxes, cabinets, top-of-the-line illusion aids. I'm talking tricks here. It's like learning a language, and you've already got the basic grammar."

Fredette was smiling but only with his mouth. His eyes were squinty and sad.

"Now name me the sucker who's going to take over the lease on a greasy spoon that's losing money."

"You're looking at him."

Recovering quickly, Fredette said, "Hey, we've got location. Students from UMass, bus station people, overflow from Legal Sea Food on most weekends. We've had some great years here. It's a kind of institution. The potential is unbelievable if you put a little money into renovation, float a loan.'' Then he became small again and said, ''You serious?''

''Maybe I want to be you for a while, Norman.''

''Lots of luck.''

Millroy put his arm around the man. ''And how would you like to be me?''

I heard a honk from Norman Fredette's nose, and did not have to wonder what it meant because it was such a serious sob. It was hardly a human noise, but it was a clear snort of pain. The man did not say anything more. He simply stood in front of Millroy and stared, and then he wagged his head and moved the way I had seen people do at the county fair Fun-O-Rama in front of the twisted mirrors in the funhouse.

And while Fredette was looking at Millroy this way, Millroy was repeating like the words of a prayer: *Tell them I'll listen. Tell them they can reach me at my new premises. Tell them you found me.*

That very day Millroy wrote Norman Fredette a check, buying the rest of the lease, and when the diner was his he closed it.

''This was meant to happen,'' he said.

In the cold, quiet days between Christmas and New Year's he began gutting the place.

''It is also a way of giving thanks.''

The planks howled and shrieked as he used a crowbar to crank them off their nails, and he splintered them when they would not give.

''I used to go to church on Christmas with Gaga.''

He was looking at the jumble of cracked and broken lumber he had hacked.

''There are all sorts of churches,'' he said in a whisper, and looked meaningfully around the gutted insides of what had once been Norm's Diner.

He began hacking again, this time with an ax. I had seen him create before, bring forth birds, vagrant eggs, lengths of bunting and missing children. I had never seen him destroy anything. He did it swiftly and with accuracy, bringing down the walls of the diner.

''I can't tell you how much it pleases me to be able to purge this place,'' he said. ''Just empty it and clean it top to bottom.''

Into the Dumpster went the counter, stools, flooring and most of the kitchen equipment. It was worn-out and sorry-looking stuff, stained, chipped, clogged with grease, smelling of cigarette smoke. Millroy sold some of the hardware, the walk-in refrigerator that smelled of rancid hamburg, the sticky Frialator, the burned-out salamander, the blackened griddle, the large scorched oven.

"Release all this blockage," he said, grunting as he yanked out the chrome stools and the rotted strapping that held the appliances in place. "Flush it away."

In a short time the place was an empty shell, and Millroy blocked out more rooms in the back, one for sleeping, with a foldaway partition— my bunk on one side, Millroy's on the other—and a rest room. The rest room he finished first—all blue tiles, with a shower, two tubs, two sinks, and two wide hopper cubicles.

"You need space in a rest room most of all—room to move your elbows and swing your knees," he said. "You notice I've got heat lamps all over the place. Warmth is a critical factor. You recognize this, don't you, muffin?"

I said yes.

"From the Airstream?"

The rest room that filled the whole front end of the Airstream was the biggest one ever installed inside a trailer home, Millroy said. This one was similar—big and blue and warm, with a skylight.

"I guess anyone who saw this would immediately think of me," he said, looking proudly at it. He jammed his foot on the flush pedal, and the water was sucked down with a thrust like a rocket. "It's a kind of signature."

My bedroom was a cupboard the same as the one in the trailer, with a bedshelf just my size that folded out of the wall. The sliding partition gave us both privacy. I had noticed that whenever Millroy had a chance he protected me—built a box for me to crawl into and made me safe.

He hammered and sawed, doing most of the carpentry himself, and talked as he worked.

He said if your shoes were too tight it was like having hooves and your body got poisons fed back into it because your feet could not breathe properly. He said we would soon need people to help us here, and that I would find them in Boston the way we had found children for the show. Maybe those same youngsters would be interested, and we would treat them like sons and daughters.

He hired some workers to help him—an electrician named Roger; a plumber, McQuinn; a tile man, Tom Hackle; and the men who disposed of the Dumpster, Vinny and George—but he hardly spoke to them because they ate badly.

People who were bad eaters were misshapen, he said, and gave off the smell of carbon monoxide. That was why he was developing a machine for doing emission tests, monitoring levels of gas from the sweat and the effort and the bad food, like exhaust fumes from a car.

"What have you got here?" asked Roger when he saw the box and tubing and probe. The others stopped to listen; they were all curious.

"The germ of an idea."

He said no more, and told me why: "These men are too old and it's not a serious question and it's too late for them." They were so weak and badly fed that they were pop-eyed from struggling to lift a little plank, he said.

Even so, it surprised me that he did not tell them what he was doing, did not tell them that he was Uncle Dick from the canceled TV program, or that his name still appeared in the newspapers. It surprised me even more that he said so little about this project to me. Every now and then he muttered, "I'm still listening," and he kept busy.

Each evening when I went to sleep he was hammering and painting, and when I woke up at dawn he was still at it, with more finished. I was used to his working magic, so at this rate he seemed slow. I wondered why he did not seem to sleep.

"I eat right," he said. "If you eat wrong you get tired."

I was trying to figure out how all this was going to end up, and I remembered his saying, *There are all sorts of churches.*

"This is how the pyramids got built."

He was hoisting a steel box into place, and it might have been an oven or the tabernacle box with a swinging door in the middle of a church altar.

"Endorphins," he said, and punched himself in the stomach.

I had thought from what Millroy had said to Norman Fredette that he wanted to make plans for a new TV show, but even after ten days he was still working in what had been Norm's Diner—painting it, the interior, the trim, with white floor tiles, white ceiling, white enamel fixtures.

"First of all we need a safe haven—a rest room, a kitchen, a place to sleep," he said. "But so does everyone."

This was what churches were supposed to do, I was thinking. Take people in and give them rest, offer them a place to pray, play music, even give them food.

"This is a way of tangibilizing what I stand for," Millroy said.

It was bright, warm, safe and clean, all the old smells gone—purged and flushed, Millroy said. It was like a little chapel, with chairs and a long, altarlike counter.

"Anyone who comes in here will know me," he said. He had a paint-brush in his hand. "This is who I am. This is what I do."

He had sent the other workmen away and now he was finished, hav-ing imagined it all himself.

"This is how we will be delivered."

"What is it?"

"It's a diner, angel." He lowered his voice, as though he wanted me to do the same.

"What are you going to call it?"

"The Day One Diner." He whispered the name as though we were in a holy place.

We were in the middle of the deliveries that made it look like a diner—bright fixtures, new tables, napkin holders, plates and bowls, just out of their crates or newly unwrapped from their bandages of bub-ble wrap—and the sun was streaming through the front windows onto Millroy's renovation, which made the diner look as clean and simple as an eggshell, when there was a knock, a clink of metal on the front win-dow that now had DAY ONE DINER painted on it.

Two men were waving from the other side of the glass; they both had the serious, beaky look of people who want something badly.

"We're not ready for customers yet," Millroy called out.

"We're from the network," one said.

So Millroy let them in. One was Walter Hickle, the other a man named Hersh. Hickle had a big pink face and a bright gob of shaving foam in one earhole, and Hersh had Smoker's Face and was sweating, even though it was a cold, bright January morning in Boston.

"It's like I told you on the phone," Millroy said. "We're currently tied up."

Hersh looked wildly behind him at Walter Hickle, thrashed with his hand and then said, "We didn't call you."

"Must have been someone else, some other network," Millroy said. "Will you excuse me? I have a few panels to deal with. Take a seat. You'll find them very comfortable and form-fitting. I hate stools. Rusty?"

In the back he said to me, "This trim needs a new lick of paint."

But while I was looking at the trim, Millroy read my mind.

"Those gents are not going anywhere. They've got a lot to think about."

He began painting and blowing air between his lips.

"Hersh worries me most. That face. Lungs full of toxins. I'd love to hook him up and monitor his emissions, just to show him the printout. Hickle's body's too big for his suit; it's as though he's been sealed into it. You know his feet are swollen."

Twenty minutes later the men were still there, Hersh fidgeting because he had seen the THANK YOU FOR NOT SMOKING sign, and Hickle on a chair, seated with his knees apart.

"Now I can offer you my full attention," Millroy said.

"Nice loaf," Hickle said.

"That's showbread," Millroy said. "You can't eat that. It's a sacrifice. But try this." He handed Hickle a hunk of some bread he had just baked in the new oven.

"Tastes great—you'll have to give us the recipe."

"It's in the Book of Ezekiel, four nine."

At first they laughed, but stopped immediately when the echo reached them, realizing that Millroy had not cracked a joke. They went on chewing the bread hunks harder, as though trying to please him.

After a while Hickle swallowed and said, "I guess you know how famous you are."

Millroy's smile was like the iron gate in front of a big house you did not dare enter, and by not saying anything he confused them.

"When they pulled the plug on your kids' show it left morning viewing with a gaping hole. *Sesame Street* is romping."

Millroy still stared with a cold iron smile.

"There is no such thing as a kids' TV show," he said. "I'm not even sure what you mean by 'kid.' Big people and small people watch TV indiscriminately. There's a huge crossover audience. Big people watch cartoons and small people watch late-night news and talking heads. I could give you the demographics."

"We have a particular program format in mind," Hersh said.

"So do I," Millroy said, "but what use is a format if you don't have substance?"

He turned his back on Hersh and Hickle and began opening and closing cabinets, filling containers, sliding pots and jars, and peeling factory labels from the legs of the new chairs. He did it all with silent efficiency, the way he prepared complicated tricks.

"And you need the face for it," he said. "If you've got the wrong face you can't sell anything. Tell me, do I have the face? Charisma is a vibration, but it is also profoundly physical."

Was it Hersh's Smoker's Face that made Millroy mention this?

"We're thinking along the same lines, no question," Hersh said.

"I could go into detail," Millroy said. "Some people get constipated just worrying about doing the right thing. Why tie yourself in knots?"

"We might need a little detail," Hickle said. "Step by step."

"I call that 'paralysis by analysis,' " Millroy said. "There's only one measure of a TV show, and that's the viewing figures. You got sponsors?"

"We're talking to people. We're looking at cable. You don't get yanked on cable for saying 'toilet.' "

"That's not a taste issue," Millroy said. "It is a matter of life and death."

"America has some growing up to do," Hickle said.

Millroy winced. He took America personally and did not like hearing that the country might be immature.

"Not everyone will love me," he said.

He had lined up a set of large canisters on the counter and was lifting them, showing that they were empty.

"But I am simply a messenger. My viewers appreciate my message, because it teaches them how to like themselves better and how to live longer."

"We might need something on paper," Hersh said. "Something about your plans, something about money."

All this time, Millroy had been manipulating the five empty canisters, arranging them in a row, moving them with his fingertips, then flourishing their shiny lids and pressing them on top.

"These are my plans," he said, holding his hands above the canisters as though conjuring. "Want to do me a favor and open them, very carefully, one at a time?"

Hersh was nearest to the canisters. He took off one lid and looked in, and then another and another, until he had opened all five. Millroy stood aside, seeming pleased with yet another no-hands example of magic.

"They got stuff in them," Hersh said, looking in. "What is it, some kind of trick?"

"Loaves. Fishes. Seethed grains of barley. Pottage. Melon balls."

"Is this the detail you were talking about?"

"Call it documentation, call it nutritional engineering," Millroy said. "Call it manna. Because you've got coriander in it. And the color of bdellium. That is, yellowish."

"What happens now?" Walter Hickle asked. He was restless and fidgeting, glancing around the way hungry people behave just before they eat.

Millroy handed them forks and kept one for himself.

"But before you dig in"—the fork he held upright to gesture with began to go rubbery and twist forward as he stroked it with his thumb—"you might want to say thank you."

Their eyes were jammed sideways at the fork in Millroy's hand coiling like a clockspring.

Knowing that he was distracting them, Millroy said, "Thank the source of all our health, or if you are inclined to put it into one word thank God, or, as I like to think of the Almighty, 'Good.' "

As he spoke, he put down the twisted fork and emptied two of the canisters, a fish in one, a loaf in the other. Then he placed the fish on one platter, and the loaf on another. He opened two napkins and covered them, flapping them casually, hardly paying attention, with the lightness that meant magic was not far off.

"This day is different from any other in my life on earth."

Hersh and Hickle repeated this, speaking together, like two big boys, their voices nudging.

Lifting the first napkin, Millroy uncovered a stack of fish; they were hot and had dark grill marks ribbing their sides. Jerking the second napkin, he showed the men ten small wheat dinner buns just like the single loaf that had been there before.

"This is not a miracle," he said. "This is deliverance." He could see that the men were amazed. He smiled and said, "This day is different from any other day of my life on earth."

Then he offered them the loaves and the fishes.

"Every day is different—every day is Day One," he said. "That is the miracle."

But the men, especially Hersh, were hesitating, as though embarrassed that they might not have said the prayer correctly.

"Eat," Millroy said, "and we'll have something to talk about. But we've got plenty of time. I plan to be around for two hundred years."

Hersh was still looking at me sideways as he began to eat, nibbling a little at time.

"What's his story?"

"No story," Millroy said.

From that moment I knew I was vulnerable. I felt weak and tricky. He suspected that I was not right, that I was hiding something—and I was, more than he could ever guess.

"What do you mean you never talk about money?" Walter Hickle complained. "Listen, we can get you a whole bunch of contracts."

Millroy placed his fingers against the counter and leaned on them.

"Don't squeeze the fish—it makes the eyes bulge," he said. "If you don't want it, just leave it on the plate."

But the men were confused. Except for the two that were picked apart on their plates, most of the fish were on the platter, where Millroy had multiplied them.

"I am the fish," he explained.

23 The first night we slept at the Day One Diner, Millroy's voice woke me like a slap in the face, saying, "No!" He thumped and fought, as though someone were trying to drag him away. He choked, then let off a thirsty gasp of fright, then there was deep silence, then another thump, then a small, sorrowing sound, *hoo-hoo-hoo,* and I could imagine his shoulders heaving.

All this worry came from behind the shutter that separated me from Millroy in the room at the back of the diner. The noise was so sudden and unusual that I imagined someone else was in there with him, but who?

"Don't, please."

The voice was so pitiful that I thought it was the other person in there with him talking. I heard it again and realized it was his voice, yet tiny coming out of his big bumping body.

"No"—he swallowed hard—"because I'm not finished."

It was the sort of confusion you have in your dreams, but when had Millroy ever dreamed like this?

"It is too soon." He sounded like a man trapped inside a box.

Struggling some more, he seemed to bang his head, a dull *pock* of wood knocking on skull-bone.

"Please don't take me," he said, and sucked his breath through the spaces between his teeth.

I was sweating.

"Aren't you going to take me?" I asked in a voice as normal as I could make it, reminding him first that I was listening to him and second that we were supposed to be picking up Willie Webb and Stacy today after breakfast.

"Who's that?" He still sounded like a man in a box.

"It's only me."

"Talk to me, muffin."

"What about?"

"Anything, but do it quick. What's your favorite color?"

"Aqua. You okay?"

"No."

"How come?"

"A black crab had me in its claws and was trying to drag me into its hole," Millroy said. "The thing had stuffed me in and I was suffocating. It wanted to eat me. Its bony mandibles were chewing my face."

"Jeekers."

I did not know what else to say, but I thought, *Suppose I was having a bad dream; what use would Millroy have been to me?*

"I forgot where I was," he said, seeming to mutter to himself. "I just woke up and got spooked." He pleaded a little, saying, "Are you happy, angel?"

"I guess so."

"Tell me why." His voice came sharply out of the dark.

"Because I made that phone call you asked me to. Plus Willie and Stacy were glad I called."

"That was so good of you, angel."

It was my new job—to find youngsters to work in the Day One Diner. They had to be the right age, neither too old nor too young. But I had told Millroy that the only ones I knew in Boston were the youngsters who had helped him run *Paradise Park,* Willie, Stacy, Dedrick and the others.

That's a great idea, Millroy had said. *They'd be perfect,* as though he had been too busy to think of other things while making arrangements with Hickle and Hersh for his new TV show, which I knew nothing about.

"Muffin, I dreamed I was dying."

"That's a real bad dream."

He sighed and said, "What do you dream about?"

That potato-head men are chasing me. That Gaga is hitting me with a strap. That I am flying with my arms out and starting to crash into a tree. That I am naked outside on the road and trying to run home to Marstons Mills. That Mumma is lying in a bed saying, *Nine, nine,* and then when she stops I realize she is saying, *Dying, dying.*

"Different stuff," I said.

"The crab in my dream was bigger than me," Millroy said. His voice had no echo. It was stifled and simple, still in a box. "And black and shiny."

"You mentioned it was black."

"I'm all right now."

I could not bear the thought that he had been frightened, because the rest of the time he was such a happy man. His fear had come quickly, the bad dream sitting on his head like a fever.

Snuffling softly, he fell asleep again, and so did I—it was always as though we slept on the same cloud—and in the morning he made a loaf of showbread as a way of giving thanks, and for breakfast served us both a piece of broiled fish and a honeycomb.

"According to Luke," he said, "this is what the Lord ate after he rose from the dead."

• • •

Cold January rain was darkening the streets and smacking the wind-shield of the Ford as we drove through Park Square, and I knew that to-night there would be black ice all over Boston. But I did not mind: I was happy again because Millroy was joyous, and I was thinking about what he had said as we got into the car: *After I cook for people, I feel they belong to me.*

"These mornings, Hersh and Hickle are saying, 'I feel good, I slept real good, I'm clean.' They're wondering what got into them."

He spun the steering wheel and laughed, and now I was less troubled about his dream.

"And the fact is that a spirit of righteousness got into them, entered them in the form of Day One food that I myself prepared. They are cleansed. They feel brilliant and hopeful, with an intimation of purity, and they cannot understand why their bowels sound like a harp."

We were driving slowly down Columbus Avenue, the rain slashing at the car like sand grains in the wind. Hearing the *whup-whup* of wipers and the hiss of rubber tires, I knew I would have felt sad if I had not been with Millroy. Rain made me feel lonely, and I never felt smaller than when I was wet.

"The pity is that it's probably too late for them," Millroy said. "That's why we need to bring our message to the young."

We were passing a row of restaurants and shops, pizza joints, signs saying FRIJOLES, LENNY'S LUNCHETTE, BARAKAT GROCERY, WHOLESALE CHICKEN PARTS. Millroy's nose throbbed as he sniffed.

"I got a little sideways last night," he said after a while.

He did not say anything more about his dream, but I could easily pic-ture the black crab squeezing him in its claws and trying to stuff him into its black hole so that it could eat his face. And because Millroy was big, I saw it as a monster black crab.

"But today's a new day," he said.

I was still thinking that the only other time he had frightened me like that was at Pilgrim Pines Trailer Park just after he quit the Barnstable County Fair, and woke up in the middle of the night and yelled, *I ain't ready!*

Whirling rain, heavier now, hit the windshield like slop from a rag. I mentioned this.

"Did you say 'peltering'?" he asked.

And it was soaking into the buildings and staining the stone black.

"Did you say 'egg-sorbed'?"

Crowding the doorways of these stores and Laundromats and apartment houses were men in heavy jackets and pulled-down hats, looking wet and angry.

"I am not afraid of anything mortal," Millroy said.

He was still driving slowly through this miserable part of Roxbury.

"Is this the right place?"

"You said to meet them on the corner."

Nowhere near their houses, he had said. *A street corner would be perfect.*

"Then it must be so."

People looked lonely, quietly struggling as they stood in the rain, heads bent, hardly moving, even youngsters like Willie Webb and Stacy. I knew they felt small like me. They were waiting at the corner of Columbus and Drayton next to a boarded-up furniture store, where a mass of overlapping signs advertised rock concerts, used-car dealers and church services. One of them called *COME TO LIFE* showed a familiar chubby face over and over on each poster, THE REV. BABY HUBER IN THE PULPIT.

"He is polyphagous," Millroy said. "I know for a fact that the Sinister Minister eats pork chops. And what about his fries and his buckets of hot wings?"

He smiled, and I knew he was remembering those sights and stinks.

Then I heard, "Yo. Big guy!"

It was Willie Webb, rushing up to the car, his hands on his head because of the rain, and Stacy was right behind him. They had thin faces and bright eyes, and though it had only been a month since the show ended, they both looked taller and bonier, with big hands and feet. They were not dressed for the rain; their jackets were soaked, their hair wet and their heads tucked into their hunched-up shoulders.

"This your vehicle, Uncle Dick?" Stacy asked as she scrambled into the backseat next to Willie.

It was odd to hear him called Uncle Dick now that the show was over.

"Hi, Alex," Willie said.

"I'm Rusty these days."

But he did not hear me because Millroy's face was pressed against the side of his head and he was inhaling. Then he did the same to Stacy, breathing them both.

"I'm trying to see whether you've changed," he said. "I'm working on a gadget that measures emissions, and I am satisfied that you've been eating right. So if you can keep a secret, let's go."

They sat in the backseat looking breathless and pleased as Millroy drove through the rain, our windshield wipers whacking back and forth. I could see that he was excited the way he had been at TV rehearsals. He did not approve of the word "kids," but he was always in a good mood when he was around them.

"Any of the others live around here?" Millroy asked.

"Berry and Kayla are down that street," Willie said. "And Dedrick's over that barber shop."

"That's good to know."

"You got a new TV show?"

"That's not the secret I want you to keep," Millroy said.

Hearing that, they both put on important-looking expressions.

"I need your full attention here. You notice I am driving you farther and farther from your homes. How do you feel about that?"

"Psyched," Willie said, and screwed up one eye and looked reckless. "Alex said something about a job."

"Not a job," Millroy said, "but Rusty might have mentioned work, and a new way of life. Do you want to be happy and live two hundred years?"

They laughed because Millroy had slipped into his Uncle Dick TV voice, but they stopped when he turned around and was not wearing his Uncle Dick smile. He was in a terror of concentration, his eyes gone black, and he said nothing more until we turned the corner at the Armory and got to the edge of Park Square, and there next to the Star of Siam was the Day One Diner—the only white storefront on the block. Even in the rain it was blazing away, shining inside and out with mirrors, tiles, white walls and chrome.

"That is our new home," Millroy said, "and you're welcome to join us if you observe a few simple rules."

He parked the Ford in front and pulled up the emergency brake. We all got out.

"Don't think about school. Don't think about money. Don't think about what your parents will say."

"My momma likes you," Stacy said. "She said your show was hot. Hey, she wants to meet you."

Millroy held Stacy's shoulders, keeping her straight while he faced her and said, "No offense, but I don't want to meet your momma. You'll have to leave your momma behind."

"That's cool with me," Willie said.

"Rusty did it, didn't you, Russ?"

"Left my Dada and my grammy Gaga."

"No burgers," Millroy said. "Now are you ready to come inside?"

We were swaying slightly in the rain.

Willie said, "Yo," and Stacy took a breath and looked at her feet.

Touching her rain-spattered face so that she raised her eyes to his, Millroy stared into her eyes, seeming to fill her with light, and said, "It's beautiful inside."

Then he turned and unlocked the front door for us and led us in, still talking.

"It was a mess before, but we got rid of its innards, gutted it, purged it—the stinks, the grease, the smoke ghosts, the dust bunnies, the opportunistic germs."

We followed him, and Willie and Stacy, holding their breaths, kept their elbows against their bodies as though they were afraid to touch anything.

"Sit on those chairs. Notice how they're form-fitting," Millroy said in the seating area, and in the kitchen he said, "Notice no frying pans. Just a grill and an oven and a microwave—we're greaseless here." He was proudest of all of the customers' rest rooms, with the space and the warmth and stalls with the skylights and foolproof locks. "How can you have a rest room if you don't have elbow room?"

"I get it. You opening a kind of restaurant," Willie said.

"More than a restaurant. Let me show you. Pass me that basket, Stacy, please."

Stacy lifted a small basket from the counter and passed it to Millroy with both hands, but still the lid shook from her nervousness.

"You did that real well," Millroy said. "Willie, do you think you could do the same thing with that next basket?"

Trying to please Millroy, Willie worked a little harder and lifted the other basket with his fingertips.

"That was superb," Millroy said, and tipped open the lid on each basket, showing a small fish in the first one and a grainy loaf in the second.

As the lids went down, Willie and Stacy were probably thinking, *Not enough food.*

"Let's say thanks. Let's pray," Millroy said. "This day is different from any other on earth. Thank you, Lord, for Day One."

We repeated the prayer, and Millroy opened the baskets and showed that they were brimming, one with fish, the other with grainy loaves.

"I like that a lot," Stacy said, looking happier than when Millroy had told her, *You'll have to leave your momma behind.*

"Eat," Millroy said. "All good food is a kind of communion."

He prayed over an earthenware bowl, his prayer like the words he called "my mutterance" before a magic trick, and when he took off the lid it was filled with cucumber-and-bean salad.

"Smells like Mexican," Stacy said.

"Christ himself used the word 'cumin,' " Millroy said, chewing, then with his cheeks bulging with food he said, "This is living your faith," and put more into his mouth.

Afterward we had herbal tea, and on the tags of the tea bags were quotes from The Book. Millroy suggested we turn our plates over. There were Book quotes on the bottom. Mine said, *I will lead you into a good land flowing with milk and honey.* The border of my paper napkin had a Book quote on it, too, but it was printed so prettily that the words looked like the design: *Ye cannot drink the cup of the Lord, and the cup of devils. Ye cannot be partakers of the Lord's table, and the table of devils.*

"Think you can shift these plates into the sink as gracefully as you set them out?"

We cleaned up while Millroy made more magic, using only his fingers darting in the air to create a power surge with the diner's lights, and he said the way we had put everything away was perfect.

Before Willie and Stacy left for home in the afternoon, Millroy said, "If I ever ask you to leave home and follow me, will you do it? Don't answer the question now. Think it over. If the answer's no, don't come back. If it's yes, I'll see you tomorrow."

Willie and Stacy showed up hungry before sunup, six-thirty or so, the next morning, rapping on the diner door, asking could they come in?

Breakfast was fresh fruit, yogurt, herbal tea, honey and toasted Ezekiel bread. Then we got to work. They helped: they swept, they unpacked crockery and flatware and glasses, and at lunchtime we took turns serving while Millroy watched and praised us. He gave us white T-shirts and white aprons, all of them lettered DAY ONE in big blue letters, with a yellow sun rising and giving off wiggly rays.

They stayed for dinner. Again Millroy did the cooking, some of it using magic techniques—praying over baskets and bowls and making food appear—but most of the cooking was the slow, fragrant kind, mixing up ingredients and using the oven or the grill, baking bread, simmering soup, grilling fish, culturing yogurt, slicing melons.

"I'd like to think you will always eat here," Millroy said at dinner. "If you get hungry at home, gnaw on an apple and drink a glass of pure water to stave off your hunger, but don't eat your folks' food. Don't put it into your mouth, and especially don't introduce their meat into your body."

"What's wrong with meat?" Stacy asked.

"Flesh?" Millroy said. "Chicken fingers? Pork knobs? Beef nuggets?"

Stacy made a face at the words and Willie snuffled.

"And there's lamb," Millroy said. "But I am looking for guidance about it. I wonder, do we really want to kill animals and bury their carcasses in our bodies?"

When they left that night to return to Roxbury, Millroy said, "This is not a job. This is a life."

And if there was anything they needed they should ask him, not their own folks.

Next morning Stacy needed a blouse and Willie needed new shoes, and Millroy bought us all warm sweaters. The diner was still not open for business, but there was work to do—putting away, setting up, training—serving Millroy as though he were a customer.

"Your folks ever ask you where you're going?" he asked Willie and Stacy after a few days of our working together.

A little awkwardly and guiltily, they said that they had quit school around the time they had started appearing on *Paradise Park*.

"That's wonderful," Millroy said. "That's why you smell so good."

There were shadows on the wall—people on the sidewalk looking through the front window at Millroy hugging us.

"Willie, you're a Day One Son," he said. "Stacy, you're a Day One Daughter."

That evening just before they left, Millroy asked, "Know anyone else your age who's hungry?"

They brought Berry and Kayla, the brother and sister from *Paradise Park,* and Kayla's friend Mickey, a tall girl with lovely eyelashes and a soft way of speaking. Millroy said that Berry and Kayla could be a Son and Daughter, but that Mickey would not be able to stay. He did not give a reason.

After she left he said, "She was gaseous. I was monitoring her emissions."

Willie's mouth was fixed in a smile that said *What?*

"I smelled her."

With five of us working, Millroy began taking afternoons off, saying, "I'm going to the station"—his new show, nothing to do with us, not on the air, but still rehearsing. He would be away for a few hours, or sometimes all afternoon. Once he returned to the diner saying, "Rest room," went into the back and locked himself in. Just before he set off for the station again, he said, "Never call it a toilet. Makes you think of 'toil.' "

"I'm glad I'm here," Stacy said. "I need to spend more time around someone like Uncle Dick."

But he was not called that. He was Millroy the Magician once more, with a new TV show that would be on the air soon. I knew nothing more about it except that it was almost ready.

The Day One Diner was almost ready, too. Everything was in place except the neon sign on the roof. The larder was full of food, and so was the hatchway cellar—full of sacks of beans, flour and barrels of dried fruit—which was reached through a trapdoor in the kitchen floor. Nearly all our pots and pans were put away, the plates and bowls stacked in cupboards. We had seats for sixty-four people—twenty at the counter, where there were high chairs ("Never call them stools") and the rest at tables. We had Day One place mats, Day One menus, the Book-tag tea, and Book-quote napkins.

Often students from UMass or people from the Armory or the Greyhound station appeared outside at the door looking hungry, knocked and gestured, asking to be let in. At lunchtime there might be as many as ten, motioning and making faces. But we pointed to the sign OPENING SOON, and we smiled like Sons and Daughters, as Millroy had told us to.

But the people sometimes got angry, seeing us inside eating.

"Can't be helped," Millroy said. "We can't open until the TV show starts."

"You're smiling, Big Guy."

"I've just realized why I was put on earth," Millroy said.

His happiness made him especially kind and generous to us during this waiting period. He worked magic for us, produced presents of clothes and money, or just tricks to amaze us, and he showed us how to strengthen our muscles. These days Willie Webb and Berry were saying *Punch me in the stomach,* and they called the diner the "Day-Oh." Millroy showed them how to get control of their bodies and, saying that speaking was also a bodily function, he corrected their pronunciation when they said *ax him* and *thow it* and *thang* and *akohol.*

We worked, we practiced, we ate, we waited. The Sons and Daughters came in the morning and left in the evening. Millroy and I lived in the back, each in our own cupboard space, with the shutters pulled down. Millroy had no more nightmares of black crabs. But when we were alone he often said to me, "I don't know what I would do without you, angel."

One Saturday Millroy was gone from early morning until late at night. The Sons and Daughters hung around and did not eat until he came back. It shocked me that Millroy did not eat. He said he was too tired. He was exhausted and hollow-eyed, his baldness white and his mustache limp, the way he looked after performing a difficult or dangerous feat of magic.

But he was smiling.

"Tomorrow is Day One," he said.

So it was going to be one of those Sunday-morning shows. The Sons and Daughters arrived early. Millroy sat us down in the diner and plugged in the TV. He manipulated the remote switch, got *Festival of Faith,* then *The Hour of Power* with the Reverend Richard Schumacher, and *Praise the Lord* and *Jimmy Swaggart Gospels* and *Healing Prayer,* a flicker of a show called *The Prayer Fair,* and a glimpse of the Reverend Baby Huber. Then he found what he was looking for.

First there was white lettering on the black screen: THE FOLLOWING PROGRAM HAS BEEN PAID FOR BY THE DAY ONE MINISTRIES.

"No one owns me," Millroy said. "No one can pull the chain on me this time."

24

My name is Millroy and I am a messenger, he said.

He leaned his wide bright face into the bigness of the TV screen.

I was once so fat I was imprisoned in the darkness of my body—trapped in my own fatness. Every day was a living hell, and I suffered just like you. But the Lord spoke to me, saying, "Change your ways, Fatso!"

He laughed a little. *I was reborn and assumed the shape of this body you see before you.*

Now you could see more of him—his health, his strength—and he smiled beautifully, showing his white teeth.

I have eaten some real strange items in my time, he went on, pushing his face against the screen.

The Millroy at the diner moved his face closer to watch himself on the TV set.

Put some real strange things into my mouth, he said. *Like this.*

He stuck his fingers under his mustache, then into his mouth, and detached his tongue. The tongue was big and pink, like a baby's arm, and after he examined the thing it vanished among his busy fingers.

Or this, he said, his face flickering on the screen, and with both hands removed a live chicken from his mouth. It was Boobie, all her feathers fussed. I recognized her confused, goggling eyes and the way she kept ducking her head.

But like I say, I have a message for you.

And here was our own Millroy in the diner watching him face to face, his real nose aimed at his shimmering TV nose. He was smiling, admiring, chuckling softly, nodding as though to say *So true* of his own revelations. That was the best part of it for me: he liked what he saw.

Willie said, "Was that your real tongue?"

"Cow's tongue," Millroy said. "People eat them. But pay attention."

Millroy on television was plucking a toad from his mouth.

"This is so gross," Kayla said.

"They wanted an arresting opening," Millroy said. "Something punchy."

And I have seen some strange items that go under the name of food.

Millroy the Messenger, working the nozzle of a stomach pump up his nose, began to squeeze the plunger, and at once his mouth was full, his cheeks bulging. He bowed his head and loosed a whole bloody hamburger onto a plate and then spat a bundle of french fries next to it.

These will not satisfy—

He yanked the tube from his nose and put down the bulb and the rubber housing of the stomach plunger.

—nor will they nourish.

''Something memorable, they said.''

Berry and Willie were shaking, their hands over their mouths, eyes popping, trying not to laugh out loud. Stacy's mouth gaped open. Kayla was watching through her fingers.

Now this message—

He was pointing to a book the size of the Boston telephone directory, about five inches thick, with a sunny Day One cover and looking like it weighed fifteen pounds.

—this message is going to let you live for two hundred years or more.

That was when the music started, blaring sunrise music—trumpets and roosters, and a movie of dawn coming up that was both egglike and spiritual. Millroy's face formed out of the yolk of the sun.

He was alone on a stage set that could have been either a kitchen or part of a church. The counter looked like an altar, the flowers looked edible, the cookware shone like church paraphernalia, and was that The Book or just a big cookbook?

But he did not mention The Book—no Scriptures, no God, no Good. No youngsters either, no puppets, no films, no cartoons, no pictures even, hardly any props, nothing at first except Millroy. It was not Millroy the Magician and it was not Uncle Dick. He was different, yet he was someone I knew: Millroy the Messenger.

I have seen, he said. *And I have seen—*

Still talking but without glancing down, he removed a shoelace from one of his sneakers, turned the shoelace into a snake, made it go rigid until it stiffened into a rod, which he twirled, leaned on, turned up and set alight, letting it burn like a taper, and then, holding it like a Roman candle, let it burst, ball after flaming ball, until there was nothing but a puff of smoke in his palm. He had not blinked once.

I want to talk a little about the darkness of the body. . . .

His right hand had been singed and blackened by the explosion. Staring at the camera, he reached down and detached the burned hand at the wrist, and when he clutched it turned it into a small bud, which bloomed tremblingly, a pure white rose that he poked into his lapel with his new hand.

We can do a whole lot better than that, he said, but not about these tricks.

He performed magic the way someone might scratch his head. With so much happening all at once, it was hard to keep track of what he was saying, and the effect was hypnotic. What made my eyes like pinwheels, and the others', too, was the magic and talk at the same time, because when the magic stopped we were paying attention, holding on to the arms of our chairs with sweaty hands.

Part of the magic also was that Millroy had pushed so far forward that he seemed to be slightly outside the screen and bulging into the room, making things happen. It was all action and suspense and the flow of his steady voice, the man juggling and at the same time preaching.

Listen and be happy, be healthy and prepare to live on earth for two centuries. Forget everything you ever learned. We are going to have a real good time.

A moment later, he said, *I am not a magician. I am not a prophet or a priest. I am not a saint or a miracle worker . . .*

As soon as he said this, you thought, *Yes, you are!*

I am a messenger.

Beside me in the diner, Millroy turned from the screen to glance at the others, the Day One Sons and Daughters—Willie Webb smiling, Stacy still with her hands over her face, Berry frowning, Kayla shaking her head. Then he looked back at the face on the screen and sat there fascinated, as though he were seeing it all for the first time, his *Day One Program.*

Moving his hands—you could not tell whether this was magic or just TV tidiness—he made some dishes of food appear: soups and fruits, nuts and grains, jars of honey, the thick reddish sludgy cereal he called "pottage."

I was sick and became well, he was saying. *I was weak and became strong. I was fat and became thin.*

Up popped some more food—cucumbers and onions in baskets, grapes, melons, figs, corn and beans.

And when I speak of being sick I don't mean some vague, obscure, oblique illness of the spirit that you shoo out of your system by praying, he said. *I mean, I felt plain rotten—fat, stupid, sick and lost. I can be specific. A weightlifter needs eight thousand calories a day. I didn't.*

He leaned into the camera again, his face filling the screen.

My bowel transit-time was seventy-two hours, minimum.

He stepped back, smoothed the cover of the big nameless book and tapped it, but did not open it. The cover of the book was like a trapdoor that he had decided not to lift.

The term "full-figured" covers a multitude of errors, he was saying, *but this book changed me. I read it and I got strong. I got healthy, I got righteous and I got thin. When I tell you it was a kind of purification I'm speaking the literal truth.*

He let this sink in. He smiled and, shutting his eyes, seemed to be reflecting on a miracle. Then he became forceful.

Pretty soon I could do this.

He punched himself in the stomach so hard it sounded as though he were punching a wall; you could hear the thud.

From his seat beside me in the diner, Millroy hitched his chair closer and watched with real pleasure.

I don't want to blind you with abstractions. When I say your bowels shall sound like a harp I mean just that—like The Book says. Heavenly music from a healthy colon. Now look at this.

And he scooped some food from two of the bowls on the counter in front of him.

This is what I am talking about. A piece of broiled fish and a honeycomb. Sound familiar? It sure will be when I've delivered the whole of my message. They taste great and they're good for you, body and soul. Bring you back from the dead. . . .

He touched the book; it was so square and solid it was as though he were steadying himself with it. He swallowed the food he had been chewing.

Who ate this in remarkable circumstances? The mystery man, who revealed himself to two strangers when he took a loaf of bread—

He did so with one of the Ezekiel loaves.

—and tore it apart to eat.

"Road to Emmaus," I said. Millroy had explained the Day One Diner menu to us, and which parts of The Book had inspired dishes.

Instead of eating the hunk of bread he used it to gesture to the other baskets and bowls.

What have we here? Cucumbers, leeks, melons, garlic, grain, pulses and pot-tages.

Fuddling some more, he conjured a spoon from his cuff and worked it around one of the bowls, pushing the thick mixture and then lifting it to his mouth and tasting it. You could hear him gulping into the micro-phone, popping and snapping like thick oatmeal on the boil.

Eat this for ten days and you'll be fair and healthy. A man once ate this, and just by eating this lentil pottage he became greater than all the magicians and astrologers. He did not want to be defiled by eating flesh. He knew a thing or two about fiber. This gave him strength. Wouldn't that make you want to try it?

"Yo. Daniel," Willie Webb said. It also was on the Day One Diner menu.

Millroy smiled at him and turned to the screen, where the other Mill-roy was placing his hand on that slab of a book.

It's all here, he said, and took up the bread hunk and the jug of water. *How a man ate this and was so strengthened by this one meal that he journeyed for forty days and forty nights.*

Stacy said, "Elijah the Tishbite."

Tapping the big book again, Millroy said, *It is all in this book. And the book advises roughage and bulk. That is why so much of this food resembles wood chips and bark mulch. But never mind, it is delicious, and it is the secret of life.*

He tilted his head again and came closer, and now he was glowing in the room again.

I want you to come with me. Let me take you away to a land of corn and wine, a land of bread and vineyards, a land of olive oil and honey—a land called America. And if you eat—

Lifting a honeycomb to his mouth, his fingers thick and gleaming with its dripping syrup, he parted his lips, tested the honeycomb with his probing tongue and then took a bite of its yellow sparkle—

Gosh, this is good! he said, interrupting himself. *And if you eat this food you will never die.*

He chewed the honeycomb again, and the sound in the microphone was of chunks of honey, sweet and crystallized, bursting against his teeth and slipping down his throat.

When I say "not die" I mean live for two hundred years. That should be your goal.

Now his teeth tugged on something chewier than the honeycomb.

Figs are nice too. Lots of figs in this book.

"Nahum," said Berry.

Listen, there's a recipe for bread in here. Shall we make some and see how it tastes?

Instead of lifting the book, he cranked himself around and heaved open its heavy cover, then flicked pages until he found what he wanted, patting that page with the flat of his hand.

Take wheat, barley, beans and lentils, he said, measuring cupfuls of them and sprinkling them into an earthenware pot. He was still reading. *And millet and fitches, and mix them in a bowl.*

"Got to be Ezekiel," Willie said.

Millroy scooped and turned the mixture with a spoon, added some water and scooped some more.

No eggs. Is there any taste in the white of an egg? He tapped the book. *The answer is no.*

He shoved the bowl into the oven behind him, then said something that might have been a prayer, or the mutterance that he mumbled over his magic.

Bread, he said, removing the earthenware pot, and broke off a hunk and ate it.

All you could hear for the next few moments was Millroy's chomping, like a backhoe hacking a hole in wet sand.

It's in the book, he said, leaning on the open page and admiring the hunk of bread in his hand. *It tastes good, it's good for your body, good for your soul. A twofold bonus—it reduces your bowel transit-time and grants you salvation. You can't ask for more than that.*

He said, *It's in the book,* a few more times, and finally, *You could look it up.*

Normally, watching television, Millroy talked to me or made remarks ("Wicked case of Smoker's Face," "Notice the woven hair"), or asked my opinion about the show. But this morning, watching *The Day One Program,* he paid no attention to me. Instead, he kept glancing at Willie and Stacy and Berry and Kayla, and now and then said, "What do you think so far, Sons and Daughters?"

They all said it was great but did not take their eyes away from the screen for fear they would miss something—instant bread, or a shoelace turning into a snake.

Millroy became quiet again and interested in the program when he saw himself hoisting a large metal box onto the counter. It had lights and dials and looked like a large boom box with a four-foot length of black tubing coiled around it. He lifted off the tubing and switched the thing on. The dials lit up and a sound came out of it, a bubbly purr with a vibrating sigh.

About time we did an emission check.

Hearing this, Millroy nodded at the TV set.

After all, we've been sticking a lot of different things into our mouths.

Millroy had begun to smile again at his image on the TV screen.

There was a small black mouthpiece on the end of the rubber tubing. Hesitating a little, as though it might be dangerous, Millroy fitted it under his nose. It covered his mouth and made him look like an insect.

His eyes popped as he breathed hard, and while his face was at one side of the screen, the face of the lighted dial was on the other, the needle trembling inside a green stripe.

Looks fine, he said. *Emission accomplished.*

He reached beyond the camera, as though into the room, seeming to beckon.

Come here, he was saying. *Just for a minute. Won't hurt a bit.*

The back of the cameraman's head appeared as he moved from behind the camera and slipped off his earphones. He looked uncertain and unprepared in his faded shirt and baseball hat, and he laughed in a terrified way as Millroy hitched him to the machine.

The human body is just like an automobile engine, Millroy said, *which is why I devised this machine. The food we eat is our fuel. Our breath is the exhaust. Toxic or unhealthy food creates a noxious gas—carbon monoxide and nitrogenous wastes in vapor form. All sorts of gaseous compounds, and—uh-oh—*

The needle of the dial had jerked sharply into the red stripe, and it jolted each time the cameraman exhaled.

I know what you had for breakfast, Millroy said, and the man looked guilty. *But Rick doesn't look unhealthy, does he? You see, the damage is all inside so far. But just how serious is it?*

The man named Rick seemed bewildered, and because he was not working the camera, the lens simply stared at him and at Millroy, who was tapping the big book.

I want you to move this book with one hand.

At first Rick hesitated; then he seemed impatient to get it over with. He put his whole hand around the spine, as though picking up a sandwich. Then he faltered and a gasping noise came out of his mouth and he compressed his face with effort. But the book did not move. You would have thought it was bolted to the counter. Rick made another helpless noise and walked away. The camera wobbled and focused on Millroy and you knew that Rick had gone back to work.

Pinching the enormous book between the finger and thumb of one hand, Millroy hoisted it a foot off the counter, holding it horizontal. It was a feat of strength, yet he was smiling gently as he performed this wonderful piece of leverage.

This is not magic. This is faith. And if you live your faith and eat right you will truly be guided by this book. This is the book of life. The book of food. The book of meals and miracles.

And still as if defying gravity, he turned the book lightly in his fingers, and only then, at the end of the show, did he reveal that it was the Bible—The Book—and when you saw his mustache move you knew he was saying it with capital letters.

I was lost in the darkness of my body, and the Lord spoke to me saying, "Change your ways, Fatso!"

The *Day One* sunrise music played and the shimmering sun covered Millroy's face as a message appeared on the screen inviting viewers to write for a fact sheet, with recipes, or to use the Help Line. The last line was the name and address of the Day One Diner on Church Street in Boston. *Join us.*

In the Day One Diner, watching the next show, *The 700 Club,* being advertised, Millroy switched off the TV, stood, kicked his chair back with his heel and stretched, seeming to expand with confidence.

''We're open for business,'' he said.

The Day One Diner was empty, the TV was blind, we were silent; as yet there were no believers, no eaters.

In this quiet new place, in the white silence, I felt happy and pure and innocent, and did not know why. Then a customer walked in and ordered something he had just seen on Millroy's television show. Soon after, there was another man and the spell was broken. On that first day it was as though the world had begun to leak through the door and eat.

25 I kept thinking that: *The whole world is leaking through the door,* and as the door flapped and banged, the world began to flood and brim inside the Day One Diner. It was Millroy's program. People came—curious ones, crazy ones, lonely ones. The hungriest came first, and then it was everyone, and we were no longer innocent and empty.

And we were not anonymous anymore, happy with our secret existence of food and work and prayers, playing the game of being alone so that we could live forever. Strangers had joined us, and because Millroy was so persuasive and the food was so good, these strangers did not take long to like us. They were quick to believe Millroy, and it happened all the faster because his message was something they could eat.

It was a weekly program, so Millroy had plenty of time to prepare for it and also to run the diner. On the second *Day One* show he said, *My text for today is—fellow Americans, virtually everything you stick in your mouth is carcinogenic and deadly.*

Within days we had too many customers to count. This made me fearful, but Millroy's reaction was the opposite. He was more hopeful and eager when there were many people listening to him and eating as he suggested. He said he had always liked large audiences. Other people made him bolder and more alive, and being alive mattered most to him. He liked the stimulus of strangers, he said, and he greeted them as though he were greeting friends.

"In a way I belong to them," he said to the Sons and Daughters. "Just as you belong to me."

Kayla said it made her happy to hear this, and the others agreed.

"Your dad is so cool," Willie said.

"He is someone special," I said. "He is everything to me," and I meant it.

"I don't like to use the words 'my ministry.' No one appointed me. I started life as a traveler. I became a magician. I realized that I had a message, and that made me a messenger. I have seen so many things that my memory is a testament. I want to tell people what I have experienced within my own body. I can help open their eyes. I want to share my revelations with them. I want to save souls by saving lives.''

Millroy did not wake up at night anymore and call out *no!*, but one night soon after we had the rush of customers, he woke me by murmuring in the darkness, ''Don't be afraid. I am the first and the last.''

I did not know what to say to this.

''I am he that liveth and was dead, and behold I am alive for evermore, Amen. I have the keys.''

''Sounds good,'' I said to remind him that I was listening and if he needed me to say something more I was willing.

''The keys of hell and of death,'' he said. ''Write the things which thou hast seen.''

But then he went back to sleep, no more mutterances, and in the morning he said he had an idea for more mirrors in the doorway, the little lobby that served as the entrance and exit of the diner. He said that optically correct mirrors were the key to understanding—big revealing mirrors, full-length and frank, showing you from all angles, especially the back. When you walked in you were revealed.

''We all with open face, beholding in the glass the glory of the Lord, are changed into the same image from glory to glory,'' he said on the next *Day One Program,* and you knew he was quoting. ''Though we often befool ourself with mirrors, this is the truth, back and front.''

It was a shock for some people to see themselves from the side, he said, and which people recognized themselves from the rear?

''Mirrors are an article of our faith. If I had a church it would be a hall of mirrors.'' He was frisky, more excited than I had ever seen him.

It all started that first morning when customers began pushing through the door wanting to be fed. The world was hungry and wanted to eat, Millroy said, and he knew what was good for them.

I also realized that everything that had happened before had been a preparation for this—everything since the afternoon at the fair when he had put his throbbing nose into my face. That *I want to eat you* day had led to the Day One Diner, all part of his plan.

Only now did I recall how, months ago, in his Airstream trailer at the fairground, he had said to me, *If I were going to start a religion . . .* It had seemed so odd a thing to say, like *By the way, I am Moses, plus I want to start a new church,* that I brushed the thought from my mind and could hardly remember what else he had said. Yet these days I knew we were in the middle of it, deep in his religion, in the Christian cuisine of the Day One Diner, getting regular.

"I saw this long ago," he said, standing in the diner's kitchen. "All this . . ."

He was talking to Kayla and Berry, who found his confidence as infectious as I did. His frisky spirit made us willing. That friskiness was evident in his appetite, eating and offering food, especially to the Day One Sons and Daughters. He lifted up spoonfuls of pottage or yogurt or melon balls.

"Open up!" he would say to Kayla.

She would hesitate, as anyone might with a fork in her face.

"Get it into your mouth, angel."

At this point Kayla would laugh, sounding terrified, and the laughter kept her mouth open.

"Eat it," Millroy would say, a bit breathless from all the coaxing, his red face swollen with eagerness. "Go for bulk. Ezekiel knew about fiber. The Lord knew about complex carbohydrates. King David fleeing in Two Samuel knew the benefit of high residue."

He was excited and happy from the day of his first *Day One* television show. He knew he had been a success and he knew the diner would be a hit.

One night after the first busy days, Millroy sent the Sons and Daughters home with bonuses, to buy sandals. *I see you all in sturdy sandals and leather footgear.*

"And this is your bonus, petal," he said to me after they had gone. He came over to me carrying a dish of reddish stew he called "parched pulse."

"I like its thick, loamy texture," he said, stirred it and indicated with his eyes that I ought to sit down.

He got his wooden spoon into it and said, "Eat."

Then he fed me, sitting across from me, his mouth open, his tongue quivering, as he eased the food into me on the big warm spoon.

"Get that into you."

I could do it myself, I was thinking.

"Open wide." His big hairy fingers had a grip on the spoon. "Chew slowly."

Still he watched, swallowing saliva and talking juicily as I ate.

"This is so fibrous," he said. "This is nutrition, sure, but a lot of it is going to go straight through you," and he spooned it into me.

"In a way, I would like you to be fat, but I know that's wrong," he said. "I want to fill you up. I want to put it all into you, be responsible for everything inside you."

And went at me with his spoon again.

He was up early every morning in the half dark before dawn, clattering in the Day One Diner kitchen, boiling the beans he had soaked overnight, mashing lentils, parching pulses, baking Ezekiel loaves, brewing tea, culturing yogurt, setting out melon balls, honeycombs and the grape juice The Book referred to as wine—the first pressing of the grapes, foaming in a jug, but not fermented. He talked mutterances the whole time to himself.

"My herbage," he would say.

Clank-clunk, gurgle-gurgle.

"My wheaten loaves."

Bip-biddle-bip-bop.

"Seethe my grains and pulses."

He was proudest of the fact that this food kept fresh without refrigeration. He had bought and installed a refrigerator only to satisfy the Board of Health.

"Ice is the American vice," he said. "Cold water is a different story. Matthew speaks of the Lord handing out cups of cold water."

After he had prepared the food for the day he sealed it in jars and bowls, many of them earthenware pots—"crocks," he called them—or straw baskets. The food was reheated in the oven or microwave before it was served by the Day One Sons and Daughters.

"The virtue of this food is its purity and simplicity. Its benefit derives from its plainness," he said, swallowing and gulping as he always did when he talked about eating. "It has been tested by generations in The Book, who are noted for their longevity."

Most mornings he roasted a lamb, turning it on a spit, where it spattered and dripped, a blackened naked animal ("Third-degree burns all over its body") being cranked by a big doubtful man.

"I am not happy about lamb," he said. "I am not happy about meat eating at all, for reasons I would rather not go into."

We served the lamb in thin slices with sprigs of rosemary or mint and side dishes of lentils. Millroy did not eat it himself and urged us not to eat it. Choose fish, he said—the market on Boston Harbor had every type of fish goggling from the marble slabs. I bought the fish for the diner. I knew about it because I was from the Cape. It was my early-morning chore. I paid cash and usually got it cheap.

"I am looking for guidance on lamb," Millroy said.

Some customers ventured into the Day One Diner simply because our OPEN sign was on and they were hungry. First they looked through the front window. You saw them staring—at us, then at their own reflections. Many of them were bewildered by our food. Not enough variety, they said, funny tastes, needs salt, too simple. They did not understand the menu. They said, "Is this all you got?" They ordered strange food and were sometimes disappointed. They were confused by the taste, whispered and went away.

"What's this supposed to be?" was a common question.

Real food does not even look edible to people who have never seen it before, Millroy said, which was why their bodies were monstrous and they died young.

Other people left the diner the minute they saw they could not smoke in it, or that we did not serve coffee.

"This is Day One," Millroy explained to anyone who would listen—and he had ways of encouraging them to listen, fixing them with his eyes. "Eat this food. All of it is nourishing and pure. It will give you clear skin and a long life. A little cautious? Just try some slices of Ezekiel or wheaten loaf with broiled fish and a puddle of honey, then finish with melon balls and a pot of warmed nuts. It is wholesome and will give you life."

He seldom mentioned The Book in the diner. He urged us to speak up about the virtues of the food, or just to smile.

"This is not my pulpit," he said, meaning the diner. "Americans lost their faith when they started to eat junk food. They don't need me to preach here. This food is communion. When people prosper and are regular, they will believe. They believe their bowels."

People either tried the food and never came back, or else they ate and returned again and again—every day even. They were from the local colleges—University of Massachusetts students from across the square, youngsters from Simmons, Emerson, Boston University, Harvard, MIT. We knew them by their sweatshirts. There were secretaries, too, and they were mostly young. Many were lonely people who came because the diner was so warm and bright and the food so inexpensive.

"I was like you once," Millroy said to the people who came every day, and it gave them heart to hear it from this tall, powerful man with the mustache and shaven head. He was calm, he was a good cook—and this reassured them, too—just the way he smiled, seemed to be in no hurry, and occasionally with the most casual movement of his hands worked magic for them, little vanishing tricks.

"I am enjoying this," he said.

We were busy, with a steady flow of customers. No tipping—that was popular. The strongest aroma was that of freshly baked loaves of bread. *My wheaten loaves.* He had rigged a contraption that funneled this aroma into the diner, and he liked watching people inhale it and smile.

"We're paying off our loan," Millroy said. "We can't ask more than that."

It was important to him that the diner pay its own way, but all it had to do was break even. Millroy's television money was his real income. The Sons and Daughters were given whatever money they needed, not a salary but an allowance—"a stipend," Millroy called it, a lump sum each week, with ten percent knocked off as a tithe for the diner.

Willie said, "I can handle this," and seemed pleased that he was getting any money at all.

"I want you to be happy," Millroy said when he doled out the money.

If you treat people right they do it back, he said. The Sons and Daughters would have moved in if there had been room for them. Millroy said they were more grateful because they spent each night at home and could see the difference between their houses and the Day One Diner— how limited their houses were.

"Their food at home must be wicked," I said.

"They are going home to houses of death," Millroy said. "That's why they are so relieved to come here."

After we had cleaned up the diner and they had gone home Millroy locked the doors and fed me, sitting in front of me holding his spoon.

"Eat," he said. "I want to be responsible for everything inside you."

And while he spooned and I ate, he came up with ideas.

"What about writing a book?" he would say. "I can't write but I can talk. You take it down."

Or maybe two books, he said. One about his life—how he had discovered the obvious secret of eating right, his personal testimony about
escaping from the wilderness of his fatness—a book called *Ever Been
Dead?* or *This Is My Body,* and how he had become a magician. The second
book would be called *The Day One Program,* about the food itself, the
diet, the Scriptures, with selected recipes for the dishes we served in the
diner: Jacob Pottage, Ezekiel Bread, Daniel Lentils, Nahum's Fig Bars,
Bethel Barley Cakes, the vegetable salad he called "herbage," and all the
rest. "It would explain how I got here," he said. "And why."

Another late-night idea was to sell all sorts of sturdy containers for
storing Day One food. Or to commission a whole new translation of
The Book—the emphasis on exact meanings of food items, with recipes
listed after Revelation.

Every morning people were waiting on the sidewalk for us to open
up. Breakfast was popular—fresh bread, honey, fruit, yogurt and tea of
Day One herbs and spices. Millroy was especially pleased to see that the
most faithful eaters were young.

Many of them came because of the TV program. The rest knew nothing about Millroy's reputation and liked the cheap and healthful food. In
the diner Millroy did not say that he was a messenger, and it pleased him
that people ate without needing an explanation.

"The act of eating makes them believers," he said. "If this food con-
vinces them, they will follow. I love the simplicity of that. That is the
meaning of a gut reaction."

He pointed out that it was generally older white males who were the
hardest to convince. Some people were repeat eaters because our prices
were low, others because they wanted to be thin, or because the food
was making them regular. The best ones, Millroy said, were the ones
who did not know why they ate here day after day. They did not ask
questions, they just opened their mouths and we fed them. Something in
their bodies told them they were doing the right thing.

It was not all smooth. Some days people cheated us, left without paying, claimed the service was bad. A man swore at Stacy for spilling hot
pottage on his leg, calling her a name that made her cry. Another man
tripped Berry. Now and then a person would say straight out that the
food was disgusting and where did we get it from?

But when Millroy praised the Sons and Daughters for not shouting back at the bad customers, there was something about the way Willie Webb smiled at Berry that made me think he had a secret.

Then one day I saw Willie squeezing a plastic bottle of Sun-Glo liquid detergent into a dish of Daniel Lentils.

"That's for the dude at table seven," he was saying to Berry. "He called me slow."

"Do it, bro," Berry said. His last name was Loomis, though we always used first names, and sometimes "Son Berry" or "Daughter Stacy," or just "Son" or "Daughter." They noticed that Millroy did not speak to me that way—I was just Rusty—and they did not know whether this meant I was more special or less so. I did not mind what they thought. I knew I mattered to Millroy.

Willie noticed I was listening.

"Just a little old squirt of this make him run all night," he said to me, laughing his growly laugh.

I said "Jeekers" because I was shocked, but said nothing more. I was too afraid. I was Jilly Farina from Marstons Mills. I was no one. Willie must have thought that I was going to say something to Millroy about him—*talk trash to the Big Guy,* as he might put it—because while I watched he threw the lentils away, got a new dish and served it to the man without soap. I hoped he had forgiven the man.

The way we waited on tables in the beginning was clumsy, but within three weeks we had the hang of it, and knew how to be busy and efficient. Millroy did not criticize us, nor did he raise his voice. *It's all a lesson,* he said.

"These people are putting their lives in our hands," he said. "Think of the responsibility. Are you aware of how awesome a task we have taken upon us? People's very lives."

The Sons and Daughters listened, feeling proud, and they thanked Millroy for giving them this chance. Then I knew that Willie must have forgiven the unkind man and regretted ever putting liquid detergent in bad customers' food so that they would get the squitters.

After a month of the Day One Diner, when we were alone at night in the back, Millroy looked at me and said, "So what do you think?" It was surprising that he asked me any question at all, especially this hard one.

"Say something, angel."

I did not know what to say—anyway, what was the question?

"Is this going to work, angel?"

"It's already working, I guess."

Looking sideways, he seemed to shrink a little; his neck shortened, his mouth fell open and he spoke in a slow stupid voice.

"I have moments of doubt."

Hearing his voice quiver, what could I say?

"Didn't you hear me? I don't want to be another Mister Phyllis on a tinky-winky show, boring people rigid with sermons and boasting of my health."

"It's working good," I said with a dry mouth.

"I want it to be great."

"Tons and tons of people," I said, "plus a neat TV show that's wicked popular and everyone watches on Sunday morning."

Now he said nothing, but he turned to face me.

"It *is* great," I said.

His face was rumpled with shadow and his whole head had creases so deep I almost did not recognize him.

"Do you honestly think so?"

"Sure."

I was afraid he might ask, *How do you know?*, but he just nodded slowly and sat down.

I waited for him to say something more, but he was asleep in his chair. I stepped over him and headed to bed, but before I locked myself into my little box of a room I looked back and saw that his lips fluttered and his cheeks blew with long, windy snores.

That fretful Millroy was so different from the Millroy of *The Day One Program*, who never doubted or looked back or had shadows on his face. The television Millroy attracted more viewers, and many of them became customers—"eaters," he called them, meaning believers.

"He looks like an eater," he often said, seeing a stranger. Or "She'll definitely eat."

One taste and they would be convinced, was what he meant.

On the show he talked the whole time, his mouth and mustache going so fast that he looked like he was chewing. It was talk and food, not much Scripture and a lot less magic.

"I think your average viewer is spooked by magic," he said. "I know from experience that your audience often regards it with palpitating apprehension, and they are right to do so because many people who work magic have an impure motive. A demonstration of magic can seem hostile and aggressive, Daughter.''

He was speaking to Kayla, who nodded seriously but looked nervous, as people often did when Millroy was engaged in an explanation.

''Something exploding in your face, or flopping on the floor, or surprising you where you least expect it—maybe bursting into bloom. That can be traumatic.''

Kayla glanced around, thinking, *What?*

''I won't have anything gratuitous or misleading on my show,'' Millroy said. ''No tricks. No nonsense.''

Daughter Kayla agreed with him, looking respectful, and I began to think both from her reaction and the way Willie had decided not to doctor the bad customer's lentils with soap that they also feared Millroy.

We all watched *The Day One Program* with amazement because in an all-Millroy show you never knew what was coming next. He walked back and forth from camera to camera; he had the knack of suddenly turning and peering into a different camera, into your face, even extending his face into your room. It was his bulging eyes that created this illusion. He told stories, he testified, he ate. Now and then he worked the old magic, doing the very things that he had told Kayla were traumatic—exploding a flower, hatching a live bird from an egg, gulping a mouthful of fire, or slipping eighteen inches of sword blade into his gullet.

''Just to wake people up,'' he said. ''Get their attention.''

The early programs were testimony and personal history, with a sideways look at The Book. They were *I am a messenger* and *the darkness of the body,* stories of how he had been imprisoned in the wilderness of his fatness. It was shocking to hear him say *Most of the food we eat causes cancer.* Flashing past was all the familiar food that everyone ate—milk, peanut butter, sirloin steaks, fat cheese, jelly, candy bars, breakfast cereal, chocolate cookies, white bread, hot dogs, burgers and bacon. Then liquid and loopy images of skulls, gravestones, hellfire and devils—obese devils.

If you still were not frightened into eating his food, Millroy had more magic, and somehow he managed to eat and chew through a whole show while delivering the message in his own voice—ventriloquism, we guessed—that America had lost the art and science of cooking, and that less than five percent of kitchen time was spent preparing fresh food.

We were unhealthy and unholy because we had stopped cooking; food companies had turned us into addicts. We warmed up chemical paste, opened cans, dumped out envelopes, whisked water into toxic powders, and then nuked them in the microwave. What we called cooking was no more than heating and rehydration. In that whole message, he never stopped munching.

After the shock of the cancer-producing kitchen cupboard, Millroy broadcast some happier *Day Ones*, recounting various meals in The Book, many of them because food was always shared. Never mind the Last Supper; what about the most profound meal in the whole Book, Jesus eating with his disciples by the shores of Lake Galilee after he had come back from the dead?

"It is impossible to eat this original and life-giving food"—Millroy was chewing and swallowing fish while he spoke—"and not sense that a mystery is being revealed to you." He gulped and said, "Go and do likewise. Imagine the prophets urging us to eat complex carbohydrates."

After he began to receive letters he spent a whole program replying to criticism.

"I am not a fanatic," he said. "I am not a fundamentalist. Not a Branch Davidian, not a Swaggart. I am not a crank."

Waving a letter of accusation, he began to laugh softly.

"Listen, I am not even religious," he said, "and I am not comfortable using the term 'God.'"

Then he leaned forward and began to smile. "I know that you can assert many crazy theories using The Book as evidence. That in pain ye shall bring forth children—no anesthetic. That the earth is four thousand years old. That women are forbidden to wear men's clothes. That adulterers should be killed. That it is death to touch a man on his stones. That a bastard can't enter a church, and neither can a man with a groin injury. That wool and linen can't be woven together. That a man who pisseth against a wall is damned. That because Jesus lost his temper once, with the money changers, we are licensed to freak out whenever we want. That wizards and magicians must be put to death."

He was still smiling as he crumpled the letter and made it disappear in his fingers.

"But where food and nutrition are concerned, The Book is subject to rigorous scientific scrutiny and the test of time. I have personally experimented with it, and so have many leading laboratories. Friends, The

Book has been validated. The Book will make you regular and grant you longevity.''

Refresh my bowels in the Lord, he said on another show. *That is my text for today.*

Already Willie and Stacy were laughing at the show, remembering the fuss over *Paradise Park,* how the sponsors had canceled after the Christmas program when Dedrick had described the ideal bowel movement.

''The Big Guy is so cool,'' Willie said.

''What it down to is, he one funny dude,'' Berry said. ''He just crank it out.''

I was proud to hear them say this, and to be reminded that being funny was a way of being strong and was another example of Millroy's magic. What the Sons and Daughters said about him was a fact, and Millroy's motto was that nothing was more interesting than the truth.

In that period I mention, my wilderness, I was trapped inside my own darkness, lost within the hellish size of my own body. The word "fat" does not even begin to do justice to my ordeal. Imagine being forced to carry a two-hundred-pound weight with you wherever you go!

He would blow up his cheeks, expand his face to fill the whole TV screen so that he looked terrifying.

And so I often vocalized my despair, echoing the cry in Lamentations, "Behold, O Lord; for I am in distress: my bowels are troubled; my heart is turned within me; for I have grievously rebelled . . ."

''Tell it,'' Stacy said, urging him on.

The prophets knew about spastic colons, pouchy diverticula and chronic obesity, that roughage is a blessing from heaven, and that goodness proceeds from the bowels. I want you to repeat what Isaiah wrote: "my bowels shall sound like a harp. . . ."

''My bowels shall sound like a harp,'' Kayla said, looking up at the TV screen.

''My bowels shall sound like a harp,'' we all said.

At the end of this show Millroy displayed the food that would accomplish this and produce the harp sound—wheat, barley, parched corn, figs, garlic, leeks and so forth.

''The elements of *The Day One Program,*'' he said. ''Why has no one made this connection before, linking health, holiness, slenderness, regularity, longevity and salvation?''

When you heard these words together, you wanted to eat and be saved.

"Never mind. In my darkness I saw the link, my bowels were refreshed, and I became a messenger."

Millroy's bowels got into the newspapers, into magazines. People called the diner to ask about them, photographers showed up hoping to get his picture. Even though he would not talk to the press and refused to pose for pictures, the program racked up more viewers. They were people who hoped he would talk about bowels again—which he did on the very next show, "The Life Wish," about how people in The Book lived a long time.

"My spirit shall not always strive with man, for that he also is flesh, yet his days shall be a hundred and twenty years"—and that is just for starters.

There was food on every program—food with a message that said, *Eat well, eat Day One, get right and live a long time. The Book is the book of life.*

He often told the story of how he had discovered the truth by reading the Gideon Bible when he went from hotel to hotel as a traveling magician, like Daniel. And when his diet improved he became a better magician, and soon he hardly understood the miracles that he could work. He got regular. He saw the face of God, or Good. He appeared to be looking into a mirror. This was not a delusion of grandeur, he said: we could do the same because we were capable of being Godlike—that is, good.

The Lord appears at mealtimes was another *Day One* text-for-today—there was usually eating or food served when Jesus showed up. All the meals in the New Testament had been validated by modern dietitians and nutritionists. It was a serious error to regard these meals as symbolic because after all the Lord himself had chewed this bread, munched this fish, drunk this inky wine, and had garlicky breath. The Lord was regular. His bowels sang.

Ye shall eat no manner of fat was another week's text. *Leviticus Seven.*

Another was *Be conscious every second of what you're putting in your mouth. If it smells like bubble gum, as so much American food does, spit it out. And no more raspberry shampoo!*

Millroy wore an open-necked shirt, and his cheeks were healthy. With his sleeves rolled up you could see his arms were strong. When he punched himself in the stomach you heard a wooden thud, as though he had smacked a chopping block. One-arm push-ups were his specialty. In the middle of a show he might pump out twenty of them, then continue talking, hardly winded.

"An unhealthy person is doing something wrong," he said. "A fat person is fallen and lost, but not forever. That is my message to America. Fatsos must be found and saved."

In The Book there was a whole eating program that we served in the Day One Diner.

I went among you from house to house, selling bread and recipes, he said on another show. He told a dramatic story about braving the winter darkness to bring a message of health and holiness. It was not until much later that I realized that he was talking about the two days when he and I had headed out of Wompatuck to Egypt and Greenbush and Marshfield with thirty loaves of Ezekiel bread to knock on doors. He had said, *Stick with me and try to look a little wounded.*

Viewing figures went up when people began to write to Millroy saying that they were losing weight. For the first time in their lives they felt well and happy. They had spirit. They even experienced a sense of holiness.

Testimonials, Millroy said. He read letters on the show about people finding health and strength through God's food. He showed snapshots they sent in: Before (black-and-white, sulky, shadows, old clothes) and After (bright colors, smiling, sunny, stylish).

"They don't know what to make of it," he said. "*The Day One Program* is unclassifiable. That's the secret of our success."

It was peculiar, he said.

To me it was all Millroy the Magician, the real Millroy, the man I knew, everything except his doubts and his bad dreams.

It was food, it was prayer, it was recipes, it was The Book. It was diet and holiness and trips to the rest room. It was sermons on roughage and bowel transit-time. It was mirrors, it was snapshots. Occasionally it was Millroy's puke-o-meter, the stomach pump for dredging food from your guts to examine it for degradation and digestion. It was checks with the emission gauge to monitor corrupt breath. Often it was magic. Whatever, it brought people to the Day One Diner. So when the program became a success, the diner did too. All the people who came to it were eaters. They believed, they came almost every day, they made us feel that we were like little holy folk and priestesses, doing something special by dishing up Day One food.

Around this time, a stranger showed up and said to me, "My name is Orlo Fedewa," and handed me his card. "You've probably never heard of me."

Probably?

"I run a charitable foundation that aids underdeveloped countries."

No tie, hairy hands, a beard and long hair parted in the middle. There were flecks of barley soup clinging to his mustache. He had also eaten a whole order of Ezekiel bread, some honey and a cruse of yogurt.

"I wonder if it would be possible to have a word with Doctor Millroy," he said. "I feel he has the answer."

All I could think was, *Is he calling himself Doctor again?*

"I'll have to ask. Mind taking a seat?"

This man's nervousness made me confident.

Millroy was in the back talking on the telephone, saying, "There is no point in a *Day One Program* for Chicago unless we also open a Day One facility—"

Using sign language, slashing, pointing and mimicking with my mouth, I indicated that a man outside wanted to see him. Meanwhile, Orlo Fedewa had crept up behind me and was waving at Millroy himself.

Millroy beckoned him in, and I went out and bussed the lunch tables.

Pretty soon Orlo Fedewa hurried past me so fast I thought Millroy had socked him in the jaw.

"He wanted me to preach Day One overseas," Millroy said. "Supposedly it would be a benefit to have overseas people in the program."

He stared in the direction the stranger had gone, and I had no idea what all this meant until the next Day One show.

The Stars and Stripes hung on a flagpole behind Millroy.

I have seen overseas, he said. *Overseas is small and dirty. Never mind where overseas, because overseas is just one place. It is outside America.*

How he got that flag flying in the studio was magic.

Overseas people eat bad food, gorge themselves on fat and die young. Overseas people squat in hideous cold toilets or in the elements and hurry their bowels, their eyes popping. Overseas kitchens are black with soot. Overseas people hardly wash. They have flat feet, corrupt breath, rotten flesh, no muscle tonus. They cook, I grant you that, but they cook swill—innards, blood, pigmeat, thick sauces, strangled animals, beasts that died of old age they stuff into their mouths.

Was it my imagination or did he flash little picture bursts on the screen of starving Africans, meat-chewing mountain men, beer-guzzling Germans and greasy little people from Europe eating dead birds?

I have seen their narrow streets and chipped sinks. I will never go overseas again. I will never have to. Overseas is overpriced, overwhelming, over there. It is riddled with opportunistic germs. Overseas is a health risk. I have been there for you.

The flag was still flying and a low, howling chorus of "America the Beautiful" could be heard behind Millroy's voice.

God has placed his hand upon America, he said. *This is the Promised Land. It will happen here.*

The show was not much more than this message about overseas, and yet it was one of the most popular editions of *Day One*. Millroy was loved for it. He was asked to repeat the message of *Overseas is small and dirty.* He seemed surprised that something so obvious made him popular. He gladly said it again, and he was not just saying it to Orlo Fedewa but to all of America.

Overseas people cannot change what they eat or think or how they live, he said. *America is receptive to my message. Yes, there is a Second Coming. It is you, reborn with health and strength, coming back to live for another century!*

After that, the phone began to ring and Millroy was discussing syndication, rebroadcasts, and branches of the Day One Diner in Chicago, New York, Philadelphia, Denver, St. Louis.

Often I heard his voice from the back office saying, *I can make America regular once again.*

26 I was walking down Boylston Street in a drizzling rain with some fish in a bag and saw Vera Turtle coming toward me. Before I could hide in a doorway she recognized my face and made a move as though to snatch me, just for fun.

"Hey, Jilly," she said and looked me up and down.

It was strange to hear a name that did not seem like mine anymore.

She wore a skirt and a plastic raincoat and looked the way people always did when I saw them away from where they belonged—unreal.

The bag of fish was flopping against my leg as I fidgeted.

"Bet you got somethun good in that bag."

I told her fish.

"So you're livun around here, Jilly?"

The way she repeated my name made it seem as though she were testing me.

"Sort of. How's Dada?"

"He got laid off at the fillun station. He does supermarket security. He's on nights. I'm up here picking up his chest X rays"—she lifted the official yellow envelope stamped MASS GENERAL—"otherwise he can't get his insurance. How about a hot dog?"

"I don't eat hot dogs."

Just my saying this surprised her so much that she looked stunned, and her face seemed to open and shut, as though she could not think of another word to say.

"Cup of coffee?" she said at last.

"Makes you hyper."

"Coke?"

"Junk drink."

"Cheese danish?" She was smiling.

"It's not mentioned in The Book."

"Anythun?"

"I'm not hungry, Vera."

I was thinking that she also appeared unreal because I had begun to think of this part of Boston as my world.

"And I'm pretty busy," I said.

"I wish I was," she said. "Your Dada's a wreck."

The way she was so truthful about her regrets and how nothing had changed for her or Dada made me sad. She set off, walking toward the bus station to get back to the Cape, and as soon as she turned the corner I had the feeling that I was safe in my own world again.

When I got back to the Day One Diner carrying the fish, a man came through the door with me. He had rain on his face, pasty skin, plastic lips, socks falling down around his white anklebones, wet boiled eyes, Adam's apple going like a yo-yo. He tripped over someone's foot but did not care because he was calling out in a loud voice to Millroy, who was behind the counter hauling loaves out of the oven.

"You're out of your mind!"

He sounded frightened. His arms were stiff at his sides and his fists were pale. It was a small diner, so this sudden interruption had everyone listening.

Millroy just smiled. Some of the students who had been eating went over to the man and clamped their hands on him, until Millroy made a gesture meaning don't hurt him.

"Leave me alone," the man said, whimpering a little and shuffling backward, but when he reached the door he screamed again, louder and less frightened, "He's out of his mind!"

Then his face was at the window, his twisted lips, shouting against the glass like a big fish gasping in a fishbowl.

"We're reaching a very wide public," was all Millroy said, and the students and the rest of the customers resumed eating. When he saw me with the bag of fish, he said, "Anything wrong?"

I said no, but I was thinking about Vera Turtle and Dada—how they were strangers now, how I was a stranger to them.

Two days later, another man came in fast, panting as he looked around, and yelled to Millroy, "So you know more than God? You think you're better than Jesus?"

He left in a hurry when Millroy made a move toward him. Millroy was fast, he was strong, his eyes burned, he had magic, he looked like a wizard.

Always check out their shoes and the way they walk, Millroy said. *Mental cases usually neglect their shoes, and they tend to stumble. Always examine their fingernails.*

"He's a cynical manipulator and a control freak," a man said another day, but he had been eating at the counter. He stood up and spilled a glass of fruit juice to get attention. "This is a distortion of the Bible—belittling the Scriptures with just another foolish diet. Jews are backing him in it to destroy Christianity—you bet they are."

"That's a spazz," Berry said when he spotted bitten nails or worn-out shoes. He and Willie wanted to chase these people away, but Millroy said it was enough to single them out, and that the law was on our side. Or, "He's angry. He sells antacid and he knows I'm putting him out of business."

Millroy was right about the shoes. *Screamers wear strange things on their feet.* Sometimes you could tell people were unstable from the way their laces were knotted. They used string. Their footgear looked trampled. They walked uncoordinated, dragging one foot or else off-balance, glancing back, with loose eyes and rigid fingers, as though someone might be following them.

"You have monstrous faults," a man with wild hair screamed at Millroy, and then began to sob. Like Floyd Fewox, he carried a cat. The cat looked unconcerned. A student helped him out the door. "A Harvard man," Millroy said. "An ardent bed wetter. Or else a retailer of slimming aids."

The hair was as important as the shoes and the walk—not enough hair, or too much, or the careful way it was combed, as though by another person, or else piled up or stuck down, sometimes looking slept on, sometimes transplanted. And there was Smoker's Hair, dry and dead before its time, not enough blood reaching the follicles.

Those were the people who hated Millroy, but the ones who said they were devoted to him could sound just as crazy.

"This man is my angel," a man said. He had all the clues—collapsed shoes, off-balance walk, sideways hair. "This man saved my life."

Food in his mouth, dirty fingernails, boiled eyes—they were obvious. But others were invisible—being quiet, neatly dressed, maybe a little too attentive and breathing in gasps. You did not know anything until they spoke up, and then you knew everything.

"Take me," a woman said to Millroy. She was clean but heavy, and she sighed when she took a breath. "Help me. I belong to you."

Then she was crying softly in a grieving way and no one wanted to look at her.

"You'll see this customer to the door, Rusty?"

Millroy was busy on the phone saying, "You want an awful lot for your dime, and you have Smoker's Voice . . ." He vanished as I guided the weeping woman out, trying not to touch her.

After all this, a man named Ed Veazie—he passed out his printed card—paid for his meal one morning (barley cereal, mint loaf, melon balls), then asked to see Millroy. He was out of breath from eating too fast (that was also a sign: "Stress or psychic instability, extreme impatience, watch out," Millroy said, "You rarely find a mental case with good digestion''). But this customer had a gentle smile, said please and thank you, looked grateful, and promised not to take up too much of Doctor Millroy's time. He carried a briefcase and an umbrella. Wackos never had umbrellas, Millroy said, which was why you could always spot them in a rainstorm. They were wet and would end up shouting at you.

Still, I hesitated until Millroy passed the cash register. The man muttered, *Could I have a quiet word? There is something I would very much like to verbalize.*

Millroy rolled his eyes at me on the word ''verbalize'' and then invited Ed Veazie into the back. He knew the man was not violent—he could see straight through someone's eyes into their brain, their heart, and he knew the contents of their stomach bag.

Some minutes passed, Millroy and the man inside his office. Then, ''I want you to hear something,'' Millroy called out. He was speaking a little shriller than usual, as though not listening to himself. He was motioning to the Sons and Daughters. ''Come on in, people. You too, Rusty.''

Ed Veazie swelled a little, grew fatter in the face, seemed optimistic and pleased with himself, but Millroy was making soft, snoring noises. I could tell by the sound of his breathing that he was impatient, a little angry, that he was listening hard. ''Go on, Ed,'' he said.

His friendliness worried me because in the past week we'd had so many crazos coming in, and Millroy was cautious around strange adults, particularly large, piggy-faced men like this one. ''Tell them what you just told me.''

Ed Veazie's eyes moved back and forth very quickly, but his head stayed motionless. ''Who are they?''

The way he said it made me feel strange, as though I did not belong here. That thought had never occurred to me, but this man was looking at us all with a sour, doubting expression, and the way he said *Who are they?* made me realize how different we were—young, inexperienced, out of place; maybe he was thinking what other people said: *Why aren't they in school?*

''These are my Sons and Daughters,'' Millroy said.

''Big family.'' But Ed Veazie was not impressed.

''I sometimes think that the children of America are my family.'' Millroy's eyes blazed at Veazie, as though daring him to laugh at this.

''Okay, kids,'' the man said.

Millroy breathed in and out, snorting through his nose, gargling air in his mouth.

"I was talking to Doctor Millroy here about the marketing potential of the diet."

"Diet" was a word Millroy hated even more than "kids." He said "diet" was misleading and made you think only of weight loss, not of health. "Food program" was the expression he preferred. He blinked, still breathing hard.

"You're selling one big package that includes God, food, weight control and regularity." Veazie began to smile in a horrible, hungry way. "I mean, who else has wrapped up Christianity and slimming? This is a dynamite product—laxatives, Scriptures and weight control. We're talking salvation in all senses. All it needs is to be packaged right and sold."

He hesitated, wondering whether we understood what he was saying.

"Television is a huge selling tool. I was telling Doctor Millroy that concepting this was a stroke of brilliance. He's combined *The Hour of Power* with *Body Shaping*. But a concept is only the beginning. Marketing will bring it to fruition."

"Tell them what your idea of fruition is, Ed."

Hesitating slightly, Veazie laughed and said, "Money."

Saying the word "money" he sounded hungry and his mouth filled with spit. He swallowed and went on. "You could pretty much name your price. There's a ton of money to be made—I mean, no end to the kind of cash flow you could create with a product like this." He swallowed again as he spoke of money, paused and gulped before he could go on.

"You mentioned merchandising," Millroy said.

"Sure thing. I see tape, I see print, I see air time, I see franchises. Plus there's clothing. You could do a whole complete line of Day One fashions. Can you imagine what a Day One logo shop would gross? We're talking about buying Chinese T-shirts for a buck, printing for twenty cents, and retailing for fourteen ninety-five. Look at the Hard Rock Cafe: all the money's in the merchandising—your T-shirts, your baseball caps, your jackets. Stick a Day One logo on it and sell it."

The smilelike shape on Millroy's mouth was an expression of pain, and because he was motionless he looked like a statue of a man who'd caught his finger in a door or else had a sudden freezing pain from a jolt of electricity.

"But you need money"—Veazie gulped again—"and to raise capital on the strength of an idea, you've got to have credibility and forward planning. I'm not saying you're not bankable, but when was the last time you leveraged a buyout on a loan for three million dollars? I've been there, and I can tell you we need to craft a proposal, design a brochure and pitch some banks for the money."

He swallowed more spit, nodded at the Sons and Daughters, smiled, swallowed again. "That's where I come in," he said.

Turning to smile at Millroy, he saw that Millroy was launching himself out of his chair, and as he started to rise, Millroy snatched the man's coat, dragged him the rest of the way, and tipped him, and marched him backward toward the office door, with his nose against Veazie's face and snorting through it. "You are nothing but a rotten thief," Millroy said, speaking so hurriedly that spit flew into Veazie's face. "How dare you talk that way in here? Did you hear him, Daughter?"

"He is a thief," Stacy said, pronouncing it *feef.*

"She sees right through you," Millroy said. "You are out of order."

I had never seen Millroy touch another person in anger, not even Floyd Fewox, whom he hated. It had been rats out of Floyd's mouth, and snakes out of his ears, a kind of cruel magic. He held Veazie's lapels so tightly, bunching them as he yanked him along, that the man was strangling, and Millroy was not hitting him, but he was steering him so hard, tramping him backward, that if Veazie had resisted he would have been choked, or worse.

Nearer the door, Millroy jerked him off the floor and, bumping tables, pushed him out of the Day One Diner, roaring, "You're a pickpocket!"

The people eating in the diner sat with their faces over their plates looking anxious and interested—kind of thrilled at the commotion, but frightened too, because Millroy was bristling, and would he hurt them?

Millroy's head was sweating, his face reddish, his muscles tight, and he breathed in gasps, his eyes shining with anger. "I should have used magic on him," he said, turning to us. "He was full of vermin. I could have rendered him legally blind for two or three days. I could have taken away his voice by just pinching his windpipe in the right place. I could have given him an itch, stung him, made him cry." With his hand clapped over his head like a cap, he seemed regretful. "Only I can't do those things when I'm upset."

After his anger drained away—it took almost until nighttime—Millroy seemed smaller but more complicated, and none of us knew what to say.

He had startled us, though, and I could see that the Sons and Daughters liked Millroy even more, seeing his strength. We had known even before he told Veazie that *The Day One Program* was not a product to sell; yet we were impressed by the way he had handled the man. We had never seen him so forceful. It was not scary—far from it, we felt safer than before, seeing Millroy take a big man and bounce him out.

The Sons and Daughters were more respectful, and after this incident they took me aside and asked me (and I asked Millroy), could they move in: leave home and live with us in the rooms at the back of the diner?

His mustache flattened and negative noises came out of it. There was not enough room, he said, and they did not have a good reason yet for leaving home. I understood him to mean that he did not want to be admired for his strength; he wanted simply to be listened to for his revelations. "I am a messenger," he said. "It should not matter if I was a fifteen-year-old girl with my thumb in my mouth."

Hearing this I slipped it out.

"It's the message that matters."

He was not proud of disposing of Ed Veazie. Why had the man come in the first place? "They're getting the wrong message," he said.

He was also thinking of the shouters—*Monstrous faults!* and *Cynical manipulator!* and *He's out of his mind!* "I must be doing something wrong."

That same week another man ate in the diner and talked in a praising way with Millroy about the Day One honeycake, then said, "But admit that you're intentionally satirizing Christian Science, aren't you? You could call it The Church of Christ the Cook."

Reaching into the man's startled face, Millroy seemed to be trying to remove a rat from his mouth, but if so he failed, and in frustration spun him around and tipped him into the street so hard—Millroy bellowing—that the man stumbled and went down on one knee, his face going green.

That night, locking up after the Sons and Daughters had gone, I could hear Millroy sighing, each sigh like many words made into one strung-together sound.

"Are you sure you haven't got something on your mind?" he asked at last. "Is it the way I handled that man and the thief, Ed Veazie?"

The answer was no, I trusted him for his strength; but he asked me again, and so I decided to tell him. "I bumped into Vera Turtle two weeks ago."

Millroy lapsed into silence, as though he were meeting Vera in his mind and thinking as he chose his next question.

"Coming back from the fish market," I said to be helpful, so that he could picture it better.

"Just like that. A face from the past. Did she seem concerned about you?"

"No, but she was wicked friendly. She offered me a hot dog."

"Poor Vera Turtle." He seemed to see her standing lopsided in the air.

"Dada's a security officer now. He works nights."

"And how do you feel about all this, angel?"

"I'm good."

"It propelled your mind into the past," he said. "Into your former life."

I nodded, afraid to speak. I thought I might cry if I opened my mouth. Dada, Gaga and Vera were small, feeble and faraway, and we had magic.

When I was sure I would not cry I said, "She thought she was seeing me, but she was seeing someone else. It was like Mister Veazie saying, 'Who are they?' He didn't understand."

"Mister Veazie," Millroy said, as though naming a monster.

"I'm different now."

"You could go back if you wanted, muffin, at any time."

"No, I know what it's like there."

"What about here?"

"I don't know. That's why it's good."

"How good?"

"Wicked good."

"Life with me could get hard, you know. Even now it's no picnic. All these crazy people."

He had been pushing a sheet of paper around the table. He turned it over, a mass of writing in green ink, all shapes of words, large and small.

"I get hate mail. This is a hate letter. Want to hear it?"

He wet his finger and skidded the letter closer.

" 'You're a despicable human being, spouting garbage on the air-waves. You have no right to use the name of Jesus to sell the gullible public on your crazy theories. You think you're wise, but you're an utter fool, but that's all right because great harm will come to you. You'll get cancer and die a horrible death, and after that death, eternal hellfire.' "

Millroy crumpled the letter and threw it into the tin wastebasket, where it hit like something solid.

"There are more like that."

He looked neither fearful nor bold but expressionless, as though he had expected this and was immovable.

"I'm staying," I said.

City noises: a police siren, traffic, laughter, a car driving over a pot-hole, its rims bumping, its springs saying *ouch,* someone's TV on too loud, the sputter of the big streetlamp, the wind like arms hugging and shaking the diner, a plane overhead. Millroy's eyes were blazing and he was biting his mustache and making me feel naked.

"You're everything to me," he said in a shuddering voice, and I got worried all over again.

He must have been thinking about this, because all night I heard him sighing down the scale and thrashing on the shelf of his bunk across the room. In the morning, when the Sons and Daughters arrived (they came at six or even earlier these days, and it was dark, this being February), he said, "You could leave at any time, you know."

Willie Webb said, "Sure I could, Big Guy," in a jaunty way, while the others shrugged, as though they did not want to think about it now.

We were putting out breakfast for ourselves before setting up for the morning opening. The ovens had been turned on at five and were fra-grant with baking bread, and awaiting us on the countertops were vege-tables to be chopped, fish to be gutted, and lamb to be cut, skewered or seethed. The pottage smelled of earth and bubbled on the stove, making the sound of a small outboard on a skiff. Kayla and Stacy were drizzling honey on bread slices.

"I'm not stopping you," Millroy said, presiding over the table from his chair in the middle.

In the glary light of the diner, darkness outside, we sat in silence chewing breakfast and passing melons, honey, Ezekiel bread, almonds, pistachios, figs, apricots, barley porridge, grapes, and some mashed seed pods that Berry was poking with a spoon.

"What's this supposed to be?" he asked.

"Carob—they're nourishing," Millroy said. "Nice and bulky. I'm putting them on the menu. You know, when John the Baptist was in the wilderness eating locusts and wild honey? That's honey locust—not insects but carob, a type of acacia tree. John ate carob. Go on, you do it, too."

Berry tasted it, smiled and said it was sweet.

"You have to do what's right for yourselves," Millroy said.

Now Willie and Stacy and Kayla were tasting the mashed carob on bread.

"Cooking food and getting people to eat it can be the ultimate way of controlling people," Millroy said. "I am aware of that, and because I know the risks of making you dependent I avoid them."

Kayla, licking her fingers, said, "Oh, sure"; and Willie went on chewing bread and measuring honey into little Day One cruses that Millroy had special-ordered. Stacy was smiling at Millroy hungrily, in a moony way. Ever since he'd jerked Ed Veazie to his feet and spun him out of the diner, Stacy had been talking about leaving home and moving into the diner. *I'll sleep on the floor,* she said. *I don't care.*

"It's funny, really," Millroy was saying.

He covered a slice of bread with "cheese of kine," scooping it from a Day One earthenware jar, and handing the large slice to Stacy, who slipped some of it into her mouth and held the rest of it to her lips as she chewed and looked at Millroy lovingly.

"I'm feeding you. I'm responsible for everything inside you. An awful lot of people use cooking and food that way," Millroy said. "Eat and you are mine, I am creating you with my food. Don't laugh, eating is a serious matter. Your folks use that reasoning on you all the time."

Listening to him, we had begun to eat and were all chewing and swallowing as though agreeing, *munch-munch, yes-yes.*

"I won't take advantage of you that way, but I need you to see the benefits of Day One. I don't want blind obedience."

Berry had an insolent and lazy way of eating, keeping his mouth open and making noise, while the rest of us chewed with our lips together, breathing through our noses. The thick bread slices dripped with slow-moving honey, and the fruit was so sweet it seemed to be filled with syrup and pulp.

"Irresponsible people might ask you what I am doing. You can tell them that I am not controlling you." He fixed his eyes on us. "What am I not doing?"

"Not controlling us," Stacy said, with that same dreamy look of loving Millroy on her face.

"I am not feeding you in that sinister, manipulative way."

"Yeah," Willie said, his mouth full, his cheeks bulging.

The rest of us agreed, and Millroy's saying this reassured us and made us feel even safer.

"Keep it up, Big Guy," Berry said. "You making me hungry."

Millroy had folded his hands and placed his elbows on the table among the baskets, bowls of food, and fruit tumbled all over the white tablecloth. Then the sun came up and shafts of light pierced the mirrors and warmed the room so that it spread the aroma of baking bread.

"We are discreet, sure, we don't like prying eyes, but that's for our safety and our sanity. It's not sneaky. There's no concealment here. You know you can trust me. We have no secrets. Ask Rusty."

When signs showing the Reverend Baby Huber's face went up on the National Guard Armory one street over from Park Square, and big letters advertised COME TO LIFE—FIRST ANNUAL BOSTON PRAYER FAIR, Millroy said, "We have to see this." He closed the diner early and led us all there.

Green-and-white Yankee Division National Guard banners hung from the timber rafters over the "Prayer Fair." There were booths along one wall, and stalls selling certificates, tapes, hats and bumper stickers that said TRY GOD. The booths sold food: hot dogs, burgers, chicken, fried onion rings and Huber's Real Good Fries.

"Smell them?" Millroy asked. He was enjoying this. "Big buckets of hot wings."

A choir onstage was singing as we came in, and when they finished "Goin on a Long Journey Bye and Bye," Huber began to pray out loud, looking up at the rafters and the banners and speaking to Jesus.

Millroy turned to us, the expression on his face saying, *Listen.*

"And Lord," Huber was saying, as though he had just remembered something else to ask for, "if you don't mind another solicitation, vouchsafe these good people to be filled with thankfulness and loving-kindness and do not depreciate their goodly gifts—nay, let them open up and flow freely."

Money, Millroy said, without opening his mouth.

Huber prayed for people to join him on the stage, where they were divided into groups—"teams" he called them—and they cried while Huber encouraged them, crying himself with big splashing tears.

Millroy was biting his mustache to prevent himself from laughing out loud.

"And Lord," Huber said, still remembering things. "We earnestly enjoin you in your goodness . . ." At last some men in long green gowns climbed down from the stage, kicking at their gold-embroidered hems and carrying heavy wooden boxes with belts, buckles and a slot in the middle.

"Release unto my stewards your worldly materiality," Baby Huber finally said. "Breathe deeply and expel these earthly riches, filling the Lord's chests, to make the Devil mad and to gain the wealth of heaven!" People pushed and plunged forward to force dollar bills into the slots of the wooden boxes.

The choir sang "The Devil Is a Liar."

"Give the Lord your material wealth! Make the Devil mad!"

Yet what does he give them in return? came out of Millroy's compressed lips. *And you can see they're hungry.*

"Are you in atonement?" one of the men in gowns said, proffering a box.

"Hear that, Sons and Daughters?" Millroy said. "The soft voice of the serpent."

Then Baby Huber saw Millroy and raged, " 'Woe unto you, scribes and Pharisees, hypocrites! Ye are like unto whited sepulchres, which indeed appear beautiful outward, but are within full of dead men's bones and of all uncleanness.' "

"That's a good Day One text," Millroy said on the way out, leading us past the men in green gowns. "A person who eats willy-nilly is like a whited sepulchre."

Stacy was making a *What's that?* face.

"A pretty coffin," Millroy said.

"Yo. That preacher was screaming at you," Kayla said.

Millroy shrugged. "Impotent rage. He's making himself ridiculous. That is ignorant, passive religion. But hey, Baby Huber came a long way. Eight months ago he was running a trailer park in Buzzards Bay, just a manager, burning weenies on his outdoor grill."

"How do you know that?" Berry asked.

"I had a trailer there myself," Millroy said. "I was hooked up to his facilities."

"So I guess you came a long way, too," Willie said, looking a little sly.

Millroy stopped in the middle of his muscular stride, hovered over Willie and said, "I am on my way back—a return journey. Remember that, Son."

27 Millroy's mention of the trailer at Wompatuck—that it was his own, and furnished, that it was a big Airstream, hooked up and empty—made the Sons and Daughters ask more persistent, blunter questions like, why couldn't they move there and live in it?

"You expect us to go home every night and not eat," Willie said, "but every five minutes someone's trying to make me eat a hamburger or a bunch of ribs."

Millroy nodded, pondering.

"I've been feeling it," he said.

We looked at him.

"*Leaving* energy," he said. "You want to leave home. I've felt that energy binding within you."

The following Sunday after *The Day One Program* we all went in the Ford down the Expressway to Wompatuck to look at the trailer. We had not seen it since moving into the diner. Millroy had just padlocked it and left it, trusting that it would be safe.

As we drove toward it we knew that something was wrong: the door was half-open, the mesh of the screen was poked out, one window was smashed. None of us spoke, but it was a sure thing that the trailer had been broken into and searched—drawers pulled out, the TV stolen, papers on the floor, the paneling broken open as though someone had been looking for a particular thing. My clothes were gone—girl's clothes, no good to me now.

The sight made Millroy silent. He looked sorrowful and guilty, as though he deserved it, and knew who had done it, and could have done nothing to prevent it.

"Yo, Big Guy," Willie said, looking amazed at the mess.

"Been some lootering," Berry said.

"Yes, we are reaching a very wide public," Millroy said, "and this is one of the unfortunate consequences."

"We could clean it up so it's livable again," Willie said, and started to pick through the litter of paper and glass.

"That's physical evidence—don't meddle with it," Millroy said, and when Willie stepped away, he went on, "Take your time, Son."

He was careful of Willie and made a point of correcting him, even being a bit harder on him than on the others because he saw him as the natural leader of the Sons and Daughters, the eldest, who had to be the most responsible and the most fearful of him, Millroy.

The other bad news was that no other trailers in Wompatuck had been broken into. But there was good news when we got back to the diner: a message from Hickle and Hersh that cable-television stations in five cities had decided to carry *The Day One Program*.

That was how it went—bad news, good news, something different every day. I had been used to not much happening in my life, but with Millroy there was always something—up, then down, up again, all new.

"That is the meaning of Day One," he said.

Until Millroy and *I want to eat you,* all I had known was Gaga's and school, and once in a while a visit to Dada's in Mashpee. Before Vera Turtle, Dada had had Cheryl, who played the electric guitar until Dada kicked it and it shorted out. In the days at Gaga's I woke up in the morning with cars passing the house, their engine noises clinging to the trees, the rooster crowing, someone's chain saw, a kid's bicycle bell. Depending on the day of the week, I knew everything that would happen—usually nothing—and the same went for tomorrow and the day after.

Almost always, tomorrow would be like yesterday. School was humiliating, I was shy, the wrong size, and the sight of the yellow school bus made me sick and afraid. After school the thing was to hide from Gaga and not make her mad.

With Millroy every day was Day One, new and full of surprises, and instead of drowsing through these winter afternoons in Boston, I was fully awake. How did it happen that several lives were rotating within me at the same time? I had not known I could manage all this activity, or that I would be so good at it.

We were not puppets. Millroy said, *Be yourself*, and made room for us. I was helping in the diner, dealing with paperwork, serving meals or ringing up checks, cleaning up with the Sons and Daughters, and running errands, like buying fresh fish. When Millroy could not be found, as on rehearsal and taping days when he was at the station, people spoke to me. They knew I was closest to him, though they did not know how close, and neither did I.

This was also why, when the Sons and Daughters wanted to leave home and went to talk to Millroy about using the Airstream in Wompatuck, living in the trailer, sleeping there, eating here, they were glad when he said, "Better see Rusty about that."

They were full of vague-sounding reasons.

"I'm, like, 'Why don't we just move in?' " Stacy said.

Kayla said, "She goes, 'This could be so cool for us.' "

"What it's down to is," Willie said, "we could just use this space so bad."

When their minds were made up they had even more reasons for moving into the trailer. They would show up earlier for work, it would be easier for them to stick to the Day One food program, they could keep the Airstream in good repair, they would not have people nagging them to eat junk food all the time.

I told Millroy this.

Millroy said, "We'll talk about it tonight after we close."

Closing time, the diner in silence, was always a good moment. Everyone was tired but fulfilled, ready to head home but a bit sorry to be separated from one another, and especially from Millroy after being with him the whole day. We usually sat together just after closing time, drinking mint tea for digestion and listening to Millroy talk about his early life, his world travel, his desperate times, his enlightenment when he was trapped in the darkness of his body and God called him "Fatso."

Tonight we sat around, the others delaying because of a snow flurry that swirled outside in the lights and floated down like pillow feathers.

"I am hearing a lot of talk about the trailer, why you want to move in." Millroy looked at the Sons and Daughters. "I don't know whether you're ready for that kind of responsibility. Rusty thinks you might be." I liked him saying that because it helped me stop saying to myself, *I'm no one. I'm Jilly Farina.*

"We'll keep it in good shape," Willie said. "I might even find some more Sons and Daughters to join up with us."

Millroy considered this, holding his nose like a horn with his whole hand.

"We'll do anything you want us to," Berry said.

"It's not a question of taking orders," Millroy said. "I just want you to respond to suggestions."

"We can do that easy," Willie said. His Day One baseball hat was on sideways and he squirmed, seeming impatient.

"You have to speak for yourself, Son."

Millroy sniffed, made a face, and then asked Willie to open his mouth, which he did.

"Wider," Millroy said, slipping the emission-check probe into it. "Now breathe normally. If you gasp or hyperventilate you'll throw off my calibration."

The wind rose and the snowflakes were blown against the front window, tumbling quickly down the flat panes of glass and gathering in a long, white heap on the ledge at the bottom. Beyond, they were lit like huge clusters of fluttering, noiseless moths around each streetlamp.

We watched Willie clamping his teeth on the probe, his eyes bulging, his nostrils flaring as he breathed.

"I'm getting lots of red in my chromoscope," Millroy said, his fingers resting on a small lighted screen. "You've been eating out, Son."

This meant sneaking food that was not Day One.

Willie yanked at the probe and said, "No way. I'm clean."

"Shall we have a better look?"

Willie smiled and said, "Okay, Big Guy, I'm down to that, but how you gonna work it?" because it seemed impossible. But he soon stopped smiling.

As though revealing the existence of a peculiar and possibly dangerous pet, Millroy chuckled softly as he uncoiled his stomach plunger, a snout at one end and a pink bulb at the other, and almost four feet of wobbly rubber snake in between. The worst was the small squares of rubber patches, the sort you find on an old inner tube. Draped in his fingers it had the look of a wounded rubber reptile.

Willie was immediately terrified because he recognized it from the first *Day One Program.* He stamped his feet, saying he was leaving. Then he got angry, and finally he said, ''Why should I let you stick that thing up my nose?''

''To find the truth,'' Millroy said. ''But this is simply a suggestion.'' He dangled the tube in Willie's face. ''I am wondering how responsive you are.''

Tufts of snow had begun to stick against the big glass panes of the front windows, and it was now so late, with so few people around, that the white sidewalk showed only scattered footprints. Snow was in motion in the car headlights, in the streetlamps and across the square, whirling in front of illuminated signs.

''You think I'm afraid of that thing?'' Willie said.

Millroy said nothing, but when he cradled Willie's head and worked the tube up his nose and plunged, the boy began to cry. He sounded pitiful, and his crying told you how young he was. He was shocked, too, and he clutched at his Day One T-shirt.

I watched—Millroy had taught me the usefulness of the stomach plunger—but the others covered their faces or looked away.

A boiling sound came from Willie, thick bubbles percolating in his throat as he gagged. All this time the snow had been falling beautifully through the square, the separate flakes blowing and lifting, making the shifting wind visible.

''Hamburger,'' Millroy said, frowning at the tin basin. Then he shook his head and flung the patched apparatus into the sink.

''I'm no good,'' Willie said, and once again when he cried he seemed much younger and weaker, not tough or funny or angry anymore, but a child who would go on sobbing until he was consoled.

From where he stood at the sink, Millroy said, ''You'll never eat that poison again. You're going to be wholesome. You're going to listen to me. Look at the dead meat you've been putting into your mouth—that's why you're confused, son.''

Willie kept sniffing and sobbing as though he were wounded, and wiped his drippy nose until the back of his hand was gleaming.

"But you're going to be all right now." Millroy knew that from now on Willie would be obedient. "Oh, sure."

There was a sudden knock at the door, and a hurried rattling of the knob, which was even more startling than it would have been at this late hour because of Willie's ordeal—the puking and sobbing.

The knocker was a policeman, with snow on his shoulders and on the visor of his cap. He called out, "Open up!"

"Come right in," Millroy said, unlocking the door.

"What's happening here?"

The policeman wore a large yellow raincoat that flapped and dripped when he unhooked its front. He was breathless from the freezing wind, with red cold splotches on his face, and he growled in disgust when he smelled the tin basin.

"A tummy upset," Millroy said.

"You kids all right?" the policeman asked, ignoring Millroy.

We said we were fine, and even Willie was smiling, although he was very pale.

"You don't look too good," the policeman said to Willie.

Willie said, "He just made me better," meaning Millroy.

Millroy smiled. He had made his stomach plunger vanish.

"Fix you some food, Officer?"

He clapped the lid onto the basin of vomit, and when he slipped it off a bowl of fruit gleamed where the tin basin had been—pomegranates, apples, grapes, melons, plums.

"What is more reassuring or vitalizing to the human spirit than the sight of nourishing food?" Millroy asked. "Go on, take a piece of fruit."

Before the fuddled policeman could react, he uncovered a chafing dish of bubbling pottage over a little flame.

"Think you're so smart," the policeman said. "I could book you for violating the fire ordinance. That there's an open flame."

He meant the chafing dish, where a tin of canned heat flickered.

Millroy picked up the flaming can of Sterno, sipped it and then drank it down.

"Not anymore," he said, gasping after his deep swallow.

The policeman squinted at him.

"What about them knives?"

They were Day One daggers, the sort that Aramaic people used for cutting fruit and meat—pounded, tempered damascene blades with bone handles. Millroy special-ordered them from the same company that made the earthenware bowls, cruses, jars, baskets, woven mats and sandals. The knives had been stacked because it was the end of the day. They had just been washed and polished, and their blades glittered.

"Them are oversized," the policeman said, pointing at them with his black nightstick. "Them are illegal."

Snatching the largest knife, Millroy tilted his head back, poked it down his throat, and then pulled it out and wiped it on his arm.

"Harmless."

Now the policeman was frowning and pinching his own face in frustration.

Millroy palmed a Day One dagger, whimpered, opened his hand and showed the policeman a cucumber.

" 'And the daughter of Zion is left, as a lodge in a garden of cucumbers," Millroy said, snapping the cucumber in half. "Isaiah, one eight."

"This guy should go on TV," the policeman said, for now he was dazzled, and it was as though he had forgotten why he had come into the diner in the first place.

"He is on TV," I said. "He's famous."

The policeman left soon after, wrapping himself in his yellow slicker and stepping into the snow, grumbling the whole time.

Willie's eyes were glazed, not just from having had his stomach pumped, but from attentiveness. He had never seen Millroy's magic up close, and the magic had been done to him. He had changed, he was silent, upright and obedient, and the others had a look of smiling admiration that made them seem small and loving.

"I always feel a little desperate when I rely on magic," Millroy said. "The Lord usually performed miracles unwillingly, as you know."

He was putting away all the paraphernalia he had produced in those few minutes when the policeman had challenged him.

"But there is something hypnotic about magic."

We stood there waiting for him to tell us what to do.

"It makes me tired, though," he said. "After all that, I have to go lie down."

We were still waiting.

"You can move into the trailer if you keep it clean and look after it," he said. "Willie's in charge."

Willie stood with shining eyes, straight and silent as a soldier, and grinding his teeth as though he were chewing a mouthful of walnuts.

"What about Rusty?" Kayla said. "He coming?"

"That's up to him," Millroy said.

I shook my head and said, "I'm staying here."

The following week Millroy appointed a clean-up crew for the Airstream, and soon after the Sons and Daughters moved to the trailer park at Wompatuck.

More youngsters joined us, some moving in at Wompatuck and some still living at home, semidetached from their parents, as Millroy put it: Daughters Bervia, Shonelle, Tomarra, Jaleen, LaRayne and Peaches, and Sons Dedrick, T. Van, Daylon, Troy, Tuppy and Ike.

"Feel it?" Millroy had said, clenching his fists and gritting his teeth.

They watched him with admiring eyes.

"It's more *leaving* energy," he said. "You're gathering yourselves with a kind of binding intensity to thrust yourselves away from home."

And they said yes, it was what they wanted. Most of them had dropped out of school or were unemployed, and one or two mentioned that they were sort of homeless.

"You're part of the program now," Millroy said, and told them he was counting on them. "Program" always meant Day One—the food, the prohibitions, the simple uniform, the exercises. No smoking, no drugs, no weapons.

There were some applicants whom he rejected. Some were too old, some smelled wrong—an odor of corruption, he said—and others were college students who would not commit themselves wholeheartedly to the program, or who were too influenced by their parents or teachers. The ones he chose were especially glad, and they always said how they had seen him on TV, and many remembered how he had been on the famous show *Paradise Park*.

Most afternoons Millroy shut the diner for an hour and led the sixteen Sons and Daughters through Park Square and the Lincoln-Freeing-the-Slave Statue, to Boston Common, where he supervised us in exercises, all of us doing burpees, push-ups and jumping jacks on the frozen ground while people walked by. We imagined them saying, *They must be Millroy's people,* and we were proud.

"This too is a form of prayer," Millroy said, and performed the exercises with us, but he did one-arm push-ups, or "uprights," making himself vertical, then raising and lowering himself by his arms.

Tuppy said that Ike was an athlete, but Millroy was not impressed. He did not like sports because most of them were gladiatorial, and what did it matter how much exercise you got or what team you were on if you did not eat right? "But don't say 'af-leet,' " he said.

By now he had a system for introducing newcomers to Day One. He had them look in full-length mirrors, he took photographs of them and urged them to study the pictures, especially the rear view, the one they never saw that everyone else saw, the lasting impression that bystanders had of them.

"I am not deprogramming you. I am not disfellowshipping you. None of that manipulation is necessary for young Americans who have not lost their innocence and essential health."

They called him Big Guy, something they learned from Willie Webb, and they often asked him questions. "Don't say 'ax' him," Millroy said.

One day Dedrick said, "I can't do the diner tomorrow. It's my ma's birthday. I got to be home."

"This is your home," Millroy said. "I am not a day-care provider."

"What about Rodessa's birthday party?"

"Every day is a birthday here at Day One," Millroy said. "That is another meaning of Day One."

"My ma be real mad."

"Don't think of her as your mother. Think of her as a woman whose house you live in at the moment."

Dedrick fiddled with his baseball cap because he had not expected Millroy to say this, and he had no reply.

"What will you eat if you go to this party?"

"There's usually tons of food."

"Day One food?"

"Ham, chicken, stuff like that. Salad. Cold cuts."

"Of course you can go," Millroy said. I knew that smile. It was not a smile but a mask, defying the person looking at him to understand what lay beneath it. "But if you do, don't come back. Ever."

"If I don't go to this party, I'll have a wicked time going home again."

"It's your choice," Millroy said. "I won't influence you, Son."

Willie said in a complaining whisper to me, "He's sweating Dedrick."

"I heard that," Millroy said two rooms away, his voice knifing through the walls.

Dedrick suffered, but he stayed that night and the next day at the Day One Diner. He said it was the end for him, his ma would be so mad. Millroy said no, it was the beginning, and because Dedrick could not go home he gave him permission to move into the trailer at Wompatuck.

"You going to start catching my face on them milk cartons. 'Have You Seen This Child?' "

Millroy thought this was very funny. "You'll outlive them all," he said. "Two hundred years!"

"How'm I supposed to do that?"

"Aim at releasing two pounds of waste every morning," Millroy said.

He looked up and realized that the rest of us had overheard him: we were watching from the kitchen, from the diner, where we were baking, sweeping, washing windows, prepping the diner for the breakfast rush.

"After that you're saved."

28 "Better see Rusty about that," Millroy had said to the Day One Sons and Daughters when they wanted to talk about moving into the the trailer at Wompatuck. And I arranged it. I listened, I passed it on, and I felt useful. I was someone again.

"Rusty will fill you in," he told customers when they asked for Day One information. By now we had pamphlets: *Food for Thought, The Day One Program Fact Sheet*. Millroy had not written them; he did not have the time, he said. They had been compiled by volunteers at the TV station. Millroy did talk about dictating a major book to me called *This Is My Body*—about his life, and how he had become a messenger.

Day One life these days was full of volunteers, many of whom were plain, desperate, pleading women with big, agitated, misshapen bodies who came to him and tried to introduce themselves. Millroy clutched his Day One apron and said, "Have you met Rusty?" and they were flummoxed.

"It's some foofy designer. Wants to give us new decor for nothing," he said one day. He dropped the phone. "Claims I changed his life."

He began to hate answering the phone. "You get it, buddy."

Later, on the days when men in suits showed up unannounced and said they wanted to talk about merchandising or franchises or endorsements—T-shirts, jars of sauce, diners in other cities, Millroy's face on food products ("Look at Paul Newman")—his answer was, "See Rusty."

"We need his participation in an infomercial," one man said to me. Another said, "We want Doctor Millroy to consider an advertorial."

Millroy did not say no. He said, "I hate those words."

I had no special talent for dealing with these strangers, but Millroy refused to see them himself, so after a while, doing it for him, I developed a knack for negotiation, the art and science, Millroy called it, of being stubborn and looking patient.

"You're learning," he said.

Was he making me do this on purpose?

"It's easy to be stubborn if you're not hungry," he said. "If you're strong. If you're regular."

As a result of *Better see Rusty,* I was more important than I wanted to be, and there were revelations. Everything that went on in the Day One Diner was revealed to me, even things that Millroy himself did not know, because many of the people I saw did not get nearer to Millroy's office than table 3. Most of them he did not meet, never spoke to, never wanted to see—the T-shirt people, the food sellers, the media lawyers, the TV station executives, the syndicators, the agents. "Creepers," he called them, fish without scales or fins, snakes, lizards, and either they chewed a cud and were not cloven-footed, or the other way round—and in any case prohibited. *Keep them away,* he said. *They are unclean.*

"Tell them I can't be bought," he said.

I told them, but they did not believe me. Millroy said this was insulting, and they made him so angry he stayed in his office, refusing to come out. "This is not me at all," he protested. "I like people. Isn't that the whole point of being a messenger?"

But he was afraid of what he might do if these people angered him more—possibly a rerun of Ed Veazie, whom he had flung bodily into Park Square, frightening the pigeons.

"Yet some of these folks frankly worry me."

That was like a prophecy because the very next day the Reverend Baby Huber entered the diner looking fat in a tight green velvet sweat suit, with two of his stewards—they still wore green gowns—and his son, Todd, in a leather bomber jacket. I had not seen Todd since Buzzards Bay. He was fatter, and had a short haircut that exposed pale folds on his fleshy scalp. He was a smaller version of his father, with his father's huge head, short stubby arms and that same fat-person's knee-knocking walk.

"He has breasts," Millroy said to us in the kitchen as he watched Huber walking over to LaRayne. "His waist is around his armpits, his thighs chafe audibly as he walks, his bum won't quit, and he think he's saved?"

Stacy, the new Daughter Jaleen, the new Sons Tuppy and Troy, and I were listening, peering over the kitchen counter into the diner.

"Table for four," Huber was saying to LaRayne.

"Got no snap in his muscles," Millroy said. "No tonus anywhere. And his colon's putting out pouches."

LaRayne welcomed the group and said it was open seating.

"Better back her up, Rusty," Millroy said, seeing Huber look around with a doubting face.

"There's your friend, Todd," Huber said when I appeared.

Reverend Huber wore a gloating smile of indigestion as he approached me, and I knew he was trying to think of something sarcastic to say to me. As he came close, his eyes hardened, went mean and lost their light. "I can never remember whether your name is Gary or Mary," he said.

"It's Alex," I said. Did he know that I was Jilly Farina from Marstons Mills? "But you can call me Rusty."

"I was very pleased to see you and the others at our Prayer Fair at the Armory. But it was so sad when you didn't come forward."

"We were cooking that night," I said.

Just behind him, Todd said, "I saw this guy on TV. I'm, like, hey, 'It's the bald guy from the Airstream, Alex's dad.' "

"That sapsucker's sure not his dad," Huber said, chuckling and still gloating and flexing his chubby fingers.

His tight tracksuit clung to his odd-shaped body, giving him the look of a stuffed toy and making him seem fatter. His body was revealed in swags and bags and bulges of fat lumped all over him, swelling on his hips and clapped on his thighs, and even the back of his neck had a chunk of pork on it.

The assertiveness of fat, Millroy would have called it, *using fat as armor and making a blunt statement with your body.*

"Where is he anyway?" Huber said, after he sat down. The stewards plucked at their gowns and sat, too. Todd was still staring at me. "I remember when he ran that kids' show in the morning—the big scandal. They told him to take a hike because it was so gross. All that toilet talk."

"Gross, huh, like 'Wanna see the train crash?' Or like your big mashed-potato factory?"

Wanna see the train crash? Todd had said to me at Pilgrim Pines as he opened his mouth wide and showed me all his half-chewed hamburger. *Look at my mashed-potato factory* was him pretending to wind a crank on his cheek as he squeezed a whole mouthful of mashed potatoes through his teeth onto his plate.

One of Huber's stewards lit a cigarette, and almost at once another customer said, "Hey!"

"I'm going to have to ask you not to smoke in here," LaRayne said, repeating the formula we had taught her. "Will you please put that out for me?"

The man stubbed it out in order to look defiant and tough.

Normally the diner was quiet, people talking softly, no music—and yet the mingled aromas, Millroy said, were like music in the air. Huber and his group seemed to bring commotion into the room. Though it was one of his rehearsal days, Millroy sensed this and, wanting to quiet the place, came over to the table to welcome them.

"We're hungry from all our fasting and praying," Huber said. "Too bad you didn't come forward and declare yourself for God."

Millroy said, "One of the obvious benefits of being omniscient is that you don't need people to inform you of anything."

"Didn't I tell you he lacked humility?" Huber said.

"I was speaking of God," Millroy said, "or, as I think of him, Good."

"How about some good food," Huber said impatiently, and began selecting on his fingers. "I'll have a large fries, a vanilla shake and a cheeseburger with a white coffee. Todd?"

Before Todd could answer, Millroy said, "You'd better see a menu," and he took them from LaRayne and handed them around.

"Fart food," Huber said, punching the menu.

"Day One food," Millroy said, smiling.

"I want a burger. And a cup of coffee."

"We can't help you then."

"Chicken sandwich," a steward said.

"We don't eat dead hens," Millroy said.

"I smell meat," the man replied.

"Lamb," Millroy said. "But I am waiting for guidance on it."

"Jesus ate meat," Huber said, looking mean. " 'A certain Pharisee besought him to dine with him, and he went in and sat down to meat.' Luke eleven."

"That's a mistranslation," Millroy said. "Throughout The Book, 'meat' is interchangeable with 'food' or 'dinner.' There is no evidence in The Book that Jesus ever ate flesh. The Lord was Day One."

"I just want a snack," the other steward said. "A fishwich."

"We serve no such thing," Millroy said, his smile pasted flat on his face.

"You got anything like a Slurpee?" Todd asked.

"Sorry."

"Ring-Dings? Yoo-Hoos? Moon Pies?"

Millroy said, "Perhaps you recognize some of the items on our menu. Jacob Pottage. Daniel Lentils. Ezekiel Bread."

"It's a mockery," Huber said.

"Some people might think that using a prayer meeting as a way of taking people's money is a mockery."

"Even the Catholic Church in Boston has denounced you," Huber said. "The Cardinal came out against you."

"Creative differences," Millroy said. "The Cardinal does not realize that eating right is a form of worship. So is exercise. So is being clean, healthful"—he winked—"and bowel transit-time."

"I remember you," Huber said.

Millroy went on smiling his flat smile.

"I remember you from way back," Huber said. "See, I've still got the trailer park. You've had visitors—I'm not saying who, but they weren't happy. They didn't know that you'd moved on, but I knew where you were hiding."

"A man who owns a successful restaurant and is on television once a week is not hiding, my friend," Millroy said, looking around.

This shut Huber up, which was odd, because Millroy was still uncertain, and when had he ever seemed awkward?

"You wangled yourself a slot on TV," Huber said, "and you're perverting the word of God. You're not making the Devil mad!"

"This food restored my powers and gave me life," Millroy said. "It might do the same for you."

"Just give us some burgers," Huber said. "What we asked for."

"You insist." Millroy's eyes went black and his smile was ferocious. He reached to the counter and picked up a basket, which he held chest high in both hands and whimpered over for a moment. Then he spun it and, with a sob, removed a hamburger bun and plucked off its top to show a bleeding piece of meat with sticky hair and broken teeth.

"Road kill," Millroy said. "You asked for it!"

There was more in the basket; Millroy's hand was large and alive with a knot of black snakes tangled in his fingers. He turned the snakes into knives and stabbed them into the table.

Huber stood up and held his buttocks in fear as Millroy produced first a weasel, then a piglet with a suffering face and mottled skin.

"Swine flesh," Millroy said, opening his hand and showing Todd a quivering fistful of wet booger gobs. "Slurpee!"

The stewards had risen, gathering their gowns and sheltering Todd, who was hiccuping in terror, as they began to lead him away.

Taking Huber by the ears, Millroy lifted him until he was level with his eyes, then pulled a black, dripping rat from his mouth as Huber drooled. "Unclean," Millroy said, and released him.

We watched them leave. They did not look back. There was a vibration of approval in the diner. Millroy was exhausted; he went straight to bed and the program rehearsal was canceled. But we had all seen his magic, and the new Sons and Daughters were so thrilled they hung around after work hoping that he would wake up so that they could talk to him.

He did not wake up, so they talked to me instead.

"I goes, 'He's not going to pull out another one,' " Troy said.

"And he's, like, 'Here's another rat for you, dude,' " Shonelle said.

"Big Guy is awesome. I'm, like, 'Go for it,' " Berry said.

Daylon said, "What it's down to is, this man is so righteous he can diss them all."

"I was, like, so scared," LaRayne said, "and then I'm, 'Check it out!' "

"He find a rat upside the guy's fat head," Willie said, "I almost dropped a log."

This went on for a while.

"What he did then was nothing," I said at last. "I saw Millroy pull wicked big rats out of a guy's ears, nose and mouth—all at once, practically. His name was Floyd Fewox. It was a psychic duel. Guess who won?"

"He outstanding," Dedrick said. "He special."

Bervia said, "I was in shock."

"He's the Boss of Diss," Willie Webb said.

Millroy did not wake up until after dawn the following morning. He was quiet. He stroked his mustache and ran his fingertips across his head, the tapered fingers of a hypnotist. "I was a little sketchy yesterday," he said.

There were other people—outsiders, noneaters—who worried Millroy and made him hide. They saw me instead. They wanted to reveal schemes for making him famous, for making themselves rich, for turning Day One into a nationwide weight-loss operation. They were always in a hurry. *Can we meet with your lawyer?* But we had no lawyer. *Can we meet your people?* There was only me. They asked, *Who are you?*

Jilly Farina from Marstons Mills. "You can call me Rusty."

They said, "We'd like an opportunity to make a presentation, Rusty," and explained what they had in mind: a weight-loss program on the lines of Weight Watchers or Optifast or Nutri-System, but with huge tax benefits.

Millroy said, "Tell them not to bother," and hid.

"We'd like to take the doctor out to lunch," one said.

"That's like offering to take Jesus to church," Millroy said when I told him.

They wanted him to start a cooking school.

"I can do these things myself."

They wanted to do business. Were we registered as a charity? Did we realize that a church was a perfect tax shelter—look at Scientology. There were enormous financial incentives in the religious angle. Had we declared ourselves nonprofit?

Millroy said, "I am an American. I pay my taxes." Before I left the room where he was hiding, he raged again. "I am not selling anything. I am sharing this secret, which is not mine alone, but stated in The Book. It is not for sale; it belongs to everyone. Tell them I don't want money."

When they asked, *Who is Millroy?* I now knew enough to say, "He's a messenger, delivering his message to America."

At times like these I realized why I liked him so much. He was generous, he was kind, he protected us, he was strong, and because he was a magician he could have anything he wanted, could do anything he liked. I pretended to be Rusty, but when we were alone and he called me "muffin" or "angel" or "sugar," I never stopped being amazed that he had chosen me as a friend.

A high-level management delegation came to the diner.

"See Rusty."

I met them at a corner table. "Pitching," they called it.

"We want to market Millroy's Day One to yuppies who are obsessed with the aging process."

Millroy said, "Don't these people realize that I am doing them a favor by ignoring them? They would be sorry if I took them seriously and dealt with them accordingly. I could blind them, enslave them, render them harmless. I could take control of all their bodily functions and send them drooling and drizzling into next week."

Some recent college graduates begged Millroy for jobs and said they would do anything to join the diner. He asked them: *What is it about Day One that attracts you?*

That Day One retards the aging process, they said.

He sent them away for having no spirit and no faith, and no amount of money could change his thinking. "I have all the money I will ever need," he said. The diner was profitable, and recently—with broadcasts in other cities—he had made more. Surplus money was one of the reasons he had recruited more Sons and Daughters, and more people meant that he could expand—more cities, more syndication. He had to expand and reinvest. It was either that or deposit the money in the bank, and in his eyes all banks were sources of corruption.

"Usurers, loan sharks, money changers, Pharisees. I don't need banks or financial institutions."

His plan was to train enough Sons and Daughters to go into target cities where *The Day One Program* was broadcast so they could staff Day One diners. The new Sons and Daughters—LaRayne, Peaches, Bervia, Tuppy, Ike and the others—were perfect, he said. School dropouts, runaways, throwaways from unhappy families, and young—fifteen or sixteen, most of them (though they looked much older), young enough to have most of the magic within them unspoiled. They loved to sit and listen to Millroy tell them that they would live for two hundred years.

"I want to commission a new translation of The Book," Millroy said. "I want to straighten it out. The word 'meat' that Huber used on me. That is a confusion that is repeated all throughout The Book, but it does not mean flesh—it means food. 'He sat down to meat' does not mean the Lord was scarfing lamb chops. Of course not. Book apples are apricots. Locusts are carob trees. Manna was probably a lichen, one of the several lecanoras. Scriptural clarification is the way to health."

He said he wanted to endow a scholarship at Harvard Divinity School, stipulating that the money be used for clarifying ambiguous words and phrases in the Scriptures.

"I envision a Day One Book," he said. "The true word. No 'meat.' No 'goodly fruit.' Get the nomenclature right in the Leviticus prohibitions. What kind of wine are we talking about, and how do we grow the grapes? All of that, and with recipes in the back, slot them in right after the Book of Revelation."

So Millroy sent away businessmen from *Slimming* magazine, potential lo-cal sponsors and all the "lite"-label people; and if they refused to go, he vanished. The way he vanished reminded us that he was Millroy the Magician.

Sometimes he found it hard to deal with eaters, as he called the Day One faithful, the believers.

"It's for you," I would say, holding the phone.

"Is it an eater?"

"Yup."

He would take the call, but squinting and holding his breath, fearing what might come next. Then, perhaps, *She sounds full-figured.*

The most convinced eaters, the truest believers, were women, usually older women, usually single, often sad. They watched *The Day One Program.* They wrote him letters. They sent him snapshots, sometimes gross ones, their bodies showing, many of them snapping their own picture in front of a big mirror, with the flashbulb popping and spoiling the shot. They came to the diner to eat, to meet Millroy. They hung around and I got to know them—Erma Wysocki, Earlitha Hurley, Amy Bamberg, Dot Sweeny—and their sad eyes. One, Hazel DeHart, was just a telephone voice. She said she wanted to become a Day One Daughter. Millroy arranged to see her, but she did not show up. She called the next day. *I must see you,* she said, *at my apartment.*

"I can't take any chances," Millroy said at the last moment. "Look at Swaggart, look at Jim Bakker. I know they had lust in their hearts but they were entrapped. People in my position have been destroyed by attention seekers."

He was much more careful these days. The struggles with Ed Veazie and Orlo Fedewa had upset him, but the visit from the Reverend Baby Huber had made him even more cautious of strangers, whether they were eaters or not.

"The words that send a chill down my spine are 'I'm your greatest fan'—usually potential assassins say that."

He seemed happy not to have to deal with the trailer at Wompatuck. The break-in had worried him. "I feel conspicuous," he said. "But why? I am merely a messenger. I want my message to precede me. I want people to know that I too am an eater."

So he sent us, Jaleen and me, to see Hazel DeHart.

"If she's genuine, let me know," he said. "I'll see her. But she certainly didn't sound sixteen. She had a fattish voice. Anyway, I have to go to Baltimore to look at a property."

On the bus I asked Jaleen how Day One had changed her life.

"I don't go to clubs anymore," she said. "And I don't smoke doobies. Plus I think I hate my family so bad it's stressing me."

Hazel DeHart's was a brown brick building at the Jamaica Plain end of Mass. Ave., and Apartment 5A was in the basement, the door down a well of steep stairs where the wind had whirled old newspapers, candy wrappers, pieces of dirty knotted ribbons, plastic bags and flattened drink cans.

A big-eyed face appeared at the window. Hazel seemed afraid seeing two youngsters in Day One baseball hats standing in the shadowy well at the foot of her stairs. She opened her door a crack, enough for one eye to look out.

"What do you want?"

"Doctor Millroy sent us."

"Why didn't he come himself?"

"He's in Baltimore."

She opened up. There was a smell of fresh Ezekiel bread in the air, and the syrupy aroma of soft, overripe fruit, and the earthier, loamier odor of vegetables. She led us deeper into these mingled odors, all the while speaking of Millroy and how she watched him on television, showing us the TV as though it were somehow sacredly connected to him.

"He is my savior," she said.

I thought, *Uh-oh,* and Jaleen's face said the same thing.

Hazel DeHart was faded and fattish, about Vera Turtle's age, forty or so, much too old to be a Day One Daughter. It seemed impolite for me to tell her this, so I kept quiet.

"This is what I used to look like," she said, showing us a photograph of a very fat Hazel scowling on a plump sofa, her hands clasped and her ankles crossed.

"That don't look like you at all," Jaleen said.

"That was the point I wanted to make to Doctor Millroy." She seemed trembly-mouthed, on the verge of weeping. She had expected Millroy himself, so she had prepared a Day One meal of red lentils, herbage and Ezekiel bread, with a plate of fig cookies from one of Millroy's own recipes. It had been set out in pretty dishes on a table that had the look of an altar.

"I love him," Hazel DeHart said, and began to cry; then she smiled, though the tears ran down her cheeks. "I do exactly as he tells me. He made me well. I wasn't well before. I was sick. I was coming apart. I was scary."

"Do you pray, like Millroy says?" Jaleen asked. " 'Eating goodness is worship, and being regular is being pure.' "

Jaleen was new, and glad to be regular, so to her all these mottos were wonderful.

"What do you do, sister?"

"I touch my body," Hazel said softly.

Jaleen whispered *Uh-oh,* and stepped away, nearer to the door.

"He gave me this body," Hazel said.

After that there was a silence, and those loud food odors.

"This is different," I said, trying to think of something more to say. It was a table, with Millroy's picture in a frame. Pictures of Millroy were always lifeless and distorted and made him look insane.

"That's my shrine," Hazel said.

The photograph of Millroy was one put out by the TV station to advertise *The Day One Program*—Millroy smiling, looking loony, in a Day One apron. Hazel had colored Millroy's face with crayons, giving it a strange saintlike glow, like a holy picture, but the color made him look even more dangerous. She said she also had one in her car stuck to the dashboard. Next to the picture was a pot of fresh herbs and a candle smelling waxily of spearmint. The shrine frightened me more than the woman. It was something about the colored-in face, the gold frame, Millroy made into a god or a bullying saint, smiling from this flickering corner of the fat woman's room.

When Hazel DeHart started to cry again, we left.

"I wanted to go, like, 'Get a grip, girl,' " Jaleen said on the bus back.

"I have no control over these people," Millroy said. "I don't ask for money, and yet they send it to me. I am not a prophet, and yet they treat me like one."

He had not seen Hazel DeHart. He had no idea, and I could not describe how strange it had been for Jaleen and me. Yet I knew. She believed—that was the worst of it—and she was the first of many eaters who frightened me. They showed up late at night wanting to see Millroy; they loitered at the door in the morning, hoping that he would talk to them, and they looked as though they had spent the night in our doorway, shivering and hoping.

These people worried him. He sent us out to deal with them.

"Day One is not a church," he said. Before he vanished again, he smiled and said, "It is a movement."

29 When I was alone with Millroy he was a different man, and not always a magician. After he came back from one of his big-city trips, after everyone had gone home, after the diner was locked and the lights turned out, Millroy sighed softly and became smaller, quieter, watchful, tired from working magic. We stepped back together, and he stood over me and took his first deep lungful of air, having held his breath all day, and it was as though a curtain had come down and we were hidden behind it.

"I need you, sugar," he said, a little hoarse from preaching, but it was the voice he used for revelations. "I don't need them."

I knew he meant eaters, intruders, and people trying to cash in on his success, and maybe he even meant the Day One Sons and Daughters, because he was not close to any of them and seemed relieved when the day had ended.

Then he watched me eat. He said that he took pleasure in watching me stuff my mouth and chew. *Don't make so much noise,* Gaga used to say, but Millroy found solitary munching inspirational. He told me this, and other things that he said to no one else. No one ever heard him say that he needed me. No one knew about his dreams, how he woke, how he might cry out. He talked to me, I realized, because he never wrote anything down himself, and talking was his way of trying to make sense of his life. His voice was the pen and I was the paper.

The only thing better than watching me eat, he said, was eating with me, sitting across the table, both our mouths chewing. One of those nights we were eating bean cakes, and he was chewing as he talked.

"Huber," he said.

From what he said next I knew he was thinking how that man had come in, looked at the vegetarian menu and said, *Fart food.*

"Sure there are complex sugars in beans, whole chains of sugars that aren't digested. They move wholesale into your lower bowel, bacteria go to town on them, and they ferment. Then you are gaseous. But hey, we're talking odorless gases—methane and hydrogen. It's the pungent foods, onions and garlic, that turn them stinky and sulfurous."

When he smiled to show he had made his point, he raised his mustache and the bean skins sticking to his teeth gave him a cheerful jack-o-lantern mouth.

"And it happens to be a fact," he said, "that the more you eat beans, the greater your body's capacity to digest these oligosaccharides."

He began chewing again, concentrating on the amount he had spooned into his mouth: think about each mouthful when you eat, was one of his sayings.

"That way you end up with an essentially gasless bean."

This was a revelation.

"I have no wind."

Those words made me think of him differently, high and bright and glittering, something like a star.

At night he slept on his bedshelf in his cupboard, but sometimes he woke flustered and wanted me to talk to him.

"It was the same dream," he said in a small, trapped voice. "I died."

And it was often the same death.

"I gagged, I smothered, lost in the darkness of my body," he would say. "I suffocated inside my own fat."

Another of his revelations was that a person's real body was hidden inside his outer body, and that some troubled people hid in their fatness to bury their spirituality in a mass of pork.

"I want to reveal the actual person," he said. "With *The Day One Program* this spiritual reality will emerge."

This was another reason he liked younger people. They had a real shape and their original bodies remained intact. "It was what attracted me to you, muffin. Your perfect shape."

I was skinny, I had turned fifteen in December, but I still passed for a boy.

"And the fact that you were sucking your thumb," Millroy said.

That was another revelation, because Gaga had always told me to stop. *Get that thing out of your mouth.* She put a bandage on it, swabbed it in iodine, dipped my thumbnail with lead-based paint.

Sometimes to please him I did it again, though I had the urge less and less, and because of this my thumb seemed bonier and had a different, drier texture. After eating Day One food I stopped liking the taste of my thumb.

If the diner was closed, the Sons and Daughters gone, and Millroy and I were still wakeful, he might say, "Let's go for a little walk."

That was a revelation, too, the first time. These days I knew exactly what he wanted, but I was not sure what it was all about.

He liked watching people eat, but not just eat—he liked most of all seeing people stuffing themselves with big helpings of junk food. I had seen him at the Barnstable County Fair watching people eating fried dough and hot dogs—*weenie worship*—and I had not known what it meant. He had liked watching Baby Huber eat hamburgers and Real Good Fries. His liking was not necessarily enjoyment but an experience he needed, as though one of his theories were being proved.

We would slip out, cross Park Square and head over to the busier streets, where the restaurants were still open—along Tremont and down Stuart, or across Boylston to Newbury, to the Copley Square area, or down to Mass. Ave. There were pizza joints, burger places, ice-cream parlors, and fancier restaurants—French bistros, Chinese, Indian, Thai, sushi bars, Cajun cafés and Italian delicatessens. Boston had them all.

At night, people eating were visible behind front windows, like smiling victims gasping on food in bright fishbowls. Even in the cheap places where the windows were greasy or steamed up, or had beer signs blinking in the middle, you could see them at small tables, chewing, looking at each other rather than the food.

"They love spaghetti because they can eat it without having to look at it—it's so easy to fork in."

He was smiling. The people attracted him, and he could stand for a long time in the clammy cold of a March night on a dark sidewalk outside a Boston restaurant watching from an angle as a man forked slippery noodles or mashed potatoes and meat into his mouth.

"And what is that woman doing," he said, leaning closer, "to that hot dog?"

It made him eager and reckless; sometimes he giggled with excitement and dragged me back to look. "Let's study this."

I tried to be serious, but it was like being very young and having a grown-up say *Look,* and you could not see what they were looking at because you were the wrong size. But why was I so serious? For Millroy this was fun.

"Isn't it awful when they can't fit it all in?" he said, his face shining with pleasure. "When it spills?" Or, "Might as well be Alpo." Or, "That individual is eating Puppy Chow!"

He seemed fascinated by dabs of mustard in the corners of a mouth, or mayonnaise on lips, gravy on a chin; and a splat of ketchup on a fore-head made him laugh out loud. He looked closely when people tidied up bits of food and tucked it into their mouths with greasy fingertips. People gorging, people chewing, people sucking on big swollen cups of Coke. Even the names—a Slurpee, an Awful-Awful, a Yodel, a Big Gulp.

"He's putting meat into his mouth," he said, staring. "She's putting meat into her body."

Though he said he hated it when people did not look at the food they were eating, when they simply pushed it in until their cheeks rounded out, he could not take his eyes off them.

"Wait," he said. "I just want to see this." See what happens next, he meant—see them gag, cough or spew. He would linger, looking furtive, his coat collar turned up, as he watched a man fill his mouth with bloody meat hunks, or a woman licking whipped cream from a spoon, flecks of white froth on her lipstick.

Sometimes those eaters in the windows of Wendy's or Burger King were very hungry.

"Look, he's actually gnawing his own fingers," he said. Or: "Burger eats burger."

He read the descriptions on the menus that were framed and hung in some restaurant windows.

" 'Delicious goujons of pork, skewered with pepperoncini and garnished with julienned baby carrots and bruised garlic, presented on a bed of rice, accompanied by new potatoes in herbed butter, with a chiffonade of warmed baby lettuces.' "

He spoke the words with a mixture of horror and fascination: veal shanks, chicken thighs, shoulder of pork, calf's brain, liver paste, blood pudding.

" 'Succulent,' " he read. " 'Mouthwatering.' "

Then, with these descriptions just out of his mouth, he widened his eyes at the people eating.

" 'They that regard lying vanities forsake their own mercy,' " he said. "Jonah."

If the people in the restaurants glanced up and saw Millroy's staring face, they stopped chewing and stared back, sort of shielding their plates with their hands.

"That's pure animal," Millroy said. "That's monkey."

Then he fixed his face on them, as though daring them to begin eating again.

But they seldom looked up. Millroy explained that it was very hard for a person in a lighted restaurant to see anyone clearly in the darkness outside the window.

"Move along, pal," a waiter said to him one night, stepping outside a French restaurant near Copley Square. Millroy did not hesitate. I knew he was ashamed—the way he walked, the way he sneaked me away and shuffled, the way he had been so sideways in his staring. He would have made himself vanish except that I was with him, and our vanishing together was magic he had not so far worked.

He seldom remarked on the eaters except to say, "That's serious stomach trauma" or "She's going to gag" or "Look at the grease on his fingers." He always said these things smiling, but there was interest in it for him far beyond anything I could understand. He lurked outside places where fat people were eating bad, gleaming food with their hands, and lingered longest when it plopped through their fingers and they licked their knuckles and dug in again.

I was always with him these nights, keeping him company, listening, trying to think of something to say back to him.

"Eaters don't do that in the diner," I said.

Walking back to the Day One Diner one night from touring restaurant windows, he said that watching the people had taken away all his hunger. Another time he said, "Eating is the most intimate and revealing act—more intimate, deeper and longer-lasting even than any other human activity. It is not eating. It is feeding."

Yet watching people feeding filled him with conviction. These people were lost—too old, too wayward ever to enter a Day One Diner. They had Fat Voices, Smoker's Face, Sitter's Hips, water retention, porky necks, belly sacks, swags and bags. They were burgers, creepers, cud chewers. They ate tuna fish and other sea creatures without scales or fins. If they knew what he stood for, Millroy said, they would oppose him. Already he had been denounced by some Boston churches—the Catholic cardinal, the Christian Scientists, who were just down the street at the Mother Church, and the Seventh-Day Adventists ("The Sevies think I'm stealing their thunder").

Some people who knew him, hated him. "I make a point of not ignoring them," he said.

This was why he went out several nights a week to watch the "feeders." He was just as interested in them as he was in the Day One eaters.

"What good is it to have blind support and well-wishers and fat crazy women making shrines to me and touching their bodies?"

He had not stopped agonizing about Hazel DeHart.

"I need these burgers ranged against me. I need to see them chewing flesh and then licking their lips, and gnawing their fingers. Their very attitude inspires revelations."

I have mentioned a thing or two about what you ought to eat, Millroy said the following week on *The Day One Program. But what about forbidden foods? What's bad for you?*

He reached to the table and with his incredible strength picked up the enormous phonebook-sized copy of The Book, as he always did, using only his thumb and forefinger, and went on holding it as he talked. You were so worried he might drop it that you listened to him.

The Book is specific in prohibiting pigs, rabbits, lizards, snails, moles, ferrets and mice. Can't eat 'em. Also weasels and tortoises—and anything with paws, anything that creeps, anything that moves on its belly. Fish without scales— sharks, tuna, catfish. We can interpret the rest—crabs, oysters, and, it goes without saying, snakes. Certain birds are bad news—herons, swans, pelicans, cuckoos, owls, hawks, and—my fellow Americans—The Book says no one can eat eagles.

Leviticus eleven is an environmentalist's charter, and it's also a sort of anti-shopping list. Now think of all the other food prohibited in The Book—prohibited by omission. There is no coffee in The Book, no tea, no chocolate, no Coca-Cola. No one drinks milk in The Book, no one eats potatoes, no one chews gum. What is so odd about that? Most of what you find on the shelves of the average supermarket is not only unclean in scriptural terms but also in rigorous medical terms. Scientists are still trying to catch up with old prophets and preachers. The Book does not advocate a single item of food that has proven to be carcinogenic. More important, all the food The Book does mention is healthful. Surely there is a message here that no one so far has entirely grasped?

He was still holding the thick Book with two fingers of one hand.

Let this be your cookbook. You will be healthy. You will lose excess fat. You will grow strong. You will live in righteousness for two hundred years.

He put The Book down and came forward until his face filled the television screen.

Other preachers will promise you heaven, he said. *But how can they? No mor-*

tal can make promises like that. I am merely a messenger. And my message is, let
The Book guide your appetite and you will know health. You will be regular. You
will be delivered from constipation.

"I never heard anyone preach a sermon like that before," LaRayne
said when the program was over that Sunday. We were eating together
as usual, having shoved four tables together, end to end, with Millroy in
the middle.

"Maybe not," Millroy said. "But I hope you listened, because it is
your message, too. Very soon I am going to send you forth with some
other Sons and Daughters to run Day One diners in chosen cities. I want
you to be ready."

"I'll be ready," Dedrick said, smiling and sitting up straight.

"That is good." Millroy hugged him and then offered him a fig bar.

"But I'd be more ready if I had my driver's license."

"Get it," Millroy said. "What's wrong with you?"

"I ain't old enough, man," Dedrick said.

"Yo, Big Guy. Dedrick's fifteen," Tuppy said.

"Does it matter how old you are if you have your health and the child
inside you still intact? With Day One you will have these same bodies for
two more centuries. Age is a meaningless number if you truly know
health."

"They still going to ask Dedrick how old he is at the Registry if he
puts in for a license," Tuppy said.

Millroy smiled, and the smile said, *Listen.* "This is a ridiculous argu-
ment," he said. "Dedrick doesn't need a driver's license. Dedrick
needs to be perfect in his eating, and so do you."

I knew what was coming, though they did not, for they were still
smiling. They claimed to be interested in the emission meter when it
was fitted and they breathed into it. They also said they wanted to try the
stomach pump, but when Millroy inserted it and worked the contents of
their stomachs—these new Sons, Dedrick and Tuppy—into two tin
trays and poked through lumps in the stew with them, identifying specific meals, they began to gargle and choke and said they did not want to
look. No smiles now.

"This is how you become a faithful Day One Son or Daughter," Millroy said. "How else can I send you with confidence to a chosen city to
carry on the program?"

He was stirring the soft chunks of pukey stew in the tin trays. "I see sodium benzoate. I see emulsifiers. I see Niblets out of a can,'' he said. ''I know your problem, fellas. You've been eating out.''

They protested, but the proof was on the trays if anyone had the strength to look at it without gagging or watery eyes.

He did an emission check on Ike and Daylon.

''You're clear.''

He did one on T. Van.

''We've got blowback.''

''So I drank some tomato juice. Hey, that's supposed to be good for you.''

''Yours was canned,'' Millroy said, ''and that's not all.''

T. Van sulked, but Millroy steered the boy's head around by grasping his chin.

''Additives. Alcohol. Your juice was stepped on, Son.''

Millroy had more revelations.

''I just had a call. People wanting to put my face on cans of beans,'' he said. ''They've seen the marketing potential in Paul Newman salad dressing, Roy Rogers chicken, Ninja Turtles bubble gum. Know what I said to them?''

It was one of our after-work giving-thanks meals, and we were all listening.

'' 'Did Quaker Oats ever make anyone into a conscientious objector?' '' Millroy was smiling. ''But I have had a true relevation. I am meant to explore the possibilities of certification.''

He knew we had no idea of what he was talking about, so he waited for this to sink in.

''Like kosher certification by those gloomy-looking rabbis on the side of matzoh boxes,'' he said. ''Free of charge, I provide a Day One statement of purity on certain foods that pass rigorous tests of fibrosity, residue content, scriptural authenticity. Anything that's stepped on gets flushed.''

The Book suggests certain foods, Millroy had said on a program, *but in most cases it does not specify how they should be eaten. In other words, we have a shopping list but we don't have recipes. That is, we didn't have any until now. . . .*

Then he explained how various recipes had been revealed to him, combining Day One food with his own ways of cooking it—almond-apricot pie, pistachio bars, melon smoothies, date squares, multigrain loaf, garlic and mint pie, apple-fig cobbler, reddened snapper, escabèche of sardines, pureed chick-peas, pomegranate jam, bramble jelly, roasted chestnuts, honey popcorn balls, and all manner of vegetable soups, bean stews and fruit breads, or loaves with olives, dates and herbs baked into them. It was not just pottage, Ezekiel bread and barley cakes anymore. The Day One Diner became known for its bakery and its desserts.

This brought a new crowd of eaters—dieters, health-food people, joggers, body sculpturers, aerobics instructors—all seeking this nutritious food. They were people who had never read The Book. "But maybe they will read it now," Millroy said, "when they realize how good The Book can taste."

These revelations took the form of recipes that he broadcast on the Sunday *Day One Program*. He wanted to publish them, too, but as always he had a problem writing them down. He had never even started his book *Ever Been Dead?* He said he got too impatient, too lonely, too distracted sitting at his desk trying to write. It was drudgery. You left it, and when you came back to your desk nothing else had been added and it was shorter and skimpier than you remembered.

"No amount of magic can produce even a line of writing," he said. "Never mind good writing. But you can write down what I say, angel."

This was how we produced some more small folded-over, four-page pamphlets. One was called *Situational Eating,* about the bad food that people ate in particular places, like sports events, banquets, or at the movies, and how to avoid falling into the situational trap. Another pamphlet was *Recreational Eating.* This one began, *"I'm bored," Jimmy said. "Let's go get a pizza."* The last was called *Sequential Eating,* and described the process by which a person became entangled in dangerous eating habits, like chewing salted peanuts and getting thirsty, then drinking a Coke, but instead of quenching your thirst the Coke only introduced more sugar and salt into your body, making you want to chew something like a burger to eliminate the sweetness, and wanting ketchup on the burger, then a chocolate bar afterward, which also contains salt, which increases thirst, and so on.

Food can make you very hungry. Food can make you very thin, Millroy said on the next program. *If it's bad food you can starve, and you can seriously damage your health.*

With his face filling the screen, he closed that program howling, *Food can kill you!*

Around this time, because of the popularity of *The Day One Program,* Millroy was working on opening Day One diners in Baltimore and St. Louis. He also liked Denver, Chicago and Detroit. Certain cities were natural Day One cities—something about the city, and where the show had a big audience. He could not succeed with the program, he said, if he could not give people a place to eat, and the diner would not work without the program. The show had high viewing figures in those cities, even though it was on only once a week—eight o'clock on an inexpensive Sunday-morning cable time slot, between *Body Shaping* and *The Hour of Power.*

When some of the diners were almost ready, Millroy sent Boston Sons and Daughters to these target cities—some of the newer youngsters for training and the original Sons and Daughters, Willie Webb, Stacy, Kayla and Berry, to supervise. They went in pairs—Bervia and Tuppy, LaRayne and Ike, Jaleen and Dedrick. The other Sons and Daughters, Shonelle, Peaches, T. Van and the rest, stayed in Boston, but Millroy said that soon they would be sent to diners that were being renovated in Chicago and Detroit.

"We will go nationwide in time," Millroy said, then took on a confiding tone, almost a whisper, that he did not want anyone but me to hear. "That is the limit of my ambition, muffin. We will never be overseas. I do not want to conquer the world. It is unworthy of me."

You would not have thought it was possible to receive more mail than came each morning for Millroy, forwarded by the TV station in bags. Millroy read every letter. Some he filed, some he burned.

"I don't care what journalists are paid to write about me in the newspaper," he said. "The trouble is that they try to imitate me—they go on the attack, they denounce, they try to be funny, they fumble with words and make fools of themselves. They know I'm not Elmer Gantry, but that's the only preacher they can think of—the drunk, the adulterer, the faithless man. Americans are trained to see the clergy as hypocrites. Who can blame them?"

He was opening a mail bag that was fat with letters in bundles, and using a Day One dagger he began opening the letters.

"Jimmy Swaggart—who has been, excuse me, muffin, a whore-hopper—the things that man has eaten!" Millroy said. "Never mind just the meat you see fleshing his face. Never mind his jowls. I'm glad we're on TV an hour apart! I want people to see us both. I want Jim and Tammy back. I want Oral Roberts and his heart attack, and trembling Billy Graham."

I have lost forty pounds and the Spirit of the Lord dwells within me, I could see in a letter Millroy was holding but not reading. "They're not looking for souls—they're looking for money," he said. "Let them come on my show and take turns trying to punch me in the stomach."

Your Day One Program *is the high point of my week, and when are you going to open a Day One diner in Albany?*

"No one's paying for these letters. These letter writers mean what they say. Some of them hate me. I can understand that. The rest of them love me in a way that makes me want to hide."

For this reason he avoided making personal appearances. He did not want to speak to large crowds, he refused to sign any of the pamphlets and he would not allow his photograph to be sent out.

"Just send the Day One logo."

He wanted the Day One idea to be important, not the name Millroy. *No one needs to be grateful to me. Thank the Lord.*

But the more he hid, the more famous he became. He refused to appear in public, would not speak to journalists, turned away people from the *Today* show and *Good Morning America,* would not return calls to *People* magazine. As a result his name was known everywhere.

"Sometimes, nothing is more obvious than the thing you try to hide," he said. "And nothing is more hidden than what is obvious. Every magician knows that, muffin."

"I've been thinking about flesh," Millroy said to the remaining Sons and Daughters and me one day. "And by that I mean meat."

He spoke in the slow, dreamy *Remember this* voice that he used for revelations.

"It is almost impossible to say the word 'meat' without showing your canine teeth. The word makes you smile and bare your teeth. The other sinister aspect is the sound. 'Meat' sounds like 'eat,' and also like 'meal.' ''

Though he roasted lamb in the Day One Diner, and served it skewered or else seethed it according to suggestions in The Book, I had never seen him eat meat himself. The Book was full of lambs frisking and also full of their crackle and smell as they roasted on a spit, he said, but he would not touch it. ''All flesh has a face,'' he said. ''All flesh has a mother.''

That was his reason for not eating it, or so I thought. But he had a deeper reason. He did not tell the Sons and Daughters and he did not tell me. Then he had a nightmare. It was worse than any nightmare he'd had so far—more noise, more clattering, more gasps. I heard it first as a commotion, the sounds of his hands clawing and banging, mistaking the wall for a door, a slapping of woodwork as he tried to get out.

Then his voice from the dark: ''Talk to me, angel.''

Darkness itself, because of Millroy's descriptions, seemed to me like smothering folds of flesh that made you desperate. Darkness was fat— that was how I thought of it now. But when Millroy sounded desperate I felt lost. What could I say to this magician that he did not already know?

''Please,'' he said.

''Were you having a bad dream?''

''A terrible dream,'' he said, his voice coming through the boards. ''That there was a woman outside waiting for me.''

''Did you know her?''

''Yes.''

''That's neat.''

''It was Death,'' Millroy said.

What could I say to that? I tried.

''I wonder if I would recognize her if I dreamed her,'' I said, hoping it would never happen.

''Everyone's dream of Death is different,'' Millroy said. ''Only you would know it. My dream would not frighten you. It was my mother wearing a pig-faced mask, standing on one skinny leg in front of the Day One door shrieking at me.''

''That's wicked scary.''

''It's not supposed to be for you.''

''The part about one leg.''

"That's the important part," he said.

He was breathing hard, as he usually did when he woke up suddenly, and although walls of wood and space separated us I was so used to talking to him in the darkness that it was as though we were in the same room.

"She was small and intense. She always smelled of flour and milk. She was a wonderful cook."

"In the dream?"

"No. When I was growing up," Millroy said, in a raspy whisper. "In my dream she was Death."

"When you were growing up," I said, trying to think of a question and making it up as I went along, "what did your mother give you to eat?"

There was one of those silences that made the darkness purr like a big sleeping animal. I counted to seventy-seven.

"One meal overshadowed all the others," Millroy said finally.

"It must have been neat."

"It was a nightmare," he said.

He made a sound in his throat that I had only heard before when he was pumping his stomach with his rubber plunger.

"Mother's leg," he said.

There was another purring, fur-covered silence.

"It was a Sunday," he said, "and my mother was roasting a leg of lamb. After she put it into the oven she realized that she had forgotten to add bitter herbs, as mentioned in Numbers—dandelion, chicory, endive, sorrel. So, with the lamb sputtering inside the oven, she went out to buy the herbs."

He took a deep breath, began again, gasped, and breathed once more.

"She died on the way home," he said. "Shooting pains probably. Chest ache. Heartburn. Shortness of breath. 'I think I'll sit down.' There was a bench at the bus stop. She sat down and died."

"Jeekers."

"That wasn't the worst part."

"Jeekers."

"When she didn't come back I went looking for her. I found her. I told my Aunt Sam. She arranged for the funeral."

"It must have been wicked sad."

"It got worse."

"Jeekers."

"A week after the funeral, Aunt Sam took me home and served me the leg of lamb. The same one. Mother's leg. Aunt Sam had frozen it and saved it. 'Eat it,' she said, cutting it with a dull knife, and then she stood over me."

Millroy gulped and made several more swallowing sounds before he continued.

" 'Eat it for your mother's sake,' she said. 'She made it for you.' "

Now the silence was vast and dark, and we were lost in it.

"It had not completely thawed, so the meat was still cold and gray and corpselike, with white strings and sinews," Millroy said in a muted way, as though his mouth were full. "You expected to find her sock on it."

The small seizures and bursts of silence were liked muffled sobs, and I was still counting.

"That's how I ate Mother's leg," Millroy said. "I never ate meat after that. Would you?"

Then the darkness closed over him, and blinded and silenced and separated us again.

In the morning Millroy said, "I have had a revelation," and seemed glad.

This was Millroy with the sun on his face ("I work magic in daylight") and a good idea, something visual for *The Day One Program*.

"You have to help me," he said. "I can't do it without you."

He dressed me as a little old woman and brought me to the studio, where we rehearsed the segment "Mother's Leg."

It was my first time at this studio, a different station from *Paradise Park* and a different world. People were respectful—the doorman, the security guard, the makeup woman, the technicians. Millroy had his own dressing room.

He was subdued on the set—people made room for him, did not speak directly to him, did not interrupt or contradict him. He appeared older and more serious, with a sense of mystery about him, something dangerous, perhaps, not magic but with an unpredictable power. It made me nervous, but after a while I knew why: there were no children here, no youngsters at all. Millroy was different among grown-ups. He was not himself. The real Millroy was a happier man, who sometimes had nightmares, sometimes needed to cruise the Boston streets looking into restaurant windows, and sometimes needed me in ways I did not understand, but was always a magician.

"I want you to think of this little old lady as my mother," he said to the people on the set at the first rehearsal, beckoning me forward.

I kept my mouth shut and prayed that my wig would not fall off.

Using the simplest props, Millroy made the story "Mother's Leg" a silent movie, with music instead of narration. It was perfect, he said—obvious, strong and self-explanatory. In my apron, wig and mask of makeup, I was Mother Millroy putting the leg of lamb into the roasting pan and pushing it into the oven. Then I died. Then I was Aunt Sam serving Millroy the leg of lamb that I had frozen—"Mother's leg" on a platter.

When Millroy refused to cut it, I took his knife and stabbed it, hacking off hunks of meat and eating them. *Push the meat into your mouth with the back of your hand and chew like a cannibal.*

Millroy refused to eat any of it himself. The message was: this is flesh.

Eat nothing that has a mother—nothing that has a face, Millroy said at the end of this program. *Never put flesh in your mouth. Never put meat in your body.*

"Sensational program, Doctor Millroy," they said at the station.

Almost as soon as we got back to the diner the phones began to ring. Millroy told me to answer them and then, sensing a new onslaught of interest in him, taped next week's show early and left on a tour of the other Day One diners. He called each night from a motel or from the diners to report that they were all enjoying enormous success.

I was alone in the diner one night, about a week after the "Mother's Leg" segment and a few days after Millroy left, when the telephone rang. It was late, after eleven. I thought it must be Millroy calling from a different time zone. Who else would call at that hour?

"Hi," I said, thinking it was Millroy.

"He's still controlling you," the voice said at once; no hello, no who-is-it, nothing else.

"Who is that?"

"Still working you like a puppet."

It was a shaky, cranky, old woman's voice, like that of an animal in a cartoon. I could only think of Millroy's mother because she had been on my mind. She was dead, but so was the voice.

"I thought he would have left you alone by now," the voice said. "But no, he's shameless, and he can't disguise you."

"I think you have the wrong number."

"I have his number and no mistake."

Where had I heard that voice? It was full of old cobwebs.

"I'm on to him."

The voice had become very angry and witchlike and echoey. In spite of the criticisms and crazy people I had still not gotten used to strangers—or anyone—saying bad things about Millroy.

"He's there, isn't he? Telling you to hang up."

I looked at the darkness around me and tried to think whether I had locked the front door.

"Yes."

"Tell him he'll be sorry. There's nothing he can do to save himself. Tell him he'll be destroyed. He'll be floating belly-up!"

Before I could reply, there was a click and a hum—the person had hung up. I made sure the diner doors were locked, and I tried to sleep. I kept waking up worried, thinking, *A person who calls you knows exactly where you are.* I wished that Millroy were there to tell my worry to, the way he had so many times with me.

"How's it going, bro?" T. Van asked me the next morning.

I almost told him about the threatening phone call, but decided not to. I was glad, though, that T. Van was so strong and that he and Troy were on duty while Millroy was away. Troy lifted weights, and the Day One food had made him powerful and pantherlike.

Millroy returned from his tour of the diners smiling. "I can't believe the hats and shirts we're selling," he said. "It doesn't seem right—we don't need the revenue. But if buying logo merchandise gets people eating Day One I guess it's a good thing. How's everything here, buddy?"

Buddy, because T. Van and Troy were listening.

Millroy was doing the accounts later the same day when he said over his shoulder, "I was thinking about Mister Phyllis two nights ago. I saw a rerun of the old *Paradise Park* on a cable station in Baltimore. I bet you don't even remember him. Creepy old Sidney Perkus."

The twisted old fruit. Yes: Magic. Two nights ago was Wednesday, the night of the telephone call. His was the voice.

"Can I tell you something?" I asked.

30 The whispers and contradictions made me feel we were in danger. Was it because April had passed, the weather was warmer, and wearing fewer clothes I felt nakeder and vulnerable? Summer, a month away, meant that soon it would be a whole year with Millroy. What had happened to that man who had put his face against mine and chosen me? He was stronger, he was weaker—me, too. I missed the old days when everything had been smaller and simpler—seeing Millroy sorting stones out of beans, talking about food and working magic for me in the Airstream trailer in Buzzards Bay or Wompatuck. What did he see in his world now?

Dressed in white—white apron, Day One baseball hat, new white shoes—Millroy looked out the front window of the diner, hands in his pockets, watching the people crossing Park Street, making deliveries at Legal Sea Food, or gathering in front of UMass or the hotel. Behind him all the new Sons and Daughters were setting up, clearing tables and serving. We would soon be open for breakfast, and the eaters would flock to us without our doing anything except unlocking the door. Millroy was thinking, *We have not spent a penny on advertising.*

"I now realize that this is a revolutionary and reforming movement," he said. "This is magic."

The smell of baking bread was like a thick gust of scorched sweet-sour perfume, and just a whiff of it filled your head with dusty pleasure, slid down your throat and made you want to chew and swallow. "Yes!" he said when I told him that a loaf of unbaked bread dough was like a baby's bum.

"We are moving mountains," he said. "We are big. I had not foreseen how big a thing I had started, and it is all Book-based and righteous. This"—he snorted in the cooking aromas—"is spiritual."

Tell him he'll be sorry, I also heard—Mister Phyllis quacking through his thin, wrinkled lips.

Meanwhile, Millroy had turned the key in the front-door lock and was shooting open the bolt. People had begun to gather with hungry looks on their faces. The idea of feeding made them seem lost and nervous and alert, like chickens jerking their heads upright at the sound of the bolt thrown on the hencoop door.

"I truly did not think it would be like this," he said. "I had a simple idea. It worked for me. It gave me vitality. I was expressing myself for my own benefit. In all modesty, how was I to know that I possessed the universal secret to eternal life?"

In the breakfast crowd came, looking obedient and hungry, all wearing the same facial expression, to be fed by Millroy and greeted by the Sons and Daughters.

I searched the faces of the incoming eaters for Mister Phyllis. He would be easy to identify, with his old clown's wrinkles and sagging mouth and eyes.

Tell him he'll be destroyed.

Somehow I felt that when he came to the diner he would be carrying his bad-tempered cat, which Millroy had called Stinky.

The past will rise up and come through the door and amaze us, Millroy used to say.

He was talking about The Book and the crowd of hungry people, but all I could think of was Mister Phyllis.

The truth—the truth is something we know, something we look at every day, without realizing it is the truth. The truth is obvious, he said. *The truth is staring us in the face.*

He meant Day One food. No church in America had made much of the food in The Book, he said. Forget the Jewish horror of pigmeat. The Seventh-Day Adventists based almost their whole religion on two pages of Leviticus. Jehovah's Witnesses were fixated on the blood of strangled animals. Mormons had simply invented a cult of money and wife-collecting, and they did not drink alcohol (although nearly everyone in The Book did). The rest—beef-eating Episcopalians, spaghetti-bending Catholics, Baptist burgers—ate any old thing that fit in their mouths.

Never trust a TV evangelist unless he can do seventy-five push-ups. If he's unhealthy he's a hypocrite—never mind who.

An article about Day One in *The New York Times* appeared under an old picture of Millroy, one of the promotional pictures sent out by *Paradise Park* at the time it surpassed the ratings for *Sesame Street*. It showed the magician smiling in his "Mealtime Magic" chef's hat, with children crowding around him. The newspaper article used the phrase *Gantry with granola,* referred to "The Day One Church," and under the silly, grinning picture the caption read, *Rev. Millroy.*

"Buddy!"

He dictated a reply to me. With my elbows sticking out, sitting at Millroy's pull-down desk, I wrote down what he told me, his letter to the editor of *The New York Times.* He hated to be compared with Elmer Gantry. He wanted his message to be printed. He mentioned food and The Book, and living for two hundred years, and the intrusion of journalists, and what could a person do if a writer had set out to ridicule him? The letter was not published *(The Editor thanks you for your communication but is unable to use it).* Millroy became agitated and I went on worrying.

These misunderstandings sometimes made him sulky, but they suggested to me that we could be in for trouble. Already there were articles in magazines and newspapers about the great success of *The Day One Program.* Day One food had influenced cooking generally, some journalists and food writers said when they called up for more information. But because Millroy refused to talk to them and would not be interviewed, mistakes kept cropping up. Many people simply assumed that Rev. Millroy had founded the Day One Church, and that it was as much a church as Assembly of God or Congregational.

Even some of the Sons and Daughters believed this mistake.

"Far as I'm concerned, Big Guy is a preacher," Troy said to me quietly.

"But he doesn't want to be."

"He sure is something."

"A magician," I said. That covered everything. If someone was a magician there was nothing else you needed to know about them.

"Where'd he go to school?" Tomarra asked me.

"Magicians don't go to school."

But I knew this was not the right answer. These questions the Sons and Daughters asked me were simple, yet the simplest were sometimes the most difficult. Was he really from El Jobean in south Florida, as he had once told me? How old was he? Did he have any real children of his own? What was the story with his magic?

"He's always saying how fat he used to be," T. Van said. "Well, what city was he in when he was fat?"

They asked me because they were afraid of him, and because these days he traveled more and more. They assumed that I must know the answers to these simple questions.

"I don't know," I said.

Willie said in a whinnying, doubting voice, "You sure the Big Guy is your father?"

"Stepfather," I said.

Willie rolled his eyes—not at me but at the others, which made me feel all the more uncomfortable.

"I'll try to remember that," he said. "If you promise to do the same."

Another time, Dedrick said to me, "What's your secret, Little Guy?"

I had no answer because Millroy had no answer for me. Was I losing him? Normally the longer you know someone, the better you understand them. Time passes and makes them familiar. You are less and less afraid. Often, before they open their mouths, you know what they will say.

It was the opposite with Millroy. The day we met at the Barnstable County Fair, I had felt I knew him well—the way he laughed, the words he used to reassure me. He knew when I was hungry and what to feed me. He knew, before I told him, what my worries were: Gaga and Dada and school. He calmed me, he protected me. *I'm safe,* I said to myself. He was a friend—more than that, he was a part of me. In a previous life I had been him and he had been me, he said. I thought, maybe, in a way. If I had not believed he was good would I have gone off with him the way I did? I used to repeat the answer to this to myself, practicing for Dada, Gaga, or anyone who might ask.

But as time passed, Millroy had become more and more a man of secrets, almost a stranger. It was the reverse of everything that I had known. The longer we were together, the less I knew him, the harder it was to predict how he would react; and I had less and less idea of how to please him. He had changed from a simple, friendly soul who did tricks to a big complicated man who worked magic.

His strength made me feel weaker, and now in these months of expansion—Day One diners in three more cities—I felt powerless. I saw that all along, while admiring his magic and being dazzled by it, it had been the very thing that prevented me from knowing him. Maybe I would never know him.

The Lord is unknowable. He dresses and talks and eats and drinks like a man, but he is God, Millroy said. *You would have to be his equal to know him—as great, as divine—and who on earth is so powerful?*

This was how I felt about Millroy, and this was why the nighttime phone call from Mister Phyllis had made me afraid. Once so close, Millroy now seemed large, mysterious and far off. I liked his surprises because he was always kind, but a person so full of surprises had to be full of secrets.

Take the Day One diners. He had not said much about them—only that he wanted to start more of them, to expand and keep growing, in order to defy the noneaters and spread the good word. This was a fine idea, I thought, but just an idea. I did not think any more about it until one night there was an item on the radio news about Philadelphia. A boy who had killed his mother had been caught using her credit card to buy a pair of expensive sunglasses.

"That's a Day One city," Millroy said. "Philly."

Meaning?

"We're in Philadelphia now," he said. "We've got a Sunday TV slot and a Day One location."

I knew about Baltimore, Denver and some others, but Philadelphia? It was in this way that I found out about even more cities. Millroy also had plans for Tampa, Memphis and New Orleans. How had he expanded Day One so quickly? He denied that it was big, and because he had nothing on the West Coast he could not say that it was truly nationwide.

"It's a manageable size and it's a straightforward retail operation. The first one was the hardest. After that it's just delegation, repetition and good quality control—pure, basic Day One food in a wholesome environment. The only thing we have in a can is the program."

It was still a weekly prerecorded show, full of cooking and confessions, but fewer and fewer bursts of magic. "It's got to stay simple," he said. "We can't let it dazzle and devour us."

Summer came. Millroy sent Day One Sons and Daughters to diners in four more cities. He visited them—"quality control." He did not say much about them. I did not know whether the diners were going badly and he was quietly concerned, or whether he was embarrassed by the suddenness of their success, creating Day One cities with his own Day One cookie cutter. I decided that it was his success that made him so secretive, because he was uncomfortable making so much money. What did he do with it?

This made me feel smaller, and made him seem large and mysterious and busy.

Left alone in the diner while he traveled, and more or less in charge of the Boston Day One, I got to know the Sons and Daughters better—the ones who were still here, and the others from hearsay. They all had scary stories to tell—of fathers drunker and sicker than Dada, of grannies crazier and crueler than Gaga, nastier people than I had ever heard of, worse than the worst people in The Mills or in Mashpee. But it was not their intention to frighten me; they were only answering my questions.

They also knew about each other. *LaRayne's brother Tooty got busted for pushing a teacher out the window. Then in reform school another dude slashed Tooty so bad with a broken bottle his eye got cut out and now it's glass. He pops it out and sucks it to gross you out.*

That was Troy speaking. But Troy himself had had a hard time, according to Peaches. *Troy's old man was set on fire and died that way. They burned him down.*

I asked why.

He was dealing crack and maybe the crack was bad, or else he was skimming money. Bad drug deal. Listen, Little Guy, it could also be mistaken identity. Who knows? But better not to ask. Know what I'm saying?

No wonder they were happy here, being fed and paid by Millroy the Magician. This must have seemed so peaceful to them.

Tuppy and Ike, they both gay.

Did Millroy know that?

The Big Guy knows everything.

T. Van had scars on his hands and his arms.

Them there's bite marks, he said. His full name was T. Van Dyer. *From teeth.*

You did not want to know more than that.

We were changing a tire on Millroy's Ford one day, Tomarra Weatherless and I, and after I jacked up the car with the long, crooked-handled wrench, Tomarra said, *I hate them things.*

I asked, *What things?*

My father went wacko with one of them monkey wrenches.

You did not want to know more about that, either.

Knives, guns, broken bottles and wicked sticks of wood figured in these stories, and so did large, destructive fires. There were wrecked houses, crashed cars, policemen, jails, drugs, thefts, alcohol, death and injury. It was no mystery to me why they obeyed Millroy and now considered the Day One Diner their home.

Dedrick had some kind of breakdown and cut his sister Jevette real bad.

What happened to him?

He's still trying to work it out.

"Don't your folks wonder why you left home?" I asked Shonelle Bigart, imagining the Bigarts having breakfast without her today.

"If my mother kicked me out of the house, which she did," Shonelle said, "why would she wonder if she already knows the reason. You see what I'm saying?"

Daylon Jefferson said he never went home. How could he? He had no home, only that old lady Bodette, who was always in the bag.

"We got thrown out into the street," he said.

They were sad stories the Sons and Daughters told. If you asked for more they obliged.

So we lived in a junk heap 'seventy-eight Chevy Country Squire, four-door, in a parking lot on Warren Street. Anyway the radio worked.

Usually they kept their past lives to themselves, as though talking about those things was unlucky, or made them seem worse—which it certainly did—or might give me the wrong idea, and I might end up pitying them or thinking I'd had it easier in my own past life, which was probably true.

That didn't happen to me, they seemed to say. *That happened to someone else. This is my life now.*

They were like Millroy. The more I heard their stories, the less I knew them, and I felt like a stranger. The question *Who are these people?* usually made me feel lonely.

They admired Millroy, even idolized him. *He's the Boss of Diss,* Willie had said. *Sometimes I pray to Millroy,* Tomarra told me. They saw him as almighty—he could destroy anyone. It made them fear and respect him.

Peaches and I were dishing up barley soup one morning when Millroy had just left for quality control in a Day One city.

"There are people you meet and you're, 'Hey, I want to be like them,'" Peaches said. "But the Big Guy is different. Suppose he's right and we live for two hundred years. Even so, as long as you live you never be like him.''

The soup brimmed and steamed in its earthenware bowls, and we served it with thick slices of rye bread and ''cheese of kine.''

''That's why I'm staying so tight with him,'' she said. ''I can't leave him, because he's where it's at.'' We were still serving and she was still thinking about Millroy.

''He's the man,'' she said.

At first this gave me goose pimples. Then I thought, *Is that why I'm still here after a whole year?* I had never looked at Millroy this way, but after Peaches said it, I began to think it was true. We could never be like him, which was why we needed him, and would go on believing, and would never leave.

''He's a learning experience that you go on learning,'' Peaches said, licking slopped barley soup from her thumb. ''He's someone special.''

There were tears in her eyes as she stopped talking and went on thinking about Millroy. She reminded me of Stacy when she looked at Millroy with moony eyes, and Hazel DeHart *(Sometimes I touch my body).* Never mind Day One food and living for two hundred years—they were all in love with Millroy.

Except me. But hearing them made me proud that I had known him for so long, and that I had been the first person he had chosen. I remembered when he was unknown, nothing in the newspaper, nothing on television, when we had lived in a trailer park in Buzzards Bay, sorting stones out of beans, and him saying so seriously, *All I want is that you be regular,* and I had thought, *What's that supposed to mean?*

Willie Webb was right. I was one of Millroy's secrets. No one knew who I really was, Jilly Farina from Marstons Mills, hiding all this time from Gaga and Dada, with a new name and different clothes. A secret, or maybe one of Millroy's tricks, a person he could make disappear— smiling one minute, gone the next, up his sleeve the rest of the time. Wasn't that my life with him so far? When I was needed, *Whango!* up I popped, blinking in the bright light, straightening my shirt. *And here he is.* I came or went according to his wishes. And not only me, but everyone who believed in Day One. He gave us life. That was a scientific fact, just as he said. When he disappeared he made the world vanish. He came back and we sprang to life.

''Going out to Denver,'' he said to me one day.

My arms flopped down straight to my sides, and my spirit began leaking out of my punctured soul. *Take me with you, please.*

"Do you want to come with me?"

We had been together long enough for him to know that my silence meant yes.

Then to the airport, my first time ever in a plane, the smell of carpets, plastic and reheated meat, two old women showing us how to wear yellow life jackets, then the plane thumping like a sled through wispy white rags of cloud that were holding up the giant metal wings and leaving long streaks of spittle on the windows.

Wind shear, Millroy said.

Four and a quarter hours of this, jammed in, five across, elbow to elbow, Millroy talking.

This is a sealed container, and when you consider all these bodies you can just figure how germ-laden the air is.

A plastic card in the seatpocket in front of me read IN CASE OF AN EMERGENCY and showed a picture of a cartoon person praying with his head between his knees. *Forget that, muffin. If we go down, we're history.*

I looked out the window and saw the land like a faded map with ponds and lakes like disks of tinfoil beneath us. I picked up the airlines magazine and flipped to an article about cuckoo clocks in Switzerland.

And the radiation at this altitude can fry your cells.

My hankie was on my nose, when Millroy reached over and plucked it away and made it vanish in his fingers.

You could break an eardrum blowing your nose. Wipe it on your sleeve for now.

Meals were passed out on plastic trays by the old women pushing metal carts.

Don't breathe, angel. There's some damaging slipstream food smells drifting around.

He brought out Day One food for us, and we ate it together like picnickers, but after he finished he watched passengers eating, and his face shone the way it did when he saw people late at night through restaurant windows.

"Water?" It was one of the old women showing Millroy a pitcher of ice water.

Millroy shook his head and smiled, and went on talking in his ventriloquist's way.

Never drink water on an airplane. It is heavily chlorinated and of course potentially fatal.

I put my head down like the cartoon man on the emergency card and prayed until we landed in Denver, the plane thumping down and howling.

Denver—Stapleton Airport—smelled different from Boston: thinner air, a drier, dustier odor. The land was hot and bright under a wide-open sky propped up by far-off mountaintops, and I could feel all that blue space like high-altitude pressure on my forehead and in my ears.

A few minutes out of the airport our rental car was heading down suburban streets, with bungalows and frame and brick houses with porches, bus stops and benches at intervals saying YOUR NAME HERE $25, and one bench nearer the city saying DAY ONE.

Millroy named all the things he saw, like a voice in a certain kind of movie. "Checker Auto Parts, Grease Monkey, Messiah Lutheran Church, Josephine Street, Gaylord Street, Cherry Creek, Footpain Clinic, Car Clinic."

A big bronze buffalo got his attention, and he stuck his head out of the car window to see the statehouse dome like a huge upside-down acorn made out of gold.

Willie Webb and Stacy ran the Day One Diner here with LaRayne and Ike. They frowned when they saw me. I knew they resented the special attention that Millroy gave me. Was this my fault? They were glad to see Millroy, and rushed out of the diner to greet him in their Day One aprons and T-shirts. They were confident, taller, stronger-looking, and strangest of all, they had shaved their heads, Sons and Daughters alike, as though to look more like Millroy.

"He's the messenger," Willie said, introducing Millroy to the customers, who were respectful and told Millroy how *The Day One Program* had changed their lives. "He's the Big Guy."

Millroy did not shake hands with them. Instead he smiled and said, "Go ahead, punch me in the stomach!"

"The Klan's real active here," Willie said over the welcome meal of Day One food in the kitchen. "Also Aryan Nation. Also another group of screamers called 'The Order.' "

"They put you in any personal danger?" Millroy asked.

"We're eating them out of existence." Willie looked fearless, as nimble as he had been before, but stronger and bigger, and his shaved head and popping eyes made him seem like a giant insect.

"Remember this," Millroy said, "you will outlive them all."

The diner in Denver was the same shape and size as the Boston Day One, and the Sons and Daughters had rooms in the back, beyond the office, where Stacy did the accounts. Judging from the reaction of the eaters, Millroy was famous here, and he surprised me by being happy the whole time. He spoke to the customers as though they were old friends, and they hung around smiling at him as he ate, waiting for him to say something more, but he just smiled back.

"And who's this?" Willie said after Millroy had gone out back. He was staring at me. "That's what we're all trying to find out," he said.

I folded my arms and pretended not to care, but I was worried and felt very small, and again began to wish I had not come here.

Millroy spent ten minutes in the back while I looked at the customers—youngsters with long hair, Indians with ponytails, students, people with the sort of muscular faces you never saw in Boston. I marveled at how like the diner was to the Boston Day One, also on a side street but in this newer, brighter city. Glancing sideways so as not to be too obvious, I studied the way the Day One Sons and Daughters had shaved their heads to look like Millroy, and wondered whether I should do the same and cut it all off.

"Watch," Millroy said to the eaters in the diner just before we left.

He was holding a big metal spoon, pinching the tip of its handle. As he held it, the spoon began to droop and then slowly to bend, like a thick spring coiling. When it had stopped bending and was wound tight, he handed it to Willie, who showed it to the excited customers.

"Bless you, Doctor Millroy," a woman called out when we drove off, and she tried to touch him.

"I find that sort of person very worrying," Millroy said. He was rattled when people touched him, especially women.

We had only been a few hours in Denver, but I was glad to leave, and so was Millroy. "Martin Luther King Junior Boulevard, Jack in the Box, Taco Bell, Nutri-System," he said. His Day One briefcase was on his lap, packed with green bricks of money. He would have nothing to do with banks: this was a money run as well as a surprise visit. "Be nice to get back to our own facilities."

We are passing over the city of Cleveland, Ohio, the pilot said on the loud-speaker on the way back. "That's a Day One city," Millroy said.

I had not known that at all.

"Someday this will be a Day One country," he said.

He was energetic, generous, flushed with success, his briefcase bursting with cash.

Never mind, the next time Millroy visited a Day One city I stayed behind in Boston.

31 Most of our food was stored in the cellar of the diner down the dark hole that Millroy called "the hatchway." Things were put away so carefully there that they seemed hidden, and because of my size and the narrow trapdoor I was usually the one who squirmed into this hole to bring food up. For Day One reasons we did not use the refrigerator.

Millroy hated ice.

Two mentions of ice in The Book and both of them are silly questions.

He liked quoting the parts of the Bible that were pointless to show that he was neither a fanatic nor a fundamentalist.

In Psalms we read, "He casteth forth his ice like morsels. Who can stand before his cold?" Then he laughed. *Anyone with a good breakfast inside them can stand before his cold!*

The Sons and Daughters loved it when he talked this way. *Yo. Big Guy dissing The Book, woop-woop-woop.*

Job asks, "Out of whose womb came the ice?" Millroy said with a grin. *Answer: no one's womb. The water froze when the temperature dropped. This is the same confused Job who said, "Man that is born of woman is of a few days and is full of trouble." You can't take him literally—the man's depressed!*

Millroy did not believe that ice had any useful purpose—it deadened taste, gave you cramps, was not Day One. Who needed it? Our refriger-

•••

ator had no ice maker, and we never plugged in the refrigerator itself anyway, since there was no food to go bad. We shopped for fresh vegetables every day and bought our fish wet and slimy from the market. We no longer served lamb.

"No muscle. No sinew. No flesh."

Early on, the Sons and Daughters had grumbled more than the customers.

"No ice cubes? How can you drink Coke with no ice cubes?"

That was Dedrick, long ago.

"We don't drink Coke," Millroy had said.

But when the Sons and Daughters found out we drank greenish, inky wine, and sometimes a lot of wine, they stopped grumbling and asked for more.

"Ice in wine is unheard of," Millroy said.

The refrigerator had been installed to satisfy Board of Health requirements for a food-service permit, but the hatchway was the answer to Day One needs. Bags of beans, parched corn, unbleached flour, crates of melons and sacks of dates and figs—all these and more filled the cellar space with a dusty, humming aroma. The space could be reached only through the trapdoor in the kitchen floor, and then down a steep wooden ladder. The entrance was narrow, but I was small, so I was the one who went down with the bucket and scoop to bring up pounds of ingredients—beans for soaking, flour for sifting, nuts and dried fruit to be washed.

The trapdoor was set in the middle of the kitchen floor, where people walked. It could be lifted only when the kitchen was empty—very late, after the others had gone.

Tonight I was working the graveyard shift, and was in the hatchway hole, up to my skinny waist in darkness. It was late, the kitchen was closed, the last eaters finishing their meals, the Sons and Daughters done with the mopping and already on the bus back to Wompatuck.

Scooping flour into a bucket for the overnight bread, I worked in a single shaft of light that came through the hatchway opening. I had my usual naked, fearful, deep-hole feeling that something heavy and hard was going to drop onto my head through the trapdoor opening. I lost count of the scoopfuls out of nervousness, took a guess, scooped some more and kept glancing up.

But I was not looking up when it appeared. I heard it instead—a spitting hiss and gargling harshness that started as a howl and ended as a shriek, with a tingling echo in the cellar where I stood, the light making my face feel like a target. The sound was like stinking wind. Then I saw it.

A fat-faced cat with its mouth open was gasping and peering across the black edge of the hole, right over my head as though it wanted to pounce onto my head and claw my scalp off like peeling a fruit.

As I watched, a shaking shriveled hand with yellow fingernails reached around and closed over the cat's mouth.

"Tinky," a voice said, quavering like Gaga's just before she turned nasty.

A granny's face that went with the voice looked over the edge of the hole. It was an old man, but the face was as puffy and womanish as the cat's face with its folds of saggy fur and crusted eyes.

"Tinky found a wee mouse."

So sudden, such a fright, with a creepy sound—a hiss, a gasp, half-human, half-cat, both the cat and the man sounding like an old woman choking. It all happened fast, and because of the speed of one awful thing after another, I was more afraid of the cat than of the man. But it was not a man—it was Mister Phyllis, with his wrinkled lips, wicked eyes, sparse orangy hair and thin, blotchy skin. When I saw the rest of him he looked like a decaying clown. He clutched the big cat like a fur bag, holding it plumply on his arm. Now the cat seemed normal and it made Mister Phyllis seem dangerous.

"Where is he?"

When he was angry, Mister Phyllis's nose tightened and turned white. I could see the gristle through the skin.

"Millroy!" he called out.

I stood trembling at the foot of the steep ladder, feeling trapped.

"Get up here," Mister Phyllis said.

Leaving my flour bucket behind, I climbed the ladder and when I got to the top and stuck my head above the hatchway, I saw that the diner was empty. The last eaters must have finished and bussed their own tables, the way our eaters did, while I was down below.

Mister Phyllis was shorter than when I had last seen him—had I grown that much?—and although he had a nasty face and yellow eyes, he seemed fragile, not sick but breakable.

"Where is Millroy?"

I was also thinking how much smaller than Millroy he was.

"He's not here," I said, and felt unsafe.

If I had known how to work Millroy's magic I would have tried to shock Mister Phyllis somehow, make him whimper and cringe the way Millroy had. Now, more than ever, I admired his power to frighten a bully with his own furious rats.

"He won't be back until Friday," I said. I was sorry as soon as the words were out of my mouth.

"So you're alone, chicken." Mister Phyllis spoke my own fearful thought.

I began to back up, to be out of his reach and away from his odor of decay and soap slime, which made me feel puky, like the smell of industrial deodorant in a public toilet.

"Your customers all went home," he said. "So it's just the four of us."

The four of us?

I turned and saw that what I had taken to be a big shadowy chair at the far end of the diner was a person—a woman, staring intently at me. She was motionless and what was most distant about her was the wisps of her white hair and her big knees.

"I brought someone I wanted your Millroy to meet," Mister Phyllis said.

He laughed in the way his cat gasped.

"But you'll do, chicken."

Hearing this, the woman hitched forward so that her head was in the light and a stripe of shadow was bent across her body like a chevron. She was very old, she was silent, she was not one of us. She was wide and pale and wobbled when she moved her shoulders, with fat legs and a peeved Smoker's Face. She sat in a lopsided way with the shadow marking her, one chubby hand clutching the other. I had never seen anyone her size or shape in the diner, though we saw them all the time in the Boston streets. She made me afraid, as Mister Phyllis and his cat did, though for a different reason. Misshapen Americans made me think of insanity and death.

"I fancy she wants to talk to you," Mister Phyllis said.

"Does she know me?"

The big, top-heavy woman moved as I spoke, and hearing a creaky noise, I imagined the sound coming from her body because I could not tell where her body ended and the chair began.

"She knows as much as I do," Mister Phyllis said, "since I told her everything I know. About him. About you. About the TV program."

He began to suck air through the dark spaces between his teeth very hard with a sudden luscious sound. "I started in radio years ago—a kids' show called *Checkerboard.* We showcased Edgar Bergen and Charlie McCarthy. We had all the top sponsors—Spam, Stern's meat patties, Hecker's Spreadables"—he looked around the diner as he spoke these food names. "I've had a massively long career. I was very big, but your Millroy destroyed me."

It had been less than a year since the end of *Paradise Park.* How was it that Mister Phyllis now seemed so much smaller than me? I was a whole head higher; he hardly came to my shoulder. This gave me the courage to face him, and when I did, he moved sideways, propping his cat up, boosting the floppy creature onto his shoulder and looking annoyed.

"All Millroy did was open your mike. You destroyed yourself."

"He tricked me."

"You hated the children. You even said so."

"Liar! Your pants are on fire."

"You threatened us."

"It was supposed to be a joke."

"We were afraid," I said.

"Then you're all fraidycats."

"You wouldn't let children be on your program and you used wicked bad language."

The cat was hissing harshly on Mister Phyllis's shoulder.

"Millroy ruined me. I have not worked since."

He spoke in the same breathless way that his cat was now hissing, both the man and the cat gasping and sucking air.

"You're sticking up for him," Mister Phyllis said. "He's using you. You're a fool and you don't even know it."

I did not reply. Maybe I was a fool, but Millroy wasn't.

"You're a silly, clucking chicken," Mister Phyllis said.

The cat had begun to gargle, all its sounds like bad pipes or an old toilet, and I backed away when I heard the word.

"But now you're all alone."

I did not know what to say. I could defend Millroy when he was at-tacked—he was a magician, he had supported us and saved us all—but I could not defend myself. When I was criticized I always thought, *They're probably right.*

"You're all going to be sorry."

He took a step toward me, clawing the air with the yellow nails of one wrinkled hand, and his cat yowled. As I whimpered out loud there was a clatter from the far end of the room. The woman I had seen earlier now stood up unsteadily and kicked her chair aside.

"That's enough of that," the old woman said, her voice rumbling, as she hurried toward Mister Phyllis. "Get away."

Smoker's Voice made her sound tough. Mister Phyllis winced as she raised her hand, and the cat screeched again.

"Leave off," Mister Phyllis protested, and made a horrible face, as though to frighten the woman.

She was bigger than I had guessed, and heavy, with an old woman's slow, thumping walk, moving one big leg and then turning her hips and moving the other leg, and not even looking at Mister Phyllis but concen-trating so hard on me that I had to glance away.

"This little bloke, Alex, was sticking up for him," Mister Phyllis said in a whining voice.

"I am flat-out not interested," the woman said, sounding like Millroy at his most definite.

More in fear than anger, Mister Phyllis raised his claws at the woman, like a cat backing up and hunching as though to spring at her.

"Do you want to be hurt very badly?" she asked him, with an edge in her voice that said her patience was almost gone. For a moment I ex-pected her to hit him.

"I'm giving you five seconds to leave this place," the woman said. "If you're not out of here, I'm going to harm you. Don't think I won't. Now git."

Mister Phyllis seemed even smaller as he snatched his hairy jacket from a chair and made for the door. All this while the cat complained and gasped and moaned, and even now it was hard to tell whether the noises came from Mister Phyllis. They were at the window, distorted by the glare, and then they were gone, swallowed up by the night.

• • •

The woman and I stood facing each other in the diner, breathing hard.

"I'm very sorry, sonny," she said in a gentle voice, and came a little bit closer.

I imagined that I had seen her clench her fists, but no, her fingers were twisted and swollen like Gaga's, with arthritis. No one in the Day One Diner was ever this old or feeble, and I was so unused to being with such a person that I was as amazed by her kindness as I had been by her threats against Mister Phyllis.

"Who was that horrible man?"

"I thought you came here with him."

"I did, but I don't know him. He called me out of the blue. He said he knew where Millroy was. I told him I was looking for Millroy, too. He could have given me directions. Instead he insisted on coming with me."

She was looking around the diner as she spoke, blinking in the bright light and glary whiteness. "He thought I might be able to help him," she said. "I probably could if I wanted to."

She hobbled nearer the counter and leaned over it to get a look at the kitchen. "Now I'm not so sure—anyway, why should I?" She turned to me. "What's your name again?"

"Alex. You can call me Rusty."

She stared at me and did not say anything, then she smiled and nodded. She said, "I'm Rosella."

I thought it was odd that she did not say my name, but she had turned away and was moving heavily to a chair. Even though she had told me her name, I found it hard to think of her as Rosella, or by any other name. Old people did not have first names, or if they did, it seemed disrespectful and wrong for me to say them.

"Got anything to drink?"

"Carob tonic. Melon pulp cocktail. Juiced cucumbers. Green drink."

She made a face.

"Anything alcoholic?"

"Grape wine," I said.

"That sounds more like it."

I poured her a glass of wine and then quickly put the bottle away. Although we had a liquor license, I was too young to serve alcohol. But it was late, we were closed and I was not charging her. Millroy would have said okay, but more than likely he would have changed the wine into water if the police had questioned us.

The woman sipped the wine, then took a longer drink, swallowed and said, "This is a nice place. He's got a marvelous eye."

She had purple in the corners of her mouth. She leaned over, put her chunky elbows on the table, sighed and looked old again, and tired. But I felt grateful that this elderly woman had frightened Mister Phyllis and chased him away.

"I'll bet you met him at a birthday party." She raised the wineglass to her lips.

"Mister Phyllis?"

"No. Harry." When she put her glass down she had a purple mustache.

"Who is Harry?"

"Millroy. What does he call himself now?"

"He was Max. He was Uncle Dick for a while. He was Archie. He was Felix. Now he's Doctor Millroy."

"He used to do a lot of children's parties. He did some acting, too. He was good."

She was still sipping her glass of grape wine and smacking her lips in admiration as she spoke of Millroy.

"He was dynamite as a salesman. He sold everything—books, exercise equipment, vitamin supplements. But he was so restless. First it was sales. Then it was schemes—grow grapes, raise ducks, make candy, Dicktronics. Always something."

The way she praised Millroy made me trust her, and I liked her kindness and generosity. She would be kind to me if she was so gentle when she thought of him.

"But being on the road—all that sitting, all that driving—he got real fat." She drank again and gave herself another purple mustache. " 'I'm a little husky,' he used to say."

Her laugh was high and youthful, a girl's reckless laugh, and for a brief moment she was beautiful. "He could get sideways, though."

In Mashpee and Marstons Mills and other Cape communities there was one reason for older men acting strangely, but this was the first time I had thought it might have been an explanation for Millroy.

"Was it because he was in Vietnam?"

The woman squinted at me and with a half-smile said, "He was much too old for that."

"He had revelations," I said. "He was lost in the darkness of his body."

The woman smiled. "You don't understand. He got very sick. He almost died. He got selfish. He got bossy. He wasn't very nice."

I said, "But then he saw clearly the truth about food in The Book, and he was saved."

I realized that I was pleading with her to agree with me.

"No." The old woman was shaking her head. "He was awful. He lost his job. He was fired. His insurance was canceled. He missed payments on his car and it was taken away. The bank got his house. He worked nights as a security guard for a while. He quarreled. He drove a school bus. After a couple of accidents he was laid off and ended up bagging groceries in the A and P, saying, 'Paper or plastic?' "

The man she was talking about, the ordinariness of him, was not Millroy at all—it sounded like Dada.

"For years he was so defeated," the old woman said. "He talked about nothing but failure. He had nothing. He said he came from nowhere."

"You make him sound so old," I said.

The woman looked sharply at me, stared and thought, and decided not to smile.

"At last he just disappeared," she said, in a gentle voice. "No one knew where he'd gone. People thought he'd turn up after a week or so, that he was just hiding, maybe having mental problems, stress—whatever." She looked up from her glass of wine and smiled. "Years went by. Years and years. Nothing. No Millroy."

"Did he used to say stuff like, 'Punch me in the stomach'?"

"No. But if someone around him was sick, he got scared. That was another reason he left, I suppose."

Now I had no idea what the old woman was talking about, and I think she saw that I was confused. "He said you got to a point in your life when you either went on living or started dying. He left, to go on living."

"He read the Gideon Bible in hotel rooms."

The woman shrugged. "He didn't come from a religious background. His mother was a runaway teenager, his father a construction worker.

The trouble with self-taught people like Millroy is that they never know when to stop.''

Even though he had mentioned them to me, it was hard for me to think of Millroy with a mother and father, bagging groceries or driving a school bus. The Millroy I knew worked magic and spoke of having the secret of life.

That reminded me. ''He works magic.''

''All that must have come later, after he left. He went to some far-away countries. That's the part I don't know. He went looking for another life.''

''Maybe he found a life.''

''Was it yours?'' the woman asked.

''I don't know.''

''Maybe he found six lives,'' she said. ''He was gone a long time.''

''He still goes away,'' I said. ''He's away now.''

The woman was smiling again. ''I was supposed to be a horrible surprise for him.''

''He'll be back.''

''Millroy doesn't like surprises.''

That was true. One moment this old woman seemed to know him perfectly, the next she did not know him at all and was describing a stranger.

''Millroy only wanted one thing in life, and I'm the only one who knows that.''

''To live longer?''

''To be a writer,'' Rosella said. ''Now you know.''

She had finished her glass of wine and was looking around, moving her head in that cramped and straining way of a fat person.

''This is a nice place,'' she said, and began to move her body as though she were bracing herself to get up and leave.

''Want another drink?'' I said.

I had been seeing her grapey mustache come and go. I hated noticing it because I liked her. Even so, purple mustache and all, I wanted her to stay. She was the first person I had met who knew more about Millroy than I did, and I found it a relief to talk to her. There was so much more I wanted to ask her.

''No thank you. I have to go.''

She got to her feet heavily and steadied herself against a chair as she clapped her hand against her head, gathering her white wisps and patting them into the great, round, falling-apart nest of hair.

"Because I don't want to hurt him," she said. Now she turned in the direction that Mister Phyllis had gone. "That horrible man wants to. I didn't realize that. I'm sorry I came with him. That man frightens me. He could be dangerous. Tell Harry. You know him."

But Harry was someone else, the man she had known long ago, not Millroy.

"At first I knew him good," I said. "After a few months I didn't know him so good. These days he seems like a stranger."

"That's him," she said, and smiled.

"I don't know what to do."

"I think you're right for him," the woman said, and reached over and patted my shoulder. "What's your real name, girlie?"

"Jilly Farina."

I thought of the sad little hidden person that name belonged to and burst into tears, and tried to stop, and sobbed even harder, with my hands trying to hide my face, and the tears running through my fingers.

"Please don't go," I said, with tears dripping from my mouth.

"I can't stay," she said. She hugged me. She was big but weak, with soft arms, no muscles, just elderly cushions. "Millroy doesn't want me here."

"I don't care. I want you to stay." I felt so safe with this old woman, as I once had with Millroy—safe, protected, needed. As I once had with Mumma.

"I want Millroy to be happy," she said. "You should want it, too. You're right—he is a magician."

"I can't help him," I said. I was sniffling. "I don't know him anymore."

"He needs you."

"He left me. He does it all the time—just goes off."

"If he went away without you, it means he's counting on you to wait for him."

I was in despair and turned away to cry again.

"He chose you," the woman said.

"How do you know so much about Millroy?" I said, meaning that I did not really believe her.

She held me, got a grip, as though feebly indicating that she did not want to answer. She shook her gray head slowly from side to side.

"Are you his Gaga?"

"His what?"

"His granny."

"No, dear, I'm not."

"His Mumma?"

"No."

With each question I had asked she loosened her grip on me a bit more, and now she let go and stood at a little distance with a sad face.

"I was like you once."

It was the saddest thing I had ever heard. She said nothing more, only looked at me with her old, sorry face and then went out of the diner, moving slowly, shifting one big leg after the other and holding her hands and fingers a certain way, as though to balance and help.

After she was gone I was alone and shivering in the dark, and I prayed hard for the night to pass.

32 Leaving Millroy and the Day One Diner and everything else would be like stripping off old clothes, I thought—but no, it was like putting them on. It was confusing going home after so long—and anyway where was home?

I crept off at sunrise and was out of the diner before the first Sons and Daughters arrived for work. That was when I felt it. Walking down Essex Street, taking the shortcut to South Station, I saw a person I took to be T. Van coming toward me in the drizzly dark. I hid in a doughnut shop and thought, *Something is different.*

At the P. and B. bus stop I had the same feeling of unexpectedness, and in the bus itself as it headed south on the Expressway, watching for busrider's landmarks so I would know that the first hills and meadows were close—the gas tanks, the *Globe* building and FINE STEAKS—it came to me again: *Something is different.* I could not understand it because I was going home. Was I getting lost?

Maybe it was my trying to hurry away from Millroy and failing. I was amazed when a man across the aisle from me raised his *Herald* and slapped the folds flat. I saw DAY ONE CHURCH ASSAILED AGAIN BY CLERICS in a headline and, in smaller print, REV. MILLROY.

He'll hate that, I thought at first, and then: *What's it doing there?*

At that moment this sense of something different became a sense of something wrong. *I don't want my name in the paper,* he used to say. My secret was out. Millroy was on the bus and I was left feeling entangled, as though I couldn't get away from him, couldn't leave the diner without running into him. Bumping into someone can be much worse than constantly being with them, and I hardly knew him now, though it seemed everyone else did.

This was why I had to leave Boston and the Day One Diner. The diner had become like home to me, and I was happier than I had ever been with Gaga in Marstons Mills, or Dada in Mashpee. But Millroy had grown less and less familiar to me, and finally, with last night's visit by Rosella, whom I thought of only as *the old woman,* Millroy seemed like a total stranger, almost an enemy.

I did not know him now. I was afraid to see him again, and each time I remembered us together I shivered. That headline in the *Herald* made me sick. What was the Day One Church? Who was Reverend Millroy? I saw him feeding me, spooning herbage into my mouth, taking me through the nighttime Boston streets to watch people eating, waking me up with the sound of his snorts and bad dreams and pleading, *Talk to me, angel.*

These remembrances frightened me like the close calls that memory makes much worse when you think about them a long time afterward. Maybe something terrible had already happened to Millroy, but I could not bear to buy the newspaper and read about it. He was everywhere, but who was he?

When the bus stopped at Plymouth to pick up and drop off passengers, I tried calling Dada from a pay phone, but a school-teacherish recording told me the line had been disconnected.

The new person across the aisle, a man in a suit who had gotten on at Plymouth, had opened his *Wall Street Journal,* and I wondered whether Millroy was mentioned in it, too.

It's not ladylike to read over someone's shoulder.

I kept reading. I never understood people's sarcasm anyway, and it was not until after four more exits that I realized the man might have been talking to me.

Ladylike? I got so confused I stuck my thumb in my mouth and kept it there until we got to the Canal.

I felt better when we crossed the Sagamore Bridge to the Cape, but after we passed the junior high, Mashpee Baptist, the Grange Hall, the Trading Post, the Gas and Go, Ma Glockner's and Mister Donut, I felt different. Looking at where you came from through the road dirt on a bus window can make you feel like a failure.

I saw stapled to a fence a poster with an elephant on it advertising the Barnstable County Fair and laughed. The sound frightened me, as though someone else had laughed. Then I walked the whole way from the rotary to Main Street and thought, *Am I walking because I'm too chicken to arrive?*

If home meant winding back roads lined with long, straggly grass, no sidewalks, twisted trees with branches growing over them, and all these little wooden painted signs, then I had forgotten it all. I felt weak and pathetic just walking along them, keeping to the side of the white line where there were torn plastic cups, crushed beer cans, here and there a dead, stiff squirrel, and cars and trucks going past me, taking no notice.

Pine Street was a lonely pair of wheeltracks, and Dada's driveway was tufty with weeds and as long as a back road. The sound of my Day One shoes crunching the gravel made me feel small, but I knew the sound would have been more terrible on Gaga's driveway, which was why I was here.

Dada's trailer was just the same, rust-busted metal collapsed off its cinder blocks. I rapped the flimsy door with hurting knuckles before there was any movement inside. Then a face: Vera Turtle. Her nice green eyes had red rims and her lips were swollen from pain, as though Dada had hit her hard. She had a balled-up hankie in her hand.

"I ain't cryun," she said, and pushed the door as though she had been expecting me.

"I couldn't call you. The phone's been disconnected."

"I use the one at the Tradun Post," Vera said. "But no one knew where you were. We looked all over. Even the police didn't know nuthun. I was a wreck."

She pronounced it *veck* with her teeth on her lips, which made the word seem worse. She was very thin. She looked unhappy but lovely, misery sharpening her features, making her gaunt and more beautiful and giving her a look of intelligence.

"Never mind," I said. "Here I am."

"You're too late, lovey. And what have you gone and done to your hair again?"

My Alex haircut, my Alex clothes. I was stepping into the body of the trailer, which still smelled of old clothes and Muttrix and Vera's cologne, a syrupy, clinging odor like fresh paint. The place was neater than I had ever seen it and there was no cooking in the air, as though she had stopped eating. The television was on, yakking—a big face on the big screen.

"So where's Dada?"

Vera let out a loud sob that rattled me so badly I burst into tears, and then so did she. The way our weeping echoed in the small tin trailer told me that it was empty and that we were alone.

It was unbearable to think of that sick man dying, all his torments, but I could stand his death, the fact of it, his being gone for good. Yet it was the worst news I could have received because I had been counting on him to take me back, so that I would not have to go to Gaga's. I was sad. I remembered how Millroy had praised Dada at the Gas and Go, and felt guilty and ashamed. When Dada had been alive he was present, huge and horrible, every minute, and so the empty space he left was bigger and more awful than average.

I was also thinking that the worst part of feeling guilty is being weak, and knowing that you will agree to almost anything. Vera was still talking but I was not listening, only thinking of Dada dead. Now it was too late to say or do anything, but what would I have said if I had found him alive? *I love you* would have been a lie. It was a truer sign of my feelings that I had said nothing, and that he died knowing that I had gone away. Today I was back, alone, empty-handed, suffering. We had had what we each deserved. There had not been time for either of us to tell lies or to pretend our feelings were different. If I had found him dying I would have said things I did not mean, and would have felt like a cheat.

"I'm not going to cry no more," Vera was saying, and then cried.

I was sorry for Vera Turtle, on her own in this small, rusty trailer. Sorry, too, because she was glad to see me.

We sat talking near the loud, crazy television, not listening to it.

"You must be real hungry," she said, after a while. "You ought to eat somethun."

I said yes, although it was she who looked starved, her grief like malnutrition.

"Let me take you for a burger up Reddy's."

I thought, *Please, no,* and felt sick.

"Sounds good," I said.

Vera snorted another sad noise, and I hoped she was not crying again. Her back was turned and she was headed for the door.

"Turn the TV off?" I said.

"Nah. We'd just have to turn it back on again when we got back. Matter of factly, it's good for keeping burglars away."

I took this to mean that it was never off, and just as we left the trailer I thought I saw Millroy's face on the TV screen; he was talking fast, his mustache jumping. Or was I imagining it because of my gloomy mood and the disruption of death?

It was early afternoon on a steamy day in July, gray skies and blowing trees, and the grass looking black from the bad light, the sort of hot, headachy day that made you wonder about summer and hope for a sudden shower to clear the air. As always on the Cape, I had the sense of other people—summer people, vacationers, people with money—driving past us on the main roads, and on these back roads there was only us, in old cars, going nowhere.

This past winter had left injuries on Dada's Toyota—rust, scratches, scummy paint, dented door panels, the coughs of its blurting exhaust. That was how I knew I was home—nothing worked right.

Vera was talking slowly as she drove us over the Mashpee line and down the Old Barnstable Road shortcut, past the public housing in the pine woods and the house trailers in the woodlots. "They get them lawn ornaments in Stop and Shop."

I heard this with Millroy's ears: *Lon onnaments in Stawp and Shawp.*

"I have no use for money anymore," Vera said, meaning that Reddy's was a fancy restaurant where you splurged.

But it wasn't. It was a greasy roadside drive-in at a little crossroads mall in East Falmouth that sold old age and heart disease with its Red

Hots, and was famous for the roaches you sometimes found in the mustard pot. Reddy's sign was flashing neon showing wiggly flames and a devil in a chef's hat spearing a sizzling hot dog with a pitchfork.

"Smoking or nonsmoking?"

"Non," Vera said before I could butt in. She smiled at me, as though apologizing, and explained softly, "It makes me throw up now."

Walking in, I began seeing it all with Millroy's eyes. Was this the difference I had been noticing since early morning? Millroy had gotten inside me and was directing my attention and thoughts, determining my reaction. He had converted me, replacing all my previous judgments, and my feelings too, with his own. This should have been helpful, yet it disturbed me because I saw Dada's death Millroy's way. It had been pneumonia brought on by a kidney ailment, Vera said, but the Millroy reasoning inside me said it was too much fat, too much red meat, too much alcohol, all that smoking. It was bad food and congested bowels. Millroy logic explained life and death, and this explanation took the place of grief.

The poisons ate him up, Millroy would have said. *His food destroyed him.*

It was a pity, but he himself was to blame.

It's not a sin—I hate that word, Millroy would have said. *It's an error—in this case, a fatal error.*

"What are you thinkun about?" Vera said, picking up a menu from the back of the napkin dispenser.

"Dada."

"God called him," Vera said.

No, I thought.

"God took him," she said.

No, Dada did it to himself.

"He tried holdun on. He was fightun hard. It was no good."

I was surprised by my calmness; yet I went on hearing Millroy's voice in my ear saying: *You do not cry over someone who turns their back on the miracle of God's food. Who does not value life enough to want to live longer. Who deliberately abuses their own body—even if it is your own Dada. Bury this mistake and walk away and learn from it. The human body is biodegradable.*

Grief was not a Day One feeling.

Was this the difference? That I was different?

"They got all kinds of good stuff here," Vera said, fussing with the menu. She was thin, but seemed more nervous than hungry.

Reddy's menu showed the same devil with the pitchfork and the hot dog, looking wicked, as on the sign out front. But it was dirty and so gluey with old jam that my fingers stuck to it and I could not let go.

"They fix some delicious chickun," Vera said. "Real tender. It'll melt in your mouth."

Poor Vera—you're killing yourself, too.

"I'll have a banana," I said.

"Banana split, honey?"

"A plain banana."

She looked at me as though I was wacko, but then winced sympathetically; maybe thinking that Dada's death had crazed me a little. That was understandable.

"Have a lime rickey," she said. "Lime rickeys are real healthy. They got juice in them."

"Sounds good."

"I should get a cheeseburger," Vera said. "I need the vitamins. I've been feelun so blah. It's the cryun that makes you weak. It drains you."

A waitress in a red dress—a devil on her apron, horns on her paper hat—said, "Can I get you a cocktail or a beverage?"

"Vodka tonic," Vera said, and with Millroy's ears I heard *vogka tawnic,* "and she'll have a lime rickey."

"D'you know what you want?"

"Chicken Wing Fingers Diabolo, a side order of Red Hots, and a vanilla frappe," Vera said. "And bring her a banana."

"Just a banana?"

"I already asked her that."

The waitress wrote this down and went to get the drinks.

We sat in silence, waiting, Vera sighing in her throat, more like grieving than breathing. I looked around with Millroy's eyes.

Reddy's was small and dark, with wisps of grease in the air, the stink of hot fat, burned meat and scorched blood. It was not the smell of food, it was the stink of death. Along one wall were booths where we sat, and on the other side of the room was a bar counter, where some big paunchy men in T-shirts and baseball hats were drinking beer and watching television. Over the bar were red dancing devils with tails, grinning, hot dogs speared on their pitchforks.

Millroy would have laughed because it was perfect, the devils cut out of red-painted plywood, with a border of flames, the pointy horns and long tails, the burgers, the sausages and Red Hots and grease, a sort of eating hell. *Weenie worship.*

Being fat is being blind, Millroy had once said. *Fat is darkness.*

In the other booths people were eating noisily, wolfing burgers and Red Hots, and even their children had big soft bellies and cheeks shining with grease. They all ate in the urgent, sulky way that had fascinated Millroy on his nighttime walks through Boston when he peered into restaurant windows. He probably did it in other Day One cities too, watching people stuff their mouths and chew. The eaters at Reddy's were pale, cranky, misshapen, hobbling, unhealthy, with a hungry look that Millroy called despair—lost souls, slowly dying, even Vera sipping her vodka tonic, watching the waitress setting out the Chicken Wing Fingers Diabolo.

"Did you ever come here with Dada?"

"All the time."

A sad, soulless place, Millroy would have said, staring with blazing eyes at the people gnawing bones, but I just felt far from home.

"How's Gaga?"

"Just about the same," Vera said, chewing the flesh and skin from a wing finger.

"Does she ever mention me?"

"Being as I never see her," Vera said, "I wouldn't know."

She sounded huffy saying this, but I knew she was hurt because Gaga did not like her. Nothing to do with being a Wampanoag; rather, Vera had a black grandfather, Hickmott, who still lived in Oak Bluffs on the Vineyard. The distant blackness had turned Vera's complexion golden and given her beautiful features.

"Didn't Gaga come to the funeral?"

"There wasn't a funeral as such," Vera said. "Just a kind of burial over at The Mills. Some of my people were there. Ever meet Malvine? Ever meet Jewel and Cory? There were a few Farinas there from New Bedford. Cheryl, his ex, came. She wanted to play something but there was nowhere to plug her guitar in. And them guys from off the boats, from when Ray was a tuna spotter."

Now she was picking at the Red Hots and there was a flick of vanilla frappe on her cheek. "Plus it rained," she said.

I was pretending to drink through the straw of my lime rickey, making serious-sounding sucks. There was nothing at Reddy's that I could eat—a whole restaurant of uneatable food. It was not a problem. I would ask Vera to stop at a supermarket on the way back to Mashpee, where I could buy beans, fish, nuts, flour and fruit to make some Day One meals for myself.

"I'm real glad you came home."

"Me too." But the word made me think, *Is this home?*

"It gave me an excuse to eat, I guess."

That made me feel terrible, seeing the chewed wing fingers, the Red Hots smeared with glops of ketchup, the dried froth of the vanilla frappe like sea scum on the tall plastic cup.

I was trying to think of what to do about Gaga (Would she lock me up and beat me? Would she kick me out and call the police?) when Vera hitched herself higher in her seat, looked out of the booth and said something that took my breath away.

"Hey, Jilly, do you think that guy Millroy is righteous?"

What? Apart from the fact that she got both our names into one sentence, I had been thinking of Millroy ever since we had come into the restaurant. Magic.

"How do you know him, Vera?"

She looked at me with froggy eyes as though I were the odd one. "Everyone knows him," she said, and blinked and smiled. She was looking in the direction of the counter behind my head. "Millroy's on Sunday TV after that aerobic show."

"Body Shaping."

"That's it. And afterward there's that guy with the glasses and the blue gown."

"The Hour of Power."

"But I hate that Pat Robertson," Vera said. "He got a dog jaw and doggy eyes, and he's wicked right-wing."

I turned around and saw Millroy's face, a photograph like the one I had seen in the newspaper on the bus, filling the TV screen.

"That's him," I said, and again I had the sense that something was wrong.

"That's what got me thinkun about him."

"Is this his show?"

"No. Like I said, it's on Sundays. There's only the Friday repeat of *Day One* after *Copwatch.*"

She even knew the name of the show!

The sound of the TV in Reddy's was turned down, yet the men were staring at the screen, and a moment later an announcer replaced Millroy's face. There were bursts of basketball, then a weather map of New England, with temperature numbers, and then the news.

"What was that all about?"

Vera shrugged. "They call it the nutty religion."

"It's not a religion."

"Because they eat nuts."

"They eat a lot of different stuff."

"Crazy stuff."

"Food," I said.

"They pray in toilets."

"Who said?"

"Everyone knows," Vera said, and laughed at me for not knowing. "Where you been, kiddo?"

At first I had the spooky feeling that Millroy had bewitched her with hypnotism, as he had when he'd gotten her to stop smoking—that this was his way of getting at me for running away from the diner. But no, it was only because she had seen Millroy's face on the TV at Reddy's and had watched the show.

"He thinks he's better than other people," she said.

Then she called for the waitress in the red dress and asked for a doggy bag—*donkey bag,* she called it—for the leftover wing fingers and Red Hots.

"You could maybe have it as a snack later on," she said.

I did not say anything on the way back. Instead of driving straight to Mashpee, Vera detoured through Falmouth and up MacArthur Boulevard to the Bourne Bridge, to Flagler's in Buzzards Bay, to buy some discount dog biscuits for Muttrix. I remembered Millroy's telling me that dog biscuits, full of roughage, were better than most human food.

We passed Pilgrim Pines Trailer Park (HOOK-UPS AVAILABLE!) and the pay phone beside it where Millroy had made his first call to *Paradise Park with Mister Phyllis,* and the little Portuguese store in Buzzards Bay itself where Millroy bought chick-peas, flour and melons. It was all history now.

That night in Dada's trailer, I thought about Vera's giving up smoking and felt, *He is here, too.* And he was, his full face all over the TV screen in a flickery late-night rebroadcast of *Day One* from one of the Providence stations, talking about controlling bodily functions and showing how he had taken charge.

I have taken command of my bowels—he peered out of the TV, his head bulging into the little trailer room—*Can you say that?*

Looking at me.

"Yes," I said.

Lying in my lumpy bed, with the smell of the trailer in my nose, I felt far from home. I remembered Millroy's picture in the article in the *Herald* that I had seen on the bus. I had not wanted to read it because I was running away. Now I felt lost and stupid. I needed to know what was in that article, and got out of bed the next morning determined to find a copy of yesterday's paper.

"Can I fix you breakfast, Jilly?"

"What have we got?"

"Anythun you like."

"I usually have millet bread, melon and honey," I said without thinking. "Or fish. Or figs."

Vera just stared at me, holding a box of Kellogg's Sugar Frosted Flakes and a sticky hunk of Danish pastry.

"Is my bike still around back?"

Looking spaced-out, as she sometimes did with sleep in her eyes, Vera nodded at me.

The bike lay in the long grass. It was rusty, the handlebars were loose, the seat was too low, the front wheel rubbed against the fork. But I wheeled it to Gas and Go, where I pumped the tires, and then rode to the Trading Post. Shorty told me he had sent yesterday's papers back. The 7-Eleven on Pine Street didn't have it, or the Riverway Motel.

What happens to yesterday's newspapers? Millroy had asked on a *Day One Program. One day everyone's reading it and worrying. The next day you're wrapping garbage in it. Cut out the middle man! Don't bother to read it—just use it for garbage.*

My search for the paper had taken me to the main road, Route 28, and seeing the Marstons Mills turnoff, which was downhill, I kept going on my wobbly bike, past Pizza Plus and Capeway Roofing and the meadow beyond the pond, where Dada was in the graveyard. I walked the bike through the gate and easily found the *Farina* stone because I had spent so much time there tending it for Mumma. I had always knelt and prayed when only Mumma was here, but it was confusing with both of them buried together, and I felt the way I once did, long ago, in the trailer, when I knew they were both in bed. I always left the trailer then. I left the graveyard now with the same sense of awkwardness, holding my breath.

I pedaled past the old grassy airport to Gaga's. Nothing had changed since my last visit, when I had come with Millroy. The house looked weatherbeaten and silent, the roof slightly crushed and sloping, the window shades pulled down, the tall orangy daylilies and some deep blue pansies at the corner of the porch brightening it, and clusters of heavy, mumbling bees clinging to the pink blossoms of the hollyhocks and making the stalks sway.

Hiding the bike behind the hedge, I sneaked around back, wondering what I would say if Gaga saw me. I got to the kitchen door and listened. The talking was not Gaga. It was the TV, a talk show, in the front parlor. There was no motion in the house, but when I looked closely I saw her at the far end of all the open doors in the house, in her chair, with her fingers pressing against her face. She was like a creature in a cage, like Yowie, like her own canary, Blossom, here by the window, all of them harmless and blinking, just waiting. She looked trapped and sad, and though she faced me she was not thinking of me, and so she could not see me.

I slid closer to the wall to look deeper into the house, and that was when I saw Millroy's face again. It was in the rectangle of folded newspaper at the bottom of the canary's cage. Part of it was torn, and all I saw was the dome of his head, his mustache, the words "Day One" and "denies." The rest of it was spattered with Blossom's green droppings.

33 "Aw, I knew it was a crock," Vera said at breakfast the next morning. She had microwaved the leftover Red Hots and was holding the ketchup bottle over them and slapping the bottom with the flat of her hand.

She was talking about Millroy and *The Day One Program*. I kept thinking, *If Vera knows about it, everybody must.*

"It's not a crock," I said.

She listened to me because she knew I never lied.

Vera had discovered *The Day One Program* when Dada was in Falmouth Hospital on a respirator. Someone, maybe Cory or Jewel or Malvine, had told her to watch, that Millroy might have the answer: if Dada ate the right food he would recover. It was the simplified, popular, misunderstood version of the program, Day One as a miracle cure for illness and aging. At the time, Dada was being fed intravenously, so it had not been possible for him to eat any Day One food.

"You think it would have worked?"

"No," I said.

This seemed to relieve her. She slapped the bottle again and ketchup glopped all over the plate.

"Like I said"—she ate one of the reheated Red Hots and gagged— "it's a crock."

Then she shook out some Kellogg's Frosted Flakes into a bowl and poured milk on them.

"It's not just the food. It's a spiritual thing, too. Dada would have been wrong for it."

"So who's right for it?"

"You might be."

She was just young enough—maybe thirty-five, innocent enough, good-hearted, and her diet was terrible. As soon as she became an eater and switched to Day One, she would sleep better, feel healthier, and her bowels would sing. Most of all, she would stop grieving over Dada. People like her showed the fastest rate of change, Millroy said; this was the reason the fattest, sickest people were the easiest to convince. For them the first month of Day One brought about dramatic results, rapid weight loss, more energy, regularity.

They phoned him and cried out, *I'm producing two pounds of waste for you!*

I knew this because I took the calls.

I told Vera some of this. I said, "Millroy's a magician."

"Them people are all the same," she said.

She meant preachers, like the one talking on TV at the moment, the Reverend Oral Roberts. Vera was not watching *The Oral Roberts Show*; she never sat down and watched TV. It was simply a light flickering at the far corner of the trailer, the screen like a hole you looked into to see the rest of the world, or else to hear the world going *yakkety-yak* in the next room, or explosions, or the *rat-tat-tat* of a far-off war, or crying, or canned laughter, or talking heads.

Plant a seed to God, Oral Roberts was saying.

"A seed—that's money," I said.

"That's what I mean," Vera said.

God spoke to me. He called me and said, "I want the name Oral Roberts to stand for healing."

"Hear that old man?" I asked.

"Sure. God talks to all of um."

"He doesn't talk to Millroy. He doesn't talk, period. God reveals his truth in other ways."

"You know all about it," Vera said, smiling. She began to spoon Sugar Frosted Flakes into her mouth and looked at me as she chewed and gulped.

"In the way we live. In the way we die. God was watching Dada in the hospital. He wanted us to watch him, too, and learn a lesson."

"You been going to church?" Vera asked.

"No."

But if I am your healer I need to be near you, and my mission needs to be on the air. Don't you want to be healed of your pain?

"How can that old man heal anyone by prayer alone?" I realized I was quoting Millroy, but Vera didn't know it. "You have to do the work yourself. Eat healthy. Switch to Day One food. Get menus from The Book. Stop smoking. Stop eating french fries. All that."

"I have to give up these Red Hots and these Frosted Flakes?"

"No one eats that stuff in the Bible, Vera."

"Well, they don't do a lot of things in the Bible, Jilly," she said. "Like there's no cheeseburgers and fried clams and prime rib and no candy bars, either!"

She hooted this, believing she had stumped me, but I said, "Exactly," and she made a face.

"Are you turnun into one of these Seventh-Day Adventists?"

"Of course not. They're all-American, Millroy says, but they're not strict enough. They eat nut cutlets and Leenies and Veggie Burgers. They believe Jesus is going to come to earth again, the Second Coming."

Vera was staring at me from behind the box of Kellogg's Sugar Frosted Flakes. That reminded me. "The Adventists did do one major thing in America," I said.

While she was munching her cereal, Vera said something, made a noise that sounded like a question.

I said, "They relocated in Battle Creek, Michigan. Get it?"

"No."

"Because they got their vegetarianism out of the Bible, they decided to invent cornflakes," and I shifted the box around so that she could read *Battle Creek, MI*, on the side, "so that they wouldn't have to eat bacon and sausages. They invented peanut butter, too."

"Who told you that?"

Millroy, who told me everything.

"I read it."

"You should go on *Jeopardy*," Vera said. "If they invented cornflakes and peanut butter I guess they're not so bad!"

"Most peanut butter is carcinogenic. That and the Sugar Frosted Flakes prove they're a wicked bad menace, Millroy says," I said. "Maybe they invented the American breakfast, but Millroy invented a whole new American diet."

The key to deliverance is instant obedience. Ask the Lord how much you should send, and then do it immediately. Keep our mission on the air. . . .

"They demand ten-percent tithes, and this old guy is begging for money. Millroy never asks."

"But they say he's as rich as all get-out." Vera was still munching Frosted Flakes, as though to defy me.

"Who says?"

I kicked back on my chair, looked at her, and marveled at the way we were talking. Millroy was a shaven-headed man who smelled of freshly baked bread and cool melons, with herbs on his breath and a dusting of millet flour in his mustache, who long ago had leaned over and put his face near mine. *I want to eat you.* Now he slept on the shelf beyond my cupboard in the Day One Diner on Church Street across from the Park Square location of Legal Sea Food. I knew more than that: he snored, he sometimes had nightmares, he took me late at night through Copley Square and Back Bay to look at people eating in restaurants, and the word "lite" when applied to food made him howl with mocking laughter.

Now here was Dada's Wampanoag woman, Vera Turtle, in a house trailer in Mashpee talking about Millroy as though he were someone she knew fairly well. I felt as I had on the P. and B. bus when I saw his picture—as I had felt each time I saw him on television, and even the glimpse of him at the bottom of the bird cage. *He is mine, I am his.*

"Everyone says," Vera said, as though Millroy belonged to the world.

Later in the day I thought it might be a trick or a trap—that Vera knew where I had been, that she was saying these things to provoke me so that I would admit that I had run off with Millroy.

To test her, I said, "Vera, do you know what I do in Boston?"

"You said somethun about a job."

"In a diner. Wait-person."

"Yeah." She did not want to know more. She accepted that, she was not interested, she trusted me.

"Listen, Millroy is different from all the rest of them."

She smiled at me. *They're all the same,* she was probably thinking. For her, Millroy was big and famous, and people talked about him, making him even bigger. He had no connection with our world. He was rich and faraway, someone half-real, half-imaginary, a star. It had amazed me that she knew his name, but she knew more than that. She had a grasp of some of the elements of *The Day One Program,* she knew that Millroy had started other diners in various American cities, that he had cured some people of serious illnesses, that the program had been recommended by doctors as effective against bowel cancer, diverticulitis, obesity, wrinkles, heart disease, aging, constipation.

"It's like a religion that makes you feel better," she said.

"Not just feel better, it actually makes you healthier," I said. "That's what religion ought to do."

"But what are you supposed to get out of it?"

"You live for two hundred years."

"You sound just like him," Vera said.

"Hey, there he is."

Vera was walking ahead of me as I stocked up at the A & P Future Store at the South Sandwich crossroads, buying melons, nuts, beans and flour. I looked around, expecting to see Millroy. She hurried to the magazine rack, picked up a tabloid, *The Examiner,* and held it for me to see. There was that same old photograph of Millroy looking like an oversized light bulb, and the headline, WHY I FIRED MILLROY FROM MY TV SHOW. It was a story by Eddie Mazzola about the end of *Paradise Park.* I bought it and read it. *Foul-mouthed preacher,* it said, speaking about Millroy's talking about toilets and bowels.

This made me more watchful for Millroy's name, and after that I took a bike trip alone to the CVS pharmacy near the rotary and looked at the magazines in the rack. On the covers of some women's magazines I found *Millroy Saved My Life* and *The Day One Diet—Does It Really Work?* A magazine I had never heard of called *Longevity* had a small picture of him in a corner of the cover, and the line *Saving Yourself the Millroy Way.*

The whole cover of *Newsweek* was taken up with the words LIVING LONGER: AMERICA SEARCHES FOR ANSWERS. I knew that Millroy was mentioned in the article inside because I had taken the call from that reporter. I bought the magazine and read it when I got back to the trailer. But there was only one short paragraph about Millroy *(The Boston-based Day One Church),* and the rest I could not understand.

I went to other stores, just to look at the magazines and newspapers. Millroy always said there was nothing in them, and there was nothing you could do about the news, so why read the papers and make yourself unhappy? People would go on starving, fighting or praying on all fours whether you read about them or not. Now he was in those publications. One magazine had nothing more than his name on the cover, MILLROY.

You had to be famous when just your one name explained everything about you. Millroy had always avoided publicity. But it had not worked; in fact, it might have made him more famous, because it seemed as though hiding only made them chase him and try to find him. He became famous by refusing to cooperate.

I said to Vera, "I had no idea Millroy was this famous."

"Where have you been?" she asked me again, and when I did not answer she said, "You were probably too busy to notice."

Not too busy, but too close to the man and his magic. All the publicity might have made me doubt him. Instead, it made me a believer. I had left him because I felt I did not know him anymore, but now I realized that no one knew him. These articles did not describe him. And I was not as ignorant as I had thought—I knew his strangeness, his kindness, his magic, his dreams. I had met him when he was a magician at a county fair. I had seen him have a psychic duel with Floyd Fewox, I had watched him destroy Mister Phyllis. I had met the mystery woman, Rosella, who knew him better than anyone. All this made me feel important, knowledgeable, strong. I knew Millroy's secrets.

Once I had thought I could run away from him—go home and be rid of him. I imagined going back to school in September, sticking it out and trying to study. Go back to raking Gaga's leaves and doing Dada's dishes, listening to my Walkman in bed, going to Craigville for pizza, fishing when the blues were running, watching TV, and maybe next year getting a cleaning job at a motel in Hyannis, saving up to buy a used car. Until last summer, when I had met Millroy at the Barnstable County Fair, it was the only life I had ever imagined for myself. Just the other day I had tried to take the bus back to this life. But I came home to find that he was here—on TV, in magazines and newspapers. Vera talked about him more than about Dada, said her friends talked about him. *No one knows me,* Millroy had said to me more than once, and it was true. But everyone knew his name, and things that had been concealed from me became obvious as I watched his show with Vera. I realized that he had revealed himself to me, that I knew him better than anyone. It made me miss him, it made me lonely. Did he know this?

It was different seeing him in Dada's trailer—not simply because Dada was dead and Millroy was where Dada had been. More than that, he had power and presence, he seemed more magical. We had sat in the diner, the Sons and Daughters and I, and we had laughed seeing Millroy work magic or listening to him describe what he called "The Journey from Fatland." We screeched when he showed us footage of people eating, and when he was not traveling he sat with us during the rebroadcasts, and we laughed even harder, knowing what was coming. Why was Millroy not funny when I watched him on the TV in Dada's trailer? He was strict. He was serious. His eyes bulged. No jokes. He ranted and did hostile strongman tricks. It was all life or death. Vera was frightened, and I did not blame her.

"If he lightened up I'd believe him," she said. She could only calm herself by being skeptical. "Hey, everyone dies eventually," she said.

I could see that Millroy terrified her.

Life is fatal, people say. But let's see, Millroy said on the next *Day One Program* that Vera and I saw. *Take this narcissus.*

"Might as well change the channel," Vera said from the far end of the trailer, where she was cowering.

But I wanted to see him and sat on the remote switch.

The Book uses the word "rose" when the actual Greek text says "lily" or "flower." But we know that in the Age of Day One the bulbs of flowers were eaten. "Dove's dung" we read about in the Book of Kings—that's an awful pretty flower, your so-called "Star of Bethlehem." You can roast the bulbs like chestnuts, or dry them or grind them with flour to make bread, as Elisha must have done in Samaria.

"There he goes again." In this small trailer it was impossible for her to back away, so Vera was making herself small.

Consider the lilies of the field—consider that they have edible rootstocks, that they're good in soups and stews, and excellent as a dessert, drizzled with honey. Chewing on a lily bulb, he said, *Tastes great. But what about this other stuff you eat?*

Before him on the table were beakers labeled MILK, BEER, WHISKEY, COLA, TROPICAL FRUIT DRINK.

What happens when you put this stuff into your body?

He lifted an earthenware pot, which held a lily flower rooted in its bark-mulch soil. The heavy, yellowy-white blossom swayed, nodding as he set it down.

Shall we try it?

"What the heck's he tryun to do?"

Millroy poured some milk into the pot, then some beer, then the whiskey, the cola and the tropical drink. The liquid dripped and drizzled through the holes in the bottom of the flower pot into a basin.

Think it's going to grow and put forth more blooms? As he spoke, the lily drooped and the blossom turned brown. The petals fell. The leaves softened. Then the whole thing flopped over the side of the pot and liquefied into ribbons of black slime. *It dies the way your body does.*

As a trick, as the truth, we would have found this funny at the diner, and Millroy would have laughed with us. But the collapse of the flower was a little horror verging on tragedy. It was serious and solemn. *The flower is here one day and then she is gone.*

Why did he say "she"?

Isn't that so?

"Yes," I said.

Vera sucked wind and stared at me.

"See what I mean?" Vera said. "You don't know what to think about that guy."

My mouth was too dry for me to say anything.

"Kill it," Vera said. "Let's watch a game show."

I did. I surfed with the remote switch, but I went on thinking about Millroy. That *Day One Program* was another indication that something was wrong. It was his quavering voice, and the way he put his face against the TV screen, in the same way you put your face against a windowpane, as though he were looking for me. *And then she is gone.* Now, at this distance, I realized that no one knew Millroy as I did. I heard sounds that were inaudible to other people, I saw things that were invisible.

Millroy was sorrowful, he was tense, he was fidgety and impatient. I knew that the whiskey and milk and the rest of the forbidden liquids had not affected the lily—there was not enough time to show it dying. He had killed the flower with his own strength—passed his hand across it and drawn out all its energy with time-lapse magic.

I don't like using magic, he had said often enough. *Miracles and magic are the last resort. Even the Lord knew that. I only do it when I'm desperate. But these are desperate times.*

Seeing Millroy on TV, I understood him better. I had needed distance to put him into focus. Now I could see that he was suffering. He was not the man described in the press. He was not the man whom Vera spoke about. He was someone I knew. He was my only friend. I remembered the old woman, Rosella, saying *He needs you.*

Still, I stayed in the trailer in Mashpee, not knowing what to do next. Vera needed me, too. She told me how glad she was that I was with her, how I had taken Dada's place. She said that with me around she felt like making plans. *I'm getting real focused,* she said. *Like I was stressun out before, but now I want to put out some good energy and stop stressun.*

Millroy's next program was about angels. *Angelology,* he called it. *There were giants on earth in Day One,* he said. *Look at the Book of Genesis. The sons of God saw the daughters of men, that they were fair, and they took them wives of all which they chose, and they bore children to them. The children of the sons of God and the daughters of men were angels . . .*

He looked so sad.

There are still sons of God on earth, he said, *and still daughters of men.*

And peered out of the TV again, looking around with big searching eyes, with such heat in them that I began to squirm when he glanced in my direction. He looked haunted, he looked thin, he was not eating. He was weak.

You have to feel that someone is watching over you. That someone cares. That you are not alone.

He missed me.

"Most of the time I don't even understand what the heck he's talkun about," Vera said, calling out from the kitchenette.

Perhaps no one did these days. He was talking to me. Now I was sure that something was wrong.

"Want some root beer?"

"No, thanks."

Millroy's voice was echoing, but I could not tell whether it was coming from inside or outside my head. It was like earphones clamped on my head, his voice in both of my ears, with the twang of Vera's voice behind it all.

"There's some Ring-Dings in the Frigidaire."

But I was listening to Millroy, who was urging me to listen.

"And a whole bunch of Bolsters in the freezer," Vera said. "Your favorite."

I just want to say one more thing to you.

I replied to him, but if I could not hear what I was saying, how could he?

Life does not have to be fatal.

I still could not hear my own voice, though I heard Vera's dark whisper like a shadow behind Millroy's voice.

"You talkun to me, Jilly?"

I made another sound because Millroy was saying, *You know?*

"I thought you said somethun to me," Vera said.

On Millroy's sweaty head, small drops were beaded all over the tight skin of his skull and some were running down the sides of his face and into his mustache.

But life seems pretty meaningless now, doesn't it?

"It sure does," I said.

That's because you feel all alone.

"Who are you talkun to, Jilly?"

I muttered something that meant I wanted her to shut up, but it only made her come farther into the room, nearer the set.

I feel the same, Millroy was saying. *I need to be in your life. And you need to be in mine.*

"Amen," I said.

I heard that. That was from the heart.

I said something grateful and made a joyful noise.

"You talkun back to that guy on TV?"

Millroy smiled, as though he had heard what Vera had said but was ignoring her and only paying attention to me. I said something more, then positioned myself so that he could see my face.

"They call him 'Anal' Roberts," Vera said. "Get it?"

"No," I said. Tears were coming out of my eyes and wetting my cheeks. Never mind, I was happy.

I need you back in my life, Millroy said. *You need me in yours.*

I shushed Vera as she tried to interrupt.

"Why are you talkun to him?"

"Because he's talking to me," I said.

"Get a grip, Jilly."

Millroy winked at me; he had heard that. He was smiling.

Life is only fatal when you're alone, he said.

"That's mind control," Vera said.

She made a dive for the TV set.

"He's trying to mess with people's heads."

"Not people, just me," I said.

When she switched the set off, I squawked and turned it on again, but before the picture flickered, shook and pasted itself on the screen the program had ended. I could hear Millroy protesting in the dark, his voice sounding suffocated as he said, *Are you there, muffin?*

I could not see him. A second later there was a Burger King commercial, and then a cartoon about Diet Crunchettes, and finally *Body Shaping* began.

"It's some kind of cult," Vera said, sounding angry and scared.

She pretended to be tidying the kitchen, but she was really whimpering with fear.

Later on, she said, "Like it just hit me, kinda. You goes to your Dada's gravestone and you gets stressed. Jason Tobey told me. The Pocknetts seen you pushing your bike. You're real stressed, so you start talkun to this TV evangelist. Hey, it's mind control."

The program had left me in a peculiar mood, as though I were a little wind chime and were still ringing softly. Vera did not know me at all. Only Millroy knew me. I had not come home. No, by leaving Millroy I had run away from home. I was lost here.

There's nothing to fear, Millroy had said. *You are not alone.*

He had been talking to himself as much as to me. These last two *Day One Programs* had been like conversations between him and me, a kind of pleading on his part, and me sitting there trying to keep my lip from trembling.

It was so strange after this last program—Vera doubting and fearful and confused, talking about Millroy as though he were the most dangerous and famous man in the world—that I walked out of the trailer and biked down to the Mashpee crossroads to the pay phone on the wall of the Trading Post and dialed the diner, Millroy's private line.

"Who is this?" he said, taking a sudden breath as he heard me say hello.

"It's only me."

"Angel, where are you?"

"Never mind. I'm on my way back."

"God," he said, and the way he said it, sounding so relieved and hopeful, made me feel strong.

"Anything wrong?"

"Everything."

It was almost inhuman that Millroy never cried, or shed a tear, and yet he spoke this word in the hay-fever voice of someone trying not to sob.

34 He was so glad to see me, coming toward me fast and looking toothy, as though he wanted to eat me, that I was almost frightened, yet there was something even worse than that. The first thing he said to me at the South Station bus stop was, "Millroy was very anxious. Millroy doesn't fret, but he was very concerned about your personal safety."

It made me look around, expecting to see someone else, maybe his brother.

"And don't believe any misapprehensions you've heard about Millroy."

That was it, the way he talked about this person Millroy, who was actually himself. It scared me, as though there were three of us now in the diner, worrying each other to death.

He did it again later on, just a mumble.

"They've been trying to start rumors about rat droppings," he said. "But Millroy docs not countenance rat droppings, or animal scats of any kind."

And wagged his head, no, no, no.

"Not Millroy."

It made him smile, and I imagined he was seeing this other Millroy in his mind.

Then, suddenly, he put his nose into my face.

"Buddy, what have you been eating?"

That was all in the first half hour. The day got stranger. I said hello to the Sons and Daughters. "We got so much to ax the Big Guy," Peaches said, which meant that they wanted me to do the asking. I went into my cubicle. My little space was exactly as I had left it, everything in place, and I sensed in the way it was so tidy that Millroy had missed me. Anyway, hadn't he said so?

A whirring sound came from his room: was he shaving his head with his electric razor, and talking? I peeked through the door crack and saw that he was not shaving his head or even his chin. He was talking on the phone and running the razor in and out of the mouthpiece of the telephone receiver.

"We can't help you," he was saying.

Whee-whee-whee, went the razor.

"We are on a plane—a flight to Denver—*whee-whee*—where we have a facility."

I shut the door. I could not stand hearing him tell lies—and who was *we?*

He mumbled all night as he lay in the dark cupboard on the shelf he called his bed, and he was gone in the morning.

That was my homecoming.

"We're working the phones," Shonelle said. "He hates that old telephone."

"Some dude's been giving out Big Guy's private number," T. Van said. "He's getting nuisance traffic, is what he calls it."

"They trying to sweat him real bad," Troy said.

"Makes him get in his car and go rollin," Peaches said, meaning driving fast, listening to gospel tapes or any music.

Two nights after I returned from the Cape, Millroy woke up and spoke to me in the darkness—one of those sudden conversations, a voice without a face, that spooked me. "You heard me talking to you on TV?"

"Uh-huh."

"I knew it," he said.

"I was listening."

"I saw you. Sitting there with your face in front of the TV screen, and that doubtful Vera woman just behind you, warning you against me."

So I had been right about his speaking directly to me, even when Vera was talking about mind control and *Who are you talkun to?*

"Only two of you. I didn't see your Dada."

I began to cry, sniffling, and trying to swallow my sobs.

"Never mind, muffin. You're home."

Pretty soon I was back at work—the Day One Diner had never been so busy—but Millroy seemed disconnected and often absent. Then, just when you assumed he was in another city or taping the program, he would show up, but more sudden and complete than just "showing up" he would burst, whole, out of the air. One moment empty space, the next moment Millroy tangibilized.

One day he tangibilized himself so fast in the kitchen that he blocked my way and I almost tripped over him.

"Where are you going, buddy?"

He looked pale and nervous, and there was pleading in his voice. He touched my shoulder lightly, but even so I could feel the trembles in his fingers.

"Just mopping," I said. "Getting some work done."

Millroy always said hard work was a form of prayer because it gave you an appetite for Day One food, and the eating experience centered you in reflection.

"This place is getting gross."

Which was unusual, too, its looking neglected. But Millroy only winced and did not deny it. He looked panicky, as though he thought I was going to run away again on the bus. He opened his mouth, and it seemed as though he were going to apologize, but that was not the sound I heard. A burst of shrill barking came out of his body, as though he were replying. The sound came from in his pants pocket, an electronic beeper.

"If anyone asks, I'm in Baltimore."

He locked himself in his cubicle, and all afternoon I imagined that he had made himself small, about the size of an Ezekiel loaf, hiding on his shelf.

People said he was amazing and they believed he was rich. Even Vera regarded him as a celebrity and a powerful man. Yet here he was, interrupting my mopping, then getting nervous, and finally lying about going to Baltimore and scuttling into a hot little corner of the diner. No one, especially an eater, would have believed it. No one knew him but me.

Mopping the floor, I thought about the way he had confronted me and said, *Where are you going, buddy?* He had seemed desperate. He had even touched me, just grazed my shoulder, but I felt it. What was the problem? He had money, he had power, Day One was a success. He was famous all over America.

"Yo. Rusty." It was T. Van. He was helping me mop. "We sure glad to see you, man."

"I am specially down to that," Troy said. "I am tripping out."

I told them that I was happy to be back, and I meant it, because now I knew I had no other home.

"We were getting real worried about the Big Guy," T. Van said.

Peaches heard us and came over. She said, "He just stands there being bald and watching us sometimes with his mouth open, and I was thinking, 'What's he good for?' "

"You could show a movie on his big old head," Troy said, and went *keck-keck-keck,* and seemed surprised when I didn't laugh with him.

T. Van made a serious rotation with his head that seemed to mean that he had something on his mind.

"Tell Little Alex about the electric razor," Peaches said.

T. Van said, "This is straight up. I seen the Big Guy shaving the telephone, running his unit over it."

"He doesn't believe you," Peaches said, meaning me.

"You don't understand," I said. "He was pretending to be on an airplane. That razor was just background noise. I already figured it out."

"Yo. That makes a whole lot more sense," T. Van said. He widened his eyes. "That's just so normal, to have his old Remington going upside his telephone." Then he turned his back and screeched, laughing hard, the same *keck-keck-keck* as Troy's. "On an airaplane!"

"But we real glad to have you back, Little Guy," Tomarra said. "This is like before."

"You mean it was different while I was away?" Because I could not imagine the diner any other way.

"It was madness," Tomarra said.

"Funky?" I asked. It was one of her own words.

"No. It was a zoo."

"First he starts that beeper," Shonelle said. "There's people after him, he says. I'm thinking, 'Which people—are they, like, real?' "

"If he thinks so, that's all that matters," I said.

"But the thing is, who's beeping him? We never figured that out."

The way we were whispering now frightened me, because we had never tried to hide anything from Millroy before, and had always spoken up when we thought something was wrong. Anyway, Millroy could hear the smallest whisper, so what was the point?

"Then he starts locking himself in the office," Troy said. "He only comes out to do the program, and that's once a week."

"Didn't he talk to you?"

"All he ever did was go, 'Anyone see Alex?' and when he came back, he's like, 'Anyone call?' meaning you, guy."

That night, while we were whispering again among ourselves, Mill-

roy went into the kitchen and with his back turned to us, started slapping dough, crushing onions, parching lentils, pouring green broth,
carving melons and making wheat balls. As it was evening in the diner, I
thought this food was for tomorrow, but no. "In here, buddy," he said,
opening the door to the back room.

He glanced up at T. Van and Peaches, who were on their way back to
the kitchen after serving customers. They stared at him with white eyes
and smooth, serious faces, compressing their lips, looking back at him
like people looking at a stranger who might at any moment lose it.

Millroy shut the door on them and locked it with a snap like two teeth
sinking into the door frame. He said, "Millroy's got something for
you."

The way he said it made me cover my face. I pretended that I needed
to rub my eyes. But with my eyes shut I smelled bread and fish and figs
and sweet melons. It was what I had missed, living with Vera in Dada's
trailer. It was the smell of home, of life and health, and it was magical. I
had not seen the food, but I knew that he had prepared it himself and
transported it from the kitchen to the back room by tangibilizing it. The
table was set—one plate, with covered dishes, earthenware crocks and a
glass of grape wine.

"Sit down, angel," he said, and when I hesitated, added, "Please."

A kind of sorrow in his begging tone touched me, and I obeyed.

He hung back in the shadow of the shut door. I did not know whether
he was cowering or crouching. Millroy was usually truthful, but he also
knew how to be mysterious.

"Go on, eat," he said. "Please."

That same almost cringing tone. I picked up the dusty, floury bread
loaf, broke it into three pieces the way he had taught us, and venerated
the food. "This is Day One, all this you have given us, the gift of life.
Amen," I said.

"The bread's fresh-baked."

I nibbled the crust.

He said, "We're opening diners in three more cities. I've got the
leases. The program's in about twenty more markets. There are repeats
most nights. The simulcasts are really popular." But he looked furtive as
he spoke. "You can do better than that, angel."

"I'm not very hungry."

"Who's been feeding you?" He sounded sad.

"I've been feeding myself," I said, "and I had a whole bunch of figs a little while ago, and some wheat balls."

"My wheat balls?"

"Troy's," I said.

Millroy blinked. His mind was whirring, and he still seemed to be thinking about something else as he began to speak again.

"We are making an unbelievable impact. We've had acceptance in the major markets. I get testimonials every day. 'You made me strong.' 'I am reborn.' 'I am cured of bowel cancer.' Muffin, I've got doctors on my side. I'm thinking of starting an Executive Club—Day One Doctors."

He went on talking, yet he still seemed uncertain.

"Eat that," he said, holding out a finger of fruit.

"I can't."

"You have to." His voice had grown fainter since he had locked us in the room. It was strange, his voice seemed to match the shadows—all this food, one plate, one glass, no windows, just the two of us. Now I could hear him breathing hard and snorting down his nose hairs.

"I'll be sick if I do," I said.

"Put it in your mouth."

The melon finger dripped and gleamed as he held it against my lips and prodded them. The syrupy juice dribbled down his fingers as he held it, but the fruit squashed like poor weak flesh as he probed with it. I resisted, and then I licked it a little. Tears came to my eyes and I began to choke. "No."

He tried again, urging it against my mouth.

"I'm not hungry," I said. I was mumbling with my mouth shut because I knew that if I opened it he'd stick the fruit in and gag me. The wordless noise that came out of his neck was a twisted sound, like a whimper. He stood there sorrowing as he watched me, and he went on making sounds, but they came out of his body. Did I know this man? Perhaps he was the other Millroy that my Millroy had mentioned.

"You didn't tell me you were planning to leave," he said.

"I didn't plan it."

"But you left," he said. "It was all a surprise. I was in shock."

He paused to let me say something, but I kept quiet.

"There was a gaping hole where you had been. I missed you. The hole was within me. I wandered through space and time in America and found myself with strange food in my hands and had to put it down.''

Now I was staring at him. ''You sound like yourself on a program,'' I said.

He ignored my remark. He said, ''There were so many things I almost ate.''

What was *that* supposed to mean?

''In many ways we have been triumphant. We've been written up in all the papers. I don't mind the persecution. What messenger wasn't mocked and vilified? Some days we do two or three hundred lunches at this location. But all the diners are flourishing.''

I knew this was probably true, yet he seemed doubtful, as though he did not believe it.

''What was it like for you,'' he said, ''as a runaway?''

As soon as he said this I felt myself about to cry, just like the other night. I tried to hold back because sobbing is like vomiting.

''Dada's gone,'' I said.

Millroy sized me up with glassy eyes, as though if he blinked he could make me disappear.

''My father.'' I swallowed and started again. ''He died.''

''It was written on his face. I could smell it in the trailer—his decaying lungs, his laboring heart. I didn't want to tell you.''

He was looking at his hands as though reading fine print at a distance.

''How did you feel when you found out?''

''Bummed.''

'' 'He that loveth father or mother more than me is not worthy of me.' ''

''I guess.''

Now the tears were rolling down my cheeks, and I was trying to keep the sobbing inside my mouth.

''I'm crying for you,'' I said, because grief was not a Day One feeling.

Millroy nodded, then picked up my spoon and used it like a dipper in the beans, scooping and stirring. ''You need this bad,'' he said.

I shut my mouth and turned my head, so he poked my cheek with the wet spoon. ''You know how bad you want it,'' he said.

''No,'' I said, half-defying him for dead Dada's sake.

''Do it for me,'' he said. ''Don't refuse.''

"I'll throw up."

He winced. His face went soft and sagged. He looked so weak. He put the spoon down. When I saw his fingers release the spoon, I felt safe and strong—not so strong that I could overpower him but as though I could protect him.

He shook his head, and when he said, "It's been terrible here," I knew he was only thinking of himself. But when he repeated, "It's been terrible here," in that dry, defeated voice, I felt sorry for him and tried not to think about Dada.

I knew that Millroy would wake me up either that night, or the next, or soon. It happened just that way a day later.

"They're after Millroy, muffin."

He was not dreaming, he was thinking, he was wide awake.

"Millroy's getting threats. They want to destroy him."

This thought made him feel important, and from the way he spoke I knew he was smiling that crooked Millroy-thinking-of-Millroy smile.

"Why would anyone want to do that?"

Now the smile seemed almost audible, like the hum of something electric, an appliance warming up.

"It's a strange story because it's also a success story."

Believing it would cheer him up, I said, "Hey, they know all about you in Mashpee and Marstons Mills. And I saw your picture in the paper on the bus."

Another kind of silence told me that he had become sad again.

"What's wrong?"

"I have enemies."

"Enemies can make you strong," I said. It was one of his own sayings.

"If your soul is right."

"Just be cool."

"Millroy is much too big to hide. All these telephone calls."

"You were always good at vanishing."

There was another silence, the darkness humming.

"If I turned myself into milk would you drink me?" he said.

For a moment I froze. Then I said, "If you're really worried I could work the phones again."

"The Liquor Commission? The tax office? Social Security? The Board of Health?'' His laughter sounded like sobs. ''Someone's paying them off, muffin. But they're officials. I can't ignore them. I've been making money. Millroy is a classic American success story.''

Even though we were separated by darkness, I knew that his hands were on his face, pulling at his cheeks, snagging his mouth—another habit of his when he was thinking.

''They claimed my toilets weren't up to code. That hurt the most. They cited my rest rooms. I never imagined that anyone would cite my rest rooms.''

''What was wrong?''

''The lettering on the sign EMPLOYEES ARE REQUIRED TO WASH THEIR HANDS was too small,'' he said. ''A clear example of persecution. They blamed Millroy.''

He seemed helpless and ignorant saying this, sorrowing for that man Millroy.

''We had a disputed liquor violation. We carded a BU freshman and let him drink, but he had a fake ID. Who's wrong? They blamed Millroy.''

There was a rumbling from his cubicle as though he had made up his mind and was settling in for the night. There was nothing I could do except wake up when he wanted me to, and listen to what he said.

''The ultimate fame is being supermarket famous,'' he said. ''Millroy is huge. He has visibility. You saw it yourself on the Cape—those newspapers, those magazines. They wanted to put Millroy on the labels of fruit-juice cartons. They wanted Millroy on a bread wrapper. The biggest weight-loss company in America wanted Millroy in their commercials.''

He drew a breath, and I could sense air in my cubicle moving toward his.

''Millroy said no. Millroy is serving Day One food in six U.S. cities, with three more facilities in development. Almost two hundred TV stations carry the program. The rebroadcasts give Day One time slots all around the clock, and we have simulcasts on almost a third of them. You do the arithmetic.''

Then he was asleep.

In the morning, in sunshine, which was always worse for its misleading warmth and blinding light, he said again, ''They're after Millroy.

They lie in wait. They talk behind his back. They pester the Sons and Daughters. Sometimes they scare me.''

I was glad he was saying this before the Sons and Daughters had arrived. It was after sunrise, but on these summer mornings it was light at five o'clock, and by this time he was on his fourth baking sequence.

"They'll be pestering you, angel.''

"I won't let them.''

"They don't take no for an answer, and they're not interested in eating. They are cynical and manipulative. They are trying to bring Millroy down.''

"I wish I knew why,'' I said. But I thought it was what he had said before: *I am not Elmer Gantry or Jimmy Swaggart, not an American hypocrite, nor a mountebank.*

"They want Millroy's power,'' he said.

He straightened, seemed proud and grew quiet, with listening eyes.

"They know I have the secret of life.''

He turned to the plate-glass window at the front of the diner and smiled at the world.

"I want them to have my secret! They don't believe me. It is so simple. It is 'Eat goodness.' It is 'Chew it slowly.' ''

He nodded at his window on the world.

"There are so many of them,'' he said. "But Millroy is winning.''

I said, "Mister Phyllis was in here while you were away.''

Millroy considered this and looked around, as though seeing it all with Mister Phyllis's eyes.

"He doesn't bother me. Never did,'' he said. "He's bitter. He is profoundly unspiritual. I can deal with him, but I can't deal with the others and their photographers.''

I wanted to tell him about Rosella. Now he was thinking about photographers, and I knew he had a fear—more than a fear, something like a horror—of having his picture taken. In the past he had sometimes dealt with it by using magic, by vanishing or else making a flash with his fingertips when the picture was snapped, which ruined the photo.

Why couldn't he do that now?

"I can't anymore. I tried,'' he said. "There was no flash, only my voice, a few choice words. I haven't worked much magic. Something's been missing.''

I knew from his gluey eyes what he was going to say next.

"You, muffin."

I nodded. Now I knew it was the truth.

"I'm surprised you haven't seen all the awful lying pictures. 'The Day One Church.' 'The man who pretends to be a prophet.' 'Money-bags.' 'Bowel movements.' 'Mysterious Millroy.' "

"I saw only good things," I said. I could not admit that I had seen the attacks on him that coincided with my running off to the Cape.

"They say we pray in toilets."

"You told us to read The Book in the hopper."

"That's different," he said, but he did not seem sure. "That's edification, not prayer."

I said, "So people are talking about you?"

"Not just talk. Millroy's had dirty tricks played on him. Someone found roaches in Millroy's pottage. They were definitely planted."

"That's horrible."

"And I've had other plants," he said. "Mouse droppings. Other scats."

"That's gross."

"I've had threats."

"What kind?"

" 'We're going to break you.' 'You're defying the word of God.' 'You're the Antichrist.' 'You're trivializing the Scriptures.' 'You're taking advantage of young people.' "

"Reverend Huber? Mister Phyllis?"

" 'We're going to crucify you.' "

"This is just so depressing."

"I've had parents in here."

"Did you say *parents*?"

" 'I am come to set a man at variance against his father and the daughter against her mother,' the Lord said, and now I know why. They are monstrous. I would not repeat some of the things they said to me."

"Parents of the Sons and Daughters?"

"You guessed it."

"They neglected their children."

"Parents' pride—think of it—the idea that it will become known that their children have deserted them. That they've failed as parents."

He had seemed tired when he began, but in defiance some of his strength returned.

" 'And a man's foes shall be they of his own household.' So true."

I said, "I thought everything was working out pretty good."

"It is. Millroy is a success. The triumph of Day One has roused this fury against us."

He turned to me as he said this and looked miserable, as though pleading for me to hold him.

"I never wanted that fame. I only wanted to save myself. I don't want to be crucified, and I feel it is going to happen. Unless . . ."

He lifted his eyes and kept his mouth open as I waited for him to finish the sentence.

". . . unless you stay with me and never run away again. I was lost when you went. I am a devil without you."

He made his hands like bookends and held me gently by my narrow shoulders. There was a smell of fear on his skin. His fingers were damp and twitching. His breath was snorting through his nose.

"I feel you are my soul, muffin."

Just his saying this made me strong, and I went another day without eating his food, so I felt even stronger.

35 Next morning Millroy tried again at breakfast.

Through the wall I could hear the clunks and thumps of a normal morning at the Day One Diner: the Sons and Daughters serving food, the oven opening and closing, the spoons rattling like wind chimes, the click and scrape of earthenware bowls being nested and stacked, the murmur of folks talking in the diner. Our eaters never raised their voices. There were no sudden movements, nothing rough. Millroy had shown the Sons and Daughters how to walk with the least noise, a sort of rolling glide *on the balls of your feet*.

If you did not know it was a diner you might have thought a religious service was taking place, involving crockery and ceremonial tasting and processing back and forth with baskets—thumps and whispers so soft they sounded like waves collapsing on a beach, disturbing the flotsam on the tidewrack and sliding away, or like a freshet, or someone holy shuffling to an altar, the baptizing drip of someone being soused with water—anything but eating. *Every meal ought to be a spiritual experience,* Millroy said.

All this breakfast time, Millroy had me in the back with a bowl of oats, a wheaten loaf and melon balls, trying to get me to eat. I heard the warm diner sounds through the wall, and for the first time I realized that they meant innocence and holiness.

Then the phone rang. Millroy stiffened and someone—probably T. Van—yelled out, disturbing the peacefulness.

"Anyone named Jilly Farina in here?"

Millroy fixed his close-set eyes on me and looked woeful, as though this were the end.

"Who on earth could that be?"

When your shoulders are very small, it is hard to shrug and be believed. I tried it, and then said, "Vera?"

Outside, in the diner, T. Van was smacking the telephone receiver into his palm.

"I might be able to help," I said to him.

"Go for it."

"Oh, God," Vera said when I answered. "I just knew it. I says to myself, 'Jilly must be at that famous restaurant of his.' So I comes down to the Tradun Post and calls Information. I was right, wasn't I? It's some kind of cult."

"No way," I said. "It's an eating program based on principles and suggestions you find in the Bible. It has been proven effective against low-grade infections, digestive disorders and even cancer. It's reversed the symptoms of serious diseases and halted the aging process. Doctors believe in it."

"It's mind control, Jilly."

It was strange her calling me that name while I was here in the diner with people who knew me as Alex.

"Malvine is going out with a lawyer. If you're trapped he could get you out."

"It's voluntary," I said, trying to keep my voice down. "There are no financial contributions. In fact, we all earn money—so much per day for every day in the diner, minus ten-percent tithe."

•••

"Tithe is a contribution."

"Tithe doesn't have to be money. You can tithe spearmint or herbs—Jesus said so in The Book. Or cumin. Jesus sprinkled it on his food like pepper. Everyone did."

"You don't sound like the Jilly Farina I know."

"That's because you never knew me, Vera, and neither did Dada or Gaga. I want you to forget you ever knew me and get on with your life. If you want to do yourself a favor, avoid all manner of fat, the blood of strangled animals, and study your stools. Your body is a temple, Vera, and it can stand for two hundred years."

"I want to help you, kiddo," she said.

I almost laughed, thinking of the things she drank and how she ate pork knobs and chicken parts and Red Hots and everything else.

"I'm fine," I said.

"When are you coming home?"

"I am home," I said, and felt happy.

This had all been said in whispers, and now I cupped my hand over my mouth so that none of the Sons and Daughters would hear me. Vera was still talking as I slid the receiver onto the hook and went back to our quarters.

Millroy was at the table with my untouched bowl of oats, his hands in his lap, looking miserable. Millroy the Magician seemed the wrong name for this sad man sitting limply in the chair, with his chin sunk on his chest.

"It was Vera Turtle," I said, and hearing myself say her name made me sad for her.

Millroy said nothing, did not even nod.

"She thinks you're using mind control on me."

He misunderstood my tears.

"That means you're leaving me," he said in a despairing voice.

I wiped my nose with the back of my hand and asked, "Who is Rosella?"

Millroy looked at me sharply, startled by the sound of the name.

"She showed up while you were away. When Mister Phyllis came. He brought her to the diner that night."

Something was happening behind Millroy's eyes. He was seeing it all—the late-night visit, me alone crawling out of the hatchway, Mister Phyllis's granny face, Rosella taking charge, how she looked at me, what she said. All this motion in his head caused flickering and eye movement, but as it passed he seemed to know me better.

"I really liked her," I said.

Millroy nodded; he knew that, too.

"Afterward, I was, like, 'That's probably his wife,' " and I was falling apart inside as I said it.

His silences and his penetrating eyes made me nervous, but I had to know.

"Hey, are you married and everything?"

There was another terrible silence before he said, "No, but she was the first Mrs. Millroy."

"Did you, like, love her and all that?"

"She was my greatest friend, and friendship can be more powerful than love—at least I thought so then."

I had known that he missed me while I was gone, but now I was convinced that he was alone. He needed me, just as the old woman, Rosella, had said. She had not misled me.

"You are giving off leaving energy," Millroy said, looking gloomy. "I can feel it."

Instead of answering, I snatched up the spoon, dug into the bowl of oats and began to eat. A warm pink light glowed on Millroy's face and shone on the skin of his bald head. He smiled, he sat up straight, he seemed to swell. Then he lifted one hand, made a fist, opened it and there, perched on his fingers, was a frantic parakeet. He snapped his fingers and the bird was gone in a blaze of explosive light, the kind that frustrated photographers when they tried to take his picture. He twisted his mustache and brought out a spoon, which glittered like gold. Magic.

"Let me do it," he said.

He fed me—I let him—and when he said he was strengthened, I believed him. For the first time since I had arrived back, Millroy looked like a magician.

Later on, he locked himself into the rest room and stayed there for four and a half hours.

When he came out he said, "Maybe plant an organic garden. Grow, package and sell food from The Book. Edible flowers. Marigolds, calendulas, borage, sunflowers, chive blossoms. Hyssop from Numbers. Tithing herbs. All kinds of beans. Company motto—'We know beans.' "

• • •

The next edition of *The Day One Program* was full of magic. Millroy swallowed a length of rope, gulped down a pair of scissors, then puked out short, snipped pieces of the same rope, and pulled the scissors out of his pants. He made Day One meals in hats. Cooked the food, produced it on camera, and then ate it all.

Then came one of the greatest displays of magic Millroy had ever managed on television—a tangibilized man. Or was it? Just at the end of the show, there was a commotion. An angry man in black, looking like a priest, began shouting in the studio.

"Welcome, Father Ratto," Millroy said.

"You are the Antichrist!" the priest yelled, and he started to do damage to Millroy's pedestal.

He looked Italian: small and beaky with yellow eyes, Smoker's Face and dark teeth the color of Moxie tonic, and his black gown flapped as he rushed around pecking at Millroy like a crow at a window.

Was this magic or an angry person who had managed to get into the studio? Never mind—you did not ask.

Millroy transfixed Father Ratto with his eyes, then dropped a silk cloth over the man's body, and when he spoke one word, "Drink," the silk collapsed and a glass of dark fizzy liquid was in his place. He had liquidized the angry priest.

Then Millroy tangibilized a porcelain hopper and poured the dark liquid in, and as he closed the show he pulled the chain. "That's all for today, people."

Now I knew what he meant when he said, *I need you* and *You are my soul.* By returning to the diner I had given him strength. I would not have believed it if I had not seen it all happen. But Millroy swore it was so, and it was proven by everything he said and did after that, the way he defied threats, photographers, parents, dirty tricks. The Sons and Daughters also vouched that his power resumed with my return, the day I agreed to eat and to stay, when I told Vera on the phone, "I am home."

I could see the difference that I made to him, and to the rest of them. The Sons and Daughters were happier, Millroy was in charge again, and I felt stronger than I had ever known myself to be.

But how and why? Millroy was a famous man, with his face in the newspaper. I was small-for-my-age fifteen-year-old Jilly Farina whom everyone thought was skinny Alex or Little Al or Rusty.

Millroy always said, *Have faith. Eat as I eat. Then all will be revealed.* I had not expected it to work for me this way, and when people asked me if I thought I was going to be strong and live for two hundred years I said, *Kinda,* because who knows? But now I had power. When I felt the surge of strength through my body, I was happy. I wanted to laugh, I was reborn, as though a light inside me had been switched on.

"Don't let it scare you," Millroy said one night in the dark.

"I'm not scared, I'm confused. Why do I matter so much?"

There was a silence that meant he was amazed that I did not understand.

"Because you are innocent," he said finally.

"You mean, not guilty?"

"No. The opposite of innocence is experience."

At first I said nothing. But he was waiting for an answer.

"Inexperienced. That's me."

"It's like being holy," he said.

I wished that Vera could hear this because it was more than I could explain.

"Just accept it," Millroy said.

So that was it: he needed my innocence, and as long as we were together, we were both strong in peculiar ways, and if we were separated, we would be weak and destructible.

"Please don't leave me ever again," he said softly.

"No." I had plenty of reasons to stay, but the best one was that I had nowhere else to go.

At some other dark hour of the night his voice woke me again, and I could not tell whether he was praying to God or thanking me.

Yet I had walked back into a new situation: he had more success and more trouble now. He told me flat-out that the more successful he had become, the more danger he was in. Everyone thought they knew him, but they did not understand him.

"They think I want to lead them," he said. "No. I want to join them."

When he walked down the street, people saw him, hollered, "Day One!" and stuck up the Day One finger.

Millroy was accosted by parents who wanted to know what had happened to their children. I worked the phones, so I knew he had incessant threatening calls: *You be sorry . . . Where my daughter, Molynthia? . . . You going to get so damn busted up. . . .*

"Yo," they said when I picked up the phone, and I knew it was a parent or a relative.

Dedrick's mother, Rodessa, threatened to burn down the diner unless her son was allowed to come home.

"Day One is his home," I explained.

Millroy was whispering this to me.

"And he is physically in Chicago, Illinois."

"You are going to be physically in the hospital if I don't find my Dedrick damn soon," the woman said.

"Will you deal with this, Daughter?" Millroy said to Peaches.

Peaches took the phone, and listened, then said, "She says she's coming down to torch the whole premises. That's what she says."

The woman was calmed down, but we were not less worried when she did not show her face. She was another angry person, and her threat was on our minds. She could easily burn us down.

I went on working the phones.

"I want to talk to Millroy."

"I am Doctor Millroy's executive assistant. How may I help you?"

Millroy was grateful, and his gratitude made me stronger. The other night, when he sounded as though he was praying? Now I was sure he had been thanking me.

The newspapers and magazines still called, the ones that had already written about him. They wanted more—*People, Longevity, Today's Health, The National Enquirer,* the others. Millroy refused, but still they wrote stories about him.

"They're angry because I wouldn't sell out," he said. "They wanted to trivialize me when I became famous and wouldn't get involved in 'Delicious Diets for Thinner Thighs.' "

He snorted and pounded his stomach with his fist.

"I wouldn't cooperate, so they feel they are obliged to portray me as a hypocrite, like all the others—Brother Bakker, Brother Swaggart, Brother Gantry, Father Mapple, or some Flannery O'Connor preacher shrieking about damnation. They have to prove I am a sinner. They don't understand that all my darkness is behind me, and that I am frank about it, that I talk about it all the time. No, they are trying to crucify me."

"You're not afraid," I said.

"Of course not. Because I have seen the truth and gathered it into my hands."

"And ate it."

"Truly, muffin. I have taken it into my body."

He sounded confident, but on the next *Day One Program,* his mood was different. He produced a globe of the world—the planet Earth popped out of his hands like a beach ball—and he spun it on one finger and spoke reflectively.

What is the commonest bird in the Bible—commoner by far than the dove?

He waited, and then chucked the round Earth up and cast a shadow on the studio wall behind him with his hands, a big bird with a hooked beak. These were the sorts of tricks that made me remember that old woman, Rosella, saying, *He used to do children's parties.*

The eagle, he said, catching the globe. *The American eagle.*

The rest of the program was about hope in America—our fresh food, wheatfields, wonderful plumbing, and his mission of ridding America of obesity, constipation and colorectal cancer, of reversing the aging process and giving each of us two hundred years of life on earth. He quoted the text from The Book that spoke to him of the American revival.

Who satisfieth thy mouth with good things, he said, holding up crocks and platters of Day One food, *so that thy youth is renewed like the eagle's.*

It was one of his most popular programs, "the American Eagle program." People wrote and requested the video, the fact sheet and the recipes.

Yet a doubt remained in Millroy's mind.

"That's the worst of it . . ."

He said this a few days later—he often did this, picking up the end of a thought and saying it out loud, so that you had to connect it yourself.

"That they might succeed. Crucify me. That I might be driven out."

I remembered his bouncing a globe of the world on that wonderful "hope in America" show, and reminded him about it to make him feel better.

"There's nowhere to hide in America," he said. "Everyone knows Millroy's face."

It sounded terrible, and he was still talking. "It is a measure of how vast a thing I have created that it has crowded an entire country with its power. Millroy is everywhere."

• • •

He was way up and then way down. Was it my fault? Never mind, I thought. I watched it get worse.

One bad situation came up with Troy. Millroy often said to me, "Is he watching you?" or sometimes directly to him, "Son, where are your eyes?"

The Son Troy just smiled and said, "I am working, Big Guy. I got no time for jammin'."

All the middle-of-the-night conversations made me sleepy, and one day I dozed off in the kitchen, squatting behind the stairs, my arms folded to hold me up, my head tipped onto my shoulder. I was dreaming that someone was breathing on my face and whispering.

I woke up to find that it was true—Troy's face in mine and his hand holding my hand too tight. His mouth was open, his tongue quivering, and he looked as though he was going to lick my face.

"I want to smoke out your secret, Little Guy," he was saying in a whisper.

Millroy must have heard that. *I can hear the grass grow.* Anyway, he saw Troy, probably through eight inches of brick and plaster. And he smelled it, had the very temperature in his nose, the awful heat of it, he said later. Millroy came out quietly, as though his feet were not touching the floor, and moved toward Troy like a knife blade, and stood before the murmuring boy. Blood streamed from the rims of Millroy's eyes and there was fire in his mouth, flames instead of teeth.

"Awp," Troy stammered, trying to speak, but he was paralyzed, could not speak or stand.

Millroy placed his hand above him, and though he did not touch him, Troy was knocked flat. He rolled over and began scrambling on all fours, like a startled woodchuck, but he could not go far. He was blocked by the counter and got slowly to his feet.

"Get out," Millroy said, "and never come back."

The other Sons and Daughters watched but made no move. I heard whispers. *What he do?*

Millroy's long fingers trembled and extended over the terrified boy, who was pleading with his eyes.

"Out," Millroy said, seeming to hold himself back for a moment. Then he let go and pointed to Troy's leg, stunning it and making it collapse.

Troy sobbed, almost fell and then dragged himself away as Millroy wiped the blood from his eyes.

"Anyone who raises a hand in anger will be destroyed," Millroy said.

"Troy wasn't going to hurt me," I said.

Millroy leaned over and his red, smeary eyes examined me closely.

"I am very glad that you believe that," he said, then hid himself.

Another day there was a scream from table 5, then a ruckus, and everyone on the front-window side of the diner kicked back and jostled and shouted.

"It's a rat!" "Aw, God, a rat!" "Get it away!"

The rat was not on the floor, where most of these people were looking—it was in an earthenware bowl, its head sticking out of some red pottage, dead and stinking, and grinning with yellow teeth, someone's lunch.

Millroy rushed out of his office before the shouts, when the first rat tremor stirred the air. He had poised himself at a little distance to do something—turn the rat into an orchid, liquidize it, anything—when T. Van punted it through the open front door while screaming his head off.

"Some devil done this," T. Van cried out. "This is evil. They trying to bring about the downfall of a great and righteous man!"

Millroy had to comfort him, and he told us that this was not the work of Troy, whom he had sent away, and not of the Devil, but simply of an unhappy person who did not want to know the truth. "It's a plant."

"May I have a glass of wine with my meal?" a man asked in the diner a few days after the rat incident.

Peaches was serving him. She brought him some Day One wine, pouring it from a jug into a cup and setting it before him.

"Now take me to the manager," the man said, pulling out an official-looking ID, which gave his name as Wayne Weible.

Peaches burst into tears and was still crying when Millroy came out to ask what the problem was.

"The girl is obviously underaged, which is a violation of the Liquor Licensing Code. We've had complaints, and now we're going to have to shut you down."

"Hold on," Millroy said. "Where is the liquor in question?"

"This thing of wine," Wayne Weible said.

Millroy said, "The specific gravity of this beverage is ought-ought-two, about the same as slightly fermented apple cider, which this much resembles.'' He passed his hand across the mouth of the cup of wine and muttered a singsong sentence. ''You're sure this is your cup?''

''Yes. And if there's alcohol in there you're in big trouble,'' Mister Weible said.

''I happen to have a hydrometer handy,'' Millroy said, taking out the sort of glass tube with a rubber bulb at the end that I had seen Dada use on car batteries at the Gas and Go. He poked the tube into the cup and said, ''Just to spare you any embarrassment, shall we test it?''

Mister Weible watched the liquid brimming against the numbers on the measurer inside the tube and became very silent.

Millroy said, ''Who sent you here?''

T. Van stepped up to the man looking as though he was going to punt him the way he had punted the rat. But Millroy cautioned him, and Wayne Weible scuttled away before any harm could come to him.

''I could have turned that wine into water,'' Millroy said. ''I could have turned that man into water, poured him into the hopper and flushed him from view, as I did with Father Ratto, and all you'd have heard was that man fizzing down the tubes and the mocking laughter of the drain.''

But these intrusions made the Sons and Daughters jumpy, and the next day T. Van actually slapped a customer who had complained that his food was cold.

There were more dirty tricks—pizzas and Star of Siam take-out food were sent to us, and expensive items from the Neiman Marcus catalog, and bunches of flowers COD. There were unexplained explosions out back and spray-painted words on our windows. There were surprise inspections of the toilets and the kitchen by the Board of Health.

The Tax Department called. We were behind on our payment of sales tax, they said.

''We pay all taxes on time.''

''They want an appointment to audit your books.''

''Millroy has no books.''

He sulked, looking as though he were going to vanish any second. ''For trying to save Americans from physical and spiritual destruction, I am being persecuted. I have had to endure threats. They are trying to bring me down.''

''Who's the person?''

"Not one person—legions of them. Because I will not allow them to cash in on this. For some it is a religion. For others it's a weight-loss program—thinner thighs, flatter tummies. For still others it's a chance to market their diet drinks. Then there are the ones who think that because I am an American preacher, I must be a villain. I am trying to stay pure, so I am being battled."

Another man came. His name was Morrie Arkle. He wore a dark suit and was smiling as he waited for Millroy. He said, "Hi," to me. He looked patient and polite.

"We are currently interested in your lease," he said to Millroy in the back. His tongue snagged on his front teeth as he lisped, and he was fat, with beefy bosoms.

"Who is 'we'? I only see one of you."

"I represent Bub City Crabshack and Carmina Burrito," Mr. Arkle said. "We heard you were closing down. We like your location."

"I am not closing down."

"We had hopes of locating a franchise here," Mister Arkle said. "One of our Bub City units."

While only I watched, Millroy uttered one furious word, worked his hands over Morrie Arkle and turned him into a glass of cloudy liquid and drank him.

"You saw that, angel?"

I nodded. I could hardly believe it.

"I am still winning," Millroy said, wiping his mouth as I watched.

But he was sick as a dog all night.

As soon as I woke, I went out and looked for someone to tell it to because I wanted to see their face when I said, *Millroy liquidized that pestering stranger and drank him, and now he's seriously ill and no wonder.* I wanted to tell someone who loved Millroy for his magic.

Millroy had groaned all night and today his skin was soft and pale like bread dough. He had thumbprint smudges all over his face. He looked at me with suffering eyes that seemed to say, *Remember this, too.*

There was someone to tell that next morning—Willie Webb, the Day One Son from the diner in Denver.

"You still here?" he said. He was so unfriendly I could not think of anything to say in reply.

His head was so closely shaved it was shiny, and he looked strong and

confident, transformed by the Day One diet into a smaller, darker Millroy.

"What is going down?" he said.

But he was too loose and distracted to listen, and before I could tell
him what Millroy had done, he was talking again.

"The Big Guy is in wicked bad trouble," he said. He turned his back
on me and looked for Millroy, who was in his rest room and had been
for hours.

"Why?" I asked.

"Maybe because you're still here," he said in a snarly way, sniffing
and blinking, hating me.

36 Then, still early that same morning, the day after Millroy
drank Mister Arkle and when Willie Webb showed up
sniffing and looking righteous, some fat men in tight suits
gathered on the sidewalk in front of the diner before we opened, and
they passed out pink sheets of paper, handbills headed MILLROY—
THE DEVIL, while the man himself was out back, moaning.

"This is not the coolest time to be locked in the function room,"
Willie said, eyeing the men in suits with the handbills.

"Who are those guys?" I was used to eaters who were friendly and
kind. These older, bossy-looking men looked like villains, just in the
clumsy way they walked without smiling.

"You're going to find out," Willie said. "We got them in Denver and
all over. It's all down to they after the Big Guy. Maybe you know why."

I said I had no idea.

"That's funny you don't know, Little Guy."

"We apprehensed them in Denver," Stacy said. She had come back
with Willie.

I told him about Wayne Weible and the phone calls and the man,
Arkle, from Bub City Crabshack and Carmina Burrito.

"We were getting fried," Stacy said.

That was the beginning, but soon two or three more Sons and Daughters showed up, returned silently like birds gathering on a tree, and they were much sleeker than when they had first joined Millroy. At first I was glad to see them, but they took no notice of me, and as though by a pre-arranged signal the rest of the Sons and Daughters appeared minutes after Willie Webb, having left the Day One diners in their cities—Kayla and Berry, Jaleen, LaRayne, Tuppy and Ike, looking strong, their heads shaved, even the girls.

This is the baldest room in Boston, I was thinking, all these hairless Sons and Daughters like monks or little Millroys.

Sometimes on the Cape at Gaga's, crows would flap around the oaks, strut on the roof, caw, and peck at their reflection in the windows. They would gather all around the house, blackening the porch, making me feel it was their house now, like the crows were taking over, each caw meaning: *Get out.*

The sudden showing up of the rest of the Sons and Daughters seemed to make the men with handbills out front more threatening; it was as though they had guessed that trouble was brewing.

"The Big Guy is overdue," Willie Webb said out loud in his new, abrupt, untrusting way.

I was looking past his shining head at the strangers outside the diner handing out the pink sheets of paper.

"He's still feeling kind of sketchy," I said. "I mean sick."

It was odd hearing Willie Webb demand to see Millroy. He had been the first Son and he knew how to talk to Millroy directly—so different from the others, who needed me to pass their messages or interpret for them. Already, in Millroy's absence, Willie was taking charge.

After a while, what I had said to him sank in, and Willie got interested again because Millroy had never been sick before, only tired after he worked magic. This was like a human illness, digesting that obnoxious man, who must have been more disgusting and dangerous than Millroy had guessed.

"So what's happening?"

I was glad he asked, and glad too that the other Sons and Daughters heard him and came closer to hear me.

"A man named Morrie Arkle from Bub City Crabshack and Carmina Burrito came in yesterday asking Millroy if he could buy out his lease," I said. "He was kind of, like, 'As you're closing down.' "

•••

Willie raised an eyebrow at me as though he was not impressed, and said, "He tried to hassle the Big Guy?"

"Millroy must have suspected it. He took that man into the back room and juiced him," I said. "I saw the whole thing."

They squinted and muttered, reminding each other of how they had seen Father Ratto liquidized on TV, but they seemed to suspect that this magic of Millroy's might be a trick.

"Make him into a glass of water?" Stacy asked. "Something like that?"

"Yup. Only it wasn't water," I said. "It was human juice, sort of a cloudy liquid, like old chicken broth."

I remembered the floating blobs of fat scum on the surface, looking like last week's soup.

"He get sick from juicing that man?"

"From drinking him," I said, and watched their admiring eyes.

"Big Guy!" Tuppy said.

T. Van got a sweaty head just trying to picture it in his mind.

"About two quarts," I said. "He drank it all."

"That is boss!" Berry said.

I said, "Except he never got sick before. Something is happening."

"You know it," Willie said and unfolded a pink sheet of paper, one of the handbills.

I got a glimpse of MILLROY and DEVIL and felt sick myself.

"We been seeing these in Baltimore," LaRayne said. "And now you got them."

"They're here, right enough," Dedrick said.

The men outside were tramping the sidewalk in a slow, shoe-squashing walk, taking fat, tottering steps and panting like the sort of angry Christians who disliked Millroy. They gave out the handbills to anyone who would take them.

"What are we going to do about them?" I asked.

Even glancing at the handbill in Willie's trembling fingers, I could see at once the news was bad. Millroy's name appeared at the top in big letters, and there was a picture of him looking evil. Certain words in different typefaces stood out, seriously ugly, such as *molester* and *criminal* and *liar*.

Glaring at me, Willie said, "Maybe the Big Guy should have wised up and drank somebody else."

He shoved the handbill at me as though he did not want to touch my fingers.

MILLROY—THE DEVIL

Millroy calls himself a Preacher, a Magician, an Entertainer and a Doctor. These are criminal lies! Millroy never finished high school! He is a flat-out fraud. He is guilty of criminal deception.

MILLROY is a

—LIAR: He has never earned a doctor's degree or any other!

—BLASPHEMER: He claims the authority of the Bible for his Godless religion. He has distorted the Bible's teaching and twisted the Word of God!

—SNEAK: He refuses to meet members of the press to discuss his hiring policies. He will not speak to parents or return their phone calls!

—INCOMPETENT: Millroy was fired from his last two jobs—Foskett's Fairground Entertainment, Inc. (who he still owes money to), and TV Station WMBH for "lewd, obscene and offensive conduct . . . unacceptable in a children's show."

—TRICKSTER: He claims to be a magician but is not even a member of the Magic Circle and is a proven fraud.

—MURDERER: It has been established that the Day One Diet can be fatal for people with weak or irregular hearts or respiratory ailments. It is estimated that Millroy has killed over 300 Americans with his diet.

—MOLESTER: Many of the young kids who work for Millroy were lured away from their homes against their will, and are forced to work long hours for nothing. They are frequently terrorized and assaulted by the man who calls himself a Prophet! He claims that the young boy he lives with is his son!

Millroy must be stopped! Call his number (617-DAY-ONES) and speak your mind! Don't eat in the Day One Diner! Put an end to Millroy's criminality!

It fascinated me, not because it was all lies, but because I could recognize the shadow of Millroy in it, all the possible rumors and misunderstandings. It was Millroy the Magician painted black.

I passed the handbill to Berry.

"We had the same one in Chicago," he said, and he looked at me the way Willie had, with hard, unfriendly eyes.

T. Van began to read it.

"It's all garbage," Stacy said.

T. Van tried to reply. He stuttered and then, as though energized by his failure to get the words out, burst through the diner door and attacked one of the men, pushing him so hard that the man stumbled and dropped his armload of handbills. Instead of kicking him, T. Van kicked the handbills, scattering them.

"That big black kid hit me!" the man said, looking pleased.

In the meantime, T. Van had found his voice and was saying, "I will mess you up good. I will kill you. I will cut you."

Just then, Peaches went out and took T. Van's arm and said, "Be cool, bro."

"Sister," he said helplessly and began to sob, his face twisting with grief.

A silence had fallen on the diner as we watched this, and it was such a powerful silence, like the thickest wall of stone, that we turned. Millroy was standing in the kitchen reading one of the pink handbills.

He had appeared suddenly, had sprung out of the air, become tangibilized. He glanced through the sheet of paper, reading quickly, while we watched him, not knowing what to say.

"I was expecting this," he said.

He had recovered from gulping down the cloudy liquid which had been Morrie Arkle of Bub City Crabshack and Carmina Burrito. His skin was pink and firm, the smudges gone from his face, his eyes clear, and he was calm.

He said, "I have been in there for four hours on the hopper. I am purged."

Crumpling the handbill, but in a gentle way, simply gathering it and squeezing it like a hankie, he snorted.

"I knew it."

Was he smiling?

"I'm surprised they waited this long."

"It's lies!" Dedrick said loudly.

"In a way," Millroy said. "It happens to most messengers. It's a horrible misunderstanding."

He was smiling, he knew I felt the same, and was startled by Dedrick's outburst.

"What are you doing here, Dedrick?" he asked.

"I'm here to help you, Big Guy."

Millroy glowed with pleasure at the sight of all the Sons and Daughters looking healthy and so much like him. He never seemed more powerful than when he had this look of serene humility.

"And is that you, Willie Webb?"

"We're hurting out there, too," Willie said. "The wackos are after us."

"I will kill them," T. Van said. His eyes were glassy, he looked stupid and dangerous.

"No," Millroy said, and got everyone's attention with his smile and his easy manner. He seemed happy, and not just contented, but fatherly in a way I had never seen in him before. Perhaps it was the sight of all the Sons and Daughters gathered here to protect him.

"They are hassling us with these handbills and hurting business," Willie said.

"They are dissing you," Dedrick said.

"I am a public figure, and the law is loosely applied to well-known people in public life."

"It says here you're a murderer and a molester."

"Hyperbole," Millroy said. "That's demonstrably false."

"What if there's more?" Willie asked, and looked at me with narrow eyes.

"I know I am not a criminal," Millroy said mildly, in the most reasonable way. "You know it. I don't see this handbill as a problem."

"They are trying to trash you, Big Guy!"

Millroy nodded, still softly smiling.

"What did you expect, Willie?"

Willie said, "All I know is, there's going to be more, and that's why we're here."

"I can say with perfect modesty that I have a certain piety. I am no one special. I was fat and I was lost until I read the Bible and made a connection."

"But you got famous, Big Guy."

"As a jobbing magician on the county-fair circuit, I learned ways of putting an idea across. I can dramatize a thought. I can work a routine. I understand audiences. That's all I did. But I was strengthened and left the fairground. I am neither a prophet nor a schismatic.''

''What fairground?'' Jaleen said.

''Barnstable County Fair,'' I said.

It interested them that he had been a fairground entertainer, as the handbill had said, and that I had known it.

''What doing?''

''He was Millroy the Magician,'' I said. ''I was his assistant for a little while.''

''Bet you was,'' Willie said sarcastically.

''Pulling rabbits out of hats?'' LaRayne asked.

''All of that,'' Millroy said.

''He juggled chain saws and blowtorches. He ate broken glass. He made an elephant disappear,'' I said.

''So it's true. You could have been a member of the Magic Circle?'' Berry asked.

''I am not an illusionist,'' Millroy said. ''There's tricks and there's magic.''

LaRayne said, ''So what's the difference?''

Millroy smiled, opened a cupboard, rummaged until he found a ball of heavy-duty twine, some duct tape, and a bicycle lock on a chain.

''Restrain me,'' he said.

The Sons and Daughters gathered around him and tied his wrists, then got him to kneel in the closet and knotted his wrists to his ankles. They twisted the chain around his arms, padlocked it, and taped it again, so that he looked like a package. Some of the Sons, like Dedrick and Willie, looked fierce as they tore the lengths of tape, slapped them on and pulled the chain tight. Most of the Daughters only looked on, seeming horrified. Before they taped his mouth, Millroy said, ''Give me a strangulation twist,'' meaning to tie the chain around his neck, looping it again so that he would choke if he moved his head. Then they shut the door of the closet and locked it, too.

There was no sound inside. I moved nearer.

''Back off,'' Willie said.

''He could smuvva,'' Jaleen said.

But less than a minute later, the cupboard door flew open.

''That's not magic, it's a trick,'' Millroy said, stepping out. ''Let's do breakfast.''

• • •

It was seven-thirty. We opened to the public just after that. There were fewer people than usual, and all the Sons and Daughters serving made the diner seem lopsided—more employees than customers. The eaters were uncomfortable about the men passing out handbills at the front door. The morning was slow, lunch was quiet, the afternoon was dead, dinner looked promising but after a busy start the diner emptied, people leaving fast and no one else taking their places.

We were occupied serving food, but even so I had a sense of doom from all the threats and glitches. Our being busy made me think that if a disaster struck, it would be worse than if the place were empty—more public and painful, more destructive, messier, noisier. I had noticed since coming back from Vera's that these days many eaters in the diner seemed curious; they lingered and glanced around, looking morbid and breathless, like people who drive slow and snarl traffic near bad fires and car crashes.

The next day business was slower, there were fewer meals, and the men were still giving out handbills. "Juice them!" Willie said. "Turn them into rats!"

But Millroy only smiled and called the police. "I wish to report an obstructed sidewalk."

When the policemen showed up they said that as long as the men kept moving they could not make an arrest. One cop said, "This all you got to eat? Rabbit food and bark mulch?" They left chuckling at the handbills showing Millroy's picture and all the vicious accusations.

In the darkness that night Millroy called out, and his voice seemed to be coming straight out of his head.

"I could juice them, liquefy them, pour them into the sewer—who would miss them?" he said. "I could pronounce a curse. I could cripple them, blind them, strike them dumb, turn them into little rubber johnnies, stare at their handbills and set them ablaze from thirty feet."

The darkness murmured back at him with sounds of uncertainty, like the tentative motion of soup about to boil, and he began again.

"I have the power," he said. "But I don't need to prove I am a magician. It is more important that I demonstrate that I am human."

I could see him so clearly and understand him so well in the dark, could almost see his words in a white voice bubble, like a character talking in a cartoon. He seemed to be trying to swallow, and I knew he had something on his mind.

He said, "I want our whole movement to be regular—the church, the eaters, the show. We have to remove all blockage. We need a smoothly flowing operation all around."

The silence in the darkness still simmered.

"But it's a free country."

After a few more days of pink handbills and declining business, Millroy said, "I don't like this. I hate their neckties. Is it supposed to be a test of my strength?" Day One diners in six cities had shut down until further notice.

"And I just realized something," Millroy said. "The way they walk. Look."

Some of us looked out of the window at the men with handbills.

"See? That's a threat posture."

Their shoulders were hunched, their heads down, their walk a kind of clumping. By now we knew them by sight and could tell that they were people who ate anything that fit into their mouths, smoked, drank raw liquor, got pale and misshapen, fat or stringy, and had that look of ill health that Millroy said was like sin, because of the way they stuffed themselves.

"Polyphagous—you can see that," Millroy said. He was smiling. "But it's sad. It's like being threatened by invalids. You feel too compassionate to hit back."

He still looked powerful and seemed strengthened by the presence of so many Sons and Daughters.

"I am not alone," he said.

He was especially glad that the Sons and Daughters had returned, each one bigger, older and more confident, sleeker and harder than before, with a glow of health and youth, looking similar with shaven heads, no longer awkward, and seeming as much like a sports team as an army or a family.

"My Daughters look so beautiful bald," he said.

"We got hassled by the Klan in Chicago," Berry said. "They came out of Skokie and burned some crosses at our diner."

"That group I told you about in Denver called The Order?" Willie said. "They showed up and made a fuss."

"That was before the handbills," Stacy said.

Millroy was smiling his crooked smile. "I like it when we are opposed," he said. "It is a test of how strong we are. Yes, this handbill is a test."

I was thinking: *This is a family, and it is the only family I want.* I waited for them to be kind to me.

"Some TV people showed up one morning," Tuppy said. "They wanted us to diss the Big Guy. Yeah!"

"We had *Sixty Minutes.*"

"*Nightline* wanted to do us."

"The Devil is a liar," Ike said.

Millroy said, "There is no Devil."

In the midst of all these young people, he was like a prophet or a patriarch with his disciples, and he seemed to get strength from them, ideas and revelations.

The subject of his next *Day One Program* was "There is no Devil."

No Devil, he said. *There is you and me. There is truth and falsehood. Eat well and be regular and you will see Good.*

His face bulged against the screen, very close and confidential.

We watched it together in the kitchen of the diner, a dozen or more Sons and Daughters, like old times.

We are strong from within and will live, each of us, for two hundred years. Nothing on this earth can destroy us.

"You believe that?" Willie Webb said to me. "That there is no Devil?"

I said yes.

He said, "You wrong. The Devil is not a spook. He is a ordinary dude, put on earth to make trouble. Dude could be anyone—could be you."

On his own initiative Willie gathered the other Sons and Daughters. They did not confront the men with handbills, but crowded them and outnumbered them. *Get in their face,* Willie said. It was wonderful to see the sure-footed and healthy bodies of the Sons and Daughters closing in on the clumsy opposition. They never stopped smiling. They had been inspired by Millroy, which made them all the more intimidating, and as he told them, their overwhelming gladness was a more powerful weapon than anger. They did not lay a finger on any of them, but at last the men vanished. Afterward the Sons and Daughters went out and scooped up the handbills scattered in the street that people had thrown away. Seeing them working together made me all the more eager to help, to be part of their group.

But Willie said, "We don't need you. Get back, Alex."

"You're out of here, Little Guy," Dedrick said.

Millroy was so pleased by the way the Sons and Daughters stood up for him that he did not notice that I had been rejected.

"A big thing has happened to these children," he said, watching from the front window of the diner. "They are gaining control of their functions, muffin."

Getting control of me, I was thinking, because they had started to scare me. *And what about* my *functions?*

But Millroy was still praising them.

They now had spirit, he said, and had gained control of enough bodily functions to sense the presence of harm and to deal with it. From this inner strength would come the ability to work magic. They were true Sons and Daughters now. It did not matter that there were only a few men passing out handbills. The Sons and Daughters had achieved a Day One by dealing with them like true magicians, sending them away by using psychic energy.

As for the media coverage, he said that the notoriety of Day One had raised awareness all over America. "If need be, I could broadcast an appeal and organize an army. How could we lose?"

Yet the magazine articles were still appearing—"The Diet Prophet." "The Church That Keeps You Regular." "Millroy's Money—The Truth About Day One."

"It's all trash," I said.

But still Willie Webb glared at me with his *There is going to be more* expression, as though I were responsible for it.

"This struggle is character-forming," Millroy preached to us. "It's like something in your body, a small poisonous worm that bloats and turns into blockage. You have to sit calmly and ruminate on it and expel it with force."

But what he called "raised awareness" was plain bad publicity. Business was poor, affected by all the coverage we had ("No one likes going into an empty restaurant"). Still, the Sons and Daughters were happier than they had ever been. I kept wishing that they would let me be a part of their group, but they were ruder to me than ever. Millroy's telling them they had power and control of bodily functions made them worse—more stuck up and aggressive—but I said nothing because he seemed so pleased.

It had all worked out as he had said. It had been a test of our food, our strength, our willpower, our belief in Day One. This campaign, which had been going on ever since Millroy became famous, now seemed at an end. The magazine articles were feeble and facetious, he said; we were winning there, too. No one cared to read about *The church that lays down complicated rules for going to the toilet,* or *What next for the Millroy church?*

"We've won," Millroy said. "It is time to go back to your Day One diners. Regroup, reopen and prosper."

But the Sons and Daughters made excuses and stayed on. They talked about gathering like this every two or three months, just to reaffirm their commitment; be strong and happy together, they said.

"You will live in health for two centuries," Millroy said, praising them.

"And so will you if you let us protect you," Willie said.

"I have all the protection I need," Millroy said.

From his expression you could see that Willie did not believe him.

I could not understand this delay. They should have left by now, at the peak of their happiness. They could have walked across Park Square to the Greyhound terminal the way they had come, and caught buses back to their diners. Yet they hesitated. Were they afraid?

"Aren't you going back?" I asked Willie Webb after a few days.

"You'd like that, wouldn't you?"

He was ladling soup, and as he turned away from me, he seemed to bump the tureen with his elbow, and it tottered and fell, splashing hot soup all over. If I had not jumped away, I would have been scalded to death.

And then Willie turned and stared at me with cold eyes, as though disappointed that I was still there.

I was too terrified to say, *I could have been killed.*

Two days later I was down in the hatchway getting some scoops of beans when the trapdoor closed on me. I tried it, but it was locked. Then there were footsteps on the trapdoor, but no one opened it. I sat on a rung of the ladder in the dark and cried until Millroy heard me with his miraculous ears.

I guess I accidentally locked it, someone muttered. But no one said, *Sorry.*

"You okay, buddy?"

I answered yes because I felt that if I said anything else the Sons and Daughters would think I was accusing them of doing it on purpose.

Willie was unfriendly in the same smiling, mocking way that he had been with the handbill men. I could not say anything to him for fear I would cry, and if I cried in front of him he would know by the way I sobbed that I was a girl.

"I think I will just hang out here," he said. "How about you, Tuppy?"

"What it's down to is," Tuppy said, over my head, meaning to slight me, "I ain't going nowhere."

It had never happened before. We had always been friends—more than friends: family.

Feeling sad, I tried a Day One remedy for depression and got some sugar into my system from Horeb Honey Squares, Mosaic Melon Spheres, Caramel Carob Cookies, and Wine Jar First Press Grape Drink. When these did not work, I went for a walk down Boylston to Copley Square. I sat in front of the library in the sunshine, wondering what to say to Millroy and wishing I were someone else. I envied the people walking by, looking busy and preoccupied, heading home to their families, paying no attention to me. *I want to be her,* I thought, *I want to be him.*

One man I saw was Morrie Arkle of Bub City Crabshack and Carmina Burrito, whom Millroy had liquidized into two quarts of gray, fatty chicken soup and drunk. It was the same pink face, the same suit, a different shirt and tie but the same shoes.

I spoke up. I said, "Um, excuse me—"

But he did not hear me. He walked into the Copley T-Station and was gone.

Shocked by the sight of him, I hurried back to the diner, forgetting why I had left it in the first place, and looked for Millroy.

"Isn't he usually in your back passage?" Stacy said.

Someone laughed out loud at this.

Then I remembered the reason I had left the diner to go for a walk. *Why were they treating me this way?*

Millroy hurried through the door and went into the back without saying a word. I followed him.

"I just saw that Crabshack man, Arkle, walking into the T-station at Copley Square."

"So?"

"But you turned him into juice and drank him. You even got sick doing it."

"Right, buddy, so obviously the man you saw was not the same. I dealt with him."

What did that mean?

"He passed through my body," Millroy said. "Stands to reason."

There was knocking at the door, so loud that it sounded like someone was trying to smash the planks.

"I am not a murderer," Millroy said to me, and pulled the door open. "I am not a molester."

Willie Webb stood in the doorway with Stacy, and six or seven Sons and Daughters were standing behind him.

"You see this, Big Guy?" he said.

It was another supermarket tabloid, The Examiner, with the headline TV PREACHER'S LIVE-IN BOY LOVER.

"Didn't I tell you there was more stuff going down?"

So that was why they had all come back from their Day Ones to Boston. They knew this was coming, but they did not have Millroy's power of foresight. Never mind what they had heard. What had they said?

Millroy did not utter a word. He simply raised his hand at the paper, and before he completed the gesture the pages began to smoke. Just as Willie dropped it, the newspaper burst into flames.

That was not the end of the business. There were more articles, there were anonymous phone calls, and this time no one in the diner said, It's all trash.

Millroy got phone calls from concerned eaters. "Is this true, Doctor?"

No one except Millroy spoke to me. I was faced all day by silent Sons and Daughters, little Millroys with shaven heads and naked ears, staring at me like bug-eyed crickets. I could smell hatred on their breath.

One night Jaleen said to me as we were closing, "He should lose you."

"Are you talking to me?"

She was staring at me poisonously. "You're out of here."

"You heard Jaleen," Willie said. "Take a hike, Little Guy."

I did not move. It was not bravery; I was too frightened to take a step. When Willie came closer I put my hands on my body, less for protection than to cover myself. Willie, so strong these days from his diligence in Day One, seemed to smell my fear.

"So the Big Man is your stepfather?"

"Yes."

"He marry your ma, something like that?"

I said nothing, and Willie knew I was cornered.

"Where is your ma, Little Guy?"

He began poking and plucking at me, and I was terrified that touching me like this he would discover my secret.

"Mumma died," I said.

This rattled him and made him step back, and the others watching us looked hesitant, since death was like a sin, the real proof that a person was not Day One.

"Mumma must have been a burger," he said. "Mumma must not have been regular."

I hated these words of Millroy's applied to my poor mother. But thinking of her death, how she had slipped away and left me, I was so overwhelmed by the sadness that I forgot my other miseries. By comparison to Mumma's passing on, all the rest—the secret of being a girl and being rejected and being bullied—was nothing. I sorrowed for her, not for myself, and this must have made me look strong.

There were tears on my face, but I did not dare cry because if I had sobbed, they would have known I was a girl. So when Willie touched me again I batted his hand away, and though I was more surprised by my strength than he was, he realized he had gone too far and faltered again.

There was a sudden noise against the wall, a yawn from Millroy's cupboard, but it was like a lion's growl, the kind of roar I had heard from the starved and confused animal long ago at the Barnstable County Fair. This harsh, distant sound seem to grind against Willie's face, and it disturbed the Sons and Daughters. That growl put an end to the confrontation and saved me.

After that, there was silence again.

But Millroy's silences were like speeches to me, and in the darkness they penetrated my brain. He did not discuss the Sons' and Daughters' attitude toward me, or that I seemed to make him look like a molester. After I returned from the Cape, he had embarrassed me, trying to feed me and saying, *You are my soul.* He said nothing about the way I was being opposed, or the way he was being slandered by cheap newspapers, about how he might have to choose between the whole of Day One and me. He did not open his mouth at all.

But I knew him so well now that when he was saying nothing, he was speaking to me, and even in the dark I knew when he was awake, lying there with his mind racing so fast you could hear the wind thrashing in its spokes.

This was why I had felt safe so far. He would not send me away. He said nothing, yet still I could guess from the pulses in the air how he felt about me. But I was no one, I had nothing to lose. Millroy's reputation, his whole career, everything he had made, was in danger because of these misunderstandings.

"Maybe I should go," I said, thinking of the Sons and Daughters.

And not only of them but of myself, when I sat on the steps of the Boston Public Library, feeling small and pointless, the day I watched people going home and got a glimpse of Morrie Arkle. I had wanted to be one of those big busy people, going home, too. Nothing made me lonelier or sadder than being in this strange city, watching people hurrying home at the end of the day, abandoning the city, reminding me that I had nowhere to go.

Soon after in the darkness I heard Millroy—one word.

"Never," he said.

37 "Millroy is now bigger than his movement," Millroy said, "thanks to his detractors."

I was a wreck, and sick—his secret, his weakness, his sin—trying to make myself small because I was responsible. I was so nervous, I started sucking my thumb again when I was alone, though it tasted awful. Millroy fed me apricots and melons and honeycombs to cheer me up, a sugar infusion, but it did not cure me. No matter how he protested about needing me or said, *You are my soul, muffin,* I suffered for him—most of all because he refused to show his hurt. You never saw his pain. Millroy the Magician could make stress vanish and fat disappear. Only I knew his wretchedness, and it was misery for me.

His neck shortened whenever a helicopter went overhead.

"I know who that is," he said without glancing up. "They want me to know they're after me."

"Why?"

"Some Judas dropped a dime on me."

He paced at the window of the diner, looking at the pedestrians heading across Park Square.

"There is a fat man frowning at me. He has the breasts of a mature woman, his name is probably Walter Gasset, his diet is crippling him, he believes in UFOs, and in a perverse way he is convinced that doing away with me will relieve his own constipation."

Willie Webb was passing behind us and, hearing this, laughed. The laugh made Millroy pause.

"Ain't you worried about them tax people?" Willie said.

"Which tax people?"

"That want to look at your books," Willie said.

"But that is just a pretext. Know what I'm saying? They want to probe me."

I stared at Willie. I wanted him to look at me so that I could smile as a way of saying there were no hard feelings.

"They are trying to give me the evil eye," Millroy said.

His eyes bulged and discolored as he gave it back. All along, he had foreseen, he said, that this was inevitable. The thing to do was regard it with cold eyes. Why panic? Part of his magic was his skill in looking unconcerned—"hiding the elephant," he called it, his greatest illusion as a county fair magician.

"And Millroy will not be probed," he said.

"Yo."

And then Millroy began working the phones himself, shouting back at his accusers.

"We do not pray in the toilet, miss—"

"No donations are solicited, sir. Watch my program—"

"This is not a religion, it is a movement—"

"My people are free to leave at any time—"

"The next sound you hear will be me putting down the phone, and then you will be all alone with your spastic colon—"

Big Guy's on a roll, the Sons and Daughters said.

"Millroy gives America an enema and look what happens," he said, glancing up. "That was *Larry King Live.*"

Because of the rumors, the gossip about Millroy's private life, lurkers were outside the diner most of the day—no law against staring, the Boston police said—hoping to get a glimpse of Millroy, the famous Christian, leader of the eaters, with his beans and figs, who was living openly in the Day One Diner with a fifteen-year-old boy, never mind that it was not true.

Inside or out he was now so well known that strangers came up to him and said *Hello* or *Where's your friend?* or *Do a trick.*

He frightened these people with his laughter, and they did not know, as I did, that all his pain was in that laugh.

"Hey, what's your message today, Doctor Millroy?" a man shouted at him in the Public Gardens.

"Keep your bowels open is my message."

His laughter flashed like magic too, with his startling teeth. *I hate hearing grown people laugh,* he once said to me. *To me it is one of the most sinister sounds in the world.* When I first heard his sudden whinny, I knew why. It had nothing to do with funniness, it was all nerves, it was electric, his tongue stuck out when he laughed hard.

As for the talk about me, he refused to deny it, would not comment at all. He clammed up and was so silent he seemed to be asking for trouble, either enjoying the danger or else daring them to hurt him, the way he often said to a stranger, *Go on, punch me in the stomach.*

"What have I done to make them doubt me?" he asked. "I offered to extend their lives. Yes, I suppose some people find the prospect of all that extra time terrifying, but that's because human longevity has not been observed on earth since biblical times. Readers are scared by the monkey people in *Gulliver's Travels* and the old crones in that Aldous Huxley novel, *After Many a Summer Something-something.* The real thing is so different."

He was looking directly at people passing by, thinking, *Smoker's Face, Smoker's Limp, Fat Voice, Water Retention, Carnivore's Hump.*

"They think dying is a way of killing time."

"You're giving them something to look at," Willie Webb said when Millroy was at the window of the diner.

He meant me, because the people outside might have been hoping to catch Millroy and me together, the big man and the small boy.

"They're not going to stop at looking," Willie said, nodding at Dedrick, who agreed. "What they're down to is totally destroying the Big Guy."

Millroy's yelp was a laugh that meant *Destroy me?* and Willie backed off, embarrassed for suggesting that Millroy might be weak.

But it was not Millroy the Sons and Daughters were after, it was me, and when they spoke up they made me feel conspicuous and unhelpful. I wanted to creep away.

"There is nowhere to hide," Millroy said, reading my mind.

Most days, he winked at me and we slipped out to take a walk. I gladly went with him, relieved to be away from the diner, the curious eaters and spectators, the whispers, and the Sons and Daughters.

There were too many Sons and Daughters—fifteen altogether—and even though they worked in shifts, the diner was always full of them, often more of them than eaters.

"You're the problem," Dedrick said to me.

I looked to Stacy for support.

"Dedrick's right," Stacy said, folding her arms. "Because we're tight."

I was a threat to them, Willie said, speaking for everyone. As soon as my existence was proved, Millroy was finished; they would hassle him on taxes, liquor, labor, insurance and health regulations. They would find underpayments, lead paint and coliform bacteria.

They muttered these things to me and I tried not to cry when I repeated them to Millroy.

"What do they know?" Millroy said. "Sometimes people get close to you only to hurt you."

I felt such misery being with him, knowing that I was one of the main reasons he was being attacked, and as we walked away I felt that he was pretending to be brave and cheerful for my sake. That I was not propping him up, as he had claimed. That he was suffering. People watched him. They knew who he was. What were they thinking?

"A lot of people would love to see Millroy have a massive stroke," he said. "When Jim Fixx died jogging, all of fat America cheered. Fixx was not a righteous eater, but the fatties didn't know that. They are even more eager to see Millroy croak. A Millroy myocardial infarction would validate their own existence. Or what if Millroy was caught joy-riding in a car with an underage girl?''

"That's me."

"No, Alex."

He smiled and raised a Day One finger.

"Most of them are just curious," he said. " 'It's that bald guy from the TV show.' "

I wondered why he did not wear a hat, or make any effort to disguise his appearance. You could see he was Millroy from a mile away. His good health made his head glow pink.

All the public attention tired me out. I thought that the worst part of being famous was the fatigue you got from people staring at you, their eyes fastened on you the whole time. It wore me down, I wanted to disappear, but this visibility often seemed to energize him.

On our walks we usually left the diner, crossed the Common to Tremont Street, and when we got to Government Center, went down the steps to Quincy Market and the Boston harbor. Millroy held his head up the whole time, as though challenging anyone to accuse him of living with a young boy.

This only made me more nervous.

I said, "Alex could just go off and disappear, couldn't he?"

I felt so strange talking about myself that way, as though there were someone with me, a friend of the man Millroy that Millroy was always talking about.

"And Millroy could go on *Larry King Live* and say it was all a mistake."

"Why give them the satisfaction?" he said.

"But Alex is a problem."

"Alex has done nothing wrong," he said. "Alex has been loyal. Alex was with Millroy from the beginning."

So there were now two Alexes and two Millroys, instead of one each.

"And what harm has Millroy done?" he went on. "Millroy has transformed the country, offered it hope and truth and pure food. Millroy put salvation on a plate and served it to the whole of America."

Walking along these Boston streets at lunchtime, what strengthened him, Millroy said, was the healthy skin and bright eyes, the rush of energy, the confident sense of well-being that he saw. It was as though he were responsible for it, had made it all, looking at Boston like God looking at the world during the week of creation. It was all new, it was Day One.

"It's unmistakable," he said. "Notice that surge? You get a sense that they eat right, that their bowels are open."

He raised his hands, seeming to praise and bless them, and wagged his Day One finger.

"I like it," he said. "It's spunk. It wasn't like this before. And Millroy doesn't want credit for it. He's just grateful that it's happening. This food culture, for example."

He meant the restaurants we were walking past—Wally Wok, Lawrence of Oregano, Dunkin' Donuts, The Old Union Oyster House, Pizza Uno, Turkish Delight, Al Bustan, and Zorba's. And there were ice-cream stands, shish-kebab stalls, people making crepes and working popcorn machines.

"Millroy was able to put this food mania to spiritual use. He got them eating wheaten loaves and the husks of fibrous seeds and grains."

Then he frowned, ducked, shortening his neck, and squinted into the distance.

"Yet some of them attack Millroy!"

"They must be afraid," I said, because I was.

"Of his power and influence, sure. So if he doesn't have a massive stroke, they will try to destroy him, make him out to be just another holy hypocrite from TV."

"People say I am your secret weakness."

"You are Millroy's strength, sugar."

"You seen these magazines, Big Guy?" Jaleen said. She was shaking a pile of them. I saw PREACHER AND YOUNG BOY and SECRET LIFE OF DIET GURU.

"I don't need to see them," Millroy said. "That's been going on for a long time."

"They are dissing you, Big Guy," Willie said.

"It was meant to be," Millroy said.

Yet the Sons and Daughters were blaming me for being "Young Boy," and I was weakened and demoralized when, after a program taping or a walk, we returned to the diner and saw the Sons and Daughters still there, still hating me.

They were thinking, *Alex is bringing the Big Guy down, making life hard for him, attracting bad publicity, detracting from Day One.*

They did not know me, but so what? They wanted terrible things to happen to me, and they resented Millroy's protecting me—the nights alone with me in the back of the diner, the *Day One Programs* that only I was allowed to watch from the control room, the walks through Boston with him, Millroy calling out to heckling strangers, *Keep your bowels open*—

And standing with Millroy at the harbor while he gazed out to sea.

"I could never leave this country," he said.

Planes were landing at Logan, boats were churning the black water and gulls were clawing the posts at the edges of the docks.

"That's why I worked so hard to get this country regular," he said. "I want America to be right, because I could never live anywhere else. I know. I tried it. Didn't work out."

He was still watching the sea, smiling a little and thinking, *Never.*

"Be happy," he said.

"I am happy, out here with you," I said.

"And the Day One—that's home, where your friends are." He nodded at me while he spoke, and smiled, as though encouraging me to agree.

"Maybe we should go back," I said.

Just as we turned to go, we saw Willie Webb approaching with Dedrick from the direction of Quincy Market.

"Don't go back to the diner, Big Guy," Willie said. "There's some dudes there waiting for you, and I know they want to arrest you."

Millroy thought a moment. I expected him to laugh, walk right back, face the men and humiliate and defeat them with magic.

He said, "What do they look like?"

"Wicked."

"I think a spell in the trailer would do me good," he said. "I've got some home movies there for a program. I've been meaning to dig them out."

Meanwhile, Willie and Dedrick were making horrible faces at me from behind Millroy's back and making me feel desperate.

• • •

We went back to Wompatuck, where the trailer was still parked, and the Sons and Daughters who had been living in it moved into the diner.

"I like this old Airstream," Millroy said. "It reminds me of my days in the wilderness."

"Those men who came to the diner," I said. "You're not afraid of them."

"No."

"You could have liquidized them and drunk them," I said. "You're a magician."

"Millroy is human," he said. "I don't want people to fear me for my magic. I want them to trust in my humanity."

The word "trust" reminded me of how little I was trusted.

"The Sons and Daughters hate me," I said.

"Use that negative energy, angel."

"They came back to Boston because they knew you were going to be attacked in the newspapers and magazines," I said. "Those lies about me."

"I guessed as much." He was smiling, and because he had no fear he never looked at any one thing very closely.

"But how did they know about the lies?"

"I am way ahead of you," he said, and I had the feeling that he was just now working it all out. "Someone started the lies. It is possible that we have a traitor among us."

He kept his smile, but the light behind it flickered out and darkened it with sadness.

"I wish I knew who it was."

"It is someone who wants me to die."

"That's kind of melodramatic, muffin."

"I almost did die," I said.

"Be serious."

"Twice," I said.

Choking with fright at the memory of it, I told him the story of how I had been with Willie near the soup tureen, and the thing had tipped over and would have scalded me to death if I had not jumped out of the way. I began to lose my voice as I talked, and then, gulping even more, I struggled to tell him about the hatchway incident.

"I remember that. Accidentally locked."

"It wasn't an accident," I said, and told him how I had been suffocating in the darkness of the hatchway with the dusty bean sacks, no one paying any attention to my yelling and pleading until he had heard me. When I finished telling him these stories, I began to cry and I knew my face was a mess.

Millroy was shocked. He said, "Angel."

"I'm glad we're in this trailer," I said, with snot and tears shining on my face.

Looking at his hands, as though he expected to see something stuck to his fingers, he said, "I don't care what the world thinks, but I do worry about my own people."

"I mean, what good is eating food that helps you live for two hundred years if people kill you when you're a teenager?"

I was still sobbing and upset from telling about my close calls.

"When they warned me about you, I began worrying about them," Millroy said. "But I didn't think it would come to this."

"They really do hate me."

"I put it down to pride. Or envy. Blockage of some kind."

"They want me to die."

He put his face in his hands and made a sorrowing noise, which meant *How could people who eat this good food be so nasty?*

He believed me. He could see that I was afraid. He did not want to lose me.

"Millroy is not happy about this," he said.

He went to bed silent, and brooded all the next day, sitting in the trailer.

At dinner, which was broiled fish and a honeycomb, bread and barley cakes, he said, "Two hundred loaves of bread, a hundred bunches of raisins, a hundred of summer fruit, five measures of parched corn. That would sustain us in the wilderness."

He hardly looked at me, and it was as though he had resigned himself to setting out and leaving everything behind.

"Maybe I didn't get them early enough."

I did not know what to say.

Narrowing his eyes he said, "The real trauma of travel is having to employ strange toilets."

Darkness fell but we did not switch on the lights. Just a lumpy shadow, Millroy spoke again. "How long have we been together, angel?"

It was now the end of September. Last September Millroy was appearing on *Paradise Park.*

"More than a year," I said.

Millroy seldom looked back except to search the distant past. He took
pride in looking ahead. But here he was, adding up the months.

Before he went to sleep he said, "But this had to happen."

We were eating breakfast in the trailer the next morning with the
television on, and a group of Olympic athletes were discussing nutrition
on one of the news shows.

*I don't think I would have focused on this competition if I hadn't done the Day
One program,* one of the men said, and the others agreed, *We're all into
Day One, yeah.*

"Ironic, isn't it?" Millroy said.

He had been up since four-thirty, moving furniture, baking bread,
mashing lentils, peeling fruit, juicing vegetables, and, from time to time,
hopping to the floor and doing knee bends and push-ups. You didn't
know whether he was genuflecting or doing exercises.

"For some people the movement is still the important thing. Bless
them."

Every American eats forty pounds of sugar a year, a long-haired actress was
now saying in a commercial for artificial sweetener.

Millroy was alert to his name being mentioned, to items in the papers
about Day One, even though he pretended not to be. It mattered to him
because it was proof that the program was established and growing, that
the work was being carried on by unknown eaters.

"Now I want to know the truth," he said, and he became thoughtful
and still, as though he had stopped breathing.

That night after dark, we drove into Boston and surprised the Sons
and Daughters, who were closing down the diner for the day. They had
locked the front doors and were cleaning the bread ovens and mopping
and fussing. There were so many of them, all looking so bald and well
fed, with scowling faces and gleaming heads, that they scared me. I
wanted to go back to Wompatuck. It looked as though they had completely taken over, and that it was their diner now.

Seeing Millroy enter, they fell silent.

Willie Webb and Dedrick were up front, Willie holding a rolled-up
newspaper, which he unrolled and smoothed onto the counter.

"That's cool," Willie said. "Now how do you aim to kick this, Big Guy?"

It was another newspaper from the supermarket, making me think of Millroy so pleased at being "supermarket famous." There was a full-page color picture of Elvis in a space suit, something about Hitler being still alive, a story about Siamese twins, CARROTS ARE GREAT FOR YOUR LOVE LIFE, SCIENTISTS SAY and SHAMEFUL SEX SECRET OF TV HOLY FOOD PREACHER—"IT'S NOT HIS SON."

"Ignore it," Millroy said. "That takes more strength than fighting lies. I've been in the headlines before, as you fellows know very well."

"Yo. Are these here lies, Big Guy?"

"They dissing you, is that right?"

Hearing these defiant questions, the other Sons and Daughters crowded around, squeezing me in their hatefulness, which was like a bad smell rising in the room. I wanted to shrink and vanish, and only Millroy's presence sustained me. He could have helped me disappear, but no.

"Don't you know these rumors are an insult to us all?" Millroy said, sounding reasonable.

"There is a big bust coming," Dedrick said. "And it is down to him."

Meaning me. I was terrified.

"He is jeopardizing the movement," Stacy said.

"I think you're forgetting something," Millroy said. "Like who started the movement."

Millroy looked at all of them with hot, searching eyes, and twitched his mustache a fraction to show his teeth.

"Millroy wants you to trust him and accept his good friend Alex," he said.

Someone laughed in the back, too loud, and it sounded like a challenge. The way the rest of them stared at Millroy after this sound seemed like more defiance.

"Threats from outside can make us strong by uniting us," Millroy said, looking sadly and pityingly at them. "But this kind of talk is dangerous when it comes from inside the movement. It is a betrayal."

"The kid's a liability," Willie said, pointing at me.

Millroy's eyes went black. I thought he was going to explode.

"He is out of here," Dedrick said.

"It's time to eat."

"Who says?"

"Millroy says." And when he told them where and when, they hardly believed him.

38

The next night, with wild, staring eyes, Millroy drove to Boston in the Ford, pulled the Airstream level with the Day One Diner and called out in his voice that penetrated brick walls,

"Get in."

While the Sons and Daughters piled into the trailer, Millroy changed places with Berry—"You're driving, Son"—and joined us in the back.

He had introduced us to some strange meals, but this was the strangest one we had ever eaten—midnight, sixteen of us going *whoopsie* in the trailer as we shoved tables together, everything tipping on the turns in the Boston streets, and then speeding down the Mass. Pike. This was just before we sat down to eat, but we never stopped rolling and the trailer swayed like a boat in a breeze.

"This is one of those dinners that is so odd it's bound to be distorted later on when people talk about it," Millroy said.

His feet were planted squarely on the jogging floor—he was the only one with sea legs. The rest of us staggered and tried to balance with the motion of the creaking trailer. We felt better when we sat down, but it was still like being at sea.

The Sons and Daughters were watching him, as though he were steering us through a storm.

"I am not a nutbag."

But they looked at him as though he were.

"I am a fugitive."

He was sad, yet there was something defiant in his sadness, as though all his anger had burned away, leaving him alone and misunderstood but refusing to give up. In this isolation he had summoned all his strength.

"Which unhappy person did that to me?"

Willie said, "We're on your side, Big Guy."

Millroy just smiled, and his body tipped slightly as a truck passed us noisily, its canvas covers flapping like sheets on a line, and we were sucked sideways by the sudden wind of its slipstream.

"You ought to know that although I can make magic," Millroy said, "I am human, like you."

Repeating "human," he swept the flat of his hand along the three pushed-together tables, and thick blue bowls appeared, brimming with reddish pottage, and platters of wheaten loaves, honey wafers, melons and grapes, fig cakes, swatches of herbs, and the leafy green stalks he called "cruciform vegetables."

"I hate sermons," he said, not even looking at the food that had just miraculously been tangibilized. "I don't address crowds."

The moving trailer gave him a trembly voice, made the crockery clink and added to the creak of the straining metal shell of the Airstream. The windows were shut, but we heard the *whup-whup-whup* as we passed posts by the roadside.

"We have no congregation—The Book is our church," Millroy said, and in a more precise gesture, stabbing his fingers downward, he added goblets to the table, one in front of each person. "When I preached to a multitude I did it on television."

At that moment, his voice deepening, he seemed to be speaking again to America.

"The great thing about the prospect of living for two hundred years is that there's time for everything," he said. "You can be calm."

Standing among us at the table in the trailer, he was calmer than I had ever seen him, with his hot breath, that whisper of passionate certainty that made him seem so strong.

"We never had services," he said. "No music, no pictures, no graven images, no gold."

He held up his index finger, his Day One finger. We looked at this finger.

"That's the beauty of Day One," he said. "Its intimacy. It is just a meal. But—"

He smiled as he smoothed the table, and in a glittering miracle under his hand a crystal platter seemed to rise out of the cloth.

"—the Lord appears at mealtimes," he said. "I am that bread of life."

Lifting the platter he raised it shoulder high and it shone like a mirror, lighting his face.

"You are my children," he said and looked uneasy. "And my life is in your hands."

Was he talking about death? Maybe not, but his tones were those of someone about to set off on a long journey. *If you go please take me with you,* I thought.

The booming of the wind rocked the trailer and made me think of this trip in the Airstream as a meal on a stormy sea.

"I was lost," Millroy said. He seemed to be talking to himself, but his confidence in this murmur also made him sound as though he were speaking to the whole world.

"I was in the belly of Hell—weeds were wrapped around my head," he said.

He switched off all the overhead lights by waving his hand, and told the Jonah story of his fatness, how he had been imprisoned in the darkness of his body. We had heard this same story many times, but it was as though he were telling it for the first time.

I was suffocated in fear because the trailer was in darkness, and the way it moved and the way it sounded made us feel that we were rattling in the stifling darkness of a whale's belly, growing pukier and more scared with every word.

"Oh, no," someone said.

Whup-whup-whup from outside.

"Cut the lights on," Dedrick said, making a barf grunt.

"Do you feel it?" Millroy said. "I was in this darkness not three days and three nights like Jonah, but forty years, day and night, trapped in my fat and lugging it blindly wherever I went."

Meanwhile, Berry was driving like mad. The trailer shook, the table moved, the crockery clanked, the food in front of us that we could not see gave off fumes, and it all made the darkness worse because the simplest odors turn to stinks in the dark.

"Everything lay around me, unseparated and decayed, and I thought that I was the Beast—not that I was inside it, but that I had become the horrible, drooling creature."

Now he switched the lights back on, and we blinked and tried to listen.

"Then I was dazzled by the word of God telling me what to eat. And I understood. I fasted, I starved, I purged myself. Finally, I filled my body with goodness, and my eyes were opened. What do you see in the word 'create'? You see the word 'eat.' "

He cupped his hands into a pair of parentheses and bracketed the platter with them.

"From that moment, I was a magician." Once again he held up his Day One finger. Then twisted it, detached it and dropped it, *fthap,* onto the crystal platter, where it lay as plump and ugly as a sausage.

One of the Daughters screamed, "Da!"

"Day One," Millroy said, looking down at his broken-off, bleeding finger.

Now it was almost impossible to concentrate on what he was saying while his big finger rolled, as the trailer swayed, and the thing paused and pointed and rolled again, the yellow accusing nail at one end, the splintered white bone showing in the raw meat at the other, two kinks at the knuckles, with a pad of hair, and a trickle of blood leaking from the flesh around snapped-off bone.

The Sons and Daughters were either murmuring in fear or else silently weeping, but Millroy carried on, hardly seeming to notice.

"As a magician—"

Facing his mangled Day One finger, you believed him.

"—I stripped my body down to its chassis and I traveled the world. I lingered in countries where people die young—and even if they were shown the truth, the miracle would be denied them because their food was garbage."

He smiled, remembering his travels, as the trailer, buffeted by wind, continued to shake.

"I was the only person on earth who saw the truth in The Book, yet it was there for all to see," he said, and laughed at his good luck. "Call it a vision—it was a humdinger, but why me?"

On the word "humdinger," we looked again at the bleeding finger on the platter. We had heard Millroy say these things before but in different words, and never when we were all together around the same table, not to mention in a moving trailer, facing the torn-off finger that indicated Day One.

"This is awesome," Stacy said.

Millroy was saying, "I have seen the kitchens and toilets of the known world, too, and they are unclean. My journeys made me love America, and made me realize that I could never live anywhere else. I wanted to grasp with my fingers and satisfy my mouth with good things, so that my youth would be renewed like the eagle's—what an amazing psalm, embodying the concepts of food, longevity and America! Meditate upon that."

But what we were actually meditating upon was the finger, and the finger was pointing back into our faces.

"What a wonderful thing to be in America," Millroy said, "where we can be saved. As I've told you, God has placed his hand upon America!"

His eyes were bleeding. If this was a trick and not magic, it was the most terrifying way of convincing us that he was sad.

"You can only truly have a sense of failure when you are rejected by those you love," he said. "Then you know what death must be like"—he grasped and smudged his bloody eyes with the backs of his hands—"I must have failed you—"

"No," Willie barked, and the others joined in, *no no no*.

"Yes! Or I would not have been betrayed."

"Did we betray you, Big Guy?" Dedrick said.

"You said it."

Millroy stared in a hypnotic way at the yanked-off finger, his eyes like raw wounds.

"Because I don't believe in the finger of fate."

His way of smiling made him look ferocious.

"Don't make me do magic."

"Why not just get rid of the kid?" T. Van asked.

They all looked at me with hungry mouths.

"That's ugly," Millroy said. "I saw this child"—he did not say boy or girl, but they all knew he meant me—"a face in the crowd, luminous with trust, like a light upon a hill. That was my strength, the trust of an innocent child. So we became inseparable, body and soul, and I was further strengthened. Can you understand how I would never violate that trust?"

The Sons and Daughters kept their eyes on me, and I wondered whether they had guessed that I was a girl.

"I regret that I am regarded as an enemy in the only country I love," Millroy said. "But I am more sorry that your faith in me has wavered. I expected more from America. I don't mind scandal and disgrace, but there's a worse aspect to being hounded."

Kayla and Stacy had begun to sob in loud goose honks. The other Sons and Daughters were muttering *no, no,* and Millroy's smile was not a smile.

"I have nowhere in the world to go," he went on. "I have seen the world and it is desperate. I am being cast out and driven to die in some terrible country. It is my worst fear."

He lowered his head and his deep voice rumbled and grew fainter.

"Millroy wanted to outlive everyone now living. Millroy was never a prophet. Millroy was a messenger and hoped to be a patriarch, doing push-ups among his people."

The wind shoved hard on the shell of the trailer, and everything moved except Millroy, who was leaning over the platter on which the finger, drained of its blood, had gone bluey-gray, like an old pork sausage link.

"Now I'm going to share a secret with you," he said, and produced a knife, which blazed as he drew it out of his sleeve. It was more a dagger than a knife, and the curve of its bright blade made it look wicked and deadly. It was one that he used to slash the side of the Indian basket when someone was inside, vanishing. With the rapid, snapping motion of a Day One chef slicing an edible root, he worked the knife over the platter and chopped the loose finger into small pieces, the blade chattering as the disks of meat and bone were dealt onto the plate. Then he shaved them from the table and gathered them flat onto the widest part of the knife blade.

All this time he was talking about his secret.

"Millroy is not afraid of what the newspapers say about him," he said. "It doesn't worry Millroy that journalists and commentators try to ridicule him. That's what they are paid to do."

He lifted the knife blade, keeping it level, looked at the raw salami-like disk of the dead Day One finger. Then he peered into each of our faces.

"I know that one of you is trying to undo Millroy," he said.

There was a silence, Sons and Daughters holding their breath.

"Not you, buddy," Millroy said.

They were all looking at me with poisonous eyes, wanting me to drop dead.

"Step into the other room for a minute. I have to divulge a secret, buddy."

I got up and went into the back bunkroom of the trailer, where a small lamp trembled on the wall from the trailer's rolling wheels. I stood in its feeble light, seasick from the swaying trailer, and hung on to the wall bracket. I shut my eyes. *Something is happening.*

I could not hear anything except the roar of the wind battering the Airstream, but when I opened my eyes I saw that I was in darkness—maybe the jiggling had killed the bulb—but this black room made me see what I had missed before, a sliver of light at the edge of the door frame.

Putting my eye against the lighted crack, I saw the chopped-up finger on a plate. At that moment our trailer must have been passing an eighteen-wheeler because I heard a racket of heavy tires, the snap of canvas and a slipstream wind like a loud machine. Millroy was speaking, but I did not hear a word.

Then he smiled, but he was the only one smiling. The others looked as though he had just given them bad news. Delivered of his secret, he seemed lighter in spirit, but the secret had settled and soaked into the Sons and Daughters.

"Now eat," he said, and hoisted the plate.

What was on the plate no longer looked like a human finger or even parts of it, because it was all separated into harmless-seeming disks.

"What's it taste like?"

"Whatever you wish," Millroy said. "Wafer with honey. Fig bar. Parched pulse. Fish. Open up."

And grasping carefully, because he was missing a finger, he put one piece into the mouth of each Son and Daughter.

"Repeat after me: 'This is not meat. It is Millroy.' "

"This is not meat. It is Millroy."

In the swaying trailer at the bumping table, while I peeked through the crack, the Sons and Daughters each received a fragment of finger. They seemed startled and relieved at the taste, and it was as though they were swallowing air, just taking a breath.

"This is not meat. It is Millroy."

After they had all eaten a segment, Millroy called out for me to return. The empty plate remained on the table. He said, "It is not time for you, buddy."

The others had shut their mouths, and they smiled and looked at me sadly. The remains of Millroy's secret lingered in the room, suggestions of it, like a dim echo of what he had said to them, or wisps of an aroma still hanging in the air.

"Now eat these cruciform vegetables," Millroy said. "Get to work on these figs and this pottage. Notice that now there is wine in the goblets."

It was a complete meal, and so it seemed ceremonial, the only sort of ritual that Millroy valued, eating together, with him doing the feeding. We ate in silence, and I could tell that the way the moving trailer shook and howled made everyone nervous. They were silent and burdened, wondering what to do with whatever secret he had told them.

It was three in the morning when we swung by the Day One Diner again, and the Sons and Daughters stood up unsteadily in the trailer.

"Now get out."

Millroy seemed so thoughtful as we set off again in the Ford, pulling the empty trailer, that I did not dare speak up. It was not until we were miles from Boston, in a tunnel of darkness that was probably New Hampshire, that I asked him where we were going.

"That's up to them," he said. He squinted into the dark beyond the yellow cones of the headlights.

I was thinking, *Up to who?* as the slanting stripes on the road put me to sleep.

In my dream there were strangers clamoring at the windows of the Day One Diner, waving supermarket tabloids headlined THIS MAN IS EVIL, while Millroy glared at them from the kitchen, yanking his fingers off one by one, like someone pulling off a pair of gloves, finger by finger. That woke me up.

"We're alone," Millroy said, hearing me yawn.

Driving like that, just the two of us, I was reminded of how we had left the Barnstable County Fair that summer day with no idea of where we were going. But this was a dark, cold morning in late autumn. There was no dawn except a gray mist rising and growing silver above the hills,

clouds squashed all over the low sky, and the clammy light that blackened the pines at the roadside. Here and there were white scarves of
leftover snow. Millroy was not driving fast, and yet there was something
final in the way he gripped the wheel and faced forward, as though he
never intended to return down this empty road.

"I could not do this without you."

"Anyway, what are you doing?"

"See? I need you to ask that question."

But he did not answer it.

As sunlight lifted the sky, the pine trees became greener. They grew
straight on steep hillsides. Beneath us a black river flowed around the ice
crusts of rocks, and crows, looking busy, screamed, beat their wings and
settled on branches as though they owned the trees.

Toward noon, we entered a small town of white-painted houses, with
a simple white fence around the village green, more snow scarves
twisted under bushes and trees, and a tarnished metal statue of an old
soldier in a baggy uniform on a stone pedestal. Beyond the statue was a
church with a golden arrow as its weathervane.

Millroy hung on to the steering wheel, adjusted the rearview mirror
and clucked. "Looks like they failed."

One burst of a siren and a flashing light behind us: we were being tail-
gated by a police car.

"Who failed?"

"It was a test," Millroy said. "I told the Sons and Daughters where
we were going. If they had said nothing, there was hope. Day One was
theirs. But you see? It's all over."

He had eased the Ford onto the shoulder, and I heard the rumble of
the trailer following as it bumped.

"Was that the secret?"

"Where we were going was my secret," he said. "But I wanted to
learn their secret—what they think of me. Now I know."

There was a man in a blue uniform at the window. He looked in at
Millroy and made a face. "You're on television." He tipped his cap
back. His badge said WOODSTOCK and the black nameplate on his pocket
was lettered KENDRICKS.

"Not anymore."

"License and registration," the policeman said. "This vehicle's been
reported."

Millroy was smiling at the policeman, who wheezed and had Smoker's Face and an assertive belly and trembly fingers. He stank of anger and had the weary eyes of someone who ached for nutrition.

"Please don't restrain me," Millroy said.

The policeman said to me, "You're going to be all right, sonny."

Millroy had not prepared me for this—for one of the Sons and Daughters, or all of them, reporting him to the police. I heard the clink of metal, the policeman fumbling with a pair of handcuffs.

"Confinement stresses me," Millroy said, making a face and clutching the wheel.

The policeman opened the door to let me out and then efficiently clamped Millroy's wrists to the steering wheel. Unclicking another pair, he fitted them to Millroy's ankles and then removed the car key.

The next sound I heard was Millroy's nag-like humming in a singsong protest through his nose.

"Better come with me, kiddo."

But I had just then thought to look at Millroy's Day One finger in daylight. He knew I was staring because the finger was not missing anymore.

"It grew," he said, and flexed it and went on humming.

I sat beside the policeman in the squad car while he spelled out Millroy's name on the radio, and filled out a printed form on his clipboard, writing slowly, pinching his pen with his hairy thumb.

"It's a mistake," I said, but the policeman did not hear me.

He was arresting Millroy because someone had ratted on him. It did not matter who. So many people believed the lies in the papers, or else planted them. I agreed that Millroy sounded suspicious and seemed worse, and what was he doing with me? But that was just looks. Anyone who really knew him, knew the truth and would treat him as a hero, not a criminal.

What made it almost funny was that this policeman was another person, along with all the reporters and people who spread the lies, who could have been saved by Millroy's message. They were trying to stop the very man who could have made them happier and given them a longer life. For their lies about him they all deserved to be miserable and sick, and yet Millroy had always said that he was nothing, that his message was everything, and that it would last as long as The Book.

As I was sitting there thinking this, there came a sudden sizzling noise like the gust of air and tiny bubbles that fizz from beneath a bottle cap when you lift it with a church key. It made the policeman stop writing.

"Excuse yourself."

"That wasn't me," I said.

He clicked his pen and began again, and there was another crack of wind, more explosive than the last one, from beyond the trailer.

The policeman looked up and listened with his narrowing eyes. Then he jerked forward when he heard the glugging, like a collapse of liquid down a tube and its watery swallowing. It was a loud flushing sound, like sudden laughter, by the roadside in this pretty little town of Woodstock, Vermont. The policeman jerked the door handle and got out of the patrol car quickly, muttering to himself, heading for the Ford and Millroy. When I heard him swear loudly, a one-word *moo*, I was sure that Millroy had vanished again. Millroy the Magician.

IV
The Big Island

39 "Fasten your seat belt, angel," Millroy said on the plane during mealtime, metal food carts shaking in the aisle. He handed me a heavy buckle and the right side of the safety belt. He wore a purple skullcap and dark glasses and had trimmed his mustache. You would never have known it was Millroy.

Just a second ago he had been talking about going into hiding in the farthest corner of the USA and dictating his life story, *This Is My Body,* to me. Then the food cart rattled past and he told me to buckle up.

I heard him snort and got worried again.

"How come?"

The air blasted across the side windows, making a muffled, blowing noise like a vacuum cleaner, but the plane was steadier than the Airstream trailer had ever been.

"You'll see."

He seemed cranky. He had been agitated ever since Boston, but why? *I've come back from the dead,* he had said, *and I can prove it.* He was always doing that, and it was true once again. When he had disappeared by the roadside in Woodstock, the policeman got cross and asked me for my ID. I knew I had none, but pretended to look. *What?* There it was, slipped into my little wallet by Millroy's magic, proving I was eighteen, while the truth was I was fifteen going on sixteen. My thumbprint and photo were a perfect match. How had he done it without my knowing? And I had a chunk of money, too.

"I can't hold you, son." The policeman twisted his face, looking piggy.

He watched me leave on the Rutland bus to Boston as he guarded Millroy's trailer. I sat on the bus and sucked my thumb. The man in front of me on the bus cranked his seat back and removed his hat. Bald, mustache, Millroy, with his finger to his lips: *Not a word.* The next thing I knew we were on this airplane. I had not realized you could fly nine hours westward and still be in the USA.

During the airplane meal he had grumbled like indigestion, and pushed the tray away with his fingers when it was handed to him. I half-expected him to use magic—melt it, set it on fire or turn it into a rat's nest.

"Take it away."

Saying that, he pinched the handle of the metal fork, made it curl like a fiddlehead and then dropped it with a clatter onto the tray.

"Meat fumes," he said.

He was talking generally to whoever would listen in the seats around us, people who looked uncomfortable jammed between their armrests.

"Grease and meat fats in the air can be inhaled into the system. Kind of a slipstream effect, as toxic as cigarette smoke. No one realizes this. Angel, breathe through your nose."

From the movement of his mustache I knew he was pressing his lips together, and he went on snorting, reaming his system with air, cleansing himself, while still grumbling and wheezing.

"Tighter," he said, tapping his finger on the buckle of my safety belt. "People have been known to hit the ceiling of these planes and sustain severe neck injuries—whiplash and so forth—during turbulence."

The sun never shines brighter than through the window of an airplane, I was thinking, and this one whooshed without any shaking whatsoever. Flying cross-country on a clear day, you saw every great thing in America, as the pilot told us: the Great Lakes, the Mississippi River, Grand Canyon, Lake Havasu, the mountains of the West, Los Angeles like a bowl of brown smoke, and then the blue Pacific under high, racing clouds.

"It's wicked calm."

I was eating some melon balls we had brought. We also had sacks of beans and grains, Ezekiel bread, barley cakes, figs, cheese and honeycombs. We had wine, we had almonds.

Millroy was not eating anything, only staring behind his gleaming dark glasses at the metal meal cart, then at a newsreel of a ship on its side leaking oil on a lovely coastline.

What do I know about turbulence? I thought. *This is only my second airplane flight in my whole life.* I did not know where we were going; I only knew that he would keep me safe, so what was the point?

Millroy was disturbed, and when he was cross, the world was deranged. So I tightened my buckle. From his look of concentration, like a man squinting into a mirror, I knew he had taken control of all his bodily openings. It was the meat fumes. He had sealed himself within his body. When he managed this, he could survive, even underwater, for hours. *You could bury me alive.*

I was glad that I did not really need the seat belt. The plane was steady in the clear air. Yet just the thought of being so high in the sky in this big metal tunnel frightened me because, after all, what held it up? I felt worse when I saw the sign USE SEAT BOTTOM CUSHION FOR FLOTATION.

Millroy seemed to be smiling, but no, he was sealed in, all his openings shut down like valves against the meat fumes from the steaming dinners being handed out by men and women in blue uniforms. The carts were rattling in the narrow aisles. He was not smiling, he was expelling.

"Enough," he said without opening his mouth, and began to tremble.

As he did so, the rounded inside of the plane started to shake, the doors of the overhead compartments, the squeak of flimsy plastic under stress. Millroy's jaw was wobbling, and a moment later the plane gave a sudden, similar tremble, then it tipped and seemed to slide at a clumsy slanting angle. A plinking sound came out of the loudspeaker, lights flashed, and the newsreel jumped off the screen and onto the wall of the plane, to the sound of clattering cabinets and hatches.

The captain has turned on the seat-belt sign. Please return to your seat and make sure your seat belt is securely fastened.

Mine was already buckled from five minutes ago. I looked up at him because of the coincidence, but he was staring straight ahead through his dark goggles, his mustache making a mask for his mouth.

"I'm scared," I said.

He had no readable look on his face, yet his mustache gave him an impassive look of wisdom. To anything I said he would reply, *I know that,* and without a facial expression he seemed indestructible.

"Honest," I said.

The worst part of this big bumbling plane was not the hardness of its shakes but the way the small children first began to cry and then the older women to scream. Behind us, jerking in his seat, a frightened man was muttering filthy words to himself.

It was as though Millroy were blowing this wild rumble of air out of his mouth and tipping the plane, using his breath alone.

Long groans of terror and frank barks of fear filled the plane and scared me all the more.

I could only calm myself by looking over at Millroy as he sat still, looking ahead like a strange, rigid prophet with wiggles of magic coming out of his head.

The windows had gone dark as though we had dipped underwater, and bright scraps of cloud flew past like misshapen fish darting in shoals. We bumped and rolled again, buffeted by winds that were tearing at the wings, and I got sick feeling the whole plane twist.

Another screech in the back sounded like a terrible accident in a kitchen, with airplane crockery smashing onto the floor and a tinkling of knives and forks.

I had taken my earphones off. I had been listening to music on "Sky-tracks," but my not concentrating on the pitching of the plane made it seem to pitch much worse.

It was now falling sideways. There were streaks of light at the windows, fleeting yellow rags of cloud, and lightning—not jagged bolts but large, soupy flashes that seemed to drown us in their sickly glare.

An old worried woman began to yell in a foreign language. I saw another sign, IN CASE OF AN EMERGENCY USE THE LIFE VEST UNDER YOUR SEAT.

Millroy saw me staring at his face.

"What's wrong, angel?"

But he knew I wanted him to protect me and hide me from this misery of fear.

"I'm wicked scared."

"Why?"

"That I might die."

"Is that so bad?"

He shifted in his seat to hear me better, and I had the idea that he was very interested in my answer.

"What if I went to hell?"

"Hell is empty," Millroy said. "All the devils are here."

This is the captain speaking. I don't know where this weather came from. We've tried a new altitude but we can't seem to get around it. So keep your seat belts fastened and when I find some smoother air I'll turn the seat-belt sign off.

It was not a frightened voice, but it was a bewildered one, vibrating with doubt, as the metal meal carts clanged and the doors overhead flopped open, spilling clothes and bags into the aisles.

Millroy's head was rigid and fearless and upright and looked commanding.

In the meantime, I'm going to ask the flight attendants to suspend the dinner service.

Was Millroy nodding or was his head moving with the movement of the plane? Whatever, the airplane still shook. It had seemed like a big rocketing bus when it was humming in the calm air, but now, the way it jounced, it seemed weak and wobbly, like a thin, bent balloon that might burst at any moment.

I reached over and took Millroy's hand, hoping to feel better. His mustache moved, perhaps in a smile, though his hand was like a piece of metal—hard and with no warmth in it. It made me afraid but I could not let go. His hand had closed over mine, and now he had a good grip. I did not feel any better. The way he held it made me think that he might change my hand into a banana or a spoon or a claw, and if I raised my arm I would poke myself in the eye.

My silent crying throbbed along my arm, and Millroy felt it, and looked at me as tears ran down my cheeks.

Did he know the reason, that it was not just the storm battering this airplane, but the unexpected violence of his magic? I knew that his eyes were black behind his dark glasses, but I wondered why.

When it was pitching, the plane seemed small and breakable, and the passengers moaned when it rose and fell, especially when the whole aircraft bellywhopped through the shuddering air.

Millroy held my hands too tightly for me to wipe away my tears, and I began to resent him for making the storm. I suspected that he had done it out of spite because of the meat fumes from the meal (chicken breast) and the poisonous airplane food.

"Not only that," he said, reading my thoughts.

Then it was also to gain control of the passengers, the way he had done with his bodily functions—first shaking them up, then stirring them, then getting a good grip.

He could see my tears and feel the terror in my fingers, and I could barely breathe, to take in enough air so that I could let out a scream.

There came a sudden squawk.

Please do not walk in the aisles. Keep to your seats, with your seat belts securely fastened. It's kind of rough out there, sir!

The "sir" was Millroy, who had gotten up and was walking down the aisle to the front of the plane, just the way he had always entered the show tent at the Barnstable County Fair, with everyone watching.

Sir, the captain has told everyone to take their seat.

In his sunglasses and purple skullcap, Millroy stood without moving, commanding everyone's attention, even the ones who were moaning in fear.

He put his fingers into his mouth and drew out a glittering stick. If this was an illusion, it was the greatest one I had ever seen him perform, because he stood there while the plane nosedived and seemed to be on the verge of crashing.

Reaching past a terrified man and woman in matching flower-print shirts, he leaned over to a porthole window and picked off the plastic cover and the glass. As the outside air poured into the plane with a sound like furious marbles, Millroy tossed the glittering stick out. At once the plane steadied—lurched straight as though he had it on a leash—and the air went calm. He wiped the glass back into the porthole window with the flat of his hand.

You expected applause. But in the sudden stillness and fanlike hum that followed, the passengers were too shocked to do anything except gasp for breath. They had seen that this strange man had stopped the storm. I alone knew that he had started it.

Millroy did not speak. He gestured with his hands, indicating *That's that,* and then *See, nothing in my hands, nothing up my sleeve,* and finally with his Day One finger, *Be very careful.*

He took his seat again. Nothing more happened. No more food. No more movie. No service. Passengers kept their seat belts fastened even after the warning light was turned off, and the flight attendants also stayed seated and buckled up—maybe out of fear or maybe because of what this strange man had done. They were in shock. If only they had known who he was.

Holding their breath, they watched when he got up to stretch. Every eye in the plane was on him, pleading and grateful but wondering who he was. If he had revealed himself, they would have recognized him as

Millroy from *The Day One Program,* and would have been confused. He was famous and in disgrace. But he kept his hat and his sunglasses on, and the passengers were afraid, as though at any moment the plane would tumble once more.

"Don't make the plane go nuts again, please," I said.

A boasting sound came out of his mouth. I had the idea that he wanted me to be amazed. Had he made that wicked storm for me?

He took my hand, his fingers stiff and cold, and hardly seeming human. After all this time I did not know his hand felt like this. He now seemed like a stranger, so far beyond me, with such unpredictable power, that I could not connect myself to him.

He had never touched me like this before. The dull, cold pinch of his fingers made me afraid, and I started to imagine again that he could do something to my hand—make it into a stabbing fork—when he suddenly dropped it.

We were in blackness, slowly passing a mountainside of twinkling lights. We landed. We hurried through a terminal of fresh, flower-smelling air, damp heat and brown laughing people in rubber sandals, and boarded a smaller plane that was drenched in deodorant. It was a short flight. Our next airport was smaller and damp, smelling of rain and cut grass and crushed flowers and there was a sharp whiff of sea salt in the air that reminded me of the Cape.

Millroy had not said a word, just pointed me in the right direction. He was in a rush to arrive, always a restless traveler, hating public rest rooms and the dangerous stink of other people's food. He was tired, having exhausted himself in the storm he whipped up, his first magic in—hey, where were we?

"Still in America," he said, reading my mind again.

"What part?"

"Hawaii. The Big Island."

His first magic on The Big Island. But there was more.

40 That same night Millroy led me into a large shadowy house by a sloshing sea. He did not say a word, and yet I could feel his hot breath on my bare shoulder and I could hear the juicy sound of his swallowing.

"Mind turning on the light?"

I sounded like a little old lady fretting in the dark.

"You're over there," he said softly, jerking the light pull on the floor lamp and pointing to an open door.

That night and afterward we heard laughing and yelling from the blue bungalow down the beach, our nearest neighbor. Sometimes there was plinking music, played too loud. Just as often, there were rackety screams, a drawn-out wailing, two or three people howling together like dogs behind a fence. It was too real to be television, but they had one of those, too. You knew when the TV was on because it sounded like too many people trapped inside a tin box. There were also rattling drums. There were hymns in another language. There was singing and a ukelele song.

> Manuela boy, my dear boy, you no more hila-hila
> No more five cents, no more house, you go Aala Park hia-mo-e.
> Papa works for the stevedore, Mama makes the leis
> Sister goes with the haole boy, brother goes au-wana.

There was more laughter.

Two weeks of it. When your neighbors are as loud as that, you talk less yourself.

Meanwhile, we lived as father and son at the edge of the black cliff on this Hawaiian island that was wrapped in air, in the middle of a bluey-green sea.

"America," Millroy said. "Are you in any doubt that God placed his hand on this country?"

He was shouting because we were so near the sea, and he had to raise his voice when the surf was up. The blue waves swelled out of the flat ocean in long, straight rows and rolled forward roughly, whitening as they steepened, hovered and dumped themselves onto the beach, adding another rib of sand to the shore, and a second later snatching it back with another wave.

The beach sand was coal-black and gravelly, smooth pellets of broken lava the color of the old volcanic flow on the hillside behind our house, big cliffs of black cinders that had tumbled to the beach and been smashed into black gumdrops and beads.

It rained most nights, and in the daytime the road and the foliage steamed in the sunlight. Dolphins plopped and played in the sea below our front porch. We heard them gasp and take sucking breaths, we saw them toss themselves in the air. Our palm trees rattled, their lower fronds thumping like brooms against our walls, and sometimes a big splintery brown frond dropped onto the tin roof. The cockroaches flew with a papery flutter, and the cane spiders scuttled with no sound at all. Heavy mangoes dropped to the damp earth like a punch in the stomach.

There was always a smell of flowers: orchids and jasmine, bougainvillaea growing in long whips of pink blossoms, hibiscus blooms bigger than lilies. Millroy knew all their names.

"Nasturtiums," he said, stuffing first the orange flowers, then the round leaves into his mouth. "You could live on these. Plumeria. Naupaka."

Rats flicked around the eaves and mice nibbled holes in the screens. The birds were loud, as talkative and friendly as the people. The little birds made a scrape like a Zippo that won't light. Some of the whitest birds had long, beautiful tails, and others looked like black kites. Small, pale lizards called geckos chirped like birds and left droppings like jimmies all over the table.

"I always dreamed of this," Millroy said. "Why didn't someone ever tell me about Hawaii? We could have started Day One here. We can still work it out. We can be entirely Day One—melons, figs, beans, pulses, grains and herbs. I've got seeds from the Holy Land—heirloom seeds. Originals."

He looked around and saw a sloping field of spindly trees.

"Papayas are a kind of Day One melon," he said. "Hey, we're not fanatics."

We were walking down the beach at the margin of the collapsing waves, where the spittle line of scum was, the high-water mark. The edge of the island was a cliff of black and spiky rock topped with hunks of soggy grass. Gray crabs scuttled away from our feet.

"I needed this," Millroy said. "A spell in the wilderness to rest and give thanks. It's a kind of exile. I've come back from the dead again."

He did not mention the police, or the charges against him (of which kidnapping and fraud and tax evasion were only a few), and neither did I.

"This Is My Body," he said.

My mouth went dry, and I stumbled in the black sand.

"We can get down to writing it, angel," he said. "No interruptions. It's the perfect setting."

There was a great black headland rising up several miles away, above it the rubbly slopes of a volcano, all cinders and smoke.

"I always thought islands were supposed to be small," I said. "But this one is wicked big."

The lava flow had wiped out a nearby town, just sizzled it, then covered it with a three-foot-deep layer of crumbly lava. Half-burned palm trunks lay on top of the lava flow, and on sunny days it all smelled like burned toast.

"This is an American island," Millroy said.

He was so happy, he worked magic without knowing it. He was rested, he was calm. He blew on buds and they strained and swelled and exploded into bloom with a sudden gust of perfume.

"Strawberry guava," he said, his mouth over a low bush.

Fierce dogs on the road stopped barking when Millroy approached.

There were also thieves in this area, Puna District. One night we were awakened by suspicious noises. Millroy was in his room, I in my cubicle. I heard him laugh, then there was a howl of pain from a startled stranger, but when I went downstairs I saw nothing at all.

"What's that funny smell?"

"Burned flesh," Millroy said. His stare said, *Remember this, too.* "Scorched hair."

I did not want to know any more.

Nearer the road there were other houses—Japanese, Filipinos, Chinese, other islanders, and people like us they called "howlies," fat boys who drove pickup trucks, skinny ones on motorbikes. There were large, hand-lettered signs that said NO TRESPASSING and PRIVATE and KAPU.

"We're alone," Millroy said. He meant that no one knew us here. He raised his eyes as though to praise the island. "Alone in America."

There was sudden rain, blinding sunshine, high winds, the sight of molten lava, and there were always dolphins.

I had the sense that Millroy had bewitched the island, that he had power over it and could control it as with the storm in the airplane.

"I can prove that I came back from the dead," he said. "I am simply biding my time."

We feasted on melons and fish, on honey and beans.

"I'll dictate my book to you," he said. "That way it will be your book, too."

Our house on The Big Island was on stilts, and secluded, just behind a high cliff on a small, empty beach in a cove, which was why the laughter and screams we heard were so strange. Those loud noises were the first we knew that we had neighbors, and then we saw the blue bungalow.

A woman shrieked, *Please don't go!* and there were the sounds of a struggle. *Doont!*

I heard them clearly from my room at the side of the house. Millroy's room faced the sea, where the waves rolled in and sometimes thudded into the hollows at the foot of the lava cliff.

I had no fear of the neighbors, not with Millroy around. He had power over flowers and winds and slanting rain. He swam with the dolphins, he calmed wild dogs. The noisy neighbors were the ones who ought to have been afraid.

We went barefoot most of the time, walking along the cliff or on the beach, cultivating our garden, sitting on the porch, looking out to the sea.

"Everyone says aloha," I said because the word came into my head.

"Aloha is love," Millroy said. "Do you think much about that?"

The word "love" worried me, so I said nothing.

"Love allows us to see people the way God sees them."

"I guess so."

"Imagine how certain achievements are possible only if you are loved."

I tried to imagine it.

"What's wrong?"

But he knew. The neighbors had stopped laughing and switched off the music. They were screaming again.

"That one," he said. "That's a Smoker's Scream."

We bought most of our whole food at the nearest town, Pahoa, at the Cash-and-Carry and Da Store and at Mana Natural Foods. Millroy said that pretty soon we would not have to buy anything; we would be self-sufficient in heirloom vegetables, beans and grains. There were howlies in Pahoa, always talking to each other. *I just did your chart, Shirley,* and *We made a new batch of candles.* Some of the women had tattoos and crewcuts, their children were barefoot, the men wore ponytails.

No one stared at Millroy and me.

"Fresh vegetables," Millroy said when we shopped. "Fresh fruit, just off the vine. There's a nut farm outside Pohoiki. Fresh nuts! I wanted this in Boston. I guess we came to the right place, sugar. We can live our faith with our friends."

I looked at him. We had no friends among the howlies, surfers, candlemakers or tattooed women.

Millroy knew what I was thinking.

"Bees," he said. "Honeybees."

Those boxes I had seen behind people's houses on the upper road to Pahoa were beehives.

"When we finish my book I'm going to be a beekeeper," he said. "We'll live on our own honey. We'll give away what we don't need."

"I don't know anything about bees."

"You'll be my queen bee."

Saying things like that to me these days, he always took a step nearer, as though he wanted to say something more and for me to respond. *You'll be my queen bee* worried me greatly.

It felt odd because he had never spoken this way to me before. The first night in our house, in the dark, his silence and breathing were a way of speaking, and they made me cringe and tell him to put on the light. His looking at me with hot eyes made me want to step outside.

We were alone now, as he said. We had not been alone for a long time. He was careful not to upset me, tried to make me feel safe, but still there was something on his mind, I was not sure what.

So I said, "What do you want?"

"To get quiet and give thanks," he said. "To watch you grow. To tell the story of my life."

That broke the spell. There was no more talk about my being his queen bee.

He was not worried about having left Day One behind. He said he disliked religion, and felt that Day One had been turning into one against his will. The Sons and Daughters could carry his teachings around the country, just the simple message "Let The Book be your cookbook."

"I have delivered my message," he said. "There will be no reruns or repeats of *The Day One Program*. I expressly forbade it. It was in my contract. I have disappeared from the face of the earth. I am invisible now."

Yet I had the sense that he was not finished—anyway, not satisfied. When I saw him looking at a flower or a fence post, I had the idea that he wanted to work magic on them. He seemed restless, though he denied it, and denying his magic made it more startling because he performed it so casually. I was impressed but I could not understand the point of it, for the only person who saw it was me.

One day we drove into Pahoa as usual to buy fruit, honey and herbs, cutting through the humid heat in our new Jeep. All around us were steaming trees, wet grass, thick flowers, a glary green that made me squint and the sweet, stinging smell of rotting manure and fresh mud.

The town was just a single street of wooden buildings, some of them abandoned, a few food stores and a noisy school. The main road continued uphill to the volcano, which I wanted to see, but Millroy did not go there, or anywhere else.

"This is all the life I want," he said. "How about you, muffin?"

"I'm good."

"But isn't this landscape ravishing?"

"It's pretty wicked."

"You could spend the rest of your life here."

That was another one, like *You'll be my queen bee*. When he said *the rest of your life* it was as though he was hinting that there was not much of it left, that we would die here, and maybe soon.

"A couple of hundred years more," he said. "Don't worry. There's plenty of time if we stick together."

He had read my mind again. What didn't he know about me?

Passing one of the larger wooden buildings in Pahoa, he said, "This was once a movie house. Probably seventy-five seats or less. A little stage, footlights, a balcony, a podium.''

The peeling name on the front said AKEBONO THEATER, and I had the suspicion that he wanted to renovate it and preach on the podium.

''We got too big,'' he said, looking at the wooden marquee with a few torn posters still stuck in patches to hardened crusts of glue. ''Day One grew so fast it created misunderstandings. I had the weight-loss people after me, the equal-opportunity people, envious evangelists, the cable bosses, the Board of Health, the tax man. Not to mention all the religious nuts and New Agers.''

''The police,'' I said.

That word shut him up fast, the memory of it.

But still he fidgeted, as though he needed to work magic or explain his message. The storm on the plane was the new Millroy—he would not have done it that way in the past. He would have been subtler, jammed the meal trolleys, short-circuited the microwave, melted the trays, instead of cooking up gale-force winds, furious downdrafts and enough turbulence to rock the jumbo. He had done it for me, I was convinced of that.

He was barefoot. He wore fewer clothes here on this warm island. I saw that he was younger, stronger, more muscular than he had seemed in Boston. His bare legs were powerful and straight, and I was reminded that he was a man as well as a magician.

''Punch me in the stomach. Go on!''

His fingers were always in motion, silently conjuring, now more than ever. Yet we were alone. I did not ask why, but still I wondered. Perhaps because there was nothing else to do. Or maybe it was the island, which itself was magical with volcanoes, honeybees, friendly fish and air sweetened with blossoms. But his magic was no longer gentle. It was sudden and explosive, as nervous as knuckle-cracking, unnecessary like boasting or loud music, and at times like showing off.

I did not dare to think these thoughts. I simply kept my mind open and watched him to see what he would do next.

As we stood before the old Akebono Theater, a rusty pickup truck drove past, then stopped, backed up and parked next to the curb beside our Jeep.

A darkish howlie girl got out of the truck and walked to the public telephone bolted to the side of the old building.

She was even smaller than me, about twelve or thirteen, with a hard, slender body, dark eyes and pretty lashes, but a smudged face, dirty knees and bony elbows, and she was smoking a crushed cigarette. One of her legs was bandaged, a leak stain on the gauze. Her lips were soft and pink, and she was mumbling. She wore a T-shirt and shorts and was barefoot with a scab on her anklebone. I imagined that her Gaga thrashed her and called her a tramp, though she was just a little howlie teenager.

Millroy took an interest, watched her dial a number, tapping the buttons on the phone and then poking a quarter into the coin slot. She had small, even teeth. Her nails, painted with red polish, were chipped and bitten. Opening her mouth wide, she spoke a loud swearword and began hitting the phone box with the receiver, smacking the steel front and still saying the same ugly word.

I stepped back while Millroy leaned over and burned her with his eyes. But I felt breathless and guilty just hearing the girl speak the word.

"Give it up, peewee," Millroy said.

She had the cigarette butt in her lips and, braced against the phone, hitting it hard, was still grunting the word.

She stopped when she saw Millroy still staring.

"What happened to your leg, sister?"

"Fell in the shtreet," she said. "Want to buy some jewelry?"

Jewelry seemed like an odd word for her to use, with her small, dirty face and bloodstained bandage, but she looked at Millroy more like a woman than a little girl, and stood with her hand on her hip, sizing him up like someone much older.

Millroy said, "Let's see what you've got, sister."

All this time the man in the pickup truck had been watching, and when the girl called out, showing her tongue and teeth, he cranked the door open and hopped out holding a cardboard shoebox. He was older, sunburned and sweaty, and had dark, swollen eyes. He might have been the girl's father, but I changed my mind from the way he touched her, and where.

"You like pulls, you like brasslets and peens? You want one necklace? What you like, good price."

He lifted the shiny pieces from the box, picking them up with dirty fingernails, while the little girl arranged them on the hood of our Jeep—a shell necklace, a string of pearls, a jade pendant, pink coral earrings, a crusty pin, a gold bracelet engraved *Rosie*.

"Where did you get these?"

"From one howlie guy in Kurtistown."

"He think we cuckaroach it," the small girl said.

"What's your name?" Millroy was looking at the man.

"Hookie."

The man's shirt was torn at the shoulder and he had scraped toes. The girl flipped her cigarette butt into the street.

"That's Lerma."

"Your daughter?"

"Third one," he said, and it sounded like *turd*.

She poked the necklace and the earrings with her tiny fingers. I found her bitten, broken nails more interesting than the scraps of jewelry.

"Now put them away."

Millroy's voice was gentle but so insistent that it sounded like an order.

The man did so, letting the trinkets slip through his fingers. His swollen eyes did not look at Millroy.

Millroy was holding his hands up to show they were empty.

"Have a look in there, Lerma," he said, "then put the lid on."

"If you don't want to buy something you could maybe just say it."

The man seemed frightened as he said this, standing sideways, because all this time Millroy's hands were above him and he was so much bigger.

"There's nothing to buy," Millroy said. "Take the lid off and look."

Lerma snatched at the box, knocking the lid aside, then shaking the box and slapping it hard, but nothing fell out. She blinked at Millroy and at the man, looking smaller and dirtier and weaker, almost a tiny child in her frustration.

The man took the box from her and punched it until it ripped apart.

"It's a chrick!"

"This guy cuckaroach my things!"

"You don't like it?" Millroy smiled at them. "Punch me in the stomach."

But it was the little girl who swore at Millroy because the man was too fearful of his magic to say anything.

"So what do you think?"

I was right: he wanted to hear that I had been impressed. I did not have the heart to tell him that the whole time I had known him he had been my hero not for his magic, which often frightened me, but for his kindness. This meaningless magic was like muscle-flexing—it had been that same way with the storm.

I said, "You didn't have to do that to them."

"That's all you have to say?"

He wanted me to marvel at him, he wanted to please me. It was not necessary, yet I did not know how to tell him this.

"Silence," he said, and kept driving down the narrow road to the black coast.

He hated it when I would not reply, but I was worried.

That was not the end of it. The next day, walking along the beach beyond our cove, we saw a small girl with flowers in her hair crouched in the sand, on her hands and knees, not playing but crying. Her sorrowing body was angled toward the blue bungalow. When we looked up at the house, we heard music and voices louder than ever.

Millroy said, "They need help," in his new *Remember this* voice, with important pauses in it.

At the stairway leading from the beach were stacks of bright flowers and green leaves, some of them twined on the handrail.

Millroy led me up the stairs and into the house, where twenty or more people were moving this way and that, island people, some of them dark, Japanesy, wearing bathing suits and T-shirts; others, wild-looking howlies—big, sunburned children, infants and dogs playing together; men with uncut beards and ponytails, tattooed women, beer drinkers, talking loudly, two laughing at a joke, most of them crying, or with wet eyes as though they had just stopped crying. There was food on every level surface—pasta salad, basins of torn-apart chicken, sausages in piles, bowls of dip, mush, crunched vegetables, crumbly cake and potato chips, with a barrel of ice and beer, and a stack of Jungle Jerky.

In the next room more children watched cartoons on a large television—a cat being hammered flat on the ground by an angry dog with a frying pan.

Though it was the same noise and music we had been hearing for weeks, it was not a party, and I sensed that Millroy was thinking, *We should have known.*

At the edge of the porch, which was at the edge of the sea cliff, there was a dead woman. She lay on a narrow bed that was upraised and covered with flower blossoms and silk scarves. She was neither old nor young; she was wrapped loosely in a white cloth, and was almost bald, though her head was pillowed in flower blossoms. A photograph of a lovely woman—the woman she had once been, you knew—was propped against the narrow bed, and her name was printed on it, MOMI.

Millroy walked across the room looking serious, as though he was expected, hurried past the weepers, the jokers, the drinkers, the dogs, the eaters gnawing at chicken drumsticks.

A man said to me, "You want one laulau. Is chicken. Is ono—numba one."

A Hawaiian woman with tufty hair and big arms held on to the dead woman's bedposts, sobbing, but the TV cartoon was louder than she was, and each time she opened her mouth I heard a cartoon dog's laughter.

"You know Momi?" the woman said to Millroy. "Tree dis morning she die."

"Momi is pow," a young man said. He wore a bathing suit and a surfer T-shirt saying LOCAL MOTION.

"She maki, die, dead," another man chanted. "She maki, die, dead."

Millroy smiled his *You don't know* smile and placed his hand over the face of the dead woman lying in the bed. Her skin had a whitish tinge, as though it were a thin and fragile wrapper that had been touched with frost, her eyes bruised-looking, her dry mouth sad.

"Momi was laying there almost a month after the keemo, with a drip in her," the Hawaiian woman said. "She didn't say nothing, but she could hear. We play 'Keiki o Ka'Aina' and she smile like a keiki, too."

The party-looking people in the room were now more interested in Millroy than in the dead woman or each other, and I thought it must have been their fascination with the way that his hand was over Momi's face, his slender fingers gripping her.

"So frushtrateen, she never get one chance to say good-bye," a man near Millroy said. He was eating a sandwich. He saw me looking at him. "Spam. You want?"

"We don't use meat," Millroy said.

"Is Spam, brah. Not like the same as real meat."

It was true, as Millroy had taught, that saying the word "meat" made people show their teeth and grin like dogs.

"We don't put meat into our mouths," Millroy said to the man. "We do not introduce meat into our bodies."

The man was staring with mayonnaise on his lips and holding his sandwich, with a bitten flap of Spam showing like a shingle between the bread slices.

"Feed your head," he said, licking his lips. "That's more better, yuh."

"Momi was one sweet lady." This was a howlie man with gold chains around his neck, looking drunk, his belly poking out of his half-buttoned shirt. "A wonderful wife."

"For the gods' sake, she didn't say good-bye," the Hawaiian woman said in a sorrowing voice.

Millroy kept his right hand over Momi's face. He raised his left one and spoke to the whole room.

"She is not gone," he said in his new *Remember this* voice.

Whatever was coming next I did not want to see, but the people in the room pressed close to Millroy and the dead woman, so I was trapped.

The music still played, but no one spoke.

Millroy's big hand spread out over Momi's face, his thumb against one of her eyes.

"She is with us," he said. "Aren't you, sister?"

Someone cut off the music with a sudden gulp, and the stillness jangled, and all you could hear were people chewing and swallowing.

"Oh, yes," Momi said.

A woman screamed. A man laughed out loud.

Shut up, Wendell!

Others hugged and kissed. Millroy's hand stayed in its bold grapefruit-testing grip on the woman's face, but he did not look at her—he was staring at the people in the room.

"She wants you all to say good-bye," he said, "and she wants a chance to say thank you."

There was now so much noise of crying and laughing, so many people jostling, that Millroy had to shout. The children went on playing, though, pinching the dogs, pulling their tails and eating food off the floor.

Lifting his hand, Millroy said, "Listen."

Very distinctly, in a gluey voice, the dead woman, Momi, said, "Mahalo for your kokua."

"She opening her eyes!" the big Hawaiian woman cried out, and began to laugh in a more frightening way than when she had wept.

A man said, "That give me chicken skin!"

"This man bring Momi back from the dead!"

"Auntee!"

Again, very distinctly, a ghost voice from the bed said, "Aloha, my dear friends. I love you all. Aloha kekakiaka."

There was a little silence before the screaming came again. "Aloha, Momi!" This went on for several minutes, until Millroy released his hand from the woman's face and let her die again, this time in peace. He faced them all with stony eyes. He was not moved, and now I remembered that I had never seen him cry.

"Who is that bald-headed man?" someone asked. "He look familiar."

I had been with Millroy long enough to know that the expression on his face, his eyes, the angle of his mustache, the way his ears had tightened were not signs of solemnity but rather of his whole head smiling.

"I am Doctor Millroy and this is my young friend Jilly."

I thought, *Jeekers.*

41 I was woken by dribbly rainfall in my dream, like the muddy spatter of a shower of pebbles falling slowly into a shallow puddle. I opened my eyes, and it bubbled to a stop. Trees dripped at my window. It had also been raining outside the house. The humid darkness that was like a blanket of night pressed against my face. In the glimmer of dropping water, I saw a tall, knob-headed man in my room, staring at me from the foot of my bed—Millroy—and I was dead scared.

My feet and legs went numb, a spike of pain tore my heart, fingers of fear gripped my throat and squeezed my windpipe.

As I strained to scream, Millroy began to dissolve, and a moment later there was only a gauzy blowing curtain where he had been standing.

My ragged heart kept me awake. The sun came up yellow-orange, rinsing the ocean with fruit juice and light as the birds clacked and chattered, and the surf grew noisier, rattling the stones at the shoreline.

Breakfast usually reassured me after a bad night's sleep, but not this morning.

"I saw you in my room last night."

Whittling the green peel from a papaya, Millroy did not even look up at me.

"Sometimes you imagine the thing you want in your heart. You call it fear, but it is more often desire."

"No. I was having a bad dream and I was wicked scared."

Millroy's silence and the way his head was tilted meant he disagreed with me.

"The guy sure looked like you."

"Maybe you put me there, angel."

"Why would anyone do a thing like that?"

Penetrating me with his eyes while he ate the yellow papaya, he seemed to be saying silently that I ought to know the answer to that question.

I wanted to cry.

"What's wrong, angel?"

"Who said anything was wrong?"

But everything was. I had been sinking, drowning, feeling lost, ever since landing on The Big Island. I had never been so far from home, from anything I had known. Before, I'd had Millroy as my protector. Now I hardly knew him, was scared of his surprises. What next? Everything was strange here except the food—Day One meals, Millroy cooking his head off, preparing his fruits and pottages, his herbages and thickened loaves. He was also a magician, but an explosive one. I took up sucking my thumb again.

This is my young friend Jilly.

Jeekers.

So it was not just homesickness in the perfumed world of this high, floating island of rain and fire, rotting earth, hot springs, wet trees, droopy ferns, muddy roads, black beaches. It was not only the tearing wind, and the waves frothing on our front steps, or the great red beaks of birdlike blossoms, leaves like sword blades, plopping pink flowers, big twisted vegetables and swollen fruits. It was Millroy himself.

I wanted to scream, *Help me!* I had always depended on him.

But he was working magic, frightening me with his power and being conspicuous, making his *How am I doing?* face. Millroy at his most magical was a perfect stranger, and *my young friend Jilly* bothered me most of all. I had felt safe when it had been the simple lie of *my son,* and I would have been able to stand his saying *my daughter.* This was different.

"I thought I was your son Alex."

"We've moved on, muffin."

I said nothing.

"Don't you want to be my friend, Jilly?"

"Friend" was one of those slippery words that could mean anything. I had gotten used to being small, slender Alex. I did not want to be skinny, plain Jilly. But what was the use of replying? All Millroy's radar had been turned on. He knew what I was thinking.

The island people spooked me with their laughter. What was so funny? They kept their distance, stared at Millroy and sometimes pointed at him. They tried to figure out who I was to him, which made me suck my thumb all the more because I did not know myself. I longed for the old days when Millroy had said, *Of course I'm not his biological father.*

They whispered when they saw him. Now Millroy had a reputation on the island for magic—raising that woman, Momi, from the dead. The exaggerated story people told was that he had brought her back to life. She was dead one minute, swaggering around the bungalow like her old self in a bedsheet the next. I knew better, I had seen it, the way he had stroked her face, how she had flickered awake, lifted her head, said, "good-bye" and died again after a few seconds of life. Yet the people at the funeral party said he had had her up, talking and laughing and swinging her arms, cured of cancer for an hour or more.

Millroy smiled and did not deny it.

Though it made me fearful to be so visible, we went on hiking the beach. Today we were down at the stone jetty near Pohoiki, where black waves from a dark sea broke on a black beach.

"I thought you didn't want to be conspicuous."

"Should I be worried, angel?"

"You raised that woman from the dead."

He seemed grateful to me for mentioning it. He was smiling hungrily at me, as though he wanted me to say more.

Okay, I thought.

"You touched her," I said.

"Yes."

"But you always said that the best magic was no-hands," I said. "That the magic in The Book was great because Jesus only said things like, 'Go home—your son is healed.' "

The light went out of Millroy's eyes, and when he turned their darkness on me, I was sorry for what I had said.

"Sometimes I need to use these to work miracles," he said, but when he lifted his hands to show me, they looked like weapons.

"People are talking about you," I said.

"I am not listening, petal."

But I was. "You're going to have a wicked reputation here."

"It's worth the risk," he said.

I did not ask why, though I was wondering.

"Because of what I have to gain," he said.

He stopped walking on the black boulders and looked at me. The light had returned to his eyes, and they were on me now, feeding on my face. I had to turn away and pretend to be interested in two men with buckets scrambling, dodging waves and chipping barnacles off the rocks next to the sea.

I envied them. Jump on a rock, scrape off a barnacle, stick it in your bucket—all the time whistling or rapping. It was more like play than work, and you ended up with something to eat. You went home with your dented bucket and watched TV, and tomorrow you were back on the rocks, barnacle hunting. Simple life was magical enough, and you didn't need miracles, only a bucket.

I said, "The woman back from the dead. The vanishing jewels. The wild dogs that lick your hand. It scares me when you do that magic."

"You've seen me do it plenty of times, angel."

"But these people haven't."

I looked up and saw the barnacle men stumbling in our direction.

"Magic doesn't have to be a miracle," I said.

"Miracles are quicker," Millroy said. "Listen, there's nothing for you to be afraid of."

"Ha. Except the police. They'll only come and take you away. Plus probably put you in jail."

He surprised me by smiling and seeming relaxed, stepping closer to where the waves were sloshing on the spiky cliffs and rocks.

"Would it bother you if I got hauled away?"

I did not want to think about it but watching him I imagined a wave rising up right now like a large, jagged crab claw, all water and froth, smashing Millroy down against the boulders, dragging his dead body into the sea while I stood there, not afraid for my own life but sorrowing that he was gone, that I would be all alone until this island sank.

"Would it?" he repeated.

How could I answer his question? I kept a straight face and kept my mouth shut so that I would not sob, but still the tears flowed down my cheeks. This seemed to excite him and he stepped over to me and put his arm around me.

His hand was cold, his arm was heavy, no warmth came from him. I should have felt safe, the way he was locked onto me, but instead I became terrified of him and worried that he could squash me, flip me over and toss me into a bucket the way those hopping men were crunching barnacles.

"Don't be afraid."

This made me more afraid. He could feel me going stiffer.

With his arm around me, I remembered some of the magic he had worked: rats leaping out of people's mouths, girls turned into milk and drunk, twisting off his Day One finger and slicing it with a knife, the jumbo jet shaking, volunteers vanishing in his Indian basket, objects tangibilized, spoons bending when he stroked them, the dead woman, Momi, raising her head, opening her white, sticky eyes and saying in a gluey voice, *I love you all. Aloha kekakiaka.*

Millroy was on the point of saying something, but he was holding back. Yes, I was afraid, because he could do anything he wanted, he could have anything at all.

"You're going to be all right."

Sometimes when a person reassures you, it is worse than an outright threat. He gave me another cold hug. Touched by such a strange magician, how could I not be terrified?

I felt guilty because I wanted to love him for his magic, but his power only made him seem sudden and unfamiliar.

"Mister." It was one of the barnacle hunters stepping near.

Millroy let go of me and the blood rushed into my arm again.

"What have you got there?"

"Ohpeehee," the man said. He was big and brown, and wore soggy sneakers.

The other man showed us his bucket, which contained bleeding fish.

Smaller than his friend, he looked unhappy and dangerous. He had inky, homemade tattoos scribbled on his arm.

We were all standing on wobbly boulders getting our feet splashed as we tried to balance.

"If the tide woulda come up, you get real wet," the big man said. "One howlie guy he get caught and die."

"You got some money for us?" the other man said.

"What's your name?" Millroy asked.

"Wendell. This is Jacklick. You see us at Momi's house."

"We do know where you live," the big man named Jacklick said. "The painted house. In the trees."

In da chrees, the way he said it, made it seem like a dangerous house.

"Have you met my young friend Jilly?"

"He asking you for money," Jacklick said, as though correcting him.

"I heard him." He faced the man, who did not know that Millroy could destroy him as easily as he had raised the woman from the dead. "Would that make you happy, Wendell?"

"Maybe it make you safe."

Millroy smiled as he considered this. He seemed to enjoy being challenged.

"I have no money," Millroy said.

He had tons of it—bricks of it, chunks of it, enough to pay cash for a house, cash for a new pickup truck, cash for air tickets, all new bills smelling of fresh ink. *A million dollars in small bills weighs just about fifty pounds, angel. Did you know that?* Why not give a little of it to nasty, tattooed Wendell?

''But you have gold in that bucket,'' Millroy said, and he winked at me.

''I got mahneenee fish.'' The man seemed fiercer and more horrible when he laughed.

''Take out the biggest fish. This one,'' Millroy said in an instructing voice, taking care not to touch anything, but pointing into the bucket at a soft, plump fish. ''Now look into its mouth.''

The man Wendell squeezed the fish, making its eyes bulge and mouth gape open, and out came a glittering gold ring, along with some blood-flecked slime and sea drool.

Walking back to the house, I said nothing, trying to figure out what all this meant, when suddenly Millroy jerked his whole body around and gasped in satisfaction.

''I didn't give them anything!''

Then I understood, and it had to do with me, because I had reminded him about the magic in The Book that was done with no hands, just a few suggestions, and when these were followed the magic was accomplished.

''What did you think?''

''Wicked interesting.''

I felt small, round-shouldered, weak, powerless. Millroy could raise the dead, spirit stolen goods back to their owners, fumble up gold from the mouths of fish. You would think, from the way he walked, that this Big Island of Hawaii was mostly his, as though he had dreamed it and breathed it into being, the way he had anything he wanted. The island belonged to him. Even the people were his—he could control them, he could destroy them.

He could destroy me. Most of all I was afraid because I did not want him to control me the way he manipulated other people. I saw power in his fingers and his eyes that I had never seen before.

Was he made of flesh? Was he human? I had never spent so much time with him all at once, so I knew him better now.

''I don't want any other life, any other place, anyone but you, on this black beach,'' he said.

I felt stifled, feared him more, and I had to drag air into my mouth to breathe. The worst of it was his soft voice and his hard hands.

''Come here, angel.''

When I did not go to him right away, he crept toward me on large, silent feet, towered above me and cast a shadow over me. I could hear his lungs working perfectly.

"Did you ever see a nugget of gold come out of the mouth of a fish?"

Of course not. But when had Millroy ever boasted before, reminding me of the amazing thing I had just seen? He was not satisfied by my respectful silence, and so he touched my arm. His touch made me pity my little arm.

"Isn't this a great place?"

His hands were iron hooks hesitating on the surface of my skin.

"Maybe learn Hebrew and Greek. Plenty of time. Just sit under these trees. Translate The Book myself."

He was very near to me. His whole body purred.

"Consider these people. This is a microcosm of the whole of America, only the weather's better. It's a garden, a kind of paradise. Ample herbage. Maybe start a global shortwave radio service. Late-night programs about food and Scripture. Mellifluous voice. 'This is the Day One Broadcasting Network, coming to you from the Big Island of Hawaii . . .' "

Not hooks on my arm but claws, and when he leaned toward me, his nose was like the beak of an eagle, sharp and hovering, a weapon with two watchful nostrils.

"But these people aren't regular, you can see that. They have a low-residue diet. They eat Spam, they eat pig meat and Hula Dogs and Jungle Jerky. I want to start all over again with these fat people, even if it takes years."

His talk of the future made me freeze, and, right on cue, an overripe mango thumped to the ground.

"Who did that?" Millroy asked, meaning he had. He picked it up, peeled it and said, "Get some of this into your mouth, angel."

He was so eager to please me that I felt trapped. He wanted to take me for walks to the nut farm and pick melons and eat flowers. "Let's swim," he said, and I suspected that he wanted me to see him walk on water.

It was unusual for him to be out of sight. Most days he hovered over me like a big bird. But one morning he was nowhere to be seen. With Millroy occupied elsewhere, I was alone, and for these hours I felt safer, happier—the sunshine blazing on the water, the rustle of the thick red leaves in the wind, the clucking of the palm trees, the screechy birds. Millroy was right; it was a kind of paradise. Never mind the big cane spiders and the cockroaches.

When the wind dropped, when the surf eased, when the birds took a breath, I could hear island music, island television, and the bumping of rusty cars on the narrow Opihikao road. Around noon there were food shouts, someone calling to his friend to get some shaved ice at Yamamoto's or a plate lunch in Pahoa.

Then I was happy. It was always summer on this island. I belonged here and even began to know the place a little. Millroy's hovering had prevented me from getting to know the island well. He had taken over my life. I had not minded this in Boston when he ran the Day One diners and the TV show, but these days—ever since the sudden storm and the plane—he seemed inhuman, like a god or a prophet, and it made me feel like nothing.

Just before lunchtime, Millroy popped up, smiling.

"I had a blockage in my bowel."

I was not alarmed. I had heard him say those words before. Talking about cramps and muscle control, he had seemed human to me.

"I have been trying to expel it since six-thirty this morning."

Even that, five hours of struggle, did not seriously worry me. He was still smiling, as though he had just chased the neighbor's dog out of the yard.

But he crossed the room to where I was sitting by the window, looking at a dark, seesawing ship in the deep sea, crooking my head to squint through the spindly branches of the candlenut tree, the leaves browned by salt splash, the bruised and uneatable fruit.

"I've been in there straining and deep breathing," he said, clenching his hands to illustrate it. "It's a species of labor."

This new information was the recent Millroy that I had begun to fear so much. Did he need reminding?

"You always said it shouldn't be work."

Perhaps he was testing me.

"Not that kind of labor, angel. I mean giving birth, gathering all your muscular intensity to extrude this blockage from your body."

Now I was simply threatened by his smile.

"Like having a baby?"

I was worried by what he had just said, and by his eager face.

"Sure. Ever think about that?"

"No," I said.

Now I had something else to disturb me.

"What are you looking at, angel?"

"The ocean. That ship."

It bobbed like a toy and the sun shimmered on the foam around it.

"Isn't that tree in the way?"

I liked the candlenut tree for its uselessness, a skinny, harmless planting you did not have to think about.

"Kind of," I said because I knew he wanted me to.

Millroy came closer and covered me with a hug—his iron claws, his hooked beak, his fish-cold skin, his big clammy, gray eyes.

I wanted to say, *Please!* but then he let go.

"Now look."

The tree was blighted, the leaves had fallen, the fruit was burned, the branches and the skinny, miserable trunk were a blackened skeleton.

I felt unsafe again, only more so.

"I am doing all this for you."

I nodded because I did not know what to say except *I'm wicked grateful.*

"Get your notebook, angel. I want you to take some dictation. Let's get going on my book."

He meant *This Is My Body,* which we had not worked on for days, and it was supposed to be our main project here on The Big Island. I found my notebook with gecko jimmies on it and opened it.

"Ready."

"I love you," Millroy said.

I wrote that down. I looked at it and waited for more. Millroy was breathing hard, and when I glanced up, I saw that his eyes had turned the sharpest blue.

"I love you," he said again.

Just then I realized that I had been dreading his saying those words ever since we landed in Hawaii. For a instant I wanted to cry out—not a long scream but an *ouch* of pain. Instead, I just winced.

He repeated the words as though I had not heard him, but each time he said them differently, so the words were like searching fingers.

I wanted to run for my life.

42 Once Millroy managed to get *I love you* out of his mouth, he kept it up, repeating the words as though he had overcome his fear of them, the way some fearful people whisper a swearword the first time, say it louder after that, and then shout it. Maybe Millroy had been trying to say *I love you* for a long time, was what I thought. Now he could not stop himself, never mind how I felt.

"I love you, Jilly Farina."

The way he said these words made him seem monstrous and desperate, with swiveling eyes.

If you could not say it back, what did it mean except *I want you body and soul, all of you,* and this terrified me worse than any threat I had ever heard.

"Quit it, please."

But no, he went on saying it.

"Please cut it out."

I winced. I was flustered because the words seemed to have fingers and hands and lips and teeth. They had hot breath. I felt caught and mauled by their very sound.

Then Millroy said, "All I ask is that you give me a chance."

Not being able to think of anything to say, I began to cry and, as always, crying made me feel small and skinny. I seemed to shrink with each sob. What made my crying worse for me was that Milloy never did it himself.

His *I love you* scared me most of all because I could not love him in return. He was Millroy the Magician. I had never stopped seeing him as the man who could turn me into a glass of milk and drink me. He was made of cold metal; he had unpredictable power. Why didn't he know that it was impossible for me to love him, or that his love made me feel unsafe?

He said, "I know how to make you happy."

If this was true, it just made him seem more powerful.

Stabbing the air with his fingers, he worked sudden magic wildly—fumbled with his hands, flicked out flower blossoms with his fingertips, darted hummingbirds into the blossoms to suck, plucked open a bubble of light, twirling his fingers and tangibilizing a round mirror, which showed me shimmering, older, fuller and beautiful.

"No," I said. "Please stop."

He unscrewed a light bulb and crunched it in his mouth.

"Anything you say." He chewed pieces of glass with a sound like potato chips.

I said nothing. I could not think of anything to say. What was more dangerous than a magician who was so desperate to have me? Seeing his cheeks bulging with glass made me picture him crunching me.

"I could teach you to do this."

He went on chewing the glass.

"I don't want to learn," I said because if I had told him I was afraid, he would have insisted.

"I've been waiting all this time," he said. "For you."

They made me rigid, those simple words.

"Just say yes," he said. "What is there to be afraid of?"

"Everything," I said with a dry mouth.

He laughed at the idea of my seeing threats everywhere.

"You," I said.

He stared at me with yellow eyes, his hands upraised, as though about to make magic. I stepped away and got smaller. I feared that he would touch me and, touching me, break me in two.

I slept badly, I could not eat, I began to pray that Millroy would be caught and taken away, arrested by the police who sometimes drove down the road to Kalapana, where the road turned into a smoldering lava flow. There was a rumor in Puna that Millroy was able to divert the molten lava that smoked and flamed at night. People believed him. I had believed him once.

He had made me different, changed the shape of my life, stolen me from my hopeless family, and I had felt safe with him. He had turned me into a young boy. *This is my son Alex.* He had made me depend on him, and then amazed me by falling in love with me and wanting me to love him back. There was no one else, just the two of us in the house, listening hard for each other.

He did not want to be my father anymore. I had known he was a magician, but I had not realized how much power he had until he flashed his whole light on me. Then I saw that he was difficult and dangerous and strange—a true magician—yet it was only when I was alone with him that I understood I had no business being there.

No more magic, I thought, *please don't freak me out.*

But I had no right to think it. What was I doing here? I needed someone else.

"There is no one else," he said.

I had no privacy, even in my thoughts.

"I have loved you from the moment I saw you," he said.

All those months, a year and a half, in the diner watching me, talking to me while I lay on my cupboard shelf in the darkness. *I never dreamed this movement would be so big, angel.* But I was embarrassed, as though only now he was telling me how long ago he had seen me naked and, reminded of it, I felt ashamed and unprotected. This whole time he had been watching me, but what could I do about it?

It was hard to be on this island with him. Even when I was alone I felt his eyes fastened on me, pressing on my head like his thumbs, a sense of squeezing fingers.

"Sorry," I said one of these times, looking around.

But it was not him, it was a stranger, one of the island people looking at me from below the black cliff.

The man was looking past me at Millroy, who was out back hammering a piece of wood on one of his new beehives.

I saw someone again the next day. The finger pressure on the back of my skull made me turn to find another stranger.

I might have felt better if we had gone on making our regular trips into town—to Pahoa, Kurtistown, Mountain View or Hilo, where we had bought the pickup truck. But we did not even go to smoldering Kalapana or to Opihikao, which was one church, one store and two barking mutts.

"We've got everything we need right here," Millroy said.

It was as though he wanted to keep me in a box.

We had no flour, no wheat, no barley, not even any honey yet. We had plenty of lentils, red and brown, we had melons, papayas, guavas and pineapples. We had other fruits and fish, nuts of three kinds, beans of all sorts to parch. Millroy encouraged a boy named Cal from a local farm to bring him butter and honey.

"What about bread?"

" 'Butter and honey shall ye eat, that ye may know to refuse the evil and choose the good.' Isaiah makes no mention of bread, angel."

He fingered up gobs of honey and licked it, looking wise. Later, instead of buying flour he produced loaves out of an empty basket with a flash of blue light that terrified me.

"Did you see that?" he asked one morning at the beach.

I shook my head. He was holding a live fish.

"I coaxed him out of the sea. The creature was scrabbling up the pebbles on its fins."

We ate, we purged, we prayed—the Day One routine. "And furious dousings"—we bathed. Millroy said there was no need to go anywhere except the beach. Before we set out he squinted right and left to make sure there was no one around.

There were hidden houses nearby, but the rest of this stretch of coast was lonely and remote. I was used to the low dunes and unsurfy shore of the Cape. Often there was someone on the beach, a fisherman or a barnacle hunter, sometimes a surfer. Millroy was not worried by them, yet it was clear that he did not know what to do with these people. Turn them into milk and drink them? Liquidize them and pour them into the Pacific? Stuff them into an Indian basket and make them vanish? Frighten them by pulling live creatures out of their ears?

More people began to appear at the edge of our black cliff; occasionally just their heads sticking up, their faces and white eyes looking curious. People paused when they passed the house.

"There's always someone out there."

"Don't worry, angel."

"I'm not worried."

"I love you."

Only this made me feel unsafe.

Soon it was Millroy's turn to be confused.

I said, "We should get a TV. There are tons of them on sale in Hilo."

"That's the last thing I would buy."

"Everyone's got one."

He did not reply. He made a disgusted sound in his nose, a grunt that swelled to a roar.

Then I knew why.

We had a strict Day One routine: walking the cliffs after breakfast, scrambling on the black beach, taking a nap or rocking on the lanai porch after lunch, walking the beach again after dinner, which was always early because Millroy said you needed at least four hours of residue formation before bedtime. *Eating too late or at the wrong time is as much of a life shortener as eating badly.*

We were heading back to our house one evening just after sundown. In that part of The Big Island, houses were camouflaged during the day, but they sprang up in the dark, their light bulbs shining through open windows. TV sets winked and flickered, washing the house walls in blue light. No one could see out, but you could see in.

We were walking slowly, side by side, neither of us mentioning the lights we both could see. The wind had dropped, the leaves on the palm trees were motionless and picked out like ragged umbrellas under the moon, and even the ocean was stiller and soupier than usual.

Our feet made chewing sounds on the gravelly beach, and then came a human murmur from up ahead, echoing in the bluish lights of the house behind the hedge.

Lost in the darkness of my body—imagine. It was my experience of wilderness, until I realized I was eating poison, the carcinogenic diet that all of you call food. . . .

''No, I am not throwing my voice,'' Millroy said. I was glad he made a little joke of it. He could have done so much angry damage if he had wanted.

Before we passed by the house, he hesitated and could not resist squeezing through the hedge and creeping up to the window to see who it was, watching this *Day One* rerun. Standing on my tiptoes I got a glimpse of his face on the TV screen.

It was another shock here. I had started to think that everything that had happened before, all the Day One business, had been a dream—unreal, anyway. There had been so much of it, all the changes, all the people, the food, the money, then the walking away. A moment ago I had heard his voice through the trees, and now I saw his big bald head, bushy mustache and wise doctor's voice, and I was frightened because it had all been true.

''A fat, dusky family,'' Millroy said, back on the path. ''They had webbed feet. They had chunky thighs and bad skin. They were feeding on a jumbo bag of Cheez Doodles and swigging Cokes. They badly need this program.''

But he was annoyed, too, because he had expressly forbidden any reruns or rebroadcasts of *Day One*.

''Someone's making a pile of money out of this, and I can feel in my bones that he's not an eater—not righteous at all.''

At the next house, jumping blue glare on the walls and the same Millroy the Messenger voice coming from the TV, he went stooping to the side window. He came back to the path where I stood and muttered. First he said that he had seen four islanders in the room watching the show.

Then he began to shout.

''I have been betrayed,'' he said. ''There was a commercial break! I never had a commercial in all the months I did that show. They were selling so-called high-fiber breakfast cereal, but you know that all processed food has been stepped on. That's treachery.''

He was furious that *Day One* was on television here. His success had been stolen from him—there he was on TV, grinning and eating, and he watched with a stony face. Most of the houses on the beach or on the cliffs had the show on, though two or three howlie families were watching *Wheel of Fortune*.

That night in the dark I heard him insisting, *I don't want a TV set.*

These reruns explained why people squinted at him at times on the beach, why they sometimes said hello and aloha, and lingered near the house.

After that *Day One* night, I noticed that there were many people lurking near the house, as though they wanted something but were too shy to ask.

''There's someone out there,'' I said.

''A dozen of them,'' Millroy said without looking up.

''Those people freak me out,'' I said.

Millroy was not even thinking about them. He looked at me sadly, and said, ''I love you.''

This was my biggest reason to leave. At night I planned my escape— the flight to Honolulu, then back to Boston, the bus to the Cape, the walk from Falmouth, the road to Dada's trailer or Gaga's house. But at some point on this imaginary trip, usually in one of the weedy driveways, I found myself hesitating, looking back, not sure what I should do next.

I sensed the dark and heavy island people watching me. *I love you* was a challenge that made me feel helpless. Millroy kept on insisting he did not want a TV set, and he listened to the wind and said, *I can hear them talking about me.*

He was right. It was our old experience of seeing strangers circling, gathering, mounting up, and getting attentive, like chickens following a feed bucket. I had seen it before at Millroy's show at the Barnstable County Fair, the people ducking under the sign, BELTESHAZZAR—MASTER OF THE MAGICIANS. They had done it again after the show in the studio parking lot of *Paradise Park,* and more recently at the Day One Diner in Boston, when the crowd clamored for Millroy on the sidewalk, blocked traffic and gave out handbills claiming he was the Devil.

Millroy attracted crowds. It was happening again here on The Big Island, people in front of the house, trying to look inside.

"Why should I mind?" Millroy said.

They were both shy and nosy, bobbing around our bushes—fat boys mostly, in faded baseball hats.

"They don't worry me at all," he said.

Trying to be quiet, they made a racket, and their loud whispers made them seem panicky and deaf.

"They're the ones who should be worried," he said.

He was not watching them, he was watching me and seemed on the verge of telling me again that he loved me.

"You're not scared, are you?"

I folded my arms so that he could not see me tremble, and I forced myself to say, "I'm wicked scared."

He made a little laughing noise that rattled behind his face. He said, "I'll be right back."

The next sound I heard was breaking glass, Millroy in the kitchen smashing a bottle into smaller pieces as though he were whacking a cake of ice with a hatchet.

"Come with me," he said, hurrying past me and out the front door, carrying a tray of broken glass.

I followed him into the sunny yard, where ten or fifteen island people were milling around as usual, looking sheepish. When they saw him, they backed up, but Millroy motioned them nearer.

"Don't rush off," he said, and went up to one man. "Tell me, friend, what are people saying about me?"

"Some people talking stink," the man said. His T-shirt was lettered VOTE SPARK MATSUNAGA.

"About me?"

The man's blinking eyes meant yes, yes.

"What are they saying?"

"That you're the guy from TV. Does magic chricks. Can turn the Devil into a glass of djuice and then pick the glass up and djrink it all."

Another man said, "And da police lookeen for you on da mainland. And talkeen udda stink."

The rest of the people stepped back when this reckless man spoke, as though Millroy were going to howl at them.

"I wonder how strong those policemen are," Millroy said. But his smile meant it was not a question.

He buried his face in the broken glass, holding the tray up and roaring into it. Then he put the tray down and brushed glass splinters off his face, unscrewed the bulb from the light fixture on the porch and bit on it, shattered it, crunched it in his teeth. He spat it out—the watching people moaned as he did it—swallowed four razor blades, and finally vomited them onto the lawn, where they gleamed.

"I wonder what those cops eat for breakfast," he said, wiping his mouth with the back of his hand.

He had always been a showman.

Someone said, "He so shtrong."

"Is anudda chrick."

Meanwhile, Millroy was unrolling a small, tight ring of rubber into a wrinkly white balloon. The men and boys in the crowd laughed and covered their faces when they saw it.

"A rubber johnny," Millroy said, and snorted it through his nose. He stuck out his tongue and eased the rubber thing out of his mouth. Then he reversed the process—into his mouth, out his nose, the thin rubber rippling out of one nostril.

They laughed hard with goggling eyes, the laughter that is the worst kind of horrified.

"Punch me in the stomach!"

When no one did it, he turned his back on the fearful people.

"You have nothing to worry about, sugar."

He did not know that it was his magic that worried me most of all.

Millroy's magic had kept me safe but had never calmed me. First it had startled me, then amazed me, and finally terrified me—ever since he changed that girl into milk and drank her. The rats of Floyd Fewox were worse, and I had been a trembling witness when Millroy said of Mister Phyllis, *His name is Sidney Perkus. He is a twisted old fruit,* and destroyed him. He had grown in power, from conjuring with flags to making a jumbo jet shudder in the sky. But his power had made him dangerously visible.

"I never wanted to be famous," he had said.

I believed that—no one else had—and he loved me for it.

Millroy's magic was so unusual on The Big Island that it had the opposite effect from the one he intended. The magic that was supposed to scare these people off only made them nosier. They kept their distance, but they did not go away. They told their friends. That was the strangest part of his magic—even when it was shocking, you wanted to go on watching, and it was at its most dazzling when it was dangerous. His magic made people want more.

He progressed from being famous on the beach to being famous in Puna District, and at last he roused the whole island.

They knew he was not just the man who chewed light bulbs and ate razor blades, not just the healer who withered trees and raised the woman Momi from the dead, or even the big kahoona who bewitched wild dogs and diverted lava flows.

He was Millroy, he was Uncle Dick, the doctor, the wise messenger of *The Day One Program,* wanted by the police on the mainland on various charges because of misunderstandings.

I had already told him how worried I was, and that I froze stiff whenever I saw a white police car on the coast road. But he could easily vanish, as he had done before, so what did he care?

"I could live the rest of my life like this," he said. "Two hundred years!"

That worried me very much.

"I love you," Millroy said.

You heard something like that and you just wanted to take off.

• • •

So I knew what I had to do, and I decided to tell him early one eve-ning while there was still time to pack my things and catch the early-morning plane out of Hilo. Home was awful, but home was simple. I remembered my old daydream of getting a waitressing job in Hyannis or Falmouth and going to work in my secondhand car. I would save up, move out of Vera's trailer, and maybe later I would meet someone—not a magician but a normal man—and raise some children. One day, when I trusted them enough not to be freaked, I would tell them of my amazing time with Millroy. I pictured myself at my own kitchen table saying, *Whatever happened to Millroy the Magician?*

They would all look at me differently after they realized what I had been through.

That little guy Alex on the show and that's mentioned in his book? I would say. *That was me.*

Twilight was not just a shadowy sky, it was also a certain perfume in the air, the cooing of a pair of speckled doves, the twitter of a bird set-tling on a branch, the hoarse coughlike bark of a dog out on the road, the dusky day winding down, the world filling with night that was like thick-ening dust. It was also how I felt about my life with Millroy, that it was ending like this, in a quiet departure.

He was cooking again tonight. Just seeing his efficient fussing in the kitchen made me nervous these days, as though he were making a po-tion, preparing to cast a spell on me.

It was his happiness, too, that bothered me because I could not share it, any more than I could return his love.

I was staring at him from the door, bracing myself to tell him my de-cision.

"Pottage," he said, batting the pot with his wooden spoon.

Did he remember that it was one of the first meals he had ever made for me?

He had not switched the light on. He moved in the kitchen like a dark sorcerer without a shadow.

"Let's go for a walk," he said, stepping outside.

He looked young, smoother in the fading light, stronger than ever, more wizardly. But I was so afraid of his power that everything he said to me sounded as though it had hidden meanings.

"I don't trust these people," I said.

"They can't hurt us."

"There are police here, too."

"You've seen me deal with the law, angel."

I kept my mind a blank so that he would not be able to read it. When he walked toward me, I stepped back.

We were in the small secluded garden behind the kitchen, where green leaves the shape and size of elephant ears trembled over my head. There were long-stemmed ferns and pink and yellow flowers and smudges of jasmine in the air.

I could just make out Millroy looking at me in a certain way, as though straining his eyes to see me. He dropped his voice, talking so softly I barely heard what he was saying.

Night fell fast on the windward coast of The Big Island—sunset was on the other side. No sooner had you decided that it would be night in a little while than it was pitch-dark, the sea blackening from the horizon, the darkness rushing in with the waves, faster than a rising tide.

Millroy was talking harmlessly about eating, and what he said made no sense to me, but his gesturing fingers stilled my eyes.

"Yes," I said, and felt my tongue grow fatter in my mouth and heard a buzzing in my brain. Even in this poor light I was aware of his eyes changing color.

He was saying, "You love me."

I jerked my head and looked up. In places between smoky twilight clouds, the sky was still blue. "What are you doing?" I asked.

He was never at a loss for words, yet he had no answer to this, and his silence perplexed me, as though I had dropped something and it had not clunked.

"You love me," he said after a pause, and this woke me up more.

"Hey, are you trying to hypnotize me?"

He looked guilty, on the verge of denying it.

"How could you do a crappy thing like that to me, you turkey!"

I began to cry and ran so that he would not see me, and when I was away from him, I got angry and was glad I had called him a turkey, knowing how much he hated it. I locked myself in my room and did not reply when he called to me, making promises, begging me to listen, telling me how much he loved me.

I was packing my bag. I was sad when I saw that I owned so few things, and all of them boy's clothes. All night I repeated like a prayer, *I am Jilly Farina from Marstons Mills,* to remind myself of who I really was and where I belonged.

Millroy was outside my door the next morning, kneeling on the creaking boards. Had he been there all night? Sleeplessness and kneeling made him look sorry. Whenever he was tired he did not look like a magician. He saw me holding my small bag and spoke to me in a weary, gentle voice.

"Angel?"

"I'm going home."

"This is your home."

"Not anymore."

He was suddenly ugly, with a frantic, twisted face.

"I'll do anything." It was a different and desperate voice. I could tell he was about to say *I love you,* but he saw me cringe and held back.

"By the way, I'm not hungry."

I had the idea that he might try to bewitch me with one of his marvelous meals and then recite, *If you feed someone they belong to you.*

I set off, walked past him, reached the door. I was surprised that he made no move, did not follow me, simply watched me foundering in the doorway, where beyond the black cliff the sunrise was blazing on the ocean and in the air.

Breathing hard, he got my attention—all those gasps.

"I know what you need me to do."

He stepped back from me and seemed to draw me toward him, yet I resisted.

"What?"

"Break my rod," he said.

I stared hard at nothing at all on the floor because I had not expected that word.

"Didn't even know you had a rod."

"Just an expression," Millroy said.

43 *I know what you need me to do?*

When Millroy sprang that on me, I felt fuzzy around the edges, and hopeful, but then I looked hard at him and my feet bumped back to the ground. I could not imagine Millroy any other way because now his magic made him a stranger to me and to everyone else. Ever since we had come to The Big Island, I had felt we were living in a dream, and now I wanted to wake up and go home. Yet this man had saved my life and kept me alive and happy most of the time, so I was willing to listen.

But *Break my rod?*

"Give me a little time."

At least he hadn't said, *Give Millroy a little time.* He had gotten over talking like that.

Yet it was odd, this bargaining with me. He was frantic, but he was also firm—desperate in a determined way, with stony eyes. He never shed a tear. Even when he woke up worried after a crab fright or a death nightmare, he never wept.

"And then what's supposed to happen?"

"You'll know. You won't be afraid."

"Anyway"—I hated asking him this—"what does 'break my rod' mean?"

He did not ask me to guess. He knew my head was empty.

" 'This rough magic of mine I here abjure,' " he said, with a strange smile, knowing I still had no idea. He added, "Renounce my magic. Drown it."

I could not picture it at all, Millroy without it.

"Then the whole thing will be my fault," I said.

He smiled at me, his shoulders lopsided, one up, one down, holding his hands out, one in a clenched fist, the other with his palm open. I knew that this crippled, weighing gesture expressed his feeling that one side of him would be relieved to be rid of the magic, and the other side of him sorry that it was gone. But if it was gone, what then?

"Then I'll need you more than ever," he said, mind-reading my question.

"Why would you give up your magic? You have everything."

"Except you."

"Here I am."

"Your love," he said.

Even though this was true, it did not make me feel important, and I wanted to cry. I felt terrible. I prayed to myself, *I am Jilly Farina from Marstons Mills, I am nobody, I am nothing.*

"Other people won't like it."

"They put me in the wrong. Most of them don't deserve me. The rest are after me."

"I am nobody."

"My whole life is about you," Millroy said.

Millroy the Magician! Not only tricks—the disappearing elephant, the Indian basket, the television stunts, flushing Perkus—but the miracles of Millroy the Messenger. He could whip up storms in the sky, raise the dead, see through walls, hear distant whispers, send jets of fire out of his fingertips. He knew the insides of things, he had fathomed the human body, had control over nine bodily functions. It might have been awful for him at times ("I never wanted to be famous"), but it was amazing for everyone else.

"Angel, you don't know how powerful you are," he said. He looked out of the window at the sound of a chirp—a tiny bird alighting on the thick velvet petal of a pink blossom. "Or how weak I am."

"You're not weak," I said.

"I am helpless," he said, and that was how he looked, sort of narrow, "without your love."

I put my small bag down on the sofa. Millroy was glad, he swelled a little.

"Eat something," he said.

I was hungry from all the stress, yet a niggling suspicion, even if it was unfair, kept me from letting him feed me. I served myself—melon pulp, nut meats, warm bread buns—while he watched.

"I need you," he said, "so that I can go on living."

I felt conspicuous, licking the sweet strings of melon pulp from my lips.

"I would sicken and die without you. But didn't I tell you that together, we can live for two hundred years?"

This made me feel worse about wanting to go. I thought, *I'll go tomorrow for sure.*

All that day in the house by the sea, I watched Millroy. He was like Dada had been the day before his gallstone operation, like anyone facing surgery or getting on an airplane, thinking about his life and what was going to happen next—like a statue, suffering in his own stony way.

I knew we were both thinking the same thing. He had made magic. It was in his head, all this supernatural power. Just standing barefoot in a pair of shorts in an ordinary room, he had worked miracles. I had seen everything—he knew that I was his witness. Now he looked sad, with streaky shadows on his face, his features heavy from all his pondering. Maybe he was also a little baffled. He must have had doubts, and he knew I was frightened. He remained silent and still, like a small bird on a cold branch.

Toward dusk he began to stir, moving through the house. His padding feet made me cautious. He always moved as though he hovered a few inches from the ground. I kept away from him, watching him from a corner of the room, near a window where more birds twittered and clacked, settling for the night.

"Magic is the power to see. That's brilliant," Millroy said. "But a magician sees everything. That's painful."

He was looking away from me, speaking through the open door as though at the open ocean.

"I have this gift. If I use it I am taking a risk. If I don't use it, I'm neglecting my gift." He looked sad. He said, "And there are limits to bewitchment. I can impress you or frighten you, but I can't make you love me."

At this mellow time of day, early evening in Puna District, the wind died, the sea looked carbonated, and it seemed as though the whole world were holding its breath to listen.

"I know my magic makes me seem like a foreigner, or an exile," he said. "That's why this lovely country matters so much to me."

In the distance where the water met the sky, a shadow surfaced from the ocean and sealed the horizon in a streak of darkness, the first stain of night.

"And there's natural magic in the real world. The miracle of life, muffin."

Bursting from the silence, from the small wooden houses hidden by trees, there came children's laughter, and he may have been thinking that his program had caused it.

"There is birth," Millroy said. "No magician on earth can give life."

I said nothing, but his fixed attention made me squirm. He was staring straight at the back of my head.

"Don't you agree, angel?"

At that moment I wanted to be doing something easy, like washing dishes in warm soapy water.

"Sounds good."

I also guessed it might be a long night, so I went outside while the sky was still pale.

In his blue shorts, barefoot, Millroy left the creaking porch and crossed the grass to the edge of the low cliff. He walked down the cut-lava steps to the beach, now at its blackest because the sand was soaked by the incoming tide.

Raising his arms—*For my last trick,* he used to say—he sent a tremble like a thrill through the water, and a split appeared and widened to a pie wedge of air where the sea had parted. Exposed crabs scuttled sideways, small fish flopped among the sea urchins, and black seaweed was pasted flat to the wet sand.

Millroy stepped into the airy corridor he had made in the green sea, and its walls quivered and then all the water closed over him.

He bobbed to the surface some distance out, then plunged into the oncoming waves, kicking hard, swimming away. He tossed his head in the foam, and I half expected him to stand up and stride across the water's surface, like a wizard in air. But he went on swimming smoothly, moving like a fish. He slipped onto his back and spouted water, and then it was as though he were taking a bath, the ocean speeding him on, until he stopped and slapped it.

It was bad when I saw him swimming away. It was worse when he was struggling. Then he sank and there was nothing left, not even his waterbug ripple on the water, and he took the rest of the glimmering daylight with him.

44 With Millroy gone, it was night and I was alone and lost. I kept watching because I had nowhere to go. Just behind me, some palm trees in a windblown clump were holding a conversation—so it seemed to me—and the wind stiffened and made their fronds even more talkative.

"Quit it," I said, as though at unkind kids.

At the edge of this island, under a hula moon, I stared at the water while ragged smoke trails of cloud drifted across the sky. Recently I had thought about leaving Millroy for good, but I had never imagined Millroy leaving me. Then off he went, splashing out to sea, while I dropped to my knees and crouched like a monkey on the black sand beach in the dark, among the chattering palms.

Wait. Not chattering now, the wind had dropped just a moment ago, the palms had gone silent, their fronds were motionless. Was it something I'd said?

Now the moon was wrapped in smoky clouds and its faint light hardly showed on the water. The wind had died, the palms had quieted, but night had gathered around me so close and so dark that it was as though I had been squeezed into a small, damp box.

Instead of speaking, I turned my face to the clouds and made a wish for the moon to shine, and for moonlight to be loosed across the surface of the sea.

It happened just that way, the clouds traipsing off and the powerful light releasing me. Had another wish of mine been granted? First the wind, then the moon. I was breathless. It was the sort of unexplainable magic that Millroy had once worked. Or was it a coincidence?

Lit by the puddly moonbeams, the rough sea seemed more dangerous, deeper and surfier, with a chop like miles of tumbling rocks.

I got up, stood before the dumping waves, raised my arms and silently commanded the water to be stilled. There came a simmering in the sea, like a pot of water going off the boil, and then a flattening and a gasp as the water, laced with tiny puckering bubbles, settled in a hush and shone with the reflection of new moonlight, like a black mirror.

I stepped back, amazed. This was almost too much, the sense that I might have Millroy's powers. I insisted to myself that it was something I misunderstood, but all this while, testing it, I was nervous and felt exposed, as though I were being fooled by the world.

I was hesitant to try again, but facing a calm sea in the stillest air I had known on this island, I knelt again and watched for Millroy. In the five hours until shivery midnight, I doubted everything that had happened. How could it be magic? It was my imagination, just nerves, because I was alone, because Millroy was gone.

It was not myself I worried about, but that good man. I was all right. In his splashing departure and in the rising of the moon, I had felt strengthened in a way I had never known before. It had nothing to do with physical health. It was something else, beyond confidence, a spirit that was like a light blazing within me. My whole being brimmed with a queenly sense of peace and power, as though I contained an enormous secret that tonight I had begun to understand. It was the simple truth that there was no death, so there was nothing on earth to fear.

Suddenly I wanted Millroy to know this, and I yelled so hard that my shrill voice clapped against my ears and I could not remember what I had said even an instant later. The force of my scream had startled me. I stayed there with my fingers in my mouth for the longest time, listening, feeling mocked by the squeezed and distant echo that sounded so merry. It was Millroy's name I had yelled. I had never spoken it before.

I did it again, calling out all my wishes and hopes in that one word, his name. Saying it again was easier, like a chant. I saw a distant motion in the sea, like a wrinkle in a rug. I yelled again and the moonlight broke and separated on the water.

Someone far off was splashing, beating the moonlight, more like a dog than a fish, he was clumsy and tired, the way the creature thrashed as though the water were an obstacle, snagging his arms and legs, trying to drown him.

He lifted his head and roared as he made the beach, flopping forward and flattening himself on the sand. Then he stood up, streaming with water that flickered, dripping moony brightness.

I was so glad to see him, I could hardly draw air into my mouth. He started toward me and stumbled—he was unmistakably a man. It was Millroy, somewhat smaller, even shy, and a little pale. I wanted to touch him to make sure that he was real.

My touch steadied him. He stood straighter. My hand did not seem so small in his. There was no pressure from his fingers. I hesitated to hold on, not knowing what he would say. He staggered and, needing my help, put all his weight against my hand to keep himself from falling. Regaining his balance, he thanked me in a soft breath that was a sigh of gratitude.

As we climbed the rocky steps that led from the beach to the cliff top, we heard loud, interrupting voices. We looked up and saw the clumsy, sweeping beams of fishermen's flashlights, three of them, with shadowy people behind them.

I had the idea that they were the police, come to take him away. But no.

"Uncle, come"—it was a young and frightened voice—"my granny just now get very sick."

Millroy waved them away with his wet hand.

"You can do something?"

"I'm awfully sorry."

It was a new voice—Millroy's without magic, apologetic, with extra syllables of hesitation in it.

"Please come." The voice behind the other flashlight was stronger than Millroy's and more insistent.

Millroy must have been shaking his head. I could not see. I had turned away from the blinding glare.

Although they had been rejected, the men did not go away. They seemed to grow more curious, and bolder, almost threatening. Black night had deepened around us like a pit.

Unafraid, they ignored Millroy's murmur for them to leave us alone, and came a few steps nearer. They saw something I could not see.

"Uncle."

The word was spoken more in surprise than in sympathy, but they said nothing more.

A spirit within me shimmered—fearless hope and a feeling for them. I realized that I knew something they did not know.

"Go home," I said to them. "Your granny is all right."

I had a vivid sight of the old woman sitting up in bed, restored to health and smiling, her dark eyes shining, a pretty shawl thrown over her lampshade, the fringes of it dangling, and long, black shadows jumping on the planks of the wall.

"She is waiting for you."

The men with flashlights hurried away, whispering loudly.

Millroy turned to me, and then the pale moonlight struck him. There were tears shining in his eyes and beginning to flow—that was what the men had seen. It had touched them to see this famous fugitive weep, a sad man with wet cheeks. They knew that magicians never cry. Now his tongue went *blort* and he began to cry.

Only I knew the reason for his tears. Now he was no stranger to me, and he knew I was not afraid. I had never loved his strength, but I loved this man deeply for his weakness.

He said, "You're happy."

"Wicked happy."

"You saved me, angel."

It did not matter. I wanted him to say *I love you,* so that I could say it back.

Instead of saying it, he kissed me, lightly at first, more like a whispered word, as though he thought I might be afraid and pull away. When I did not move, he kissed my upturned face again, pressing harder, and in that moment I grew even stronger. All the strings of my muscles in my arms and legs were quickened by this kiss, drawn tighter as his lips parted. Then I knew what to do and how to kiss him in my way.

Long ago at the county fair I had wondered what it must have been like when Millroy changed that girl into milk and drank her. Now I knew.

I clung to him, whispering, *Carry me,* and I gave him the strength to lift me. He hoisted me, still kissing me, in his adoring way. Even so, half-devoured, I yearned for more of this glory. His kisses opened my body and filled me with light.

Never mind that they were still hunting him all over the island, or that one night they would locate him in our house by the sea. We would be holding each other as they knocked and rattled the doorknob. These days he was not afraid of anything, and neither was I.

Let go, angel. I won't be long.

Never mind that they would detach him from me and make him famous all over again. Never mind that it was another national misunderstanding. Time would pass, but he was truthful and he always kept his promises. It was not magic but love that made me patient.

Never mind. Millroy would come back to me—back to us.